END OF DAY

JEWEL E ANN

Copyright © 2015 by Jewel E. Ann

Second Print Edition

ISBN: 978-1-7359982-4-4

Cover Designer: Jenn Beach

For kick-ass women

CHAPTER ONE

DAY

Four graves.
Four caskets.
Two bodies.

A THRONG of family and friends mourned the loss of four innocent lives under dapple gray skies in a cemetery nestled at the bottom of a hillside just miles from the Golden Gate Bridge. A DEA agent and his wife were murdered a week earlier and their two adult children were reported dead in an apartment building the following day. Investigators reported the cause of death—self-inflicted gunshot wounds. Those same investigators collected a bag of cash at a drop location in exchange for their report which led to two empty caskets and headstones carved with the names Jessica Maeve Day and Jude Paxton Day.

"How many people live to see their own funeral?" Knox, the lead Agent for G.A.I.L, mumbled from the driver's seat of the SUV custom built to meet presidential motorcade standards.

"I could snap your neck and not shed ... One. Fucking.

JEWEL E ANN

Tear," Jessica Day answered.

The cocky agent chuckled, as any asshole that treated life and death like a business would do. "I taught you everything you know. I'm not too worried."

"No, you taught me everything *you* know."

"Jess," Jude warned, grabbing her fisted hand and holding it until she relaxed.

"I've seen enough. Let's go." Jessica turned away from the window and closed her eyes as she released a slow sigh. Why couldn't she have a normal life? A husband who worked too much but adored her, a daughter with long black hair and an ornery son that loved to pull it, and a dog that dug up the flowers planted along their white picket fence.

How could fate be so cruel?

"We're gridlocked. We won't be leaving early without busting up a few cars, which would make a scene. And the last thing we want to do is make a scene."

Every word Knox spoke brought Jessica closer to the edge. She needed to hit something. She needed to hit *someone*. The most painful hour of her life passed with every second and felt like an eternity. Jessica didn't want to live to see her own funeral. She fought the urge to jump out of the vehicle and race to the casket—*her* casket—climb inside, and let them bury her alive. At that point, no death would be as excruciating as the alternative—living.

"Look at me." The uneasy tremble to her brother's voice made her skin pebble, hair standing on end.

Jessica's heart hid in her throat, sending waves of throbbing pain through her body as tears stung her eyes. She knew why Jude wanted her to look at him. On the other side of the privacy-tinted window was her *everything*.

How could fate be so cruel?

2

"Jess, don't do it ... just don't."

Jessica looked at her brother the way someone would before pulling a trigger pointed at their own temple—lifeless and regretful. "I have to ... I have to see him one last time."

The heartbroken shell of a woman turned toward the window and there he was, surrounded by his family. Sunglasses hid his deep navy eyes that had pieced her back together as much as his most brilliantly spoken words. His signature tailored suit he wore was black that day. She cursed him for not being more original—a splash of flare in honor of her funeral.

Her gaze drifted to his shoes. Inside she felt a blink of reprieve from the pain, a smile that didn't reach her lips. He was wearing those argyle socks; she couldn't see them ... she just knew. Jessica knew that man. Jessica loved that man. And in that very moment, she said goodbye to that man. In another blink, the pain returned.

How could life. Be. So. Cruel?

Jude squeezed her hand. "He could come with us."

"I know." Her voice cracked under the weight of pain. He already thought she was dead. "I can't take him from them. I want him ... but they *deserve* him."

───────────

THE DAYS WERE TRANSPORTED to an undisclosed location that defined middle of nowhere, a million miles from civilization—no cell phones, no television, no computers ... no alcohol. They were dropped off by plane, literally dropped from the plane with parachutes on their backs. Jessica and Jude were members of G.A.I.L. (Guardian Angels for Innocent Lives) and therefore they were experts in two areas: combat and survival.

Weekly food rations were deposited from the same plane, like aid and sustenance to soldiers. But their war was not a physical war; the enemy targeted their emotions. There were no hidden cameras, but those six months living by themselves in a tiny cabin as they moved through the stages of grief felt like a cruel psych experiment. They mourned the loss of their parents and the loss of themselves.

Cheating death more than once, Jessica had seen so much in her short life. Not once did she contemplate the worth of her own life. Not once did she think a single suicidal thought—until she said a silent goodbye to Luke at the cemetery. Jude spent months pulling her from the ledge, offering his shoulder, and sometimes beating some sense into her. How could the person she mourned the most be the only one still living?

Unfortunately, there was no room for error in their new lives. Severing emotional ties would keep them alive. Time. It would not heal them, but with each passing day it hardened their emotions, leaving them feeling numb.

Jude marked off each day on their calendar until the one with the star finally arrived. It read: fin de journée—End of Day. A knock at the door had them bodychecking each other, desperate to see a different face after six long months.

"Greetings!" Knox smiled as he stepped inside.

Jessica never imagined feeling excited to see Knox. In all respects she hated him. However, by then she would have welcomed the devil himself into their cabin. She loved her brother, but six months alone with him, living in such primitive conditions, tested her already-questionable sanity.

"So I see you haven't killed each other."

Jessica and Jude shared knowing smirks. On several occasions they sparred one blow shy of knocking the other one unconscious.

"Did you do your homework?"

"Homework?" Jessica looked at Jude. "You mean there was more than just not killing each other?"

Knox groaned. "God! Can't you two just do what you're told for once? We insisted on grief counseling and you refused it. We suggested Jude have all visible tattoos removed, and he refused that. Now you know damn well we asked you to give yourselves a past and plan out your future —think of new professions or new skills you want to acquire —and you've not done that either? I'm tempted to put a bullet in each of your heads myself and call it a day!"

"We picked out names." Jude grinned, eyes wide. He couldn't feign an ounce of sincerity in his expression.

"Well, thank fuck for that." Knox took a seat at the kitchen table and pulled a computer out of his bag. "I'm going to go over a shitload of information with you. Our main goal is to keep you safe so if you listen and follow the rules, there shouldn't ever be a problem. Our second objective is to make sure the discovery and identification of G.A.I.L is never revealed or compromised."

Jessica and Jude nodded.

"So let's get started."

Four hours later they completed their exit training and packed their minimal belongings for the transport to their final destination.

"Got everything?" Knox asked as he finished typing a few things into his computer.

They looked around the small cabin one last time.

"We're ready," Jude affirmed.

"Alright, one last thing so they can have your new IDs ready by the time we get there. What's it going to be? What new names have you chosen?"

The Days looked at each other and grinned.

CHAPTER TWO

KNIGHT

FOR NINE MONTHS they were inseparable in the womb. Thirty years, two murders, and fifteen hundred miles later, Jillian Knight rolled down the smoked Escalade window. The pungent stench of manure was no longer detectable inside the city's limits. Her life was supposed to be a self-induced state of amnesia, only she remembered everything: the therapeutic monotony of her job, Samovar Tea Bar for plum pu-erh and scones with her mom every Saturday morning, and strolling for miles with Jones—the greatest of all Great Danes—along the scenic trails on the high bluffs of Fort Funston overlooking large sand dunes and the rolling waves of the bay.

"What did you tell the realtor?" Jackson Knight asked, drumming his thumb on his leg with the intensity of a smoker in need of nicotine.

Agent Knox McGraw glanced over his shoulder, beady eyes narrowed against the rays of the June sun cutting through the moonroof. "About?"

"Us," Jackson replied as he pushed his black-framed glasses up his nose.

"Nothing." Knox shrugged.

"He didn't ask about the new owners?"

Jillian smirked while she dabbed her pinkie toenail with blood red polish.

"He did, but I told him it was none of his fucking business." McGraw winked at Jillian as she capped her bottle of polish.

Somewhere over the previous few days and long hours in the SUV, Jillian bonded—a little—with her nemesis, Knox McGraw. They shared a love for driving her brother crazy.

Jackson caught their exchange. "I'm intelligent, not paranoid."

Jillian laughed. "One word: Luke." His name tasted equally bitter and sweet as it slid across her lips, the one person who loved her, all of her—the woman, the survivor, the monster. She imagined Luke taking Jones on those long walks. Her boys. That's what she called them. And now she'd never call them anything ever again because the woman they loved died.

"He snuck up on me." Jackson rolled down his window as the vehicle turned into the Peaceful Woods townhome development.

"He tapped your shoulder." She chuckled. Her dear brother was a hair trigger. She'd adopted sarcasm to hide her nerves. Jackson used the Japanese Chokehold to hide his.

"When he *sneaked* up on me." Jackson narrowed his eyes at her.

Jillian slipped her feet into her flip-flops, careful not to smudge her shiny wet toenails. "In the *grocery store*! You had him on his knees, an inch from his life, in under a second."

McGraw shook his head. "Enough, you two misfit

7

psychos. Out! Good riddance. Utilities are due on the fifteenth. I'd say try to stay alive, but you're not the ones I should be concerned about. So don't kill anyone but yourselves."

The Knights stepped out of the vehicle that sped away the moment their doors slammed shut. They stood in the two-stall driveway, making a 360-degree survey of their new neighborhood: grey cookie cutter homes in groups of two and three, each with a small, staked maple tree in the front yard.

In that moment they were reborn.

"Kansas?" Jackson asked.

"Omaha … Nebraska." Jillian nudged his shoulder, a snicker vibrating from her chest.

"The Cornhusker State?"

"Yes."

"Warren Buffet?"

"Yes."

"Malcolm X?"

"I don't know, Jack. You're the geek."

He looked down at her, pushing his Clark Kent glasses high on his nose. She ripped them off his face and snapped them in two.

"What the hell?"

Jillian tossed them over her shoulder. "You have twenty-twenty vision, and if I have to give up my *everything,* it's not going to be to stare at you in geek glasses that make me want to punch you squarely between the eyes."

The bitter sister with a penchant for snark opened the front door to their three-bedroom fully furnished ranch. "Yeah, no one will ever find us here. After all, who voluntarily enters the gates of Hell? I bet the bathroom is wheelchair accessible."

Jackson feathered his hand along the floral wallpaper that plastered every inch of drywall like geriatric graffiti in the story-and-a-half great room. Jillian eyed the polished brass fixtures, none more nauseating than the gaudy crystal chandelier over the dining room table.

"McGraw is going to die."

Jackson nodded. "I won't be getting laid here anytime soon."

"Not unless she's blind. Then again, I think *you* could manage to get laid in the front pew of a Baptist church during communion." Jillian wrinkled her nose, walking toward the master bedroom. "It even smells like old people."

"And what is that smell?"

The bedroom was a replica of a 1980's Motel 6 room, complete with a dusty rose bedspread and a brass-framed knockoff of Monet's *Blue Water Lilies* over the white wicker headboard.

"You know ... Bengay and carnations."

"What's in the garage?" Jackson walked past her.

"I told McGraw a Harley Davidson for me and something sophisticated like a BMW or Mercedes for you. I miss my bike, I miss ..."

Jackson turned, giving her a sad smile. "It's okay. I miss Dad too. He would be pleased to see that your love for his hobby was genuine."

Jillian nodded as he opened the door to the garage and flipped the switch for the florescent lights that flickered in protest with their last bit of life.

"So. Fucking. Dead."

Jillian squeezed past him. "Oh God."

"Yup." Jackson chuckled until it grew into a full-out hysteria-filled laugh.

She didn't share his humor. Her eyes flitted with disbelief between the pink Vespa with a cream seat and chrome mirrors and the eggplant PT Cruiser with wood panels.

"I'm calling him Woody." Jackson opened the driver's door and slid down into the tan leather seat, hands clenching the steering wheel. "You should call your motorcycle Candy."

Her nose wrinkled in disgust. "It's *not* a motorcycle and you know it. I wouldn't be caught dead on this thing." She made a full-circle inspection without touching it. Jackson and his friends used to call her a tomboy because she liked motorcycles and tools. She hated that stereotype. There was something in between a frilly girly girl and a tomboy. Jillian called it badass sexy.

Jackson climbed out, shut the door, and leaned back against Woody, arms crossed over his chest. "I think not being caught dead is the point."

She riffled through the contents of the red, five-drawer Craftsman tool chest she requested. "No, the point is to fit in, not look like a Mary Kay consultant."

"I think they drive Cadillacs."

The daughter with her father's temper slammed the drawers shut and balled her hands at her hips. "Look at us." Her emotions warred between laughing and crying, but Jillian Knight didn't cry, or maybe she did. She didn't know this Jillian woman well enough to say for sure. Years of repressing her true feelings and hiding any weaknesses had left her emotionally disoriented.

"It all sounded so easy. New identities, new appearances, new location, new professions. But I can't ... I can't let go of that life. Thirty years. It's too much to just forget in six months. Hell, it's too much to forget in a lifetime."

Jackson shared a pained smile. "You don't have to forget, but you do have to let it go. Those caskets ... they represent that life. It's dead, but we're not. We have each other. I still get to look at you and see my sister, and that's enough for me to move on."

"How can you look at me and see anything? Have you looked in the mirror? You have a disturbing mess of dark hair sprouting from your head with *gel* in it. You haven't had hair in over a decade. And this..." she held her long platinum blond hair out from her ear "...my IQ went down ten points in one hour at the salon."

"But our eyes..." Jackson pulled her into his strong, safe arms and looked into her eyes "...they're—"

"Amber ... like the desert sunset." She'd lost count of how many times their mother had said those words—at least a million.

"I want to go back, even if I die. I just ... I don't want to be here." The honesty ripped from her gut. They were conditioned as teenagers to show no emotion, to find strength in bravery. But no one could live that way forever. Everyone needed a safe harbor to release their rawest emotions. Jackson was hers.

"Jess," he whispered her name as if it was the last time he'd ever say it. "Now. Right now. You need to channel that strength I know you have, and feed off it until it numbs the pain. You no longer have a choice. Okay? Fin de journée."

Jillian averted her eyes, pulling away. Empty. Lost. *Numb.* "Fin de journée."

End of Day

"We need a plan." Jackson opened the garage door.

Weak moments had to be brushed away like pesky bugs. Jillian took a deep breath and exhaled all her emotion. Some days it felt like letting go of her humanity. Who lives that way?

"Vehicles, gut the place, then jobs." She sighed.

"Jobs, gut the place, then vehicles," Jackson countered. They grinned at each other. "Alcohol."

By THE TIME they pulled Woody in the garage, the back-seat filled with liquor and a few essential groceries, the neighbors were out in droves walking dogs, spit shining old cars, grilling, and watering potted plants.

"We moved to Jurassic Park." Jackson gave Jillian a side-long glance before opening his door.

Jillian shrugged. "I didn't want to live in an apartment. You didn't want to worry about running over neighbor kids. So our only option was the old fogey development."

"Yoo hoo!" a voice singsonged before Jillian could tag the down button to the garage door. "Hello, hello, hello. You must be the new neighbors."

"We are-are-are," Jackson sang back.

Jillian stifled a snort as she unloaded the sacks and cartons from the backseat. Her brother had three talents: computers, hand-to-hand combat, and random sex. Acting out niceties with strangers that wouldn't end up in his bed was not part of his arsenal of social assets. However, this Jackson guy poured it on thick and sweet. Jillian cocked her head sideways, intrigued by the Oscar-winning performance.

"I'm Jackson Knight and this is Jillian."

"Oh, well *hello* there. I'm Greta Housby. I live right across the street. You two seem too pretty ... I mean *young* ... well, pretty young for our community. These ranch-style homes seem to attract the fifty and over group."

"We were looking for a quiet community." Jackson smiled.

Greta homed in on his arms. "Oh those tattoos are really something. I bet they don't end there ... not that it's my business ... but they don't ... do they?" She bit her lip, missing sexy by about thirty years. It was oddly endearing.

Jillian swallowed back her amusement as Greta stumbled over her words unable to keep her eyes on Jackson for more than a few seconds at a time before her face blushed to a cherry Dum Dum. Jackson shoved his hands deep into the pockets of his shorts, looking the part of an innocent boy. He wet his lips as they pulled into his signature sexy grin that rendered women speechless and usually naked too.

"No they don't." He wiggled his brows.

"Oh ... uh ... good, I mean okay..." Greta took a second to catch her breath "... so, no kids I take it?"

"Nope, just us." Jackson winked at her like a pro.

"Well, your timing is perfect. We're having an association picnic this weekend. Everyone is just dying to meet you. Sarge should be home by then too."

"Sarge?" Jillian questioned, a little uneasy at the word and the memories it conjured.

"Yes, he lives in the unit right next to yours. He works at Offutt ... the air force base. We're all just so proud of his accomplishments. Kind of a quiet guy. I think he's seen some pretty horrific stuff during his career. He's divorced and I'd love to see him find a nice girl. He always seems so sad."

"A nice *girl?* How old is Sarge?" Jillian questioned as if it didn't matter, even if it did.

Greta's skin flushed a bit. "He's young, maybe not as young as you two, but I think he's in his early forties."

Jillian nodded, deep in thought.

"And he's so handsome." Greta gave Jackson a timid glance as if she was worried he'd be jealous of a little competition. "He looks like a body builder with a half dozen abs and all that."

Jillian grinned. "You mean a six pack." She took an instant liking to Greta, admiring any woman who embraced her sexiness no matter her age. Jillian could see herself working the shameless flirt well into her nineties ... if she lived that long.

"Oh yes, that might be it. But that's just hearsay. It's not like he walks around the development without his shirt on." She cleared her throat. "I mean ... he could, there's nothing in the association guidelines that prohibits it." She beamed at Jackson. "In case you were wondering."

Jillian looked at Jackson. Neither one jumped in to rescue Greta from her nervous pool of chatter. After a few moments, Greta's gaze drifted to the pink Vespa.

"What a darling little motorcycle."

Jillian's nostrils flared while malevolent thoughts of breaking McGraw's neck jigged in her mind. "It's not a motorcycle. It's a scooter. Would you like to have it?"

Greta's expression grew wide with surprise. "Oh, I couldn't—"

"Jillian, don't be ridiculous. You won that on the *Price is Right*. It's your favorite souvenir." Jackson grinned.

Her brother may have been a special neurotic breed, but he could crank the crap out of his mouth at a moment's notice. It shouldn't have surprised Jillian, but it still did. When would she ever learn? They had a story and deviating from said story was unacceptable. In less than two hours of their arrival, Jackson had gone rogue. Brother dearest would pay for his indiscretion.

"The *Price is Right* ... yes. What was I thinking? Though maybe you could take it for a little spin sometime."

"Oh dear. I don't know. My hands are a bit crippled with arthritis."

"No worries, Greta. Jackson would love to take you for a ride." Jillian kicked the back door of Woody shut.

"I would?" Jackson raised a single eyebrow at his sister.

Greta's cheeks pinked as she traced invisible circles on the concrete with the toe of her chunky, tan orthotic shoe, hands clasped behind her back. Jillian waited for the bashful "aw shucks" to fall from her lips.

"I ... I would. I'd love to take you for a ride sometime." Jackson grabbed the last two sacks from the back of Woody.

"It's a date!" Greta waltzed backwards. "Well, not a date. We're all married of course. But Marvin takes a nap between three and five every day ... if that works for you. Not that I'm hiding anything from him—"

"Bye, Greta." Jillian pushed the garage door button and reentered the gates of Hell. "If Candy doesn't do it for her, I bet Mrs. Marvin Housby would like the smooth ride of your Woody."

"You're going to get your ass handed to you later. I'm still pissed about you snapping my glasses. Don't even get me started on you pimping me out to the blue-hair."

Jillian popped the caps off two bottles of beer, then handed one to Jackson. "I like her. I bet she's a real cougar."

Jackson took a long pull. "I don't know. The whiskers on her chin bear greater resemblance to a wild boar than a cougar."

Jillian laughed. "Can you hear that? It's Satan cackling as the inferno flames lick our asses because we're close, buddy, really close. As we speak, there are babies being born that will be calling us walking fossils in thirty to forty years. Your toenails will be yellowed and six inches thick, and I'll be using a tree spade to remove the whiskers from *my* boar chin."

———

By MIDNIGHT JACK and Jill had finished two six packs of beer and declared it was time to spar in the basement.

"This might not be such a good idea." Jillian hiccuppped as her body swayed on its own accord.

Jackson stumbled over his impaired feet while shoving all the furniture to the far side of the walkout basement. "We don't have to go to work in the morning." He laughed. "Cuz we don't have jobs. And I haven't been this drunk in years—cuz I used to be responsible. And I need to beat the shit out of you—cuz you pissed me off today."

The equally drunk and pissed off sister kicked out one leg then the other, sending her flip-flops flying. "Fair enough. But if you mess up my nail polish, you'll be eating out of a straw for the next week. And I'm not holding back because that *Price is Right* shit was ridiculous."

Jackson brought his fists up in front of his face. "This is for my designer glasses." His first attempt was sloppy, but he landed his second.

Their bodies were fit and cut to perfection. Their skills —mastered. Sparring was their favorite workout and a necessary part of their survival. Only on the rare occasion did either one emerge with marks, cuts, or bruises. However, on that particular night, under the heavy influ-ence of Heineken, the Knights busted each other up as well as the drywall.

"Why is the floor wet?" Jackson mumbled from his corpse position, knuckles bloodied. Heineken distracted the Knights from wrapping their hands first.

Propped against the wall like a rag doll, Jillian pried open the eye that hadn't caught Jackson's fist. "I think 'Sarge' has a fish tank. Scratch that ... *had* a fish tank."

Jackson eyed the huge hole in the wall. "Oops."

"Coffee ... lots of coffee, then you patch the wall and I'll replace the tank and fish." Jillian moved to all fours then lumbered to vertical.

Jackson took her offered hand. "Where are you going to get fish and a tank in the middle of the night?"

"Sam Walton's."

"Jillian wouldn't know that." Jackson flicked her ear with his finger, reaffirming their sibling antics would stay frozen in time at age ten forever.

"Everyone knows Sam Walton founded Walmart, you idiot." She rolled her eyes at his paranoia.

Their grandfather had been a professor at UC Davis and thanks to him they knew the founders' names of the top Fortune 500 companies before they knew the states and their capitals. Ever since then she referred to major businesses by their founder's name.

CHAPTER THREE

Senior Master Sergeant Monaghan was career air force. When his son, Cage, was ten, his wife—a dental hygienist—left him for her boss. At the time he didn't care; Sarge was happily married to his job. At least that's what he told himself to keep the pain at bay.

"Son, are you ready to talk about the fish tank?" Sarge asked as he inhaled his eggs, hash, and sausage at the kitchen table. He'd already run seven miles, surged through an hour of weights and abs, spit shined the bathrooms, and devoured the paper cover-to-cover.

Twenty-year-old Cage, starting quarterback for the Huskers, made the short hour drive home most weekends to hang out with his dad. He lived on the football field—hard-working, dedicated, and focused just like his father. But on the weekends he did what most college students did over summer break—drank too much and slept until noon.

"Yeah, Dad, I'm dying to know how you managed to break the tank, replace it with the cheapest piece of crap I've ever seen, fill it with Betta fish, which are known for fighting to the death, and then paint the wall behind the tank a completely different shade of gray than the rest of the wall. Are you having *issues* again?" Cage raised a cautious eyebrow.

"I'm not laughing." Sarge cleared his throat, a stern glare shooting over the rim of his coffee cup like a missile taking aim at its target.

Cage poured nearly an entire box of cereal into a popcorn bowl and flooded it with milk, then took a seat opposite his father. "Of course you're not. Come to think of it ... I'm not sure I've ever seen you laugh."

"I don't mind you staying with me on the weekends, but I have zero tolerance for parties."

Cage paused mid-shovel, milk dripping from his spoon as he leaned over the trough. "You're serious? I arrived around noon yesterday, met up with a few buddies downtown, then crashed by eleven. The tank and fish massacre happened before I arrived here. Maybe Ryn broke the tank and replaced it."

Sarge studied his son through narrowed eyes. Not only was Sarge a human lie detector, he'd also raised his son to value integrity and honesty.

"Ryn came last week. I was home three days ago." Sarge knew his housekeeper would not try to hide something as blatantly obvious as that from him.

"What else could it be? You had some nice fish but they weren't anything worth stealing. Besides, when someone breaks in to steal something they don't replace it with a cheaper version ... or replace it at all for that matter."

"If this is some prank or practical joke ..." Sarge warned.

Cage shook his head. "I don't have a death wish, so stop trying to pin this one on me. Maybe you should ask the new neighbors if they heard anything going on over here."

"New neighbors? They've moved in?"

Cage nodded. "Mrs. Housby dropped off an invite for tomorrow's association picnic. She said they're young and 'utterly delightful.' She thinks it's going to be 'fun' having a young married couple in the neighborhood."

"Kids?"

"I don't think so. She didn't say. I haven't met them, but I saw the woman when I arrived yesterday. She was ..." Cage shifted in his chair.

"She was ...?" Sarge looked up at him while loading the dishwasher.

"Getting the mail ... in a white tank top..." Cage cleared his throat "...no bra, lace panties, and red rain boots."

Sarge straightened with a stiff air of readiness. "I see. Was anyone else outside witnessing it?"

Cage grinned. "Oh yes. It was like the second coming of Christ. The women gasped, nearly fainting, and the men..." Cage winked with an easy nod "...well, a *part* of them was most likely resurrected."

Sergeant Monaghan thrived on order and regimen. He couldn't shake the unsettling feeling Cage's revelation gave him about the new neighbors. Peaceful Woods was a quiet development free from the chaos of young children and even barking dogs. Only a few of the residents had pets and most were cats or small dogs that used piss pads indoors. The forty pound weight limit on pets served both to discourage ownership and keep the peace.

"Clean up your mess when you're done. I'm going to go introduce myself to the new neighbors."

WEEKENDS WERE a rare opportunity to catch Sarge out of his uniform. He needed the aura of authority it gave him.

Lingering stares that conveyed both respect and intimidation. It made it easier to pretend he wasn't losing his fucking mind. However, he deemed it best to make his first encounter with the new neighbors a friendly one. There was no need to intimidate anyone—yet.

"Just a minute!" a female voice sounded.

Sarge tried to peer through the sidelight window, but all he could see were a few boxes and some tied up black trash bags. The door flung open giving way to a woman. A woman who did not belong in Peaceful Woods. She couldn't have been more than a buck fifteen in weight and maybe five-two with arms and legs wrapped in muscle and taut tan skin. Her long blond hair hung in messy strands over her chest, not completely concealing the fact that she wasn't wearing a bra under her tight T-shirt and frayed denim shorts that would violate most public school dress codes.

"Are you more of the welcome wagon?" She smiled, but not just any smile. Sarge knew her type. He was certain she was used to men frolicking around in her presence—men with a fraction of Sarge's discipline and devoid of all dignity.

"No. I don't bake," he deadpanned.

Her grin crept its way up to her golden eyes. She looked humored by his comment; little did she know, Sarge was born without a funny bone. He too was used to women frolicking around him, but it pissed him off that his *married* neighbor was so blatant with her eyes all over him.

"Neither do I. Beer?"

Sarge glanced at his watch. It was ten minutes past noon. "If I say no thank you, are you going to give me the 'It's five o'clock somewhere' line?"

She turned on her heel with a chuckle. "No."

He followed her inside, weaving his way through the maze of boxes. "Still unpacking?"

"Nope, just the opposite. We bought the place unseen and furnished. We won't be making that mistake again. Everything in those boxes and bags is too nauseating to keep." She handed him a beer.

"No, thank you."

The petulant woman with seductive curves and a wicked smile shoved it into his chest until he wrapped his hand around its cool neck. "It's five o'clock somewhere." She hopped up on the counter.

His eyes narrowed.

"Your line, not mine." Jillian winked then took a long pull of her beer.

Showing no humor or interest, he set the beer down on the counter. She glanced at it with a frown.

"I just came over to introduce myself. I'm AJ Monaghan. I live in the unit next to yours."

"Mmm ..." she swallowed "...yes, the uh ... GI Joe guy. Greta speaks highly of you. In fact, I think you were her neighborhood crush until Jackson caused her fragile heart to go all a flutter."

She chugged down the rest of the beer. AJ had never seen a woman drink quite like that. "Rumor has it you have the best abs in the neighborhood. Mine aren't too shabby either. Want to compare?"

"Excuse me?" He shot her a piercing glare. Her uncensored personality was three times the size of her body.

Jillian's eyes danced with mischief. "Maybe some other time, then. Jackson's out in the garage cleaning up his Woody. I'll have to introduce you two."

AJ wasn't going to touch the "woody" comment. "I'm a Senior Master Sergeant, not a 'GI Joe guy.'"

She grabbed AJ's beer and gulped half of it down, then wiped her mouth with the back of her hand. "Good for you. I'd hate to invite you to my wedding. It would be a real bitch trying to fit all that in calligraphy on a five-by-seven envelope. So what's AJ stand for?"

He tipped his chin up. "How long's he been hitting you?"

The not so innocent victim touched the mottled skin around her eye, then feathered her fingers down to the small cut on her lip. A devilish grin appeared. "As long as I've been hitting him." She hopped off the counter, landing so close to AJ her chest almost touched his stomach.

AJ retreated until his back pressed flush against the refrigerator. She moved with him like a slow dance. Her lips grazed his shirt at his sternum. The pint-sized man-eater inhaled a slow breath as if he were going to be her lunch. Then she met his gaze, peering at him through long lashes.

"Why? Are you going to save me from the Big Bad Wolf?" she whispered then let her tongue make a lazy drag across her bottom lip.

He'd always imagined the devil being taller. AJ didn't care that she most likely felt his erection against her stomach. It wasn't much of a compliment to her. Guys could get erections from tampon commercials; it was simple anatomy.

"Doubtful. You probably deserved it."

Pleasure spread across her face as she stepped back, taking another swig of beer. "I'm Jillian. And I'm sure you're right. I probably had it coming for one thing or another. But thanks for your concern."

He stared at her, willing her to back off. Her complete disregard for his personal space pissed him off even if his dick was having a lapse in judgement. "I wasn't concerned."

"Oh, well then that just shows your lack of manners for

23

pointing out a woman's flaws to her. You must be a real lady killer." She gestured with her head. "Come on, I'll introduce you to Jackson."

AJ's head pounded with dizzying confusion. He couldn't figure out how this sick and twisted couple found their way into Peaceful Woods. The rest of the residents may have had impaired vision, but the moment Jackson turned his attention away from the most wretchedly hideous car AJ had ever seen, he knew—Jackson and Jillian were siblings. Their eyes weren't similar, they were identical. Identical shades of a rare golden-amber. *Fucking inbreds.*

"It's a pleasure to meet you." Jackson offered his hand.

AJ returned a firm shake while he inspected Jackson's face that resembled a boxer's after a title fight.

"Don't mind my ugly mug. Jillian got me drunk; it's the only way she can land a solid hit."

Jillian tilted her head, giving Jackson a subtle shake and challenging glare.

AJ had seen and heard enough. The unexpectedness of the situation crippled his thoughts. He couldn't remember the real reason for his visit.

"Anyway..." he cleared his throat "...I just wanted to introduce myself. I'm not home much, but my son is here most weekends so maybe just keep things ... *appropriate* for his young eyes and ears."

Jackson and Jillian shared an indecipherable look—maybe amusement but most definitely disrespect.

"How old is your son?" Jillian asked.

"Young," AJ replied with a matter-of-fact finality.

"Young, huh? What two numbers is that between?" she goaded.

AJ's heart hammered as he clenched his jaw, reaching

deep for control. His brain was fucked-up, but not without cause. Never before had a woman made him feel so enraged. And never before had such lewd acts felt so tempting ... so inevitable. He'd found a woman who could take pain. But Jillian didn't just take it—she beseeched it.

CHAPTER FOUR

JILLIAN'S MIND lingered on the image of AJ long after he'd vanished from her sight. It was obvious he made weightlifting his bitch, his definition a little more than just long and lean. The short black hair with a few highlights of grey and his strong jaw bared resemblance to Hugh Jackman. His broad shoulders seemed to bear the weight of the world as much as his dark intense eyes reflected it.

Confusion set in. Did she want to lick every inch of him or beat the shit out of him just to see if she could? What did he look like in uniform and would the sight of it awaken the demons?

The buzz cut he kept would prevent her controlling hands from making claim, but Jillian envisioned her fingernails digging, ripping, and scarring the muscled terrain of his back while his stormy eyes held hers, narrowing with every stab of pain. Pain she knew he would feel at her merciless touch. In the suppressed, rational corner of her twisted mind, she knew he defined wrongness and at least a dozen other synonyms. He woke something inside her that threatened her new existence.

Was there enough room in her head for this Jillian woman and the life she was trying to make for herself? Was there room in her heart to build a wall—a tomb—around her past and start anew? She had to find out because every day without Luke in her life felt like death, and there was nothing worse than feeling dead but still being alive. Maybe if she let her body move on, her mind would catch up.

"So AJ's the sergeant?"

"Senior Master Sergeant Monaghan." Jillian stood at attention and saluted.

"A guy in a uniform. Sounds like trouble ... as in a mind-fuck of trouble." Jackson frowned as he turned and walked inside the house.

Jillian followed. "Maybe, but don't worry, he's not my type. I'm trying to rehabilitate my uniform 'fetish' to strictly FedEx and UPS—bigger packages."

Jackson sighed like he'd been choking on the words he wanted to say but decided to gut them back down. "Let's rip this wallpaper off today." He pinched a peeling corner and pulled a small strip from the wall.

"I know what you're thinking."

"No, Jess—Jillian." Jackson closed his eyes. "You don't." His pain was hers too. They were bonded by so much more than blood.

Jillian couldn't remember a time where she didn't sense his thoughts, feel his pain. She pressed her forehead to his back and wrapped her arms around him.

"You have a jaded history with older women, but I didn't get all judgmental with you when Greta showed such blatant interest."

Jackson's body vibrated with laughter, and she melted into him, grateful for the break in tension. "With one thrust, I'd snap her in half."

They laughed.

"McGraw was right. We're going to ruin these poor old people." She handed him the wallpaper scorer. "Here— score, mix, soak, strip, clean."

They spent the rest of the afternoon "de-elderizing" the place. Their neighborhood turned into a multiplying herd of onlookers roaming past their house, eager to catch a glimpse of the mysterious young couple who seemed to be gutting their entire place.

"Knock, knock," an unfamiliar male voice sounded through the screen door.

Jackson climbed down the ladder while Jillian tied the last trash bag of wallpaper scraps.

"Hey, not trying to bother ya. I'm Stan Renner."

"Hi, Stan. I'm Jackson Knight and Jillian is around the corner."

"Be right there," she called.

"No hurry. I live up the street, the only one with the four-car garage."

"Did you stop by to see if we wanted to trade places?" Jackson smiled.

"What? Oh ... no, no. My garage is my man cave. It's temperature-controlled, finished floor, heated walls. Basically it's the only thing that keeps me sane when my wife goes off on her rants about ... well, everything. No, I'm just stopping cuz I'm the association president—nobody else wanted the job—but that's neither here nor there. I think it's great the way you're updating the place, but you might not be aware of the fact that the garbage doesn't come until Wednesday. If it were only a couple of trash bags, I'd tell ya to just keep them in your garage until trash day. But you've got a real mountain out at the end of your driveway, and I just don't think you can leave that sitting there until Wednesday. I'm not trying to be a bad guy, but—"

"Hey, Stan ..." Jillian enjoyed Stan's incessant rambling too much to interrupt, but she also loved her brother and felt the need to save him from President Stan. "I'm Jillian. How lovely to meet you."

Stan smoothed his hands over his salt and pepper hair that looked like it had once been curly, but suffered from the thinning and slow physical deterioration of time.

"Hi ... uh ... I'm Stan ... Stan Renner." He fell hard and quick, like most of Jillian's victims.

His introduction was either naturally James Bond or simply a case of nerves. "I apologize for the heap of garbage in our driveway." Jillian flipped her hair back over her shoulder, in case Stan wasn't working with twenty-twenty.

As if on cue, those old-man eyes slipped to her breasts that were enjoying yet another day of freedom from the confines of a bra. "Ya know what? I'm just so tickled that you two are such diligent workers, which is hard to find in this day and age, that I don't see any reason why I can't bring down my pickup and get this hauled off for you."

"Oh really?" Jillian proved to Jackson that he wasn't the only one who could pour the honey slow and sweet. "That would be amazing! Make sure you check with me when you're done. I was just getting ready to throw a batch of chocolate chip cookies in the oven."

Stan backed out the door. "Well, young lady, I might just take you up on that. The only thing the missus does anymore is sit around watching Netflix on her computer all day. I think I've forgotten what a woman's sweet treats taste like." Stan waved then walked his tall, bony body back up the street—hands gesturing every which way, lips moving like he was talking to someone, but no one else was around.

"Let's just be clear on this. First, it's a little disturbing that Stan can't remember the taste of a 'woman's sweet treats.' But what's even crazier is the fact that we have beer, half a loaf of bread, a jar of peanut butter, and three brown bananas, yet somehow you're going to wave your magic wand and make homemade chocolate chip cookies appear in our oven?"

Jillian bit the edge of her thumbnail. "Yeah, I should have said peanut butter cookies."

WITHIN TWO HOURS, Stan had hauled away all of their trash, swept their driveway, pulled weeds in their front yard, edged along their walk, and planted three hostas below their deck that he'd split from the north side of his own house. The Knights were dealing with a seventy-something who had a severe case of ADHD. Luckily for everyone involved, Stan enjoyed staying busy and they had no qualms with taking advantage of their elderly neighbor, who had the energy of someone half his age.

"Peanut butter, banana bread balls ... and he ate them with a smile."

Jillian fought to contain her own amusement. "Do you think it's my blond hair?"

Jackson nudged her shoulder as they sipped their beers and watched the slow motion of life in Peaceful Woods from their front door step. "No, it's your tits."

"I should start wearing a bra."

"I doubt it would matter. It's still lingerie. From what I've seen, I think once women hit sixty they start buying their bras from the Army Surplus Store. You know what I'm talking about, the ones with seven rows of fastening hooks, six-inch wide shoulder straps, and such thick material and complete coverage it could double as a bulletproof vest. These men around here ... they've been looking at vests for years."

Jillian laughed, almost to the point of tears. "You're so mean."

"Astute."

"Shrewd." She sighed. "God, I can't believe this is our home now."

"Well believe it. And I know you don't want to talk about it, but we're going to be attacked from every direction at the picnic tomorrow. These people have nothing better to do than live vicariously through us because let's face it ... they have no life. So we need to get our shit together. We've agreed on a past, now we need a future."

"A future?" Jillian finished the rest of her beer.

"Jobs."

"You know what we should do?" Jillian's eyes widened.

"Professional beer tasting?"

"Is that a real job?" Jillian couldn't hide the excitement in her voice from the fleeting moment of promise.

"I'm joking."

"About it being a real job or our job?"

Jackson shook his head. "Both, neither ... I don't know. You'd suck at it since you don't like beer."

"No, that other girl didn't like beer. Jillian Knight is quite fond of it."

"You guzzle it down to expedite the buzz so you no longer care what it tastes like."

He had a valid point. In the past thirty years she'd had maybe a grand total of six bottles of beer. Since their arrival in Omaha, she'd been averaging a six pack a day. The beer did two necessary things: one, it made her Jillian Knight, and two, it made life as Jillian Knight in Omaha, Nebraska, *tolerable.*

"Back to my idea." Jillian stood and offered Jackson her hand.

"Where are we going?"

"Inside for paper, pens, and hats."

As only two thirty-year-olds on a new path with way too much alcohol circulating through their veins would have done, the Knights decided to write five jobs for each other on ripped pieces of paper then drew them out of a hat.

"What if I don't like the first one I draw?" Jackson asked as he went first.

"Then you can draw another, but there's only five so you have to choose one."

"No way." Jackson ripped the first piece of paper in two.

"Which one was it?"

"School bus driver."

Jillian giggled, tipping her beer toward him. "Yeah, I didn't think that one through. It would require you to be sober."

"And like kids. Your turn."

"Don't act so callous. Why exactly is it you don't like kids? I mean ... I've assumed for quite some time now that it's because you still are one and you don't like competition."

Jackson shrugged. "They remind me of what I may never have."

"Oh ... that's ... deep."

"God, you're gullible. It's been my MO for years. The downside to dating older women is their damn ticking biological clocks. If a woman knows I don't like kids and still ends up in my bed, then I know it's for the right reason."

"Which is?"

"Duh ... sex." Jackson took a swig of his beer.

"Yeah ... not so deep after all."

Jackson smirked and held out Jillian's hat. She stirred her hand around and picked out a piece of paper. "What the hell?"

Jackson snatched it from her. "Oh, this is a good one. And I'm sure the demand is high here in Nebraska. The downside is the risk of injury."

"It's not even a real job, you perverted fuck."

"It most certainly is."

"Then do share, oh wise one, what exactly a *barnyard masturbator* does."

"It's self-explanatory. They collect bovine sperm for research and breeding purposes. You can use a rectal electrifier to stimulate its release, or an artificial vagina on its penis, or good old-fashioned manual stimulation." Jackson wiggled his brows.

"Bullshit."

Jackson laughed. "Technically it's bull sperm."

"Give me your hat. I need to add some better job options." Jillian tried to take Jackson's drawing hat.

"Nope. Too late. And just remember ... we shook on it. We *both* agreed we would choose one of the five jobs, *no matter what.*"

"Draw," Jillian grumbled, sitting back in her chair.

"Personal Trainer? No way." Jackson narrowed his eyes at her.

"Don't even look at me that way. You cannot honestly say working as a personal trainer is worse than jacking-off barnyard animals."

"It is if you spent most of your senior year in high school being jacked off by your personal trainer."

"She wasn't a personal trainer, she was a P.E. teacher." Jillian laughed. "And don't act like you didn't like it. Luke said it's probably what started your older woman fetish."

"Nice to know you kept that shit confidential."

They both paused for a moment. Just the mention of his name sucked the air out of the room, even in their inebriated state.

Jackson held out Jillian's hat. "Go."

Jillian grinned as she read the paper. "Pampered Chef? Is that company still in business?"

"Absolutely. Then maybe you'd learn to cook."

"Not happening. Next."

Jackson drew. "Piano teacher?"

"You'd be great at it!"

"No jobs with kids."

"It's a half hour lesson, not a commitment to be their big brother. Anyway, you could always teach adults."

Jackson shook his head while Jillian took her turn.

"Sex toy party consultant." Jillian raised a lone brow. "These home party jobs are usually evening work. Why don't I just turn tricks? The pay would be better."

"Patience. You still have two more options."

Jillian kicked his shin. "Prostitute is one of the last two options, isn't it?"

Jackson snickered. "My turn." He fished a piece of paper from the hat. "Discount mattress store mascot?"

"Yes. You've seen them—the guys that dress up in a mattress costume and stand on the street corner. I bet it would increase your chances of getting laid."

Jackson took a pull of his beer. "I've got Woody, what more could women want?"

Jillian drew again. "A psychic?" She giggled as the endless possibilities played in her mind.

"I knew you'd like that one."

"I do, but I think it's best we stick with jobs that won't have disgruntled customers seeking revenge."

"You're probably right. Give me my last choice." Jackson unfolded the paper. "A prostitute? You bitch! You put that one in *my* hat?"

Jillian hugged her stomach. There was nothing she loved more than getting the best of her brother. "Don't act all offended. That was basically your life before, I'm just suggesting you get paid for it now."

"These suck." Jackson wadded the paper and tossed it back in the hat. "Every single one."

"Yeah, because my choices are so appealing. Let's see what your last ingenious idea is." She pulled the last piece of paper from her hat. "A surrogate? You think I'm going to spend the next ten years, fat, swollen, and pissing my pants every time I laugh?"

Jackson shrugged. "What could be more beautiful than giving the gift of life?"

She flicked the piece of paper at him. "Ending yours, you barnyard masturbating jerk!"

He sighed, eyes red and glassy. "This is fucked. We shouldn't be doing this. This is our life, we should take it seriously. I want my old job—the one where I'm actually using my computer engineering degree."

"Join the club. Do you have any idea how many tests I took and how hard I worked ... all for nothing. I say we just do it. You start your own business and I'll start retaking my exams."

Jackson sighed. "God you're pathetic. You have a weak moment and I'm there, pulling you back to reality. I have a weak moment and you're like, 'Yeah, fuck it, bro, let's jump off that cliff.' McGraw said no to anything close to our old professions. It would give us an unnecessary hint of visibility, put us on the radar."

Jillian slumped in her chair, finishing the last of her beer. "I know, I know. Karma hates us. We shouldn't even be here, but we are so screw it. Money's not an issue, so for now I say we live with reckless abandon, shunning all reason and responsibility. Accountability is overrated. Let's just *be*."

Jessica and Jude Day had been overachievers in every sense of the word. Could Jillian and Jackson let go of their inner drive for success and just *be*? Not likely, but it was worth a try.

Jackson slid her a pen and piece of paper. "Ok then. You're right. It's too hard to choose. So you pick *the* job for me and I'll pick *the* one for you."

"Just like that? Out of the five choices I gave you, I get to pick *the* one?"

"Yes. Just like that. And I get to pick yours."

The Knights stared at each other in a drunken gaze showdown. Luckily choosing random and meaningless professions didn't require sobriety.

"Fine."

"Fine."

CHAPTER FIVE

AJ LOOKED for every possible excuse to skip the association picnic. He even entertained the idea of a self-inflicted gunshot wound. Unfortunately, Cage was still home so he considered any form of self-mutilation to be extreme and a bad example.

"Everyone is going to hound you about the upcoming season and guilt you into getting them tickets for a game." AJ made his last appeal as he packed their plates and utensils in a brown bag while Cage loaded the cooler.

"What's your deal? I'm usually being guilted into attending these things." He laughed at his father's peculiar mood.

AJ shrugged. "No deal. What's your deal today? Why are you so enthusiastic about attending a picnic with a bunch of people from your grandparents' generation?"

"Our new neighbors are close to my age."

Once. AJ had met her once. Jillian was a goddamn train wreck. He couldn't get her out of his mind and Cage's comment only aggravated AJ's already edgy mood. "No, she's not."

"She?"

"They," AJ corrected. "*They* are older than you."

"But younger than you. It's not like they're old enough to be my parents. I haven't met them, but they or *she* seemed pretty cool."

AJ sighed. "You saw her in her underwear."

"Let me repeat ... she seemed pretty cool." Cage smirked.

"Behave."

AJ CURSED God and the local meteorologists for the blanket of blue sky that kidnapped the seventy percent chance of rain. Cage pulled his red Husker cap over his unkempt blond hair he inherited from his mother—along with his blue eyes—then grabbed the cooler from the back of the truck—sporting a shit-eating grin as the residents of Peaceful Woods greeted him like a celebrity.

Smoke billowed from the large grill as the men huddled around it while the women arranged side dishes on the picnic tables in the pavilion. The glaring contradiction to the scene was Jackson Knight surrounded by the flock of women shoving food at his pretty-boy face as they vied for his attention.

"Sarge, where's your meat? We'll throw it on the grill," Dodge called.

AJ raised his chin. "Cage is getting it." He grabbed a beer and navigated to the smoke. Cage handed him their brats, and AJ dropped them on the grill next to what he thought looked like the most pathetic excuse for a hot dog ever.

"Watch it, Senior Master Sergeant. I don't want my

Tofurkey dog touching your *big sausage* or I'll be tasting it all night."

AJ turned. Jillian peered at him over the frames of her sunglasses that sat low on her nose. Stray hairs from her ponytail whipped in the wind as reckless as the rest of her.

"It's a bratwurst and what the hell is a Tofurkey dog?" Hidden by his dark aviators, AJ's eyes roved her pint-sized body barely covered by a strapless sundress that was a good six inches too short. Why did that bother him? Simple. His dick had lost all self-respect.

"I don't eat meat. It's tofu." She winked and pushed her glasses high on her nose.

"My ex-girlfriend is a vegetarian." Cage managed to physically and verbally squeeze his way into the conversation as he nudged AJ to the side. "Don't mind my old man, he wouldn't understand. I think he brushes his teeth with bacon-flavored toothpaste."

"No. I don't," AJ grumbled.

Cage winked. "It's a joke..." he cupped his hand at his mouth "...but he doesn't understand what that is either."

Jillian's smile grew exponentially as she held out her hand. "Jillian Knight. And you must be the *young* son."

Cage took her hand with an eagerness that tipped AJ even closer to the edge. "Cage, and yes I'm young, twenty to be exact." He looked around. "But that's not saying much with this crowd. I'll be twenty-one next month."

"Well, I might have to take you out for a celebratory drink." Jillian teased the neck of her beer bottle along her blood red painted lower lip.

AJ cleared his throat. "You're married." *To your brother, you incestuous whore.*

"I am?" Jillian raised up on her toes and looked around. "Hmm, I don't see my *husband*. I think we're good." She

39

stepped closer to Cage. "It's just a drink. I'm not going to take your virginity."

Cage adjusted his hat and AJ suspected that wasn't all he needed to adjust.

"I'm not a virgin." Cage wet his lips and chuckled a bit.

Jillian moved her head in a conspiratorial side-to-side glance, then whispered, "Neither am I."

"Speaking of drinks..." AJ gave Cage a firm squeeze on the shoulder "...why don't you grab me another beer and go entertain the ladies that I'm sure are dying to chat with you."

Cage walked off with a quick look back at Jillian.

"Entertain the *ladies*? Am I not a lady?" Jillian sipped her beer.

"No. You're not." AJ tried to look anywhere but directly at her.

"Have I done something wrong?"

How was he supposed to answer that question? Especially since she failed to deliver her words with an ounce of give-a-shit. "Do you have any morals?"

She twisted her lips. "I think so, unless they were lost in the move. Why? Do you need to borrow some?"

AJ shook his head. "Just stay away from my son."

"Is everything okay?" Jackson slid his arm around Jillian.

The roiling in AJ's stomach intensified, festering like a flesh eating bacteria. "Keep your *wife* away from my son." He brushed past them, enraged that he was the only one who didn't think they were God's gift to Peaceful Woods.

"Here's your beer." Cage handed him another can and a plate for food. "Jillian's—"

"Trouble. Just ... keep your distance." AJ mentally reprimanded himself. Cage was a good kid, but he also had a wild side that was drawn to *trouble*.

"Hey, Sarge."

"Dodge, good to see you." AJ smiled. "How's Lilith?"

"She's okay. Katie's been visiting the past week so I've been able to sneak out on a few occasions."

"Any luck finding some part-time help?"

AJ was close to Dodge and Lilith. His father and Dodge had been in the service together then lived next to each other in Portland for years until Dodge was transferred to Omaha. His wife, Lilith, suffered from severe rheumatoid arthritis and Ménière's disease which required constant supervision.

"Until today, no."

AJ followed Dodge through the food line. "Oh, yeah?"

"Yeah. Jillian."

AJ paused. "Jillian?"

"Yes, she's offered to look after Lilith on Tuesday and Thursday afternoons."

"Jillian Knight?"

Dodge laughed. "Yes. What an angel."

Angel? AJ had many words to describe his new neighbor, but angel was not one of them. "Doesn't she have a job?"

"Said she works nights."

AJ glanced over a few tables at Jillian who sat next to Stan Renner, throwing her head back in laughter as he talked to her using his animated hand gestures. AJ tried to sound casual with his words. "Did she mention what she does at *night*?"

"Hmm ... I couldn't say for sure. Something to do with a private consulting business, personal equipment sales of some sort. I wasn't following. After she offered to help out with Lilith, I couldn't concentrate on anything else she said." Dodge nudged AJ's elbow and lowered his voice to a whisper. "It's hard to concentrate around her in general. Have you ever seen anything quite like her? She looks like one of them superhero girls straight off the movie screen."

Superhero—another completely inappropriate word to describe Jillian. AJ had at least a dozen more accurate ones: black widow, serpent, man-eater, mindfuck, wicked, twisted, deceitful, Satan ...

"Ya know what's even better?" Dodge continued as AJ's mind went where it always did with Jillian—to that very dark place. "She's offered to help Bill with the mowing while his son's wife is on bedrest until the twins are born."

Bill and his son Todd owned a lawn and snow removal business. Since Bill lived at Peaceful Woods, his company was the obvious choice, however, AJ wasn't fond of his mowing method—scalp the yards so he didn't have to mow as often. On the flip side, the chemical company they'd hired made more money because the only thing that survived in the lawn after Bill mowed was the weeds.

"Good talking with you, Dodge." AJ drifted through the rest of the picnic on autopilot, doing what he did best—keeping an eye on the enemy.

The Knights left not long after the meal was over, but AJ and Cage stayed another hour enduring the endless chatter over how wonderful the new neighbors were. AJ lost count of the number of times he had to swallow down his own vomit.

"Oh, Sarge! I forgot to say something to Jillian and Jackson," Stan called.

AJ scowled, jaw clenched, then turned around. "About?"

"I hauled away some trash for them the other day, and I

noticed there was a broken fish tank in the pile. Looked like a pretty nice one. Anyway, I was going to see if they had a new one yet. My daughter has one she no longer uses and I'm sure she'd be willing to sell it to them for a decent price."

Red. That's all AJ could see, and he could feel his pulse in the vein on his forehead. "Something tells me they've already replaced it. But I assure you, I'll have a word with them about it."

"Great, let me know what you find out."

AJ shot Cage a belligerent look, slit eyes daring him to so much as let his lips twitch into anything resembling a sign of amusement. "Let's go."

CHAPTER SIX

THE WOMAN that attempted to settle in Jillian Knight's body would never have been able to sell sex toys. She knew the only people who required battery-operated plastic and silicon devices were lazy and unimaginative dolts who didn't have a clue how to use their God-given parts for pleasure. If a guy wanted her restrained during sex, he would have to physically overpower her. But in the spirit of new beginnings, Jillian decided she'd sell sex toys better than the Pope sold religion.

Jackson left to get paint and more alcohol. They both agreed when their new jobs started they would cut back on the booze and act like grownups again instead of college kids during rush week. Jillian took the opportunity to soak in the huge master bathroom tub, in need of some peace and quiet to reflect on her new life. Much to her aggravation, the doorbell rang just as she settled into the steamy abyss laced with her favorite fragrance: gardenia.

"Go away," she mumbled to herself with her head resting back, eyes closed.

It rang again and again at more frequent intervals until

she was ready to break the finger of the perpetrator. *Go the fuck away!*

The water sloshed everywhere as she stepped out and wrapped a satin robe around her soap-slicked body, cinching the tie with a few expletives whispered to no one in particular, then slapped her wet feet against the hard floor to the front door.

"What?" she answered, throwing open the door.

For the second day in a row, AJ stood on her front door stoop wearing a pissed-off expression that somehow excluded his eyes, which took liberty with her body in ways that both exhilarated and frightened her. "How stupid do you really think I am?"

Jillian narrowed her eyes, lips twisted to the side. "Well, given your high military ranking I would have said average to normal intelligence, but since you decided to incessantly ring my doorbell like a five-year-old doped up on sugar, I'm now inclined to say somewhere between borderline deficiency in intelligence and feeble-mindedness."

"I have an IQ of one-twenty-two. Where's your *husband*?" He stepped into the house, forcing Jillian to retreat.

She loved watching his whole body tense as his strong chest heaved with each wrathful breath. "You tell me, Sherlock. Where is my *husband*?" Jillian rooted herself in place. She vowed that no man was going to intimidate her, not ever again.

AJ barged past her to the living room, then the bedrooms. Yet, somehow she knew he wasn't looking for Jackson. A few minutes after he stomped down the stairs. She decided to follow him.

"Find what you're looking for?" she asked, stopped at the bottom step.

AJ stood with his back to her, thick muscled arms crossed over his chest. He stared at the patched wall. "You broke into my place."

"No ... more like broke through. We were exercising, sparring actually. It was Heineken's fault."

He turned. "I'm not talking about the wall! I'm talking about the cheap-ass fish tank full of fucking Betta fish that have killed each other and the piss-poor paint matching."

Jillian waved him off. "I didn't break in for that. I went through the front door, without breaking it. Someone wasn't using their *one-twenty-two* IQ when they decided to hide their house key in the most original place ever—under a planter."

Her muscles clenched in rigid defense from the speed that AJ used to close the distance between them. The extra few inches of the bottom step put them closer to eye-level.

"Jackson is your brother." His deep voice vibrated, devoid of any question. She felt his warm breath inches from her mouth as his icy words wrapped around her nerves.

"He is." She eased a slow swallow, unwilling to show emotion.

"So are you a liar or just a real sick bitch?"

Jillian shrugged as her eyes focused on his lips. But she didn't crave their warmth or the feel of them against hers; she craved the metallic taste that would bleed from them. "Depends on the day."

He grabbed her left arm and just as quickly she struck his nose, not enough to break it, just enough to give a warning and make his eyes water. She surprised herself. That survival instinct was still there and it smothered the quick flash of regret.

"Chain of command, *Sergeant*! You touch me without permission and there will be consequences."

AJ released her arm and dabbed the slow drip of blood from his left nostril. A grin pulled at his lips—a grin that surprised Jillian and she let her guard slip. As if he timed her blink just right, he had her pinned facedown on the stairs, hands restrained at her back with his whole body bearing down on hers. "That's *Senior Master Sergeant* to you," he whispered in her ear as she struggled beneath him.

She gasped as he sucked and bit the back of her neck with bruising force, his erection pressed to her ass. Why did that turn her on so damn much?

"Fuck you!" She wriggled an arm free and landed a solid blow to his ribs, allowing her to break free for a split second before he had her pinned down again, chest-to-chest, face-to-face. The sash to her robe loosened in the struggle and left her robe open, her naked flesh against his clothed body. His eyes searched her face for a long moment, and the instant his expression softened, lips closing in on hers, she head-butted him.

"Goddammit!" AJ growled.

Jillian wiggled out and shoved him back onto the floor. She re-tied her robe, wild eyes holding his gaze, both of them breathless.

Luke ... she couldn't stop thinking about Luke. The stranger on her floor was Luke. He had to be Luke. Her body belonged to Luke. He was her heart. Luke was her entire world.

She closed her eyes and told her brain to stop! Luke was gone ... forever. Even if her mind couldn't accept that and move on ... her body needed to. Jillian was not Jessica. Period.

"Is it weird that your coveting-the-neighbor's-wife thing

turns me on?" Straddling his body, she lowered one inch at a time. AJ's hands slid up her bare legs beneath her robe.

"You're fucked-up."

"Pot. Kettle. Black." She smirked.

His jaw clenched as she pressed her lips to his neck; his hands made a painful claim to her hips. Driven by a need with a pulse and voice of its own, she curled her fingers around the neck of his T-shirt, stretching it down until hungry lips brushed over the firm ridge of his collarbone.

His body was stone beneath hers as she moved her mouth back up his neck, slow and calculated like a wasp getting ready to sting. And that's what she did. She flicked her tongue against his, then taking his lower lip between her teeth, she bit him—hard.

"Fuck!" Releasing her hips he brought his hand to his mouth.

Jillian stood, smiling as her tongue swept along her lips tasting his blood. It tasted like control. She wasn't an animal —she was a survivor. It was a ridiculous justification, but it's all she had. "My water's probably cold. Show yourself out."

Without so much as a curious glance back, she walked up the stairs, shed her robe, slipped back into the bubbly water, and gave herself the most explosive orgasm she'd had in too many months to count.

SMOKE AND RUST. Jillian specifically told her *ignoramus* brother she wanted to paint the living room pewter and pumpkin.

"Close enough." Jackson dipped the wooden stirrer into the thick, dark orange liquid.

"You're such a guy," she mumbled, arranging the drop cloths.

"Why the mood? I thought you were going to take a relaxing bath."

"I did, but it got interrupted, and then I had to finish in lukewarm water."

"Interrupted?"

Jillian bit back her grin. "Yes. Sarge."

Jackson poured the paint into the roller pan. "What did he want?"

Twisted lips hid a dubious smile as her eyes rolled to the ceiling. "Hmm ... let me think. He wanted to know where you were, and then he made the brilliant observation ... well, at least I think it was an observation and not a question ... that you are my brother."

He glanced up, one eye squinted. "It's pretty messed up that we let anyone believe it in the first place."

She grinned. "Yes. But in our defense, we never told anyone we were married, and the truth is ... we're about as messed-up as they come."

"So he came over just to let you know he's on to us?"

"Not exactly. I think he was on a mission to solve a mystery."

Jackson pulled off his T-shirt exposing his freakishly fit, tattooed torso that always seemed to clinch the deal when he wanted to get laid. "What mystery is that?"

"I think he wanted to see our downstairs wall to confirm we were the perpetrators that broke into his house. Apparently Betta fish don't get along."

Jackson rested his hands on his hips and leaned forward. "*We*? *You* broke into his house, and why the hell didn't you replace the fish with the same type he had before?"

Jillian pinched her bottom lip between her thumb and forefinger. "I was tired, and hungover, and—"

"Stupid?"

"It was just a lapse in judgement. Sam Walton's will do that to you."

He handed her a beer, a paint brush, and a side of disapproving brotherly eye rolling. They tapped their bottles, cranked up the music, and attacked the white walls. By midnight they were delightfully buzzed, covered in paint—some of which did make it onto the walls—and ready to dive into the next color when the doorbell rang.

They shared blank stares, of course wondering if the doorbell did in fact ring or if their ears were as impaired as the rest of their bodies.

"Who could that be? Don't these people go to bed by eight?" Jillian snickered.

Jackson lifted his shoulders then opened the door. "Hey, AJ. Is everything okay?"

Jillian peeked around Jackson. With wide, glassy eyes she checked out AJ's swollen lip and small knot on his forehead. Hers was concealed by hair.

"No. Everything is not okay. It's after midnight and you've had the music so fucking loud over here I can't sleep!"

Jackson's lips puckered into an O as he grimaced. "Sorry about that. I think we're ready to call it a night." He turned. "Right, Sis?"

Jillian's wry grin was meant for Jackson, but AJ's eyes narrowed into slits of displeasure as if they were making him the butt of their joke—and maybe they were. But even in her foggy, relaxed state, she couldn't stop thinking about the heat from his lips, the taste of his tongue, and how his hands sliding up her bare legs took her halfway to her bathtub orgasm.

"Yes, we're going to bed, but not together. We only do that on April 10, National Sibling Day. Oh and Twins Day, which is coming up sometime in August ... I think. But it's an unofficial day so we don't always celebrate it."

Jackson snorted out a laugh. "She's full of shit."

Jillian found her intoxicated eyes lingering on AJ's bare feet and large defined calves. The right one had a serpent tattoo wrapped around it. She imagined tracing it with her tongue.

"I'm aware of that. Just try to be more respectful of the noise level." AJ cleared his throat.

Jillian's eyes flicked up to his, but his quickly cut to Jackson's.

"Will do. Good night, AJ." Jackson shut the door before AJ even turned away.

"Fuck, Jill! You have to stop that shit."

CHAPTER SEVEN

Most brothers remember how bratty their little sisters were or how they were treated like a princess. Jackson's sister hated being called "younger," but that's what she was, at least in his mind. Jillian was born seven minutes after Jackson, and rarely did a day go by that he didn't remind her of it.

When he thought of his sister, it was usually the ghost of her innocence. It was the young teenage girl that watched a video on slaughter houses and declared never to eat meat again. He remembered the shrill scream of her racing across a room to save a spider from its near death as their father prepared to snuff out its life under his shoe. She shooed him away then coaxed the spider onto a piece of paper to set it free in the backyard.

Jillian walked away from the front door, refusing to acknowledge him. She always hid her regret behind a pile of denial.

"What happened to you?" he asked, his voice a notch calmer. "You're not that person anymore. You shouldn't even want to be that person. She died. Let. Her. Go."

Jillian pounded the lid back onto the can of paint. "I don't know what you're—"

"Don't! You can lie to anyone, including yourself, but you can't lie to me no matter how hard you try. I saw him." Jackson grabbed her arm and turned her toward him then brushed her hair off her forehead.

Jillian blinked at the floor.

"You head-butted him."

"He grabbed my—"

"You *bit* him! I saw the *bite* mark on his lip."

She turned her back to him.

Jackson sighed. "This is your chance, Jill. You can be whoever you want to be. It's not perfect, I get that, but you can find normalcy. That part of you doesn't have to die. You were quirky, and a little weird, but in a completely endearing way. Remember when Dad would go to Home Depot and you'd beg to go with him because you loved the smell of the place? Even when Mom told you it was just chemicals off-gassing, you didn't care because your other little secret was how you'd crack open the door when they filled the car up with gas because you loved the smell of those fumes too."

Jackson grieved for his sister—what she'd seen, who she'd become. He suffered from his own denial. They were told she'd never completely recover, but he refused to believe it. She was too strong. He wanted to believe that she could prove everyone wrong.

"Do you remember when you got your first babysitting job how you blew your whole paycheck at Staples because you had an addiction to office supply stores? I miss that girl. I miss you showing me a carton of Sour Cream and Chive Pringles, an ice scraper, toenail clippers, a bulk box of red Bic Pens, and a box of tampons, then asking me if I knew where you got everything just so you could yell 'Staples!' before I had a chance to answer."

Jillian turned back around. "No, I don't remember because that girl is gone. She *died*. Let. Her. Go." She sulked toward her bedroom.

"What's going on with AJ? What is he to you?" Jackson called after her.

His sister had mad talent for compartmentalizing her emotions, almost to the point of OCD. Every situation had a little shelf in her head and she never took more than one thing down at a time, never mixed feelings, always kept a sense of control. Sometimes she sounded like she was regurgitating lines from a self-help book. The problem was, when she couldn't mentally or emotionally handle a situation, she tried to physically control it. AJ was clearly one of those *situations*.

She stopped at her door and released a slow, *controlled* breath. "He's therapy."

Out of a million answers she could have given him ... that was the one he feared most.

Take away a college education and all previous work experience and the only thing that's left is one unmarketable loser. That's how Jackson felt. Even as the movers were delivering his piano, the daunting task of finding students—adult students—drove him back into the warm comfort of a cool Heineken.

"It's a grand piano." Jillian observed as the movers situated it in the middle of their great room. "And it takes up the whole room. If we sit on the sofa we won't be able to see the T.V."

Jackson laughed. "We don't have a sofa or T.V. anymore, remember ... you had Stan haul them off."

"The sofa smelled like Febreeze and the T.V. was a box —with a turn dial."

"It didn't have a turn dial, you goof. And this was your job choice for me."

Jillian pressed her foot into the back of Jackson's knee causing him to falter a bit. "Yes, but I envisioned an upright piano on the sun porch."

"Then clearly you don't know me as well as you think you do." He ran his hand along the sleek black lines of wood then feathered his fingertips across every ivory key without making a sound. He loved music, it conveyed emotions much deeper than words.

They both had taken lessons from the tender age of four, yet Jillian had merely managed to butcher each note of every song that was set before her. She practiced. Jackson played.

"Well my Lascivio kit should arrive later today, and I'm watching after Lilith this afternoon, so I think it's official: We are back to being responsible adults." Jillian snatched his beer. "Starting now." She sneaked a swig, then dumped the contents down the drain.

"Buzz kill," Jackson grumbled. "Did you know some of history's greatest composers were alcoholics?" He tipped the delivery guys before shutting the front door.

"You're so full of shit." Jillian plopped down on the piano bench.

Jackson sat next to her and played "Chasing Cars." "I'm not. Have I ever steered you wrong?" He smirked.

Of course he'd steered her wrong. That was his favorite game. He believed you could convince people of just about anything as long as it was said with complete and unwavering conviction. Jackson told her it was human nature to doubt oneself, even in matters of factual certainty.

Jillian nudged his shoulder. "It's the *only* way you steer me. I have to go. If my Lascivio stuff arrives, stay out."

Jackson laughed. "I'm not into sex toys."

"Too intimidating?" She winked, slipping on her shoes. "Vibrator envy?"

Jackson looked down at his fingers as they danced over the keys with effortless grace. "Nah, it just makes me sad for all the women that will stick anything in their pussies."

Jillian paused before closing the front door. "Huh ... interesting. Those are the same words I used to say about all the one-night stands you had over the years."

CHAPTER EIGHT

BENEATH THE EMOTIONAL armor of self-preservation, Jillian Knight wore a cloak woven with threads of deep love and compassion. She knew it was there, but she hid it well. All it took to see that intricate fabric of her heart was someone who needed protection more than her. Lilith Kepler was that someone.

"She just ate, but if you wouldn't mind washing up those few dishes I'd gladly pay you extra." Dodge slipped on his shoes. "She may need to go to the bathroom and being the stubborn old woman she is, she won't ask for help but eventually you'll have to go in there and pull her ass off the toilet. I need to get a rail put up, but I just haven't yet."

Jillian sucked her lips in and nodded. She imagined Dodge's seemingly insensitive persona was nothing more than a mask to hide how much grief he felt for his sick wife. Masks were sometimes necessary. Jillian had many of them.

"Oh, and don't forget. She's deaf ... mute would have been nice, but I guess we don't get to make those decisions." Dodge winked while scratching the bald spot on his head surrounded by a halo of gray hair.

"We'll be fine and I don't mind doing the dishes, no need to pay me extra. In fact if you have laundry or some other cleaning you need done, I'd be happy to do it. She doesn't look too demanding." Jillian looked over at Lilith in her recliner chair, head bowed into a book.

"She'll be out before too long. Might want to bookmark her page though, before it falls out of her hands. Pisses her off when she loses her spot. I'll be back in a few hours." Dodge gave a final wave before shutting the door.

Jillian inspected the familiar surroundings. Most of the townhomes had a similar floor plan. She was impressed that the Kepler's was updated with tile, hardwood floors, brushed nickel fixtures, and earth-tone paint on the walls.

Lilith's eyelids closed, head tilted off to the side. Jillian eased the book out of her hands and slipped the bookmark in place, then draped a blanket over her lap. The T.V. was turned down, closed caption along the bottom of the screen. She grabbed the empty coffee cup on the end table and took it to the kitchen to wash with the rest of the dishes. On the granite bar top was a silver-framed photo of a dog, a yellow Great Dane with a black mask.

"Pretty dog." She looked back, not knowing why. Lilith was deaf and sleeping. "I had a dog once." Jillian began to fill the sink with hot soapy water and the silence with a story. "I'm not supposed to tell anyone, but..." she shrugged her shoulders "...I think I need to." She grabbed the sponge and laughed. "I bet you can keep a secret, huh?" She didn't look back again. Jillian knew Lilith was nothing more than a warm-bodied statue that made her feel as if she wasn't just talking to herself like Stan did, even if she really was.

"Jones was white with irregular black patches over his entire body. He was small and pudgy with big paws and so ornery. But that's not where the story begins." Jillian closed her eyes for a brief moment. "I was Jessica then ... Jessica Day."

Day

JESSICA DAY WAS an actuary intern by day and vampire by night. At least that was what she put under *reason for visit* on the health form she filled out at the office of Dr. Luke Jones, Psychiatrist. Her brother got his name from a friend who said Dr. Jones was stern, unconventional, and had already received high praises from other more experienced doctors in the field. He was known as the go-to guy for the more challenging psychological issues.

"Dr. Jones will see you now." The sixty-something receptionist smiled.

Jessica looked up from her computer resting on her lap. She was studying for her next actuary exam, and after that she would be studying for the next and the next ... That's all she did, worked, studied ... oh, and made people bleed.

"Psst." The receptionist beckoned her with a crooked finger as Jessica walked past her desk. "I tell everyone this on their first visit. He's young but he graduated top of his class and he's just ... brilliant."

Jessica's eyes widened, her lips parted into an O as she tucked her long brown hair behind her ear. "O-kay." She gave a slow nod. "Like Doogie Howser young?"

The receptionist's brow lined with confusion. "Of course not. He's thirty-two."

Jessica winked. "Good to know." As she opened the door she stopped before clearing the threshold.

Perplexed. That was the only word to describe the look

on Dr. Jones's face as he leaned against the front of his desk, one ankle crossed over the other, hands resting on the edge. She felt him making a ten-page assessment of her before she spoke her first word. Her assessment of him was much shorter: sex in a suit.

"Come in, Miss Day."

Jessica peeled her eyes off him and turned to shut the door. "I'd like to come alright," she mumbled to herself. Turning back to him she smiled.

Dr. Jones exuded confidence with his neatly parted black hair, a gleam in his blue eyes that tracked her without a single blink, and the way he held his shoulders back, chin up. He pushed off the desk and offered his hand with an air of calm self-confidence. "I'm Dr. Jones. It's a pleasure to meet you."

His steadfast professionalism was reassuring and continued to feed her new naughty-doctor-troubled-patient fantasy. "Call me Jessica." She gave him a firm shake, a very firm shake.

He raised a single brow, undoubtedly questioning the reason for her iron grip, but he didn't back down from her non-verbal challenge. Her body language said more than she did that day.

"Please, have a seat wherever you'll feel most comfortable." He gestured to the chairs facing his desk and a brown sofa against the wall to the right by a fish tank.

Jessica surveyed her options. "Hmm ... everything's covered in dead cow. You don't by chance have something in cotton or polyester do you?" She wanted Dr. Jones to feel distracted, slightly off kilter. She needed the upper hand. After all, that was the reason for therapy.

He straightened his light blue tie that looked sharp with

his steel gray three-piece suit. Jessica expected a slight grimace, or some sort of stumble over his composure. How was he going to counsel her if she refused to sit on leather? Which of course she didn't really have an issue with it, but wasn't going to tell him that until she'd made him squirm a bit.

Dr. Jones tipped his chin, gesturing to the floor. "I believe the carpet is a nylon blend. Have a seat."

She looked at the floor then back up at him. He held her gaze with eyes that said checkmate. Jessica ran her hand along the leather chair in front of him.

"Feels like aged leather. I bet the cow died of old age before they claimed its remains from a large grassy field under the arch of a late spring rainbow." She stepped forward and slid down into the "humane" leather chair.

Dr. Jones studied her for a few intense moments before sitting in the chair next to hers. He looked over her paperwork without so much as a pen tap or lip twitch. Every move he made was controlled, calculated, and immune to her provoking antics.

Smooth. She thought of him claiming equal ground instead of the authoritative position behind the desk. So in an act that could have only been called "An Act of Jessica Day" she stood, walked around his desk, and sat in his chair. He glanced up from her chart, lips slightly parted. Jessica leaned back, hands interlaced and resting on her stomach.

"Well, this chair is ridiculously comfortable and neither one of us sitting in it seems like a waste of probably what..." she bounced a bit, spinning it side to side "...one? Two grand of complete comfort?"

After several slow blinks, he looked back down at her forms. "Tell me about your job."

Jessica smiled, tilting her head to the side, unable to hide the amusement that trickled through her whole body. Actuary intern by day and vampire by night and he asked about her job? "It's a lot of qualitative and analytical stuff. I help put together spreadsheets and presentations, including researching information about clients and issues affecting them now or in the foreseen future. I spend way too much time justifying and explaining myself to others, but I guess that comes with the territory."

Her job was not only confusing, but extremely boring to the average person. Why she was good at math and where she got her talent was a mystery. Neither one of her parents liked math, nor did Jude, her twin brother, although he was still good at it. Jude was good at everything.

"Do you like your job?" Dr. Jones looked up for a second then jotted a few notes.

Jessica shrugged. "I'm good at it."

"That doesn't necessarily equate to liking it."

She drummed her nails on the arm of the chair. "Is your secretary your mom? She seemed very proud of you, more like a mother than a receptionist."

"Let's talk about you." Dr. Jones looked up again, lips in a firm line.

"So she's your mom, right?"

"No. How would you describe your relationship with your brother?"

Jessica leaned back, swinging her feet up on the desk, legs crossed at the ankles. "I'm not here to talk about my brother, even if he's the reason I'm here. Bossy bastard thinks I need 'help.'"

"You don't want to be here?"

"I'm fine with it. However, I wish we could just get to

the point instead of engaging in meaningless small talk about my job and my relationship with my brother."

"And what is the point?" Dr. Jones folded his hands in his lap on top of Jessica's chart.

She stared at his long fingers wondering if they'd ever seen a day of manual labor in their life. Dr. Jones was handsome, but not ruggedly so, more preppy handsome like a Hugo Boss model: clean shaven, neatly trimmed nails, and perfect white teeth. But he stood easily over six feet with broad shoulders and those soft hands were *large*. Jessica imagined the body hidden beneath the immaculately pressed layers of his suit far exceeded handsome.

"I can't be intimate with a guy until I make him bleed." Her gaze inched up to his face.

Surely a whisper of a voice in his head screamed "cuckoo."

Jessica wrinkled her nose. "That's messed up, right?"

Dr. Jones rested his elbow on the arm of the chair, his chin on his fist. He'd perfected the stoic thinker pose. "And why do you feel the need to do that?"

"I need the illusion of control ... not the blood, because I'm a vegetarian." She twisted her lips. "Hmm, maybe it is the blood. Do you think I have a vitamin deficiency?"

"Why do you say illusion?"

Maybe he'd address the possible vitamin deficiency later.

"Because I don't need my lovers to roll over and play dead. And I don't need them tied up. It's really more of a healthy respect. Okay, maybe not 'healthy' but a mutual respect. Fifty-fifty." She rolled her neck to one side and then the other. "Fifty-one-forty-nine ... sixty-forty. Well, you get my point. I just need a guy to think I have control, even if I don't ... which I usually do. My father has a high risk job so he's made sure my mother, brother, and I have the proper skills to defend ourselves."

"I see. However, self-defense requires self-control. Making someone bleed just to prove a point is not self-control."

Jessica spun in the chair a few inches so she could see out the window. Dr. Jones's twenty-seventh story view of San Francisco Bay was stunning. "Don't you think there should be some law requiring all psychiatrists to have ground-level offices?"

"Have you ever had suicidal thoughts?"

Jessica turned her head toward him. "Is this about my 'control' issue? As in I probably feel the need to control my own destiny, including the way I die?"

He jotted down a few more notes. "No, this is about your suggestion that I have a ground-floor office. I want to be sure you have no intention of throwing yourself out my window."

She looked back out the tall glass panels. "That might be bad for business."

"I was referring to the window. I don't own this space, I just rent it. I imagine replacing that window would be expensive and might prevent the owner from renewing my lease."

Jessica grinned until she felt it tugging the corners of her eyes. Dr. Jones had a sense of humor, even if dry, which proved his approach to treatment was in fact unconventional. And that made Jessica happy ... very happy.

"Maybe you should include a damage deposit at the beginning of treatment." She spun back around to face him.

His head was still bowed, left hand frantically working the gel-inked pen over the paper. "I just made a note to have my receptionist revise the New Patient Agreement later this afternoon." He kept writing but looked up at Jessica and for the first time he gave her a smile.

In that moment she was certain of only one thing—she needed him.

CHAPTER NINE

KNIGHT

THREE NIGHTS in a row of rain had the grass climbing to the sky on the first sunny day. A red-streaked tornado ripped through Peaceful Woods with a long ponytail of wavy blond hair, aviator glasses, frayed denim shorts, a silver bikini top, and red rain boots to protect her legs while weed eating. The same boots she'd been wearing with her panties and tank top to get the mail on the previous days. Jillian Knight was subconsciously hell-bent on giving every man in her path a massive heart attack. They were, however, destined to die with a smile.

"Bill has run his mower into three different trees and the corner of one garage. Maybe you should throw on a T-shirt before he ends up in the pond," Jackson yelled.

Jillian killed the weed eater and popped out her ear buds. "Shut it."

Jackson handed her a bottled water then leaned back in his lawn chair positioned in the middle of the driveway. He'd taught four piano lessons already that day and was enjoying watching his sister work her third job.

"Excited for your big night?"

"Shut it." She twisted the cap back on the bottle. "It's just sex toys. It's the job you picked for me. Besides, I'm only training. I don't make any money off the sales tonight."

"Is your mentor having you demo stuff?" Jackson smirked.

"Shut it."

"My my, someone's grumpy today. Are you shedding the lining of your uterus?"

Jillian didn't want to let Jackson see her grin, so she turned away, cupping a hand over her eyebrows to see how many more lawns she had to go. Ever since they had sex education in junior high, Jackson referred to her period as "shedding the lining of her uterus." And years later she still got the giggles when he said it with the same seriousness as their instructor had in class.

"No, I'm not, so just *shut it*."

"Then what is it? Your Harley arrives at the dealership tomorrow. You have boxes of vibrators and nipple clamps at your disposal. Dodge said Lilith enjoyed you being there to watch her the other day, so that's going well. And you're making money as we speak while getting a tan."

"Dodge said Lilith enjoyed me being there? That's weird, she slept the whole time while I did the dishes and dusted the furniture." And told the deaf sleeping neighbor about her past. But she didn't share that bit of information with her paranoid brother. "I don't know." She sighed in equal parts frustration and disappointment. "Have you seen AJ the past few days?"

"No. And *why* do you ask?"

Jillian brushed some grass off her arms. "No reason."

"You don't ask for 'no reason,' so what gives?"

"We had a … moment. That's all."

Jackson chuckled. "A moment? You're kidding, right? I

67

don't think roughing him up then piercing his lip is considered a *moment*."

Jillian noticed Bill gaining on her so she slipped her earbuds back in and picked up the weed eater. "It was for a few brief seconds between the roughing up and the piercing. But it was definitely a moment."

Jackson shook his head, tilting it back with the contentment of a dog in the sun. "It's too soon."

"It's never too soon to take your next breath."

"He's not a breath. He's a step backwards. And he has the marks from you to prove it."

Jillian yanked the pull cord on the weed eater and finished her work.

———

THAT BREATH PULLED his black Jeep Wrangler into his driveway as Jillian hosed off her red boots. She flashed him a killer smile with the devil's wink when he glanced over at her. He turned ahead without acknowledgement, pulling the rest of the way in the garage. Jillian shut off the water and hustled across the short patch of lawn to limbo under the descending garage door, clearing the beam by just millimeters.

"Sarge."

His visual assessment of Jillian started with her boots and ended with her sexy grin. Any other day she would have been disappointed that he didn't share her enthusiasm, especially after their *moment*. But on that particular day Jillian fought the onslaught of cold fear mingling with the heart-pounding blaze of adrenaline. She felt anxious, alert, and *alive* as he stood before her in his combat fatigues. His top was unbuttoned, revealing a fitted khaki T-shirt that hugged his hard muscles.

"*Miss* Knight." He shut the driver's door and slung his messenger bag over his shoulder. "Do you need something?"

"What does AJ stand for?" She inched forward until they were toe to toe, red rain boots to tan combat boots. Jillian loved how her skin tingled in his proximity, how she felt dominated by his stature but not submissive to his strength.

"Your shorts are too short." The authoritative intonation of his voice felt like a tongue dragging over every pleasurable nerve ending in her body.

"Too short for what? *You*, Sergeant Monaghan?"

"We don't have a club house or swimming pool. Why the bikini top?" AJ clenched his fists as Jillian moved her feet between his. Her cleavage-bared chest pressed against his stomach.

"Is my body appalling to you, Sarge?"

"The old men in this neighborhood don't need to have their wives pissed at them all day because the new neighbor gets her mail wearing a little bit of nothing." His voice escalated with each word as it muffled into pure grit.

"Sarge, are you upset about my mail-retrieving attire or that I get the mail after you've already left for work?"

He narrowed his eyes.

"Because you've already seen more than the other neighbors."

AJ maintained a scowl, but his deep swallow gave him away.

"How's your lip?"

The tip of his tongue instinctively glided over the small red spot that was still there. "Tell me. Are you one of those kinky dominatrixes that like it rough?"

Jillian twisted her lips and rolled her eyes, diverting her gaze from his. "Hmm ... no, that's not an accurate assessment." Dr. Jones ruled out that possibility years ago.

"And why is that?"

She yanked his T-shirt from his pants and snaked her hand up a few inches against his taut, bare skin. It felt warm, unmarked, and tempting.

"Because I don't want you to submit to me," she whispered her words like a potion meant to cast a spell.

AJ secured her ponytail in his fisted hand. "I assure you words like surrender, succumb, and *submit* are only under the list of things I'm incapable of doing."

Jillian smiled. She never considered her *issue* an addiction, but at that moment it was powerful and all-consuming. "I'm going to bring you to your *knees*, Senior Master Sergeant Monaghan."

"Only if I'm straddling your body facedown on the ground."

Jillian heard Dr. Jones's voice in her head, but saw Luke's face. The duality was always present: the man who saved her and the one that set her free. She hated as much as she loved that one man possessed so much power over her. But he was gone—forever, and so was Jessica.

It's in here, Luke would kiss her forehead, *and here,* he'd kiss her chest over her heart that had found love with his. *Not in here,* he'd lace his fingers with hers and squeeze hard until her body was the first to surrender. That ability to surrender was the greatest power anyone had ever given her, and when Jessica died, she took that power with her.

Jillian Knight could never surrender.

When Dr. Jones's voice faded, all she could hear was her racing heart and shallow breath. The tension between Jillian and AJ could spark a blackout across Omaha. Her attraction to him was fueled by her past, but she couldn't make sense of his unnerving mix of hate and desire, or maybe she could ... she just didn't want to.

As he held her hair tight, he lowered his lips towards her mouth. She inched her hands under his arms and up his back. There was nothing right about them. The distrust— thick. The fear—heavy. The sexual tension—suffocating.

There was no closing eyes and melting into a moment of passion.

He watched her. She watched him.

When their lips touched it went from soft to punishingly hard in an instant. Their tongues dueled like swords. Their lips vied for control. AJ jerked her ponytail back until she opened wider for him and with his other hand he gripped her ass like he was trying to rip through the denim. Jillian yanked the chain off his neck, letting it drop to the floor. Her hands made swift, precise moves with his belt. With one quick, forceful tug she snapped it completely out of the loops, a whip crack piercing the air.

It's here ... that voice.

AJ released her ass and cupped her jaw. His hand slid down to her neck and she could feel his fingers wrapping around, crushing her windpipe even though they were relaxed.

Fear.

It's here.

Jillian's hands navigated to his back. *Don't do it,* her mind chanted. But her fingernails curled into his flesh on their own accord. AJ dragged his hand from her neck to her chest between the exposed cleavage from her bikini top. She waited for him to push the material aside exposing her hardened nipples, but he didn't. He left the heel of his hand pressed to her sternum. Her heart tried to beat it away, but he left it there until she swore she could feel his pulse surge against hers. Slipping ... her control was slipping as the moment blurred into dizzying confusion.

"Fuck!" AJ growled as he shoved her back. "Knock that shit off!"

Stumbling to a halt, eyes wide, Jillian opened her mouth to speak but nothing came out. Any other woman would have been flat on her back with the force he used on her. She looked down, twisting her palms up and fisting her fingers. Blood. Her nails were smeared with his blood. She closed her eyes for a brief moment.

"I-I have to get ready for work." She smiled with child-like innocence as she wiped her fingers along her shorts, kissed him on the cheek like she didn't just dig a garden into his back, then slipped out the side access door. "I go for a run every night at ten if you care to join me," she called two seconds before the wind slammed the door shut behind her.

JILLIAN KNIGHT BROUGHT one thing with her that used to belong to Jessica Day—killer sales skills. The Lascivio consultant that "trained" Jillian at the bachelorette party found herself being schooled in the sales department. Jillian spent the whole night number crunching and making up statistics about nipple clamps and breast cancer prevention, vibrators and decreased yeast infections, and strap-on penises and longevity.

Her mentoring consultant sulked with guilt that she'd allowed Jillian to sell the products under such false pretense, until Jillian made a quick calculation of the commission that the party brought in: over twelve-hundred dollars.

"Hey, working girl! Did you bring home the bacon?" Jackson grinned as he finished playing a familiar Bach piece.

Jillian loved listening to him play. Part of it was envy because she didn't inherit an ounce of musical talent, but most of it was honest adoration for his insane ability.

"Tempeh bacon, and no I didn't bring it home, but Sara, the Lascivio consultant that 'trained' me, her family is celebrating bacon fest, thanks to yours truly."

Jackson whistled.

Jillian shrugged, gulping down a glass of water. "Sex sells."

"You, my dear sis, could sell purity rings and abstinence to pimps and call girls."

"Speaking of call girls ... what are you doing here anyway? Have you gotten laid since we arrived?"

Jackson closed the lid. "I think this Jackson guy is going to keep his virginity for a while."

"Excuse me?"

"How many people get the chance to start over from scratch? Very few. So I'm saving myself. Maybe I'll find some nice girl who's not a virgin and would be willing to teach me about sex and intimacy."

"You fucked half the West Coast!"

"I don't know what guy to whom you're referring."

Jillian shook her head while unbuttoning her white blouse. "I'm going to change. I need a run and an escape from this impostor who claims to be my brother."

"No sparring tonight?"

"Maybe when I get back."

"You're just upset that I'm making a change for the better, a true fresh start."

Jillian stopped in the hallway. His words, even if not

intentional, were a jab to her gut. "Here's the thing ... I had it as good as it gets. I have nowhere to go but worse." She shrugged off her shirt and tossed it onto her bed.

"Let's talk about it." Jackson stood at her door while she changed in her closet.

"I can't talk about it with you."

Jackson chuckled. "I'm the *only* person with whom you can talk about it."

Lilith. She couldn't wait to be with her again because she was the one person Jillian could tell about her past without putting her safety in jeopardy and without judgement.

"If I tell you how painfully hollow I feel inside because I miss Luke and Jones, then you're going to rationalize everything, reminding me that we had no choice. If we wanted to live we had to leave. Then you're going to pour on the guilt about how I have you and how our bond is stronger than anything."

Jillian came out of the closet with the posture of a rag doll as she sat on the edge of the bed to tie her running shoes. Truth—every breath was a silent whisper of gratitude to her brother. She knew she was alive because he saved her time and time again.

"But right now I don't want to be rational and, I don't want to feel guilty. I just want to wallow in my misery of missing them." She sighed with defeat etched in lines across her face. "Strength acknowledges weakness, it doesn't ignore it." She stood, looking up at her brother, no longer trying to hide the agony in her eyes. "For now I'm going to acknowledge it and later I will be stronger for it. Okay?"

Jackson nodded then pulled her into his arms. "Fin de journée."

"I know—fin de journée."

JILLIAN SLIPPED IN ONE EARBUD; she still couldn't do both at night. Surrendering to the unknown wasn't possible yet, maybe ever. The pulsing music opposite the quiet darkness of abandoned streets and sleeping dogs was a needed escape from the cacophony of morning chaos that Jackson preferred when he jogged.

The cooler evening breeze, the grinding beat, her past, and the nagging fascination of a certain uniformed neighbor fed the surging energy inside her, propelling her legs to the point of exhaustion. Her lungs stretched to capacity, a simmering burn in her chest. The only thing that moved faster than Jillian's legs was her mind. It was an endless loop of the last ten years of her life playing in a roller coaster highlight reel: the drizzle of mist from the fog rolling in over the bay, the doctor, the dog. She missed it all.

After five miles of pure adrenaline-fed exertion, Jillian laced her fingers on top of her head and walked in slow circles on their driveway.

"It's probably not safe for you to be running by yourself at night."

Jillian mustered a small smirk with her back to AJ. She'd seen him in the shadows of his front stoop when she jogged the last few feet to her house. She was trained to notice everything and everyone, but she wasn't in a hurry to acknowledge him. Her thoughts of Luke, Jones, and the normalcy she'd lost had left her feeling melancholy. As much as she loved playing cat and mouse with AJ, her inner fight was gone that night.

"Yeah, well I think you have a scar on your lip and fresh branding on your back that says otherwise." She turned as he stepped into view under the moonlight.

It had only been hours since she'd seen him, but he looked different. It may have been the dark whiskers surfacing along his strong jaw or maybe his casual attire of shorts and a T-shirt, or the absence of his usual scowl, but something about him made Jillian's guard slip.

"This thing..." he motioned between them before shoving his hands in his pockets "...it's not a good thing. Cage is coming home tomorrow and I don't want him to think anything is going on between us."

Jillian gave careful consideration to her response because while AJ's mouth said one thing, his eyes said the opposite. They lingered on her bare legs then her exposed abs below her sports bra. He must have swallowed after every third word. She craved intimacy, to the point of feeling a physical pain inside, from nothing more than the way his gaze traversed her body.

You miss me ... She heard Luke's voice in her head. *More than my heart would miss its beat,* she thought, closing her eyes for a brief moment before letting his image fade from her mind.

CHAPTER TEN

Living through the trauma was easier than reliving it ...
Every. Single. Day. AJ counted himself lucky for having
served so many years, seen so many things that no one
should ever have to endure, and yet he made it home to his
family. Many of his comrades did not. He played the part of
the grateful soldier who served his country, then slipped
back into the role of husband and father. If only that would
have been the case, the truth. But it wasn't.

His PTSD took its time lurking in the distance, waiting
to strike like a battalion waiting command. And when it did,
he lost his wife, the man he was, the father he wanted to be
—his whole world. The worst part was the unpredictability
of it. Some days he felt like the victim of dissociative identity disorder. Nearly every woman he'd tried to be with
since his wife left because after a few dates they caught a
glimpse of the man he'd become.

The half-pint of solid muscle that stood before him with
a dewy sheen of sweat kissing every inch of her silky skin
stirred something inside him. Jillian Knight was clearly a
hundred ways of fucked-up, and the warning sirens blared

in AJ's head every time he neared her proximity, but he was deaf to their warning.

Jillian was either fearless or scared to the point of ruthless insanity. Either way, AJ wanted nothing more than to exhale ... relinquish control, and let her see the monster inside. Beat him, break him, destroy him, and maybe in the wreckage find the man he used to be. But he had a son and for once in his life he was determined to put him first, no matter the cost. Cage was the only thing AJ had left that was worth fighting for, even if the protector was also the enemy.

Jillian tugged at her ponytail until her sweaty platinum blond hair fell in tangled waves around her shoulders. "What is this *thing*, AJ?" She stepped closer until there were no more steps to take. Personal space was not something she acknowledged with him.

His hands twitched, desperate to clutch her hair and pull those pouty lips to his. He knew their seductive taste, their arousing touch, and their demanding control.

"Dangerous," he whispered. His fingers grazed the line of her jaw. She closed her eyes. With firm pressure, he dragged his thumb along her bottom lip. A storm raged inside that left him teetering on a razor's edge of control.

On an exhale, her body froze at attention with the exception of her chest that heaved with building intensity every second his touch lingered. She parted her lips and he slid the end of his thumb over her bottom teeth. He swallowed and suppressed a guttural moan when she flicked the tip of her tongue against him. The hard pulse of his erection grew torturous.

AJ knew what was coming, but some alien masochistic part of him needed it to justify the moment he willingly gave in to. Like an angry serpent, he hissed when Jillian clenched her jaw, but he didn't pull away. Instead, he curled his thumb until she released him. There was no blood, but the deep indents of her front teeth were molded into the pad of his thumb, and he felt confident his nail would be black and blue within days.

He wrapped his lips around the tip of his thumb, and Jillian's golden eyes—the ones that only existed in children's fantasy books—shimmered in the full light of the moon. There was no way to read into her dubious expression. Did that twinkle in her eyes spell challenge or conquest? Either way he knew for certain it glimmered with the element of surprise.

"Dangerous, huh?" Jillian rubbed her lips together, as if she wanted to savor the taste of him. "To whom?"

AJ pulled his thumb from his lips, rubbing his forefinger over the indentations. "I'm not sure, yet."

Her gaze faltered. Several thoughtful blinks later she met his eyes again. "Pleasant dreams, AJ." She lifted on to her toes, but without him bowing, she couldn't reach his lips. He closed his eyes in a silent prayer for control as she pressed her lips to the hollow of his throat. By the time he opened them and unclenched his fists, she was gone.

THE NIGHTMARES WERE RARE, one every month or two. And even those were more often flashbacks to the months that led to the demise of his marriage.

The anger.

The fighting.

The reflection AJ no longer recognized.

It was the pain. If not the physical agony of the migraines that came at more frequent intervals, the emotional anguish over his inability to control his temper. One minute he raged out of control over Cage forgetting to make his bed and the next he withdrew, sometimes leaving for days—sleeping on base, or even in his truck. He was never suicidal. There were just times he didn't want to be found, didn't want human contact, not even a knock at his door.

"Dad?" Cage whispered.

"Yeah?" AJ answered, his voice gravelly from lack of sleep and muffled from the pillow that covered his head to block out the morning light penetrating his shades like a thousand knives to his brain.

"Um ... it's almost ten-thirty. Are you okay?"

AJ cursed even the dimmest reflection of light as he peeked out from under his pillow to confirm the time. "Dammit!" he mumbled to himself. "I'm fine."

He wasn't fine. He was two and half hours late to work and the devil was still drumming in his head. After pulling on a T-shirt and shoving his legs into a pair of jogging pants, he lumbered into the hallway.

"You look like shit." Cage grimaced as he handed his father a glass of water and a couple Advil.

"Sounds about right." AJ tossed back the pills.

"Bad one?"

AJ nodded, swallowing the last of the water. "I've got to get to work."

"Take a sick day. That's what they're for."

AJ pinned Cage with a piercing glare. "I've never called in sick to work." He also hadn't ever had to jerk off twice in less than an hour before going to bed because a certain neighbor had him so painfully turned on. He thought the overdue release would have lessened the severity of his migraine, but it hadn't.

Cage shrugged. "Whatever. Jillian caught me when I arrived earlier. Jackson's working until later this afternoon so she asked if I'd give her a ride to Dillion Brothers' this morning."

"The Harley Davidson dealership?"

Cage grinned. "Yep. She ordered a bike for herself. Jillian rides a *motorcycle*. Jackson's one lucky bastard." Cage shook his head.

"Why do you say that?" AJ brushed past him in desperate need of coffee.

"A wife that looks like a fitness model, wears virtually nothing, and rides a *motorcycle*—not the stereotypical butch-looking broad that you usually see on a bike. I'm talking every guy's fantasy ... times one hundred, and he's tapping that every day—probably more than once."

"Cage!" AJ growled with his back to his son, nearly overflowing his coffee cup.

Cage fought to hide his smirk. "Sorry, he's gently making sweet, sweet love to her every day—probably more than once." His voice rose an octave.

AJ pinched his temples. "Jackson's her brother, not her husband."

Cage's eyes grew wide. "Really? Why does everyone seem to think they're married?"

AJ sighed as he glanced at his watch. He needed to get his ass to work and call to let them know why he was running so late. "I don't know. They're two grown siblings living together; that's messed-up enough. I don't have the time nor the interest to dig any deeper into that situation." He also didn't know why he'd fucked her in his head while he got himself off in the shower once and again in bed a half hour later. "Stay away from her ... *them*. Got it?" AJ warned as he brought his phone up to his ear.

"It's just a ride, and I already said I would." Cage grabbed his keys and waved to his dad.

"Wait—" AJ didn't get a chance to finish as work picked up on the line and Cage shut the front door. While he explained his situation, he looked out the front window. Jillian slipped on her sunglasses, walking toward Cage's old black pickup. It was the first time AJ had seen her in jeans. Jeans that hugged her curves a little too much and black leather boots.

Cage held up one finger and jogged back to the house as AJ ended his call. "Forgot my phone." He took the stairs two at a time.

AJ endured the excruciating pain of the sun to go have a few words with Jillian who was waiting in the truck.

"Sarge," she said, looking not the least bit surprised to see him as he opened the door. "Playing hooky today?" She eyed him in his casual attire.

"I told you to stay away from Cage."

"Don't sweat it, the only thing I'll be mounting today is my Sportster SuperLow." Jillian applied lipgloss in the visor mirror. "And even that ride will be cut short since I'm watching Lilith this afternoon."

"He's..." AJ grimaced while bowing his head and clenching one hand on each side "...just ... a boy." The Advil wasn't touching the pain and his coffee threatened to come up as a wave of nausea hit him.

Jillian flipped up the visor. "He's a young man and—" She looked over at AJ. "Are you okay?"

AJ hissed in a breath as he clenched his jaw. Jillian unbuckled and turned toward him, resting her hands over his. "AJ?"

He held his breath, fighting to keep the nausea at bay, not wanting to vomit or pass out. Jillian slowly wedged her hands under his and with a pressure that wasn't normal for a woman's hands, she massaged his head, thumbs digging into his temples with small circles. He left his hands resting over hers as he moaned like a wounded animal.

"Migraine?"

"Yes," he seethed against the pain.

She continued to massage his head and as much as he wanted to fight it, he let his body begin to relax into hers. The pain was still murderous, but the nausea started to subside.

"Dad?"

AJ jerked away from Jillian and the sudden movement shot daggers through his brain. "Fuck!" He squeezed his eyes shut and stumbled toward the house.

"Here's some money and a list of things I need from Home Depot for Dodge and Lilith's bathroom. I've got your dad." She caught up to AJ and wrapped an arm around his waist, guiding him into the house.

"What about your motorcycle?" Cage called.

"Another day." Jillian helped AJ down the hall.

"Go ... I don't want your help." Pain bled from his voice, intensified by the humiliation he felt having Jillian help him. How could a fucking headache turn into such a degrading moment?

"Shut up." Jillian pushed him past his bed into the master bathroom, leaving the lights off. The glass block window allowed enough light to see.

AJ had a large tiled walk-in shower and she turned it on to hot.

"Go," it came out as a desperate plea.

"No." Jillian wrestled his shirt off.

The unbearable pulsing in his head rendered him incapable of fighting her any longer. She pulled down his pants and helped him step out of them. Then, leaving his briefs on, she nudged him toward the shower.

"Sit."

He stepped inside and slid down the wall, knees bent, head cradled in his hands as the nearly scalding water rained down on his head. AJ wasn't sure if it was the pain of the hot water distracting him from his head, but within seconds he could breathe again. The throbbing eased to just bearable.

Jillian toed off her boots and removed her clothes, leaving on her bra and panties. No one had ever taken care of AJ like that before. His voice caught in his throat, trapped by confusion. He wanted her to leave, but needed her to stay. As if defying a law of nature, his body shivered when she kneeled before him, squeezing between his knees and taking his head in her strong, capable hands. He rested his forehead on her chest as she pressed her fingers into his scalp, magically landing on every pressure point.

"Feel good?" she whispered so close he felt her lips brush his ear.

"Yes," he breathed out on a slow sigh.

Jillian worked one area, then made a slight shift finding more points that eased the pain. Her fingers kneaded their way down the back of his head, putting firm pressure with small upward strokes at his nape. He moaned and she continued to his shoulders, digging into tight knots of tension.

"God ..." he breathed.

She rested her cheek on his head, and he swallowed a large gulp of ego, confusion, and a shitload of garbage from his fucked-up past. They stayed resting on each other until the water faded to warm.

"You're running out of hot water."

For the first time since she stepped in the shower, AJ opened his eyes and slowly lifted his head. Surprised and relieved that the pain was nearly gone.

Jillian stared expressionless with rivulets of water racing down her face, lips parted. AJ's eyes homed in on a single bead of water on her neck. He watched it make a leisurely descent to the swell of her breast. His gaze flicked to hers for a split second before finding that drop again. He leaned in until his lips pressed to her wet flesh, his tongue capturing that single drop.

Her breath hitched. AJ lingered, his hands resting on her legs.

"I'm soaked and Dodge is expecting me by noon."

AJ nodded, keeping his head down.

She stood and offered her hand. He took it and let her help him up, pausing a moment to gather his bearings.

"Okay?"

He nodded. She grabbed a towel and wrapped it around her body, then grabbed another and dried him off.

"You might need some dry underwear." She smiled and handed him the towel.

AJ relinquished a small grin that felt foreign to his lips and wrapped the towel around his waist. He collapsed on his bed, completely exhausted. Migraines drained all of his energy. After a long sigh he opened his eyes capturing Jillian in the bathroom with her back to him. She unhooked her bra setting it on the vanity. Then she removed her wet panties. He had never seen the human body in such perfect form.

She stepped into her jeans and glanced back. He held her gaze without apology. Jillian wasn't embarrassed, or angry. She looked ... sad. Turning back around she finished pulling on her jeans, shoving her feet into her boots at the same time. He closed his eyes. Nothing about the morning felt like reality to him in that moment.

When the edge of his bed dipped, he opened his tired eyes again. Jillian traced the pad of her thumb over his eyebrow.

"What does AJ stand for?" she whispered.

He closed his eyes again. "Why do you live with your brother?"

He felt her lips curl into a smile as she pressed them to his forehead. "Feel better, Sarge."

CHAPTER ELEVEN

JILLIAN SNEAKED in the garage door. There was a car in their driveway which meant Jackson was in the middle of a lesson. She tiptoed to her room trying to avoid the two creaky spots on the wood floor.

"Is it raining?"

She jumped, whipping around. "Jesus! You scared me."

"Jackson, not Jesus. Why is your hair wet?" He looked at her hand. "And why are you carrying your undergarments instead of wearing them?"

"Where's your student?"

"Bathroom. Are you going to answer me?" He crossed his arms over his chest.

"Are you seriously wearing those stupid glasses?"

Jackson pressed his finger to the white taped bridge of his black *nonprescription* glasses. "They make me look professional."

"Pfft, they make you look like something for sure, but professional is not the word." She turned, heading to her closet.

"Jill—"

"Yes, it rained," she hollered. "One of those pop-up storms. I saw it on the horizon so I pulled over and stripped down to my bra and panties so my clothes wouldn't get wet. You know what a pain in the ass it can be trying to peel off wet denim. I dressed again in the garage when I noticed you had a student."

"Screwing AJ is a bad idea." He peeked his head into her closet as she shrugged off her shirt.

Jillian covered her breasts with one arm and tossed her shirt at his face with a menacing scowl. "I'm not screwing AJ. But if I were, I'm quite certain it would be the best idea I've had since we landed in this whole big mess."

"Jackson?" a female voice called.

He adjusted his glasses. "We're not done talking about this."

Jillian rolled her eyes after he left. She had done a good deed that morning, one that warranted a merit badge not an interrogation.

By the time she dried her hair and donned new undergarments she found herself skidding onto Dodge's front step at exactly noon. She would have been there sooner had Stan not stopped her to talk about the upcoming board meeting that he thought she should attend. There was an open spot for Treasurer and he'd asked if she was good with numbers. Jillian shrugged and said she was competent in basic math skills. That was all he needed to hear and somehow she got the impression the job was already hers. Just what she needed: another job.

"Hey, young lady!" Dodge greeted her with his usual exuberance.

"Hi, Dodge. Did Cage drop off the supplies?" she asked while he stepped back to let her inside.

"Yes, but I don't think you have any idea how much

Stan is going to bust my chops if he finds out the neighbor *lady* installed a handicap bar in the bathroom for *my* wife."

Jillian laughed. "Then tell him you did it."

"Nah, he's knows I don't have a handy bone in my body."

Lilith looked up from reading her book in her favorite recliner and waved at Jillian.

"How's she doing today?"

"It's been a good day. I think it's because she's getting rid of my old ass for the afternoon and she gets you instead."

"So what's on your agenda today?"

Dodge sat on the bench by the garage door, tying his shoes. "The usual. Bank, grocery shopping, wash the car, and maybe I'll pick up some perennials at the nursery." He stood. "Lilith's lunch is in the oven. Leftover tuna noodle casserole."

"Okay, I'll get her lunch then start working on the bathroom."

"Thanks, Jillian. You're a savior." Dodge winked before shutting the door.

She smiled at Lilith's expectant blue-gray eyes. "I'll check on your lunch." She pointed to herself and then the oven because miming was as close to sign language as Jillian could get.

Lilith smiled back. She hadn't asked if Lilith could read lips or if she knew any sign language; not that it mattered because the only real sign language Jillian knew was *please*, *thank you*, and *sorry*.

"I think it's done," Jillian called. Why? She wasn't sure. There was something comforting about thinking aloud without feeling like a mental patient. She didn't dwell on the fact that Lilith couldn't hear her.

"Shit!" Jillian fisted her hand, sucking her knuckle that

grazed the oven's heating element. After handing Lilith her lunch she ran cold water over her knuckle. "Luke still has a scar on his finger from dinner that night." Jillian rubbed her middle finger, not where her burn was, but where Luke's had been.

Day

JESSICA HAD BEEN SEEING Dr. Jones for three months. They hadn't made much progress in her mind. Dr. Jones assured her once she stopped asking questions about him and started focusing on her past she'd see improvement and small breakthroughs that would lead to an emotional healing or at least an acceptable means of coping.

He tossed her a morsel of information on a rare occasion. She'd learned that he wasn't married, wasn't gay, and wasn't related in any way to his secretary.

"Tell me about your childhood." He'd asked on more than one occasion. It had become clear that he didn't believe her childhood could be summed up in less than five sentences.

"My dad worked long hours as a DEA agent and my mom was a stay-at-home mom. In school Jude and I were placed in different classes, as was customary with twins, so we could establish a sense of 'individuality.' I played every sport, got good grades, had lots of friends, and went on my first official date when I was fifteen."

Dr. Jones latched onto the date disclosure. "Tell me about your boyfriends in school."

"Why? Are you sizing up your competition?" Jessica

wiggled her eyebrows from her designated spot—*his* desk chair.

He never took the bait, not even with an eye roll or smile. Jessica felt certain psychiatrists were trained to have selective hearing. Then again, she also considered the possibility that it was a guy thing.

"My boyfriends, well, let me think…" she spun around in his chair like a five-year-old on the teacups, head back, long dark hair dangling behind the expensive leather ride "…mostly jocks who wanted to see how far they could go with me. I wasn't a slut so at best they'd get to second base." She grabbed the desk, coming to an abrupt halt. "I didn't have large bases at the time."

Jessica waited for Dr. Jones to react, but as usual—nothing. She grinned and shoved off the desk, sending the chair whirling again. "I bet you hit some serious home runs in your day, Dr. Jones." Early on, Jessica had given up on keeping her attraction to him a secret. It was also her way of testing his professionalism. *And damn if he wasn't militant about it!*

"What age were you when you lost your virginity?"

Jessica let the chair slow to a stop, with her back facing Dr. Jones while she admired her exorbitantly expensive view of the bay. "Physically or emotionally?"

"Both."

After fifteen minutes of silence Jessica answered. "I was nineteen when Pete claimed my hymen." She closed her eyes. "I was seventeen when Four stole my emotional innocence and killed my best friend."

"Tell me about Pete."

Jessica laughed out loud, spinning around to face Dr. Jones. "Pete? That's the direction you want to go?"

He capped his pen and rested his ankle on his opposing

knee. His black pants rode up showing his argyle socks. Only Dr. Luke Jones could make argyle sexy. Luke made everything sexy.

"Fine ... Peter McAllister played guitar at a jazz club. I met him when I was on a date." She wrinkled her nose. "Sadly, I don't remember the guy who took me there. I just remember leaving with Pete. He was *older* and sexy as hell." She pinned Dr. Jones with an intense stare as a wry grin captured her lips. "You know what that's like, huh?" She winked.

Dr. Jones blinked on cue, keeping his expression neutral.

Jessica sighed. "I knew rules and regimen. Pete broke the law and answered to no one. Nothing major. Possession, I think. I know, what are the chances of a DEA agent's daughter getting involved with a druggie?" Jessica shrugged. "What can I say ... it happens. Anyway, on our third date he took me to the club and dedicated this amazing song to me. I felt like a queen and later that night I treated him like a king, until..." She stared at the aquarium, lost in the past.

"Until?" Dr. Jones prompted.

Jessica smirked. "Until I made him bleed." She met his gaze and waited patiently in their customary standoff.

They both knew when she was waiting for a reaction, and they both also knew he wouldn't give her one.

"I sank my teeth into his carotid, drained his blood, then called in the clean-up crew." She faked an exaggerated smile with clenched teeth.

Dr. Jones tugged on the cuffs to his shirt then removed a hair from his sleeve. "And how did he react?"

He was no fun, a buzz kill, and a complete stodgy grump. "He called me a fucking lunatic, insisted I untie him, and had me banned from the jazz club."

"Why did he have you banned from the jazz club?"

Jessica sat erect and gripped the edge of the desk. "Are you kidding me? We've been dancing around the entire point of all this bullshit therapy for weeks and weeks, and you're still not ready to address why it is I need to make these men bleed? You don't want to know about Four and my dead best friend?"

"Time's up."

She slammed her hand on the desk. "You're damn right! Time's up. We're finished." She grabbed her purse and stomped to the door.

"Jessica?" Dr. Jones called, not bothering to stand or look at her.

"What?" she grumbled before shutting the door.

"You're making progress."

A sarcastic chuckle vibrated from her chest. "Yeah, well I have a date tonight. We'll see if he agrees with you by the end of the night."

In college Jessica's roommate, Kelly Gunner, persuaded Jessica to do a few triathlons with her. Jessica, a self-professed exercise junkie, was an easy sell. After graduation Kelly continued her role as Jessica's training partner and also took on a new role as her designated matchmaker.

"Please tell me this guy is sex personified, not full of himself, and good in bed," Jessica said to Kelly over the phone as she zipped the back of her white strapless dress and slipped on her heels.

"Don't be pissed, but honestly I don't know anything about him. Gabe's known him since preschool. Their parents are still neighbors."

"And?" Jessica combed her fingers through her long dark hair that she'd spent over an hour straightening.

"And what? That's it. I've only known Gabe for two weeks. I haven't met his parents, so of course I don't know anything about his friend. But Gabe said everyone loves him."

"Pfft, then why is he still single?"

"Probably the same reason you are."

Jessica camouflaged her lips in blood red as she considered that possibility. Was her date for the night single because he was a vampire too? "I doubt that, but we'll see. I had a shit day with my psychiatrist so I need a no brainer evening with a guy who can give me an orgasm with a simple handshake."

"You see a shrink?"

"Saw. Today was my last day."

"What on Earth were you seeing a shrink for?"

"To exercise my brain," Jessica deadpanned.

Kelly laughed. "Whatever, you weirdo. Gabe's here so we'll meet you there soon?"

"Yep."

"And you have his address?"

"You messaged it to me twice and e-mailed it five minutes before I called you."

"Okay, hun. See you soon."

Jessica slipped her clutch under her arm, rolled her eyes to the ceiling, and crossed her fingers. "Please, please, please let this guy be normal, very hot, and not afraid of a little blood." Before she opened her door she sensed God giving her an affirmative wink.

The double date that night was at said date's place, a twenty minute drive from Jessica's apartment. It was the epitome of a blind date—more like a blind, deaf, and mute date. She didn't know anything about him, not his age, a physical description, profession, or even his name. One thing, his address, was all she knew. He lived in a newer condo in the Mission Bay area.

She took the elevator up to his floor, checking her makeup in the hall mirror before knocking on the door. Long hair, short dress, and high heels, she prayed it would be enough to put a smile on said stranger's face.

When the dark paneled door opened, Jessica exhaled in relief. The man before her was an easy eleven out of ten.

"Oh, hi there." He smiled and Jessica's mind already had him naked, branded, and kneeling between her legs.

"Hi, I'm Jessica." She held out her hand.

"Oh, I-I'm Darren." He shook her hand, and she didn't orgasm but she knew the night was still young and there was definite potential.

"So ... are you going to invite me in?" She tried to look past him to see if Kelly and Gabe had arrived.

"Yeah, I'm sure you can go on in."

"Jess!" Kelly squealed.

"Well, nice to meet you." Darren smiled and walked past Jessica as Kelly grabbed her hand and yanked her inside before she could respond.

"Oh my God! Jackpot, baby. Wait until you see him!" Kelly made an effort to whisper but failed by several decibels.

Jessica pointed back at the door with her thumb. "Where's he going?"

"Who?"

"Darren?"

"Oh, home I suppose."

"I thought we were having dinner at his house."

"What? Oh ... no, Jess that was the neighbor. He was dropping off his key or something like that. I think he's leaving town for a few weeks. Come, come, come ..." Kelly looped her arm around Jessica's and pulled her down the hall to a large open room with sleek modern lines and shades of gray on the walls.

"Gabe, Luke, this is Jessica."

Two men stood in the large kitchen leaning against the island, each with a beer in hand. Jessica hadn't met Gabe before, but she knew which one he was because the other guy was her *ex* shrink, Dr. Luke Jones.

"Nice to meet you, Jessica." Gabe held out his hand. "This is my friend, Luke."

Dr. Jones was no longer wearing his signature three-piece suit. He'd traded it in for dark jeans and a light blue button down shirt with the sleeves rolled up to his elbows. The only thing that felt familiar was his stone poker face, never giving away anything.

Jessica smiled while shaking Gabe's hand. "Nice to meet you too. And ... Luke, is it?" Jessica offered her hand. Luke accepted it with a pleasant smile. "Yes." His eyes tensed a bit as Jessica held his hand with bone-crushing intensity, reminiscent of their first encounter.

"It's *Doctor* Luke Jones," Kelly gushed while wrapping her arm around Gabe.

"A doctor, huh?" Jessica raised her eyebrows at Luke.

"I'm a psychiatrist." Luke took a sip of his beer, eyes tracking Jessica's every move.

Jessica accepted the glass of wine that Kelly handed her. "So not a real doctor then."

Luke smirked. "I think four years of undergrad, four years of medical school, and a four year residency qualifies me as a *real* doctor."

"But you're not saving lives or anything like that, right?"

"Luke was a volunteer firefighter when we were in college, so he's definitely had his days of saving lives. Now he just deals with the crazies of San Francisco." Gabe was kind enough to jump in on Luke's behalf.

Luke cleared his throat. For the first time ever, Jessica sensed his discomfort—his humanity. She wondered if "crazies" was Luke's description or Gabe's assumption.

"So what do you do, Jessica?" Gabe asked.

"Waitress during the day, strip at night."

Gabe choked on his beer. Kelly patted his back while shaking her head. "No she doesn't. Jessica's a brilliant actuary intern. She does two to three triathlons with me every year, and she teaches self-defense classes at a battered women's shelter." Kelly laughed. "Well, come to think of it, Jessica's a shit cook so she spends a lot of time eating out and when we shared an apartment in college she used to run around the place half naked like her body physically rejected clothes, so I suppose the waitress/stripper scenario isn't too far off."

Jessica shrugged and took a sip of her wine. It didn't matter what she did, the night was a shamble of wreckage. She thought of the wasted hour on her hair, the dry-clean only dress getting another night's wear, and the expensive perfume she only wore when her vagina needed some manly attention.

"Isn't Luke's place amazing?" Kelly kept the conversation flowing in a non-confrontational direction.

Jessica looked around. "I suppose it's tidy enough." Kelly and Gabe laughed at her comment that wasn't meant to be funny. Luke ... not so much.

"I'll give you a tour." Luke smiled.

"Mmm, yes we'll meet you out on the balcony when

you're done. The view is amazing." Kelly pulled Gabe toward the French doors.

Jessica and Luke stared at each other until the door clicked shut.

"This can't happen." Luke set down his beer. "If you choose to tell them you're my patient, that's your choice, but legally I can't tell them."

"Whoa, first, I'm not your patient anymore. I've done the financial risk assessment and based on our *progress,* I should have ended treatment weeks ago. Second, *this* is nothing." Jessica gestured her hand between the two of them. "So don't get your over-starched flannel boxers bound in a wad up your tight ass thinking anything is *happening.*" Jessica glanced over her shoulder at two sets of eyes peering in at them. She smiled. "Now, weren't you going to show me what all my money has bought you?"

Luke drummed his fingers on the counter in a steady beat of contemplation. "We'll make it through the evening and after you leave I'll tell Gabe you're not my type."

"Not your type?" she mumbled to herself, following him down the hall. Apparently his type was submissive giraffes with weak personalities. Jessica inherited her mother's verti-cally challenged gene and her father's strong but colorful personality which was often intimidating to men. It was possible the blood "fetish" played a minor part in her one-and-done dating streak.

"Bathroom ... guest bedroom ... office..." Luke droned with zero enthusiasm "...master bedroom ..."

Jessica veered off the tour into his bedroom. The view of the bay was nearly as amazing as his office. The bedding on the king bed was a mix of white, grays, black, and a few pillow splashes of blue. Everything was a perfect geometric configuration of modern design and immaculate order.

"This is my bedroom." Luke stood in the doorway.

"I know. That's what you said." She dusted her fingertips over his dresser then the foot of the bed, mesmerized by how turned on she felt being in his personal space. "You have OCD."

"I don't. I'm simply entertaining guests tonight."

"In your bedroom?"

"It's on the tour."

Jessica continued to his large walk-in closet.

"That's not on the tour."

It didn't matter to her. The light automatically came on when she opened the door. With the same delicate touch, she ran her hand down the sleeve of one out of maybe twenty flawlessly ironed dress shirts. From a dark wood cubby she pulled out a folded hoodie and brought it to her nose.

"You're in my closet ... smelling my clothes. I think you're crossing a serious line, Jessica."

She turned, hugging his sweatshirt. "I hate how good you smell all the time."

Luke leaned against the door frame with his hands casually resting in the back pockets of his jeans, shoulders pulled back, shirt hugged to his defined chest.

"It's been distracting me for the past three months." She took calculated steps toward him.

Luke tracked her every move with spine-tingling intensity. There was a predator and its prey, but neither one showed signs of submitting to the lesser role.

"My apologies," he whispered.

"Liar." Jessica rested her hands on his chest.

He regarded her with undaunted control, not retreating an inch or relinquishing so much as the slightest flinch. "What do you want?"

Jessica circled the pad of her finger over the buttons of his shirt. "That's simple—you."

She slid her hands up his chest to the back of his neck and pulled him toward her as she lifted on to her toes. When their lips touched, it felt like someone poured gasoline onto a small ember deep inside her that Dr. Jones had been fanning for weeks with his eyes, his smell, his militant control.

A painful urgency to feel his hands on her body set off a familiar panic in her mind. Control—she was losing it. His hands remained static in his back pockets, but for some reason that felt more dominating than if they'd been tangled in her hair. Luke controlled her with just his presence. Jessica was drowning in his taste, the way his tongue manipulated hers, and his lips overruled the urgent pace hers were desperate to maintain. It was too fast and too slow, too much, yet not enough. It was in her head—*he* was in her head.

"Shit!" Luke pulled away, eyes wide for a split second before narrowing into small slits. He touched his middle two fingers to his bloodied lip.

Jessica rubbed her lips together as they curled into a smirk; blood red lipstick hid the evidence. She brushed past him. "Can't say I didn't warn you."

CHAPTER TWELVE

KNIGHT

JILLIAN RUBBED HER LIPS TOGETHER, still tasting the one kiss that would forever linger with equal parts pain and pleasure. She glanced up from the sofa where she was folding some clothes. Lilith smiled. She was always smiling, even when she slept. But each smile was unique. Jillian knew Lilith couldn't hear her story, but the way her smiles changed throughout parts of it made Jillian wonder if she had a sixth sense for the emotions in the air.

"I'm going to work on the bathroom since you're done with lunch." Jillian stood.

Lilith squinted a bit, then nodded as she tried to get up from her chair.

"Do you need to use the bathroom first?" Jillian asked, helping Lilith to her feet.

Lilith shook her head.

"Do you want to nap in your bed today?"

Lilith hobbled down the hall as Jillian held her arm. When they reached the master bathroom, Lilith pointed to the floral upholstered vanity chair.

"Oh, you want to watch me install the bar?"

Lilith smiled again, and Jillian helped her sit on the chair. She had about an hour to get the handicap bar secured to the wall before Dodge would be home. Jillian had learned her handywoman skills from the most unlikely place, but that was a story for another day. She still hadn't finished her blind date.

Day

JESSICA LEFT her wounded ex-shrink behind to think about his wrong doings. She felt no remorse. He needed to adjust his treatment plan to actually address the patient's problem before any more innocent victims were affected. Even more than that, he needed to stop wearing that cologne or using that soap, or whatever it was that made her have such an insatiable craving for him. It could have been those sharp navy eyes too, or his thick black hair he always wore styled just so. In Jessica's eyes it begged for her fingers to mess it up and yank it hard.

"Hey, Jess. So what'd you think? Isn't this place amazing?" Kelly moved her feet from the opposing patio chair at the table so Jessica could sit down. Gabe grabbed Kelly's foot, pulled off her heeled sandal, and began massaging her foot. Gabe was a keeper. It had to be in the stars for them. They both had curly blond hair, his just long enough to tease his ears and hers midway down her back. Their children would be ridiculously cute and sweet. Both Gabe and Kelly were nauseatingly lovey-dovey.

"Yeah, it's pretty amazing." Jessica sipped her wine.

"Dinner will be ready soon. Is everyone good with eating out here?" Luke asked, peeking his head outside.

"Oh my God! What happened to your lip?" Kelly gasped.

"Jessica bit me."

Jessica whipped around, dragging her jaw along the ground.

"What? No, seriously what happened?" Gabe laughed. The idea of Jessica biting her blind date within twenty minutes of supposedly meeting him for the first time was beyond crazy.

Jessica stood, giving Kelly and Gabe a nervous smile. "Kudos, you two. This guy is a real jokester and I love a good sense of humor." She motioned to the door with her thumb. "Just relax. I'll help Luke finish up in the kitchen." She turned on her heels and marched toward Luke without any more confusion as to who was the predator that day.

Luke walked back to the kitchen like he didn't just toss her off the ten story balcony.

"What the hell was that? What happened to doctor-patient confidentiality?"

Luke grabbed the plates from behind the glass-doored cabinet then turned toward her. "I didn't disclose anything about my patient, Jessica Day. I simply shared the incident that happened in my closet five minutes ago with my blind date, Hannibal Lecter."

"I was just proving a point." Jessica leaned over the island, teeth clenched.

Luke leaned in from the opposite side until there were only a few inches between their faces. "So. Was. I."

She huffed in exasperation while reclaiming her space. "I trusted you to help me."

Luke's brow creased. "I *was* helping you, but I didn't get to remove anyone's appendix on my first day of medical school. I had to study and master the human body first. It's the same way with the mind. No two people are alike. I need to study and understand you before I can help you. There's nothing textbook about thoughts and feelings." He took a breath and closed his eyes for a brief moment, like that speech had been playing in his head for weeks, desperate to be heard.

Jessica's shoulders slumped as defeat hijacked her voice. "I spent three hours getting ready for this date, shaving almost everything except my head—lotion, makeup, hair straightening, ten wardrobe changes—because I haven't had sex in over six months. Six. Months!"

Luke gave her a sad smile. "You look truly stunning tonight."

Jessica forced her gaze up to meet his. "If I wouldn't have bit you would we have had sex tonight?"

He laughed, a real laugh. It was a foreign sound that Jessica had never heard him make. "Honestly I hadn't thought that far."

"Why not?"

He pulled the large dish from the oven. "Shit!" He sucked his finger just below the knuckle having burned it on the top of the oven. "Because..." he sucked it some more "...I was waiting for you to make me bleed."

Jessica cocked her head to the side. "Why were you so sure I'd make you bleed?"

Luke ran his hand under cold water, looking over his shoulder at Jessica for a long second. "Because I've been studying you for the past three months."

She fell into a brief, rare moment of speechlessness. Her eyes blinked in rapid succession. "You think I look stunning tonight?" she whispered.

"Painfully." Luke's gaze slipped as his hands commenced arranging the food on the plates.

They served dinner, enjoyed a mild sixty-five degree evening on the balcony with their friends, laughed at jokes, sipped fine wine and beer, and shared an occasional glance. But they never spoke directly to each other again until the evening came to an end.

"We're going to head out so you two can have some time alone, exchange numbers, plan your wedding." Kelly giggled as Gabe pulled her out the door with his hand over her mouth.

"She's clearly had too much to drink. Thanks, Luke. Dinner was great." Gabe gave a final wave before Luke closed the door, leaning back against it with his hands in his pockets.

She always remembered that image of Dr. Luke Jones as her favorite: casual and blindingly handsome. The evening had bestowed a few wrinkles to his clothes. The messy contrast to his perfectly parted, neatly combed hair gave him an unforgettable boyish appeal, and there was a soft surrender in his blue eyes.

"I-I'm at a loss for words."

Jessica nodded. "What were the chances, right?" She shifted slightly from one foot to the other in an attempt to ease the murderous torture of her heels. "I think I'll keep my appointment with you for next week after all."

Luke squinted as he shook his head. "I can't be your doctor anymore."

"What? Why not?"

"Our friends set us up on a date tonight. We kissed. The grid of lines we've crossed is so far beyond ethical I can't see straight. I'm not going to end my career over this. And you need help, but it can't be me. I'll refer you to someone else, but—"

"Someone else?" Jessica's voice strained in disbelief

against her wavering anger. "I'm not doing this shit again. I've spent the past three months with you. Opening up to you. Being *studied* by you. Now I'm just supposed to start over?"

"It wouldn't be like that." Luke pushed off the door.

Jessica retreated a step in response.

"I'd bring your new doctor up to speed on our progress—"

"Progress? Really? Have you looked in the mirror? Do you call that progress?"

"I can't see you. Period."

Jessica crossed her arms over her chest. "You can't see me as my doctor or—"

"At all." Luke's words held a cold finality. "I'm not an ER doctor that stitched up your wound. I'm a psychiatrist and in my profession it's not ethical to get personally involved with patients—not during treatment and not even after the professional relationship has been terminated."

"But you kissed me back."

He shook his head, squinting a bit. "I should not have."

Jessica drew in a shaky breath and closed her eyes, willing what was happening to just stop. She needed him and she had to make him see that. "I'll never forget how her body looked drained of its blood."

"Jessica, don't. I'm not your doctor anymore." Luke opened the front door.

Memories of that crippling fear seized her body. She opened her eyes and stared at an imperfection in the dark wood floor next to a small steel-framed credenza. "He always wore combat fatigues with brown boots. I estimated his shoe size to be a ten from the blood-stamped boot prints on the floor."

"Jessica! Stop. Now."

"That's what I said ... every time he'd cut her. He was in control, total control. And when he'd start to lose it, he'd cut her again. Just the sight of it calmed him. I don't remember when I stopped crying and started placing bets with myself as to where he would cut her next. Every time I guessed correctly I felt stronger as Claire became weaker. It was as if I was taking his control. If I could predict his next move I could save us, get us out of there."

"I'm sorry. I can't—I *won't* do this with you. Call my office on Monday and Eve will give you a referral." Luke grabbed her arm.

It took a moment for Jessica to register what he was doing and by the time she did, the door was closed and she was on the opposite side. She rested her cheek and flattened her hands against it. The magnetism to Luke was more than she could resist. He had something so vital to her survival that walking away would feel like a slow death.

"He was her boyfriend. Claire had met him online. They dated over the internet for almost a year before they decided to meet. He wanted to wait until she was eighteen so Claire asked me to drive down to San Diego with her on her birthday. It was the summer between our junior and senior year. I didn't turn eighteen until that October." A lone tear smeared down her cheek. "Luke?" she whispered, closing her eyes.

She sucked in a shaky breath. "Our parents thought we were going to LA for a concert. Jude was the only person who knew where we were going. Claire didn't know I told him, but I did. Jude and I don't keep secrets; we never have." She opened her eyes and started sliding her fingernail along the grooves of the woodgrain door.

"It wasn't the best neighborhood, but when I tried to warn Claire she berated me for being so judgmental. The houses were all small and rundown with cars parked on the streets and so much junk in the driveways it looked like everyone was having a rummage sale. Four lived in a green house with half the siding ripped off, an old brown stained sofa on the weathered gray porch, and the storm door with ripped screen that rattled on its loose hinges like an earthquake every time the wind gusted."

Jessica chuckled, the trail of her lone tear washed away by an uncontrollable flood of many more. She missed Claire. Every. Single. Day. "You want to know what was so ironic? When the police told Claire's parents, they visibly relaxed with relief that she hadn't been raped. She bled out of her femoral artery in just under two minutes, yet her parents were relieved that she died a virgin. How fucked-up is that?" She sniffled. "I know what you're thinking: not nearly as fucked-up as me." Her voice cracked on the last word. Could he possibly know that she never let anyone see this vulnerability?

Without warning, the door disappeared. Jessica stumbled to the ground, quick hands saving her from a face-plant by less than an inch. Those same quick hands pulled her to her feet.

Luke sighed and waited for her amber eyes to find his through her long wet lashes. "When I'm the most overeducated barista at Starbucks you'd better come in every day to remind me why I trashed my career. And since you'll be the most psychologically stable actuary in the history of the profession, you'd better leave me one helluva tip."

Jessica nodded while wiping her tears. Relief mingled between her laughter and sobs. "I'm sorry I bit you. It won't happen again."

"No, it won't." Luke framed her petite face in his strong hands. "Because if it does I'll have you muzzled, put in a straitjacket, and committed to a mental institute. Are we clear?"

She swallowed with a slow nod. "Dr. Jo—"

"No." He shook his head. "I'm not your doctor. You will see me *here* three times a week, no more no less. You will clean my apartment and tell me about your past. I will listen and offer *friendly* advice. There will never be an exchange of money. You will never come to my office again. You will never tell anyone. As far as Gabe and Kelly are concerned, we just didn't have that much in common. Are. We. Clear?"

"Can I call you Jones ... just Jones. I like it."

"No."

Jessica sighed. "You're no fun." She pulled from his grasp and opened the door.

"Jessica?"

"Yes?" She turned.

"That's another thing this will not be."

"Huh?"

"*Fun.*"

CHAPTER THIRTEEN

KNIGHT

JILLIAN FINISHED INSTALLING the handicap bar minutes after ending her story for the day.

"Hey, look at that!" Dodge stood in the doorway admiring Jillian's handy work.

"I think she'll be able to use the bathroom by herself now."

"Thank God for that. There's nothing worse than pulling her ass off the toilet after she's shot out one of them toxic loads. I think them meds are messing with her plumbing. I sure as shit won't miss breaking that seal."

Jillian looked at Lilith who was smiling at her without regard for Dodge's crude and cruel comment. "Your husband doesn't think his shit stinks. Typical guy." Jillian winked at Dodge.

"Come here. I want to show you something before you go." Dodge waved Jillian toward the back door.

"Bye, Lilith." Jillian helped her up from the vanity chair.

"Thank you," Lilith said, and it was the first time Jillian heard her speak.

"You're welcome." Jillian gave her hand a little squeeze.

As soon as she opened the garage door, Jillian froze —speechless.

"Just got the new rims on today. What do you think?" Dodge sat in a golf cart that occupied its own garage stall. But it wasn't just any golf cart. It was red with a white top, red and white painted rims, custom white leather seats with a red N stitched into the back of them. The rest of the body looked like the Cornhusker apparel store exploded onto it— decals, a flag, and a built-in Cornhusker cooler on the back.

"Wow, it's ... wow. I didn't know you golfed."

"Oh, I don't."

Jillian raised her eyebrows. "Um, okay so what's with the *golf* cart?"

"I'm a Cornhusker fan."

She laughed. "I can see that."

"My knees have gone to shit so I use her to get around the development. Mainly to get the mail and stuff like that."

Jillian peeked around the garage door opening to the grouping of mailboxes. "Yeah, that has to be a good fifteen ... twenty yard walk."

"Nineteen and a half to be exact. Stan measured it for me awhile back. We were just curious."

"And you pack a cooler to get the mail?"

Dodge grinned. "Nah. I sit out here with Stan and shoot the breeze or watch the games." He gestured to the TV in the corner of the garage. "Sometimes I take a cold one down to Stan when he's working outside—hand trimming his lawn or sweeping the street with his big push broom."

Jillian smiled. She didn't just relocate to Nebraska, she landed on an entirely different planet called Peaceful Woods, which ironically had no woods at all, rather small algae-infested ponds behind each grouping of townhomes.

"Well, I'm going to head home now."

"Want a ride?"

"No ... I'm good." She winked at Dodge who had retrieved a beer from his cooler.

"Beer for the road?"

Jillian didn't have to sell sex toys that night so she shrugged. "Why not. Thanks."

Dodge tossed her a can. "Thanks again for everything, young lady."

"You're welcome." She raised her can to him before heading down the street. After popping the top, she took a big gulp. It was cold and tasted only mildly gross after her long and unexpectedly emotional day with AJ, then reminiscing about her blind date with Dr. Luke Jones.

"Jillian," a familiar voice called as she neared her driveway. Cage stood behind a grill.

"Hey, early dinner?"

He smirked. "Late lunch."

"Whatcha grilling?"

"Steaks and not the kind made from soybeans, sorry."

"Don't be. I'm good." She held up her can of beer before taking another sip.

Cage laughed. "Looks healthy."

"How's the big guy?"

He flipped the steaks and closed the lid. "Grumpy. He didn't end up going into work today so now he feels guilty."

Jillian handed Cage the rest of her beer. "Here, drink up. I'll go cheer him up."

Cage sat in the folding chair next to the grill and tipped back the can for a long swig. "Good luck with that. I don't think you bring out the best in him."

Jillian turned before opening the door to the house. "Really?" she asked with a hint of surprise in her voice.

Cage chuckled. "Really."

She shut the door and padded down the hall toward the kitchen.

"Better not be burning my steak," AJ called from the kitchen with his back to Jillian as he sliced vegetables and slid them off the cutting board into a large salad bowl.

"I love how protective you are of your meat," she whispered, sliding her hands under his shirt and around front to his chest.

AJ stiffened. "What are you doing?"

"Trying to un-grump you."

He turned. "That's not a word."

She stepped back and leaned against the opposite counter. "Thanks for the grammar tip. How are you feeling?"

He cleared his throat and turned back around to continue working on the salad. "About that. What happened earlier ... it shouldn't have happened."

She rubbed her forehead. Jillian wasn't sure when she became such a guilty pleasure, but she had always been Luke's, and AJ, with that statement, joined the list too. "Because ...?"

"Because I have a date tonight."

She pushed off the counter. "Well, that must mean you're feeling better. Good for you." She headed to the back door. "I have one too." The statement came out of nowhere, an ego knee-jerk reaction, but it was too late. She had to own it.

AJ started to say something, but she shut the door before he could finish.

"Hey, young buck. What are your plans tonight?"

Cage retrieved the steaks from the grill, setting them onto a plate. "Not sure yet. Why?"

"I think you should take me around town and show me the nightlife in Omaha. What do you say?" She continued walking to her house.

"Like a date?"

Jillian grinned to herself. "If your dad asks, then yes—definitely a date."

"Will I be getting lucky tonight?"

A giggle bubbled from her chest. "Sorry."

"But I don't have to tell my dad that, right?"

"I'd be disappointed if you did."

"Jills, get your ass down here. I need to hit something."

Jillian rolled her eyes, smirking as she slipped off her shoes. "Let me change my clothes, *Jacks*." After a quick change, she joined her brother downstairs for some friendly sparring.

"My four o'clock student raped my piano. I didn't think it was possible for such a hideous sound to come out of Black Beauty."

"You named your piano?"

"Yes. Hit me."

Jillian pulled one arm across her body then the other, stretching her shoulders. "Anxious?"

"Restless ... agitated ... I don't know." Jackson rolled his neck.

"You need to get out of the house, have some fun. Get drunk with purpose."

"And what purpose would that be?"

She jabbed at him, but he was too quick for her. "To get laid. You're much more charming once you've had a few beers."

Jackson landed a kick just below her ribs. "I think I wrote the book on getting laid."

She swept his leg, landing him on his ass. "Don't be cocky."

He jumped back up. "You and I. We're going out tonight."

Jillian ducked and weaved to avoid the knuckles aiming for her jaw. "Can't..." she breathed "...I already have plans."

"Plans?"

"A date of sorts."

He T'd his hands. "Timeout. A date?"

"Of sorts." She guzzled down half her glass of water.

"With whom?"

"Cage."

"The neighbor boy?"

"He's a young man, but yes." Jillian could see the lecture being composed in her brother's incessantly churning brain. "And before you go off about it, I can assure you it's nothing. He's just showing me around town."

Jackson cocked his head, hands rested on his hips. "Did he ask you?"

She shrugged. "I don't remember." Her grin called her out before Jackson had the chance.

"Liar. You asked him, didn't you? Why? There has to be a reason. He's not your type."

Jillian shot him a scowl. "Then what type is he?"

"Young, weak, and not Luke."

"He plays football. I'd hardly call that weak."

"You know what I mean."

She sighed, lips pursed.

"This is about AJ. You're trying to piss him off by going out with his son. Or are you trying to make him jealous?"

"I think we both know Sarge isn't going to be jealous."

Jackson nodded. "Pissed. He's going to be really pissed. But why?"

"We had another *moment* this morning." She leaned back against the wall with her arms crossed over her chest.

"Was this before or after you got caught in the rain wearing only your bra and underwear?" He mirrored her stance against the opposite wall, a single brow peaked.

She bit her lip to hide her smile. "Somewhere in the middle."

"Uh huh ... I don't know why you're going down this road. It can't end well."

"Because he wears a uniform?"

"Because you've already lost control ... reverted back to *old habits*."

She stared at the floor. "I didn't today. I didn't even want to."

"And?"

Jillian looked up, nose wrinkled. "And he has a date tonight."

Jackson stood erect with a puffed chest. "You had sex with him this morning and he has a date tonight?"

"No! We didn't have sex. I told you that earlier. We ... ugh! It's complicated."

"Want my advice?"

She pouted. "No."

"Un-complicate it."

IT MAY HAVE BEEN OBSESSION, compulsion, or just flat-out insanity, but for whatever reason Jillian wanted to make a statement. A tube top with a spaghetti strap tie around the neck, a good two inches of exposed abs, and a short flowing skirt said a lot. What? She wasn't sure, but she'd know when AJ saw her.

"Hi, Sarge. Is my date ready?" Jillian threw down the gauntlet while batting her eyelashes when AJ opened the door.

"Excuse me?"

"My date ... Cage. Is he ready to go?"

"He's your date?" Each word fought for air between AJ's clenched teeth.

She beamed with delight that Cage hadn't told his dad yet, and she was getting to see his initial reaction firsthand.

"Every young, *firm* inch of him."

AJ stepped outside, closing the front door behind him. "What the hell is going on? Is this some joke?"

"It's dinner, a private tour of Omaha, maybe a thank you kiss good night ... second base tops."

"Is this about this morning?" AJ leaned in closer, his voice low, the dam of control cracking. "Because I didn't ask you to do anything for me—"

"Wow! Aren't you the self-centered bastard. The world doesn't revolve around you. I'm going out with Cage tonight because I want an evening out and he's *fun.* Clearly something that is completely foreign to you." Jillian stepped closer, not willing to back down for a second. "And as far as this morning goes, fuck you. Fuck you for being too stupid and stubborn to ask for help and fuck you for not having the decency to just say 'Thank you.'"

Cage opened the door. "Is ... everything okay?"

Jillian flipped in a single breath, finding her happy face for Cage. "Everything is perfect." She grabbed his hand and tugged him out the door. "Remember what I said about you not getting lucky tonight?"

Cage took a nervous glance back at his dad as they walked toward his truck. "Uh yeah."

"Well, I might just change my mind."

JILLIAN LIKED Cage too much to risk taking him to clubs or bars since he wasn't twenty-one yet. After he gave her an hour tour of Omaha's hotspots, they settled for casual dining on pizza.

"So starting quarterback, that's pretty awesome."

Cage had the most endearing blush. "Yeah, last year was my first season to start."

"Are you hoping to go Pro or are you going to settle for a low-key respectable job where all the women aren't stalking you."

He laughed. "I'm not sure yet. I'm studying for a degree in elementary education, so one life would be polar opposite of the other."

"Oh, that's unexpected. I rescind my earlier comment. You're going to have girls stalking you no matter what. Women dig strong, sexy guys with a soft side." She chuckled. "And nothing says soft quite like the male elementary school teacher. Especially kindergarten or first grade."

Cage nodded, face still rosy with embarrassment. "So what about you? What do you do?"

"Well as you know I help Dodge with Lilith two days a week and the perfectly trimmed yards in the development, which I'm sure you've noticed..." she winked "...are the fine work of yours truly. And I've also been doing some home parties."

"Home parties?"

Jillian smirked. She knew Cage was about to go from rosy face to inferno red. "Have you heard of Lascivio?"

Cage choked on his pizza as he pressed his napkin to his mouth.

"So you have." She smiled.

Cage nodded while he cleared his throat. "Sex toys?" he whispered.

"I like to think of them as PPDs: personal pleasure devices."

"Uh, how did you get into that job?"

She twisted her lips. "Just by chance ... luck of the draw, you could say."

"Do you *like* your job?" He risked a glance up from his plate.

She shrugged. "There are worse jobs. I mean, I could have been a barnyard masturbator."

He snickered. "Really? That was on your list of dream jobs?"

Jillian grinned thinking it was on a *list,* but not her dream job list.

"A kid in my Poli-Sci class has an uncle that does that."

She licked some sauce off her finger. "I bet they're in high demand in these parts."

Cage stirred his straw, poking around at the ice. "My dad likes you."

Fiddling with the corner of her napkin, she met his eyes. "What makes you think that?"

"You irritate the hell out of him."

"And that equates to him liking me?"

Cage nodded. "He suffers from PTSD. The migraine this morning ... that's part of it. Doctors say they're stress-induced. Anyway, he only lets people he likes get under his skin—me for instance. Everyone else he deems not worthy of his time, attention, or reaction. But you..." Cage shook his head and whistled "...you are thoroughly under his skin. I've never seen anything like it. You were gone by the time I got back this morning, but he didn't even go into work and he's been a hair trigger all day."

Jillian let his words simmer for a few minutes before she decided to ask the question that had been on her mind all evening. "His date tonight ... is she—"

"Serious? No. She's the sister of one of his buddies from work. They go out maybe once or twice a month. I'm not sure, but I wouldn't call it serious. I think he uses her for a convenient hook-up, but don't tell him I said that."

Jillian didn't know how she felt about AJ hooking-up with a woman ten hours after he'd stared at her naked body.

"Excuse me." Cage held up a finger as he answered his phone. The confusion in his face and clipped, one-sided conversation led her to believe he was talking to someone about later that night. "Uh ... I sort of have plans." He looked up at her.

She reached across the table and patted his hand. "I should get back," she mouthed.

"You sure?" he whispered, holding the phone away from his mouth.

Jillian nodded.

"Okay, sure. In about an hour? Cool. See ya then."

When they arrived back home, Jillian hopped out of his truck. "Thanks, young buck. It was fun." She blew him a kiss and smiled.

Cage shifted the truck into reverse before she shut the door. "Probably means I'm not getting lucky now, huh?"

Jillian grinned. "Depends. Who are you going to meet up with?"

Cage smirked. "Good point. Good night."

The dangerously sexy neighbor waved as the innocent young man backed out of the driveway. His fading taillights were replaced with blinding headlights. Jillian squinted against them as they drew near. The moment she recognized the Jeep, she wished she would have hurried inside. AJ stared at her, devoid of any discernible emotion like he was looking at a lamppost. She was too busy playing her lamppost role to question why he parked in the driveway or notice the passenger door opening at the same time he opened his.

"Jillian," AJ greeted in a monotone voice.

That's when the woman from the passenger side walked around the front of his Jeep and slid her arm behind his waist. Jillian smiled at her, *not* him.

"Lovely evening. You two just get back from dinner?"

The blonde with plenty up top and a spare shoved in the trunk furrowed her brow at AJ then met Jillian's pointed gaze again. "Um, yes. Do you live here? AJ didn't tell me he had new neighbors. I'm Carin ... with a C."

Jillian stepped into the grassy easement. "Nice to meet you, Carin with a C. I'm Jillian with a J." She shook her hand.

Carin homed in on Jillian's biceps. "Damn girl, you've got some serious arms. I'd kill to have those."

AJ frowned at Jillian. Jillian smiled at Carin. Truthfully, Carin's body was beautifully all woman: nice curves, soft, and feminine. Jillian's curves were rigid and defined lacking any sort of softness. She had sex appeal but lacked that classic graceful beauty.

"Are you married?" Carin asked.

"Yes, to my brother."

AJ shot Jillian a raised brow that she opted to ignore.

"Oh ... um ... I didn't realize that was legal."

Jillian slipped off her heeled sandals, relishing the feel of the cool grass as she curled her toes into its soft blades. "It's not, but we've been together since ... well, birth so we consider it a common law marriage. Neither one of us had to change our name, and I don't know if it was a sharing the womb thing or what, but the sex is ... *incredible*."

AJ rolled his eyes and it was the closest thing to showing a side of humor that Jillian had ever seen from him.

"That's well ... I mean ..." Carin looked like someone just shoved the end of a shovel up her ass so Jillian decided to put her out of her misery.

"I'm bullshitting you."

An uneasy smile touched Carin's lips as she looked up at AJ, who had yet to join the conversation.

"Oh, you had me ... that's funny ... I think," she mumbled.

"Carin, why don't you head inside. I'll be in, in just a minute. I have a neighborhood matter to discuss with Jillian."

"Oh, sure. Well, it was nice to meet you."

Jillian winked. "You too, Carin with a C."

AJ wasted no time before his face transformed into a scowl. The kind that could be molded into a villain's mask for Halloween.

"Oh stop!" Jillian shook her head. "You're such a killjoy. You have no idea how bad I want to wipe that ridiculous frown off your face, and don't think I can't."

"You took my son on a date and then insulted mine."

"Whoa! Insulted your date?"

"You insulted her intelligence with your 'bullshitting.'"

Jillian reared her head back in laughter. "Oh my god! *You* are the only one who insulted her by eye-fucking me with her on your arm. If she were that intelligent, she'd be thumbing it home to get away from your cheating ass."

AJ stepped closer, but Jillian would not be intimated by his size or growly demeanor. "A, I'm not *with* Carin so cheating is a non-issue and B, I wasn't *eye-fucking* you."

"You were ... you still are." Jillian tipped her chin up in defiance.

A sense of foreboding hung in the air as he squinted at her a split second before yanking her arm toward his garage door. He typed in a code and pulled her inside before pausing the door to send it back down. Jillian covered his hand that was clenched around her arm. As her heart began to race her fingernails began to breach the first few layers of his skin. Her eyes locked to his.

AJ clenched his teeth, his breath heavy, his intent clear. "Do it."

The rest of Jillian's body relaxed as just her hand curled with strength and complete control, drawing blood. AJ closed his eyes, opening them again when she relaxed her grip. They both stared at the micro pools of blood clotting at the surface. He grabbed the back of her head. Their lips collided with anger and raw need. Jillian ripped open his shirt, sending buttons scattering in every direction. She moaned, clawed, and ignited from his touch.

AJ grabbed her wrists and held them behind her back as he pushed his erection against her. Breathless, he broke from her angry kiss and rubbed his rough face against her cheek until his lips brushed her ear. "What do you *need*?" he whispered.

Short, quick puffs of breath escaped her parted lips as she wriggled her hands free from his. She pushed down on his shoulders. AJ lowered to his *knees* in front of her. Jillian fisted the material of her skirt over and over until it was gathered near her waist.

He looked up. She looked down. Their breaths were the only sound mingling with the sticky summer air. The tension in the garage could be felt like the crack of lighting and crash of thunder vibrating everywhere with the eerie descent of a mid-summer storm.

AJ curled his fingers around Jillian's panties and slid them down her legs, keeping his eyes fixed to hers. He gripped the firm muscled tissue of her legs and pressed his lips to her. Jillian swallowed hard, flattened her hands to the drywall, then curled her fingers until a dusting of it began to collect under her fingernails. Her skirt fell over his head like a mechanic under the hood of a car. *God, did she need to be serviced.*

His tongue eased along the apex of her legs. Her head fell back against the wall with a soft thump, eyes closed, fingernails chiseling small divots in the wall. It was the closest she'd felt to Luke in months. His voice whispered in her head.

"You can touch anything ... but me."

As AJ teased her opening and massaged her clitoris with expertise, she bit her bottom lip until she tasted her own blood. Another coping mechanism that she'd given up, but once again needed. Jillian *needed* so much more, but she took what AJ gave her and knew that it would be enough ... it *had* to be enough.

The pressure built with momentum. Jillian wanted to let go as much as she wanted to hold on. She tried to pull away as he pushed her closer to the edge, but her silent pleas to wait just a little longer went unheard. He slid his hands up the back of her legs and palmed her ass *hard*, holding her to him as she went tumbling out of control down the hill of a body-seizing, mind-blowing orgasm. The sound of AJ moaning against her sensitive flesh, like he was getting off from just the taste of her, echoed in her ears.

AJ emerged from under her *hood*, wiping his mouth with the back of his non-bloodied hand. He looked like hell and Jillian rather liked the dark side at that moment: his right hand smeared with blood, his shirt torn open exposing his rock-solid physique, and his lips swollen from administering an unforgiving assault on both sets of her lips.

Jillian bent down and grabbed her shoes and panties. "So ... tell Carin I'm sorry for keeping you." She considered saying thank you but decided to just bite her lips together and leave it at that. AJ gave her his signature blank stare so she turned to leave through the side door.

"Jillian?"

She looked back, feigning confidence because she wasn't. She was flustered with a nauseating mix of embarrassment and guilt.

"Thank you for not taking advantage of my son tonight."

A grin pulled at her lips. "You're welcome." She turned without looking back.

She was greeted by the smell of popcorn the moment she walked in the door. Jackson sat at the dining room table enjoying a late night snack while messing with his computer. He clocked her the second she closed the door; his eyes moved to her hand that held her sandals and panties.

"You know, there's a reason they call them *under*garments."

She dropped her shoes on the floor and padded off toward her room. "Good night, Jacks."

CHAPTER FOURTEEN

Jɪʟʟɪᴀɴ sᴛɪʀʀᴇᴅ to consciousness by Für Elise, the worst possible, nearly indistinguishable version of it. She suspected that to be the "rape" to which Jackson had made reference. On a long groan, she reached for her watch on the nightstand. It read five after noon.

"I'm a complete lazy-ass," she mumbled through a lion's yawn as she stretched into an X on her big bed. Confirming the time of day, the shrill screech of the mail truck's brakes sounded in the distance. Jillian traipsed to the front door, earning an exaggerated eye roll from Jackson sitting next to his student. She stuck her tongue out at him before stepping into the sweltering sun, wearing only her thread-bare tank top, hip-hugger panties, and of course red rain boots.

"Oh, man. My dad's going to crap his pants." Cage grinned while circling a soapy sponge over the hood of his truck.

Jillian padded toward the mailboxes, squinting at him. "Why? Did he have undercooked chicken for dinner last night?'

Cage laughed. "No. He's usually not home to see you

get the mail, but he just pulled in. Came home for lunch today."

She retrieved her three pieces of junk mail. "Is my 'getting the mail' an event around here?"

"If you lived in college dorms, no. But around here, yes. You getting the mail is *the* event of the day for these guys. Except my dad. I don't think he approves of your ..."

Jillian raised a hand to her brow, blocking the sun. "My?"

Cage shrugged, "Your ... *free spiritedness.*"

"Can you elaborate?"

"He means the strip show you give the neighbors." AJ stepped out from the corner of the garage. "Give us a minute, son."

Cage's face looked pained as he fought to hide his monstrous grin. "Told ya." He chuckled before going inside the house.

Jillian eyed AJ in his uniform. "Back to work today?"

"Go put some clothes on."

She laughed. "I'm not naked."

"You look cheap and easy strutting around wearing next to nothing in front of your neighbors."

Jillian wet her lips then bit them together. "I see. Did I *taste* cheap and easy last night?"

AJ's eyes slipped from her gaze.

"I'm probably more than ten years younger than you. What will the neighbors think when they see you looking at me like the perverted dirty old man you are, like a dog salivating over a piece of meat."

AJ's face masked into an unappreciative scowl, focusing his gaze back on Jillian's. "I have to get back to work."

"It must be exhausting being grumpy all the time. When you're alone do you roll around on the floor, hugging your belly while laughing hysterically? Because it's human nature to smile and laugh, so holding it in for the sake of keeping up this stern façade of yours must feel like torture sometimes. Am I right?"

AJ turned. "You don't know me."

"I don't. But I feel you."

Jillian's words stopped him like a fired gun. AJ looked over his shoulder.

"Good day, Sarge." She took her barely-covered body back in the house. A dreary cloud of sadness weighed on her. Luke had said those same words.

I feel you.

JACKSON FINISHED his two lessons for the day and took Jillian to get her Harley. They grabbed an early dinner, then she set off for the open road while he headed home for his first official date since arriving in Omaha—the daughter of a student. Jillian warned him it wasn't going to end well, but Jackson returned with the look-who's-talking face.

She arrived home just after seven. The whole neighborhood was outside watering plants, walking dogs, chatting in driveways. The trademark rumble of her hog pulling into the development turned heads and unhinged jaws. Jillian smirked behind the shielded face of her helmet. If there was a noise limit for Peaceful Woods, she was most likely breaking it.

"Yours?" Stan asked as she pulled off her helmet. He and Dodge sat in the pimped-out golf cart parked in her driveway just feet from her garage.

She shook out her long blond hair ... just because.

Dodge and Stan shared a pleased grin that Jillian caught out of the corner of her eye. "Yep, it's mine. You like?"

One by one more neighbors gathered around because they really had nothing better to do than keep tabs on the new neighbors.

"It looks like a sweet ride. It doesn't have any Husker decals or a cooler on the back, but it's not bad at all." Dodge winked.

Jillian grinned. "Oh, Dodge. I knew when I saw your baby that any attempt to compete would be futile at best. But she's an okay ride, even if I have to stop at an actual bar to get a drink." She ran her hand over the seat.

"Hey, Sarge! Whatdaya think of Jillian's Harley?" Stan handed AJ a beer from Dodge's cooler.

Jillian looked up, not realizing her surly mannered neighbor had joined the evening's circus gathering.

"Looks like she has too much time on her hands and too much money in the bank for someone her age."

"Yeah, Jillian. That's quite the purchase for someone mowing lawns and watching Lilith part-time." Marvin Housby, Greta's husband, piped up.

Jillian squinted at AJ for a second before moving her focus to Marvin. "I do home parties at night too."

"Oh yeah? Like candles or the gourmet meal type stuff?" Greta asked with complete innocence.

Jillian smiled. She did offer edible underwear and edible chocolate body cream, as well as some scented candles that gave off an aphrodisiac aroma. "Sort of, along with some other PPDs."

The small gathering looked at each other in confusion, but nobody wanted to admit they didn't know what she meant by PPD ... except AJ."

"PPDs?" he questioned.

Wicked delight danced across Jillian's face as she looked at AJ. "Personal Pleasure Devices. Can I interest you in a *private* demonstration, Sarge?"

The cricket chirps amplified in the silence her words created. Then faces morphed into shock as everyone stared at Jillian and AJ. They, however, looked only at each other.

Dodge cleared his throat. "I've ... uh ... gotta get back to Lilith. I told her I'd only be gone ten minutes." With his cue everyone else mumbled a few excuses and wandered back to their houses, leaving Jillian and AJ alone.

"Sex toys?"

"Come inside, AJ." Jillian shrugged off her leather jacket as she walked in the house.

"I don't want to see your—" The door shut before AJ could finish his protest.

Jillian snagged an apple from the counter and washed it. The grin on her face grew as she waited for the backdoor to open. She knew AJ was standing in her garage, grumpy as hell, contemplating his move. There was little doubt in her mind that he would eventually come inside. She knew underneath that seemingly impenetrable layer of stubbornness was an undeniable curiosity that made him just as human as everyone else.

"You realize half the damn neighborhood thinks you're married, and now you've got them thinking there's something going on between us—" AJ let his cheery self into the house.

"Is there *not* something going on between us?"

He helped himself to a seat at the table. Jillian plopped down in the chair next to him, propping her boots up on his legs. He frowned at her boots.

"What do *you need*, AJ?" She threw his words back at him. "Do you want to go downstairs and duke it out? Do you want to fuck me doggie style until I howl at the moon? Do you need me to suck you off to help relieve a bit of that pent-up anger you carry around all day?"

His jaw twitched as he stared at her with such intensity it nearly cracked her own façade. "Yes." Just one word.

Jillian paused mid-chew, waiting for more, but he offered nothing. She continued eating her apple. "What did you see that messed you up so bad?"

"Who said I'm messed-up?"

She chuckled. "Fair enough. Why don't you ask me out on a proper date: flowers, cloth napkins, fine wine, a chaste kiss goodnight?"

AJ raised a suspicious brow. "Chaste kiss? Has a guy ever given you a chaste kiss and lived to tell about it?"

"So you won't ask me out because you're afraid of me?"

"I fear no one."

Jillian's eyes widened. "Wow. Lucky you."

AJ shoved her boots off his legs then dusted off the nonexistent dirt. "Who do you fear?"

Jillian finished her apple, core included, then tugged off her boots before drawing her knees to her chest. "Where to begin ... uh ... I don't trust women with more than three children under the age of eight. They have to be ticking time bombs. I've seen it at the grocery store—one in the cart screaming with his hand stuck between the metal bars, one under the cart eating cookies out of the box that hasn't been paid for yet, another bear-hugging her leg because he didn't get the pack of gum he wanted, and one in a carrier latched-on to the breast, but occasionally popping off to look around and the mom doesn't realize her body is in letdown mode so she's spraying breastmilk everywhere."

Jillian met AJ's gaze and although his lips were set in a

hard line, she swore his eyes sparkled with a glimmer of amusement.

She continued, "People who drive ice cream trucks. I mean come on, parents tell their kids not to talk to strangers or take food from strangers, yet they send them down the street with a five dollar bill in hand chasing some old truck that probably has three kids gagged and bound in the back already. It's like they're saying 'Hey, here's five bucks, take my kid.' And don't even get me started on people whose second toe is longer than their big toe."

That's when it happened. As hard as he tried, AJ couldn't stifle his laugh any longer. Jillian took advantage of the moment by climbing onto his lap. He had a smile that was boyish yet handsome. She rested her hands on his broad shoulders and pecked at the grin that lingered on his lips. He tensed when she drew his bottom lip into her mouth, trapping it gently between her teeth. Then she released it and kissed him with a patience that threatened to drain her last bit of control.

Making someone bleed just to prove a point is not control. Luke's words calmed her urge.

Jillian pulled back even as AJ's mouth continued to reach for hers. "Take me out on a real date."

She felt his heart thumping against her chest, his arousal between her legs, and his quick breaths against her face.

"No." He claimed her lips once more with demanding force. His tongue as desperate as his lips. Before Jillian could bring the moment into focus, his hands slid up her shirt and he moaned when he discovered she wasn't wearing a bra. He pushed her shirt up and released her lips. Jillian hissed in a breath as he sucked her nipple into his mouth. Closing his eyes, he took pleasure in her body.

The woman in her, the Jillian in her, wanted to let go and feel her own pleasure, but she couldn't. The recent rebirth of her life had left her lost in self-discovery. Passion wasn't love and love wasn't passion. Her physical urges felt like emotional needs, yet she knew that wasn't possible. She'd been several pieces away from solving a puzzle, and then some bully came along and wiped all five thousand pieces onto the floor like the ruins of a small town after an EF-5 tornado.

"Enough," Jillian said, swallowing hard.

AJ continued.

"E-nough!" Jillian raised onto her knees until her right one was applying firm pressure to his crotch.

"Dammit!" AJ jerked his head back and grabbed her waist to lift her off him. "What is your deal?"

Jillian walked into the kitchen and jotted down her phone number on a piece of paper. "Here." She handed it to him. "Congratulations for not being messed-up from your past, but I kind of am. So when you're ready to treat me with respect give me a call."

AJ stared at it then stood. "That won't be happening." He tossed the piece of paper on the table and walked out the door.

Jillian laughed to herself. She didn't think it was possible to find someone functioning in society that was as messed-up as she was. Wrong!

———

FIVE DAYS PASSED before Jillian saw AJ again. The complete lack of activity next door led her to believe he had disappeared like Cage said he did on occasion. She kept busy with two lucrative Lascivio parties, keeping the yards looking trim, and her favorite job: watching Lilith.

"Jesus, Dodge! What the hell happened?" Jillian winced, looking at the stitched-up gouge between his two black eyes.

"Nasty leg cramp in the middle of the night on Sunday. Fell out of bed and the corner of the nightstand high-fived my head before the rest of my body hit the ground. Stan had to take me to the emergency room at two o'clock in the morning. But don't worry, it looks worse than it feels."

"I don't doubt that because I'm going to be honest with you, Dodge, it couldn't look much worse."

"Just as well, young lady. At least now you won't be flirting with me so much and making the missus jealous."

Jillian looked over at Lilith, who was enraptured with a grin on her face while reading what must have been a good book. "Yeah, I'm sure that's been a real issue."

Dodge looked down at his phone. "Stan should be picking me up soon. You two ladies have fun."

"Where you off to today?"

"Lumberyard. Stan's going to get some boards and stain them to match my headboard. Then he's going to build a railing for the side of my bed that locks in at night to prevent future injuries."

Jillian grinned. "Like a baby crib."

"No! Like ... like ... uh ... well, like a hospital bed."

"Okay, whatever makes you feel better."

Dodge shook his head and left.

Jillian giggled to herself as she walked to the laundry room to see if there were clothes that needed folding or ironing. She brought the ironing board and pile of shirts to the kitchen so she could keep an eye on Lilith. The first shirt she laid on the ironing board was missing a button.

"Hmm ... missing button. What are the chances you have a spare one?" Jillian smiled to herself. "Not that it would matter. I can hang kitchen cabinets and weld pipes but the simple task of sewing on a button is something I've never mastered. But ironing ... ironing I can do."

CHAPTER FIFTEEN

DAY

JESSICA DAY WAS GETTING a second chance at life, a glimpse at normalcy again, all thanks to the good Dr. Luke Jones. Of course she was bound by verbal contract to no longer call him doctor, or Jones, or Lucas, or Lukey, or Lulu, or anything other than plain old Luke. It was like the sun refusing to shine after the rain, leaving the rainbow invisible. She felt certain that he popped little kids' balloons, gave out toothbrushes at Halloween, and went to bed before the ball dropped on New Year's Eve.

Their first unofficial counseling session resulted in her cleaning his kitchen sink and oven, then removing all the dishes from the cabinets and wiping the shelves down. Everything was spotless before she started, which made her job that much more difficult because he insisted she go through the motions like some sort of Mr. Miyagi training. She in turn got to talk about whatever she wanted to discuss or share. For some reason since the night of their agreement she hadn't been in the mood again to talk about the kidnapping or anything related to it.

Jessica found herself running ten minutes late for their second meeting as she raced across town after work.

"You're late." Luke greeted her with a frown as she slipped off her heels.

"Astute observation, genius. I also forgot a change of clothes, so tonight can we stick to meaningless chores that can be performed in a tight skirt?"

"Do you sew?" Luke asked while walking toward his bedroom.

"No."

"Do you iron?"

"Why? Do you have some boy scout badges that need to be ironed on to your button-down khaki before the next meeting?"

"Boy scout badges are stitched, not ironed on, and no that's not why I'm asking."

"The dry cleaners under starch your whitey tighties? Your hang low swaying despite your robotic gait?"

"Nice try. I cleaned out my sock drawer and found some old dress socks that I'm going to donate, but they're a bit wrinkled so you're going to iron them for me. Well ... really more for the lucky recipients."

"You've got to be kid—" The moment she turned the corner to his bedroom she saw the ironing board set up with a huge pile of argyle socks next to it.

"Some of the pairs are the same design, so make sure you match right and left ones together." Luke sat in a leather chair by the window with his feet propped up on an ottoman.

"Are you high? There's no such thing as right and left socks." She held up two matching socks as if to prove her point.

Luke glanced up from the crossword puzzle he was working on. "Those are both left."

"Oh my gosh! I knew it! I knew you were a whacked-out OCDer. I can't believe they gave you a license to practice psychiatry."

He stood and took the socks from her. "See how this area in both of these is worn thinner than the rest, both on the right side under the big toe? That's how you know they are two left socks." He handed them back before resuming his position by the window.

She plugged in the iron. "You need to get laid. Normal people don't think like you. When was the last time you had sex?"

Luke ignored her. It was his usual MO when she tried to pry into his life.

"I bet you're a missionary man. By the book: seven-point-five minutes of foreplay, thirty seconds of clitoral stimulation to get her lubed up, and exactly thirty five thrusts until climax, followed by ten minutes of spooning, a kiss on the cheek, and maybe even a gentlemanly 'thank you' before insisting she leave so you can get your necessary eight-point-five hours of sleep."

Luke didn't flinch.

"Do you suppose there's a high demand for argyle socks at Goodwill? Do they even accept socks there? It's like donating underwear. Really, who wants to risk athlete's foot or toenail fungus? I don't know … it freaks me out a little, like bowling allies. You ever get a pair of rental shoes that are still warm inside? How about hotel rooms, talk about crazy. I know the sheets and towels are washed, but at what temperature? When you dry your face with one do you ever wonder how many butt cracks that cotton has slid through?"

Luke submitted a quick glance.

"Of course you do. After all, I'm ironing your *right* and *left* socks for Pete's sake."

An hour later, Jessica completed the last set of socks then wrote off another useless hour of her life that she could never get back. Most of that hour was filled with silence.

"I'm trained to kill people with my bare hands." Jessica plopped down on Luke's bed with her fingers interlaced behind her head and legs crossed at the ankle. Luke glanced up in her peripheral vision, but Jessica kept her gaze fixed to the ceiling.

"I can't share anymore information such as how and why, but I can say that something shifted when I realized the power I had. The thing is ... I didn't feel empowered. There was this transformation. I went from trusting to fearing to an unavoidable distrust. Now I trust very few people and the person I fear the most is myself. I'm constantly on high alert. When I walked into your office for the first time I noticed you, but I also noticed all possible exits, places you might be concealing a weapon, and all objects I could use as one."

"Do you feel safe right now?" Luke asked.

Jessica closed her eyes and exhaled. "Relatively. You have three things plugged into the walls of this room. I could use any of those cords to strangle you. I could bludgeon you with either weighted bookend on your shelf, or the statue in the northeast corner of the room. However, the only weapon I've found was a pocketknife in your closet the first time I came here and it's barely even a weapon so I'd most likely kill you with my bare hands before you'd have a chance to release the money clip in your pocket that you habitually rub between your thumb and middle finger."

"Is that a threat?"

Jessica laughed, opening her eyes as she turned toward

him. "No." She rolled her eyes to the side and pursed her lips. "Well, maybe. If you ask me to iron your socks again I cannot be responsible for my reaction."

"Have you ever killed anyone?"

Jessica's smile slipped. "If I told you then I'd have to kill you."

"So you're a secret agent?"

She flipped onto her stomach, resting her chin on her crossed arms. "If I said yes then it would no longer be a secret. Come on, Jones, you're losing your focus. Don't let me feel smarter than you or our time together will be over and I rather like hanging out here."

"Luke," he corrected.

"Lucas."

"Luke."

"Lukey."

"LUKE!"

"Lulu."

"I mean it!" Luke showed another rare moment of teetering emotion.

Jessica chuckled. "What are the chances of us having sex? I've never done it missionary, but you could possibly counsel me through it."

He refocused on his crossword puzzle, filling in a word in *pen*. "Less than zero percent."

"So, not in my favor, eh?

"Why not missionary?"

Jessica smiled in delight that Luke continued with the topic of conversation.

"I'm sure you already know, but if you want me to say I need control, then sure, I need control. But the truth is I'd control any sex position you want to put me in." Jessica winked as Luke gave her a fleeting glance. "I just don't want you thinking you have control, even if I know it's not the case. Pisses me off to see the smirk on a guy's face when he thinks he has control."

"Tell me why you need control." Luke continued with his crossword.

"In bed?"

"Yes."

"Someone has to have it."

"Why?"

"Because someone initiates it."

"So if I initiate sex with you will I have control?"

"There's only one way to find out." Jessica wiggled her eyebrows at an ill-humored Luke. "Fine." She huffed. "So you're telling me when you have sex you're not in control?"

"Depends."

"On what?" She sat up straight with her legs crossed.

"The level of intimacy."

"Love versus sex?"

"Yes."

"So you've been in love?"

"Have you?"

"Come on, Jones! Answering a question with a question? You can do better than that."

"*Luke!* And yes, I've been in love. Tell me about the men you've loved."

Jessica was once again impressed with his swift and accurate diversion. "I shared the womb with one and was conceived by the other. We've never had sex. I bet you'd charge me extra for that added problem."

Luke tossed the newspaper on the side table along with the pen. "And exactly how much am I charging you now?"

"Thirty pairs of ironed socks, which let's be honest ... who owns thirty pairs of socks? Do you do laundry once a month? And then there was a complete kitchen cleaning. I'm just saying, incest would probably have me on my knees in front of your toilet scrubbing it with a toothbrush."

He folded his hands in his lap. "That was the longest answer ever for what could have been a simple 'You're not charging me anything and I've never been in love.'"

"Wow! Are you counting my words now?"

"If I kick you out early, are you going to give me a month's worth of useful information in under ten minutes on the other side of my door?" He glared at her.

Jessica leapt off the bed. "Real professional, asshole! I can't believe the Board of Medical Examiners granted you the right to fuck with people's minds and emotions."

"I'm not your doctor, Jessica." Luke held steadfast to his composure.

"Then you're a shitty friend!" She stomped out of his bedroom.

"I'm not your friend either," he called after her as she marched toward the front door.

Jessica whipped around as Luke caught up to her. "Then who or what the hell are you?"

Luke shook his head. "I'm nobody ... just a guy that wants to see you get better."

A caustic anger roiled in her chest. "Well I don't need nobody. I need somebody. I trusted Dr. Jones, and I trust my friends, but you're neither, so I'm not going to lay my whole fucking world at the feet of *nobody*!"

Luke stepped toward her until her back was pressed to the wall. His blue eyes turned to coal. "Your problem is you don't trust *anyone*—not me, not your family, and not your friends. Maybe what you need right now is a nobody, a dumping ground for all of your problems, someone who's not your past nor your future. I won't feel responsible, or guilty, or judge you. You can make up a hundred pet names for me, plot out my death in fifty different scenarios, and question me about my favorite sex position, but it won't make you better."

That was the first time Luke broke Jessica's heart. She didn't want him to be a nobody. During the months that they'd been together she'd convinced herself that he would make her better—not his willingness to listen, not his words of wisdom, but *him*.

The first tear surrendered. "There were two of them. One served as the decoy, the other shot us with a tranquilizer gun like we were rabid animals. I wasn't sure if it was hours or days that we spent coming in and out of consciousness. I remember vomiting on myself at one point and wetting my pants. Then we were dying of dehydration: swollen tongues, confusion, dizziness, heart palpitations. Finally they offered us water out of a shared dog dish. We were almost too weak to even drink. Then they offered us food, actual dog food. I didn't eat it, but Claire did. Four said he'd cut her if she didn't." Each blink released more tears. Her eyes never strayed from Luke's.

"He never cut you?"

Jessica shook her head.

"Do you know why?"

"Because I wanted him to. I dared him, taunted him, practically begged him. It was like he knew."

"Knew what?"

Salty tears melted onto her tongue when she sucked in her lips and swallowed back the words that she hadn't said in almost a decade.

"Knew what, Jessica?" Luke cupped her face in his hands.

"I'm hungry." Her tears dried up as her expression softened to a blank stare.

He nodded, releasing her. "We can be done for tonight."

She drew in a breath and released it with absolute control, putting away the past in its safe spot and focusing again on the present. "Want to go get something to eat with me?"

"I can't." Luke took a step back.

"Are you on a diet?"

He smiled, barely, but it was a smile. "No, *we* can't be seen together."

She slipped on her shoes. "Are you famous? Because I'm not and the only people who know both of us are in New York for the next two weeks, so unless we happen to pick the same restaurant as your receptionist, Eve, then I think we're good."

Jessica's area of expertise was risk assessment, but Luke's overthinking and excessive contemplation made her reserved personality look utterly reckless.

"Never mind." She slung her purse over her shoulder. "I'll eat by myself or find *somebody* who might enjoy my company. Don't sweat it, Luke."

"Jessica?"

She stopped, inches from shutting the door. He pulled it back open.

"Pizza delivery? We can eat out on my balcony."

"Is this pity?" She squinted.

"It's pizza. What kind do you like?"

She stepped back inside and kicked off her shoes. "Are we making out later?"

"No."

She brushed past him toward the French doors to the

balcony. "In that case—red onions, banana peppers, fresh garlic, and pineapple."

"*Pineapple?*"

"Did I stutter?"

"We'll go half and half. Thin crust okay?"

"Nope. Thick." She stepped outside and drew in a shaky breath. Sharing her past felt like an emotional game of Jenga. How many pieces could he extract before she'd completely collapse?

After he ordered the pizza and changed into something more casual, Luke joined her on the balcony. "Beer or wine?" He held up two bottles of Heineken in one hand and a bottle of white wine and a wine glass in the other.

"Wine. Never beer, it tastes like piss."

Luke shook his head, his usual sign of annoyance. "Wine for you, piss for me." He sat opposite her at the table and poured her a glass of wine.

"I use beer to drown out the world. Haven't had it in years. So if you see me drinking beer think of it as an SOS."

Luke popped the cap off his beer. "I drink wine when I'm trying to impress a woman I really like. So if you see me sipping a glass of Pinot, then try to avoid embarrassing me." He raised his bottle of Heineken. "To you not needing to drown out the world."

Jessica grinned and tapped his bottle with her glass. "To you not trying to impress me." She took a sip of wine. "So if you *were* having a glass of Pinot tonight, what would you be sharing about yourself that would sound impressive?"

Luke tapped the mouth of his bottle against his bottom lip, once again contemplating his response. "I'd say I shouldn't really be drinking wine or eating *thick* crust pizza tonight because my best friend, Gabe, has talked me into training for a triathlon with him and his girlfriend."

"They asked you?" Jessica's voice squeaked as her back straightened.

"Gabe did."

"Huh ... Kelly didn't say anything. Long Beach?"

"Yes."

"I'm signed up too."

"I know, that's why I suggested thin crust."

She laughed. "Triathlons for me are like a 10K to a marathoner. I 'train' so Kelly has a partner. I overdress so she sees me sweat, I fake labored breathing, and I stay three steps behind her when we jog so she thinks she's setting the pace. Then she heads home and I put in five more miles at double the pace, an hour of sparring with my brother, and an hour of abs. I swim three times a week and bike on Saturdays. But don't tell her any of that, please."

Luke set his beer down on the table. "And you call *me* OCD?"

"I'm disciplined, not obsessed."

"Okay, I've failed to impress you with my piss beer or triathlon training. What do you have?"

Jessica's eyes grew wide. "You want me to try and impress you?"

"Yes."

"And what I just said didn't do it?"

"It only explained why you have too much muscle, too little fat, and a personality stuck in overdrive."

"Overdrive? Hmm ... I'll take that as a compliment."

Luke shrugged while smothering his smirk that confirmed it was not a compliment.

"Fine, let's see ... when I'm not wearing a skirt or dress, I'm wearing jeans, black boots, a helmet, and riding around town on my motorcycle."

Jessica had learned that Luke wasn't easily surprised and rarely impressed, but she had captured his attention.

"Surprised? Impressed?"

The doorbell rang. "Yes and a little. I'll be right back."

He returned with the pizza and plates. "A motorcycle girl, huh?" The glimmer of curiosity in his eyes compounded everything else she already found irresistibly sexy about him.

"Anything with a motor really. My dad likes to work on cars and motorcycles in his rare moments of free time. He says it's de-stressing and therapeutic. So at a young age I learned that if I wanted to spend time with my dad, it was going to be under the hood or beneath a car, handing him greasy tools."

"Your brother too?"

"Jude? No way. Jude didn't even care to get his driver's license at sixteen. He's a computer geek or 'genius' in his words. The first car he bought himself was a Jetta ... a *Jetta!* Can you believe that?"

"I hear they're reliable cars." Luke took a bite of pizza.

"Oh my gosh! You have one, don't you?"

He shook his head, dabbing his mouth with a napkin. "No, I'm just making an observation."

"Well, don't." Jessica rolled her eyes at her brother, knowing that he was somewhere sensing her disapproval.

After a dinner that felt a galaxy away from their doctor-patient relationship, Jessica looked at her watch that read a quarter to eleven.

"Oh crap! I've kept you up way too late." She stood, grabbing her plate and wine glass.

"I've got it." Luke took them from her. "And it's fine. I've ..." His face tensed into his signature contemplative look that Jessica had come to recognize.

"You've?"

He smiled, but it was almost painful looking. "I've had a nice evening ... with you."

Jessica opened the balcony door for him and risked a quick glance. "Me too. Thanks for dinner and *everything*."

"You're welcome." He set the plates on the counter and walked her to the door.

"I'll see you in a few days."

Luke nodded, shoving his hands into his back pockets. "Good night, Jessica."

She stopped before shutting the door. "I gotta know ... the socks ... that was a game or lesson right? You don't really iron your socks do you?"

He smirked, but just barely. Leaning down next to her ear until his lips gently brushed it, he whispered, "Good night." Then he pushed the door the rest of the way closed.

The deadbolt clicked as she stood in the hall, eyes closed, skin tingling with goosebumps, fingers ghosting over her lips that curled into the most smitten smile ever.

CHAPTER SIXTEEN

KNIGHT

IN THE SPIRIT OF WHY-THE-HELL-NOT, Jillian accepted a working lunch date with Rick Willey, the boss of her most recent Lascivo party hostess. Rick, by any other woman's standards, was a handsome, successful bachelor. He had a good-ol'-boy look with his ten-dollar haircut, Lee jeans, and boyish smile. Rick ran a multi-million dollar construction business by day and immersed himself in the world of kinky sex toys by night. Enter Jillian.

"Thanks for lunch. I have to admit, I've never had a picnic in the back of a pickup before."

Rick nodded with ignorant pride. "I had to keep an eye on my crew, but I couldn't pass up the opportunity to have lunch with you. Gina said you're my soulmate. Thought you might like seeing me in action, you know ... dominant and *in control* of my crew."

The poor attempt at sexual innuendo brought a mini-vomit up Jillian's throat. She swallowed it back down and held open her front door.

"Uh, yeah ... there's nothing sexier than a guy that

knows his way around a walkie-talkie." She rolled her eyes as he followed her into the house.

"So ... how does this work?" He bit his lower lip and nodded slowly.

Jillian fought the grimace that pulled at her face as his eyes roved her body. "Eww ..."

"Excuse me?" He leaned closer.

She cleared her throat. "I said *you* need to try the new vibrating pleasure pocket."

"Oh yeah?" He strutted his neck like a bird.

"Yeah, just a second." She retrieved the pleasure pocket from her box of toys.

"What if it doesn't fit?"

Jillian made a quick inspection of his scrawny body. "Sorry, it doesn't come in a smaller size."

He smirked, wiggling his eyebrows. "I'm not talking about it being small ... if you know what I mean."

More bile crept up her throat. "I'm sure it will be fine."

"Maybe I should try it first. Maybe you could demonstrate it on me."

There were indeed a lot of maybes, but Jillian's were more like: Maybe I should be selling you a strap on penis or a magnifying glass to find yours, or maybe I should shove my thumb into your jugular and put us both out of our misery.

Jillian held up a finger and ran back to the bedroom, returning a few seconds later with a condom. Rick's eyes lit up. Another *eww* escaped Jillian's mouth. "Here, go to the bathroom and try it out."

His brow furrowed. "With a condom?"

"Yes. If you don't like it I can't very well sell it to someone else after you've shot your spunk into it."

He took it with a reluctant look on his face. "Okay. Are you going to wait out here?"

"Yes."

"Will you talk to me while I'm in there trying it out?"

"No."

His shoulders slumped as he went into the bathroom.

A shivering jolt of heebie jeebies wracked her body.

"I'm removing my pants," he called.

"I don't need to know that." She cursed Jackson and his stupid job choice for her.

"I'm sheathed and slipping it on my *big* guy," he continued his commentary.

She stuck her fingers in her ears and squeezed her eyes shut.

"Oh fu-fu-fuck! This is g-good!"

"Yoo-hoo?" Greta called though the screen door.

"Shit! Who's that?" Rick yelled.

"My neighbor. Just ... finish up."

"What? I can't. What do I do? Oh God! It's going f-faster. Shit, fuck, shit! I-it won't sh-shut off! Help!"

"Jillian?" Greta called as the screen door opened. "Is that you?"

"I'll be right there, Greta."

"My dick's going to break off!"

"Shh! Calm down and open the door."

The door flung open and a panicked Rick shuffled toward Jillian with his pants at his ankles and his hands gripping the pleasure pocket like a fireman with a hose.

"Don't come out—"

"Get it off!" Rick charged toward her and Jillian stepped to the side. He tripped and flew forward into the newel post. "Ahh ... fuck."

"Jesus! Are you all right?"

"What's going on in there?" Greta's voice drew closer. "Is everything okay?"

"Don't touch me!" Rick grabbed his pants, pulling them up his legs with one hand while the other covered his bloodied nose, shoving past Jillian and nearly bowling over Greta as he shot past her and straight out the front door.

Jillian smiled at Greta as if nothing happened. "Hey, Greta. What's up?"

Sergeant Monaghan slept in his office for three nights, worked out with punishing intensity, and snapped at everyone around him until his superior sent him home for a mandatory week's vacation. Exactly what he did not need: close proximity to his neighbor. Cage started daily practice which meant AJ did not see him very often. As much as his son pushed his buttons, he also knew how to handle AJ's episodes of anger and pain.

"Yoo-hoo ... Sergeant?" Greta waved at AJ the moment he got out of his Jeep.

He forced a smile. "Hi, Greta."

"Oh my, I just feel terrible. I made a complete inaccurate assumption and now I feel obligated to set the record straight before any rumors get started around here. Not that we're a bunch of gossipy people or anything."

"No, of course not." AJ choked out the words lacking any sort of sincerity.

"Any hoo ... I know this is going to come as a shock to you, it's been for everyone else, but the Knights ... they're not married. They're actually brother and sister."

"No!"

"Yes, I know. Who would have thought, right?"

"Yeah, who would have thought? So how did this get brought to your attention?"

"Well, it's rather embarrassing but Stan's wife, Lynette, saw Jackson kissing some woman in the driveway that was not Jillian. So she told Stan, Stan told Dodge, Dodge told Marvin, and when Marvin told me ... well, my heart just broke for poor Jillian. In spite of her questionable attire and well ... *evening profession*, we've come to adore her. She's done so much for Lilith, you know. So I gathered up my courage, made a batch of fudge, grabbed a box of tissues, and paid Jillian a visit when Jackson's car was gone."

"And what did she say?" AJ widened his stance and crossed his arms over his chest.

"Funny thing, actually. The front door was open so I hollered through the screen door and the next thing I knew there was this big commotion and this strange guy came running out, tugging up his trousers and blood was dripping from his face. Then Jillian came to the door looking as calm and collected as ever."

"Who was he?"

"Well, at first she told me he was an interior designer and he had a seizure on the toilet, felt utterly embarrassed, and then ran out."

"What?"

"I know, Jillian has exceptional taste why would she need an interior designer? It just didn't add up. Then she saw the fudge and box of tissues, so I decided to forge ahead with my original mission. And when I finally worked up the nerve to tell her, she fell into a fit of laughter and proceeded to tell me that Jackson's her brother. *Then* she told me on the, and I quote, 'down low' that the guy I saw running out of the house was actually her date and he injured himself..." Greta looked around then lowered her voice "...with a PPD."

AJ cleared his throat. "Excuse me?"

Greta made another visual sweep of the area. "Personal Pleasure Device," she whispered closer to his ear. "But you didn't hear it from me. I'd hate to start any rumors."

AJ's jaw clenched while the silent pulse of a headache grew with each passing second. "Thanks for clearing all that up, Greta."

"Don't mention it, dear. I'd better get back to Marvin. He's trying to shove a beer can up a chicken's ass for dinner tonight."

AJ nodded. As soon as Greta crossed the street, Jackson pulled out of their garage in Woody. He shot AJ a smile and waved as he drove out of the development. AJ needed to start doping-up on pain meds, but his urge to pay Jillian a visit hijacked all commonsense and urgency for self-preservation.

"Coming!" Jillian called when AJ rang her doorbell.

"Sarge." She glanced at her watch. "You're home early. But then again it's been days since I've seen you around at all. Did you take a trip or have you been avoiding me?" She opened the door to let him inside.

"Someone witnessed a bloodied victim of yours fleeing the scene of the crime."

Jillian smiled as she leaned against the piano. "Good news travels fast around here. I thought it would. Yes, I had a date. The hostess from my Lascivio party last week fixed me up with her boss. No need to be jealous, AJ. I made him take me to lunch before he got to second base. I also made him ask for permission, which you didn't do."

AJ stared at her through slit eyes. "Greta said he ran out with his pants down!"

She chuckled. "So you are jealous. I told you, all you had to do was take me on a date."

AJ shook his head in disgust and walked toward the door. "If that's all it takes, then you're a cheap fuck."

———————

AJ GULPED down two pills with a tall glass of water before his doorbell rang. He hated his temper and the sharp words that sliced through his mouth. Even more, he hated that his neighbor robbed all his control.

"What?" he groaned, seeing Jillian on the other side of his screen door.

"You are such a stubborn ass!" She threw open the screen door and shoved his chest, forcing him back a few feet.

"What the hell?"

"It was a vibrating pleasure pocket. Rick Willey loves two things: softball and sex toys. That's why he got fixed up with me. We went to lunch and then I offered to show him a few things. He was interested in the masturbation aids so I sent him into the bathroom with it and a condom. A few minutes later Greta hollered into the house, Rick flew out of the bathroom door with his pants still around his ankles, thinking the pleasure pocket was malfunctioning, then he face-planted into the newel post. Before I could help him with his bloodied face, he ran out the door."

AJ shook his head and stepped farther away from Jillian. "I don't care."

"Well I do! I'm so sick of you going from hot to cold with me. Like I'm some snow white virgin with you but the moment you think I'm with some other guy I become the neighborhood whore. It's been well over six months since I've had sex, AJ. So stop with your narcissistic bullshit because I'm sure you've planted your dick in plenty of women over the past six months."

"Shut up."

"Don't tell me to shut up!" Jillian stepped closer.

"Shut. Up!"

The most inevitable explosion happened in that moment. Their lips collided and the pain was stronger than the pleasure, but the undeniable *need* trumped everything else. AJ slammed Jillian into the wall and removed her shirt with brute force. She fought back, shoving him against the opposing wall sending a framed picture crashing to the ground. Their bodies pinballed from wall to wall as each vied for control. AJ's pants were yanked down with expert hands that clawed at his briefs until they too were tangled at his ankles.

AJ fisted her hair with both hands as she licked a trail up his leg, tracing his line of muscles while a dark predatory look burned in her eyes. An involuntary jerk of his hips pushed his strained erection closer to her as she dragged her tongue along his hip bone. He wanted, he *needed* her mouth sheathed around him, but she wrapped her hands around his wrists as he tried to bring her head to the place he wanted her mouth.

Jillian shook her head. "Not yet." She pushed up his shirt and traced his flat, dark nipple with the tip of her tongue before sinking her teeth into the taut skin of his pectoral muscle.

"Fuck!" he groaned against the burn, yanking her hair until his mouth was on hers again.

She stroked his erection then cupped his balls with a firm grip.

"Shit! N-not yet ..." He broke their kiss and rested his

forehead against hers, whispering his plea through labored breaths. "Not. Yet."

"Now." She narrowed her eyes and slid her hand up his shaft, circling the pad of her thumb over the bead of cum on the head.

"Dammit!" He pumped himself into her hand over and over thinking each time would be the last. Thinking he'd find the control to stop.

Jillian shoved him away, leaving both of them breathless. "Take your shirt off," she demanded as she removed a condom from the pocket of her jeans.

The swollen tip of AJ's erection thickened even more when he saw confirmation of Jillian's intentions. Leaving her gaze fixed to his, she held the foil square between her teeth and removed the rest of her clothes. AJ shrugged off his shirt and stepped out of his boots and pants. He reached for the condom. Jillian shook her head, grabbing one end and ripping it open with her teeth.

She stepped forward and stroked him over and over until he began to feel weak in the knees, then she rolled the condom onto his hard length.

"Bedroom."

She shook her head and turned, planting the palms of her hands on the wall, legs spread wide. AJ stepped closer and began to fist her hair.

"No. You can grip my hips, touch my clit, or massage my breasts. No hair, and don't touch my hands or arms. Got it?"

AJ didn't answer. He bent his knees and guided his erection between her legs where she grabbed it and rubbed it along her wet folds until the firm tip grazed her clit. She moaned, dropping her chin to her chest. She watched them and it nearly sent him over the edge. The deep hum of her pleasure quickened his pace. He was losing control. Every time he angled his pelvis to gain entry she denied him, taking her own pleasure as he slid across her swollen sex.

AJ rested his left hand flat on the wall above hers without touching it and squeezed her breast with his other hand. His legs burned from squatting behind her, his back ached from bending over her.

"Shit!" She cried out as he pinched her nipple, tugging at it with firm pressure. Jillian slid her hand along his erection until she had him literally by the balls.

"Fuck! Right. Now!" he growled, sliding his hand down from her breast.

On his next thrust he engaged the tip into her opening and impaled her with such desperate force that the moment her tight muscles gripped him he released. He continued pumping his hips into her as she milked his orgasm. It wasn't his proudest moment, but her words had been licking his dick for weeks.

He dragged his tongue along her back while massaging her clit.

"Oh God ... I need this," she groaned as she came apart under his touch. Her body sagged into his hold and he relished the fleeting moment of vulnerability—surrender.

He pulled out and slid two fingers inside her. Jillian responded to his touch with renewed vigor. She wasn't done and AJ knew one thing ... neither was he.

"WHY ARE WE ON THE FLOOR?" AJ mumbled with Jillian's body draped over his chest.

She'd been tracing random things on his chest with her fingernail. After the wall, he lifted her onto the kitchen counter and spread her wide, and then a third time, on the floor, with her on top. Every time he tried to lead them to his bedroom he was met with adamant refusal. Sex had never felt like such a power struggle. It aroused him and frustrated him in equal parts. Jillian took control then relinquished it only to take again, like putting something in a shopping cart and then back on the shelf over and over. Indecisive. It wasn't a word AJ ever imagined using to describe sex, but that's exactly what it was with Jillian.

"I only brought over three condoms, but if you have some we could test out the stairs."

He closed his eyes and rolled his head side to side. "You can't make up for a six month dry spell all at once. And I hate to play the age card, but dammit, woman, I'm exhausted and my back is killing me. What do you have against beds?"

"It's getting late. I need to head home."

AJ grabbed her ass and she grinned. "What in the hell is a vibrating pleasure pocket?"

"Think of it as a dildo for men. Would you like to give one a try?"

"Fuck, no! Why do you sell that shit?"

Her lips pressed to the dried blood where she'd bit his chest. "If I told you, you wouldn't believe me."

"You're probably right," he mumbled in exhaustion.

She eased off him and grabbed her clothes, opting to wear her undergarments too instead of carrying them home. AJ peeked open his heavy eyelids, admiring her body, remembering the salty taste of her sweat-glistened skin and the feel of her muscled legs clamped around his waist as he rocked into her. She was dangerous, unforgettable, and lethally addictive.

"Thought you were too tired, or are you just saluting me goodbye." She fastened her jeans.

AJ was fully erect again. Just the thought of her played havoc on his control. "I might need an extra *leg* to help drag my tired ass into bed."

She laughed at AJ's rare moment of humor that he still managed to deliver without a smile. "Good night, AJ ... best sex I've had in over six months."

He waited until she shut the door and then he grinned.

"I see you smiling, you grumpy bastard!" she yelled while banging her palm against the sidelight window.

CHAPTER SEVENTEEN

THE LOVING chime of "ass up, shoes on" woke Jillian three hours before her usual time. She took refuge under her pillow and comforter, a symbolic *bug off*! Jackson snagged the covers then yanked Jillian's pillow from her grasp before taking them hostage in the living room.

"Asshole!"

"You've been slacking, so I'm taking you for a run this morning," he called.

Jillian reached in every direction for something, a sheet or blanket, but Jackson took them all.

"Why?" she asked with the most aggravated tone turned up one hundred percent as she plopped down in the chair to tie her running shoes.

"You need exercise like other humans need food and water. This past week you've been skipping your evening run and avoiding me every time I mention sparring."

"Not the same, dickface. I won't die without exercise."

Jackson walked toward the door. "No, but I might kill you if you get too bitchy, which is inevitable when you go too long without expending some of that energy."

Jillian shut the door behind her and raced out in front of him. "For your information, I exercised yesterday while you were on your date."

"Doing what?"

"Things ... like ... stretching and *endurance* type stuff." Screwing the neighbor. "How was your date?"

"Fine."

"Fine? Well you've seen her three times in the past week, so fine must be code for she's boring but good in bed."

"We haven't had sex."

Jillian nearly stumbled over her own feet. "You *what?*"

"She's younger than me."

"That *is* a surprise, still doesn't explain anything."

"She's an easy eleven out of ten."

"Yada yada ..."

"And she's ... a virgin."

Jillian grabbed onto Jackson's arm to keep from falling over. "No way ... how young is *young?*"

"That's just it, she's twenty-two and her body is ..."

"Pig!"

"No, she's not fat at all."

She rolled her eyes and shoved him off the sidewalk.

He recovered with a grin plastered across his face. "It's not my fault. I honestly had no intention of sleeping with her anytime soon. I was serious when I said this Jackson guy is going to take it slow. But on our second date when I leaned over the front seat to kiss her good night she attacked me. The next thing I knew she was straddling my lap and dry humping the hell out of me like a bitch in heat. I actually came in my jeans! What thirty-year-old guy gets dry humped in his car?"

Jillian's legs couldn't keep up. Her laughter zapped all

her energy, so she bent over resting her hands on her knees. "I can't ... b-breathe." She hackled out of control.

Jackson rested his hands on his hips and walked in circles around her. "That's not the worst part."

She shook her head. "No more ... my sides hurt."

"I have to say it. I mean ... I don't think this girl's normal, but maybe they're just bred different here in the Midwest because last night's date could never be outdone. Apparently she's a big Sesame Street fan so she wore this tight-fitting Big Bird shirt to the bar. She only had one glass of wine but by the time we got to her apartment she was seriously horny."

Jillian glanced up, wiping tears from her eyes. "Big Bird makes her horny?"

Jackson grimaced. "Not exactly." He dug his teeth into his bottom lip and looked around for unsuspecting ears. "Mr. Snuffleupagus makes her horny."

Jillian's brows knitted and then it hit her. "Oh my god. Your..." she motioned toward his shorts "...is Mr. Snuffleupagus?"

Jackson nodded.

She fell to her knees in the grass—laughing, crying, and hugging her stomach.

"There's more."

She shook her head. "No ... no way."

"You know my glasses that you love so much? Well, she wanted to give me, or *Mr. Snuffleupagus,* head while *he* wore those glasses."

Jillian collapsed onto her side and not a single word made it past her laughter that was nearly silent because she couldn't catch her breath.

"The chick's messed up, right?"

"Y-you ... l-l-let her?"

"She had on the tightest damn shirt I'd ever seen! And she wanted to suck my dick and it's been a *long* time since I've had a woman's mouth on me like that, so ... yeah, I let her. I was so fucking hard by the time she asked, I think I would have let her add a wig, lipstick, and clip-on earrings to Mr. Snuffleupagus."

"Stop! Pee ... I'm going to pee my pants ..."

"The worst part ... I'm seeing her again tonight."

Jillian wiped her swollen eyes and exhaled several slow breaths. "Never and I mean *ever* have I heard anything so flat-out hysterical. The sad part..." she fought back more giggles "...is I will never be able to do that to a man without thinking about my *brother's* penis dressed up like Mr. Potato Head. You've completely ruined that for me."

Jackson held out his hand and helped her off the ground. "Just as well. I don't like to think about my sister giving some dude a blow job."

"Way to make it sound completely random, like I'm a total slut." Jillian jogged to catch up on the run Jackson decided to resume.

"You're not a slut." He paused before his next statement. "Have you had any more *moments* with AJ?"

She pushed out in front a few steps. "Uh, well, I don't know what your definition of moment is so—"

"Have you had sex with him?"

"Sex? With AJ? I mean we've done ... *stuff*, and we sort of ... yes. We did it yesterday three times in a row, just ... bang, bang, bang and it was so good and the most incredible release and—"

"No, no, no, no, no! Jesus, Jillian! It was a yes or no question."

"Are you kidding me, *Mr. Snuffleupagus*? You get dry hump and penis dress-up, but all I get to share is yes or no?"

"So what's the damage?" Jackson's voice began to sound labored.

"Bite mark on his pec." Jillian knew the question and she refused to lie to her brother. First of all, he knew when she was lying, and second, she never *wanted* to lie to him. Jackson had always been her truth, a litmus test of her sanity. Luke took over that role for a while, but he wasn't there anymore so she needed Jackson.

"Why?"

"I'm trying to figure out who I am."

"Then start with who you're not, which is Jessica Day. She was fucked-up. You don't have to be. Jillian Knight can be whomever you want her to be."

Jillian chuckled. "As long as she sells sex toys."

"Exactly."

The conversation died when they became too winded to talk.

"Knights."

Jillian glanced ahead as they neared the entrance to Peaceful Woods. The familiar voice was her uniformed lover jogging toward the entrance from the opposite direction.

"Hey, AJ." Jackson nodded.

Jillian hadn't prepared for the awkward-next-day moment, but at that point she knew there was no way around it. She had only a few seconds to react.

"Neighbor." Brilliant reply.

Jillian had a half dozen names for him, but neighbor wasn't one. Maybe her subconscious was reminding her the man she'd been *very* intimate with was in fact her neighbor and that nothing good could come of their admittedly volatile relationship.

"So ... I have a lesson in an hour. I'll..." Jackson played

his part as cool as the ninety-degree day "...see you two ... uh ... crazy kids later." He continued jogging home.

Jillian and AJ were too enthralled in each other's reaction to give Jackson's gibberish much attention.

"I thought you jogged at night."

She shrugged. "I do. This wasn't a jog. It was one sibling dragging the other around the block a few times by her hair."

AJ nodded with his usual stoic expression. Jillian's sarcastic personality was always received with rotten tomatoes when AJ was her audience.

"I'm off work for a week."

"Oh ..." It was hard for her to process the meaning behind his statement. It could have been an offer for more sex, but that was too risky of an assumption to make without more to go on. "Well, what are your plans for your time off?"

He stepped closer until she was forced to strain her neck to look at him. "I haven't decided yet."

"You might as well know, I suck at beat around the bush. So where are you at with *this* this morning? Are you wanting to pretend that nothing happened? Are you getting ready to have the 'it was a mistake' speech? Or are you entertaining the idea of doing it again, in which case the answer would be no because ..." Jillian hated herself for not having a good reason and for wanting to tackle him right then and there.

"Because?"

"Because ... because you don't even like me! You're always so damn grumpy and implying that I'm a whore because I'm confident in my own skin and I sell PPDs for a living and not even by choice. And I'm trying to be happy and feel settled here, and I know you're going to screw that up for me—"

She didn't even realize what had happened. Her face was in his hands and his lips were pressed to hers. He tasted like mint gum while she couldn't even remember if she'd brushed her teeth, but he didn't seem to mind.

"I apologize for being grumpy," he whispered over her lips.

Jillian covered his hands that were still framing her face, just to keep her balance before he literally swept her off her feet. She knew she'd never remember the words he said, but she'd never forget the way he said them. The heart never forgets skipping a beat.

She smiled. "I apologize for being too sexy for this neighborhood."

AJ hugged her to his chest so she couldn't see his face, but Jillian knew he was smiling. She just ... *knew*.

JILLIAN WAS INFURIATING. She was also strong, sexy, playful, and *compassionate*. AJ thought of her as Wonder Woman, Judge Judy, Mother Teresa, and Ellen Degeneres molded into a wet dream. She was seriously flawed and had a fucking larger-than-life attitude. But what drew him in was her vulnerability; it was fleeting like a shooting star. It was there and gone in a blink, but he'd caught a glimpse of it and he recognized it—it was his reflection.

"You *are* too sexy for this neighborhood ... any neighborhood, really." He started walking toward home, chastising himself for making what was a true compliment sound like a grumpy complaint.

"But ..." Jillian followed a step behind.

"But what?"

"Compliments like that usually come with a but."

"No but, it's just a fact."

"Oh."

Jillian at a loss for words wasn't something AJ ever imagined he'd witness. The irony was her silence left him speechless too.

"Can I make you breakfast?" AJ spoke the first words that popped into his head as they neared his house. He hadn't set out to shock her, but the wide-eyed look she gave him made it clear that's what he had done, yet again.

"I'm a veg—"

"I know. I'll keep my big sausage to myself. Oatmeal fine?"

She laughed. He made an attempt to smile, but it was difficult. Anger, pain, and resentment had hardened him over the years. He felt undeserving of those rare moments of pleasure and happiness. They felt stolen, as if around the corner someone was waiting with their hand out demanding he give them back.

"Oatmeal sounds perfect." She followed him inside.

"I'm going to take a quick shower first."

"Want some company?" Jillian offered before she gulped down the glass of water he'd handed her.

Confusion impaired his ability to find actual words, so he just stared at her. "Uh—"

"I'm kidding. Go do your thing, but hurry up because I'm starving."

After a slow nod, he pivoted and walked toward his bathroom, hands fisted while he released the breath he'd been holding. Of course he wanted to shower with Jillian. The aching need he had to feel her body against his was almost unbearable. But whatever was going on between them had not been defined and was the anti-normal of any relationship he'd ever imagined, possibly of any relationship that had ever existed.

In a blink he was showered and back in the kitchen.

"That was fast. Were you afraid I might rob your hidden treasures?"

AJ pulled a sauce pan out of the cabinet. "No, just kill my fish. Oh, that's right ... you already did that."

Jillian smirked. His attempt at humor was borderline pathetic, but she didn't seem to notice.

"Where did you and Jackson move here from?"

"The East Coast," she answered almost before he finished asking the question.

"The East Coast, huh? Why not just say North America?"

She laughed. "New York."

"Is that where you're originally from?"

"Yes."

"And what brought you to Omaha?" AJ continued as he stirred the oatmeal.

"We've just always dreamed of living in a more *mature* community but everything out east is too expensive."

He shook his head. "I'm serious. Do your parents live in New York?"

"They died."

AJ grimaced. "I'm sorry."

Jillian shrugged, casting her gaze out the window. "Me too."

"It's a little odd that at your age you decided to relocate with your brother. Were neither of you in a serious relationship?"

"Jackson doesn't know what a serious relationship is."

"And you?"

Jillian's brow set with firm lines. "You've met me ... been with me, what do you think?"

"I think you ran out of submissives and had to move because of your reputation."

She laughed, even though he wasn't smiling. "Bingo!"

"How did your parents die?"

Jillian's face drained of all color as she cleared her throat. "Car accident."

"Jillian ... I'm—"

She shook her head. "It happens. People die every day. What about you? Are you originally from here?"

AJ placed a bowl of oatmeal, maple syrup, spices, and milk in front of her. "No, I was born in Portland, but my father was in the service so we were never in one place for all that long. My father is retired now and he and my mother live in Portland again. Actually, Dodge was in the service with my father and he and Lilith were neighbors for a while until Dodge transferred a few years before he retired and moved to Omaha to be closer to their daughter."

"Really? Funny, Dodge never mentioned that to me. Then again, he has a way of talking about a whole bunch of absolutely nothing."

"They're good people."

"The best. This looks great. You're quite the cook."

"Oatmeal and water doesn't qualify me as 'quite the cook.'"

"Yeah, well you haven't seen me cook."

"Did your mom not cook much?"

"She was an amazing cook." Jillian grabbed her spoon and stared at it for a moment. "Do you want to talk about last night?"

The popping sizzle of bacon AJ tossed on the griddle

bought him a few extra moments of time while he gathered the courage to answer her. "Sure. You start."

Jillian stirred her oatmeal. "It was good sex ... I mean, it's been well over six months so my standards may have slipped a bit, but nonetheless, it was *decent*."

"Decent. Nice word choice."

She smirked.

"You like to inflict pain." He stared at the bacon.

"No."

"No?" AJ looked over with a wide-eyed incredulous expression.

"I like to make a statement."

"That says?"

"I'm not weak."

AJ nodded as he set the bacon on a paper towel. "Were you abused?"

"No. Were you?"

He flinched. "Why would you ask that?"

"Because I've made you bleed more than once, yet here I am sitting in your kitchen, eating breakfast. Is it the PTSD?"

"Who said I have PTSD?"

"Cage."

AJ sighed. "Doctors are full of shit. It's some goddamn forgone conclusion that any problem a soldier has after they return home is fucking PTSD. So if that's what you think too, then just leave."

There it was, the monster that resided in his head. He could never predict what would trigger it. Sometimes AJ felt as if he was on the outside looking in. He recognized the figure, even the voice, but the words belonged to someone else and they wouldn't be silenced.

Jillian pushed the rest of her oatmeal away. "I have to shower anyway."

"Cock tease," AJ grumbled as the anger spread like poison though his veins.

"What did you just say?" Jillian turned.

He felt the burning heat and tumultuous chaos of rage building inside. Jillian needed to leave, yet AJ needed an outlet. He could never explain the most excruciating pain was always the personality that hijacked his brain without warning.

"Go fuck somebody else today. I'm not in the mood." He looked up at her, his mind willing her to just leave, but the monster growling out his words beckoned her to stay and take every insult like an emotional punching bag.

Her jaw clenched. "Don't push me, AJ."

"Or what?" he challenged.

"Goodbye." She walked toward the door.

"You're all talk." AJ couldn't keep the words from coming out. It was like two personalities duking it out in his head. His body and everyone in its wake were nothing more than collateral damage.

Before he had a chance to think past his last breath, he was gasping for his next while he buckled over in pain. Like a quick flash of light, he saw her face, then grabbed his nose and his world went black.

An incessant sting to one cheek and then the next, over and over as a familiar voice droned on, brought him back into the light.

"Wake up, asshole." Jillian gave each cheek one last wake-up slap.

He peeled his eyes open and Jillian's face, directly above him, came into focus. Her soft feminine features were hardened, eyes squinted.

"Your nose isn't broken, but it's bleeding like a son of a bitch, so get your ass off the floor and pinch it before you stain your grout." She tossed a dish rag on his face. He grabbed it then rolled to his side. "If I were you, I'd accept the PTSD label otherwise you're just a prick."

"Like you're a fucking angel," he grumbled while lumbering to his feet, right hand squeezing his nose.

"Not even close, but at least I acknowledge my dysfunctional behavior and recognize the cause." She slammed the door.

CHAPTER EIGHTEEN

JILLIAN RESERVED the right to hate AJ for his venomous words. However, she knew that wouldn't happen. He couldn't control his behavior any easier than she could control hers. He'd been verbally abusive and she'd been physically abusive. Neither were excusable. His refusal to acknowledge his PTSD left them in a complicated situation. She had a slew of questions about his past, including the demise of his marriage. However, questioning him would have been an open invitation for him to continue exploring the life of pre-Omaha Jillian, which was impossible because it didn't exist ... it couldn't exist.

"Dahlia wants to 'go all the way' tonight," Jackson announced as Jillian shoved some snacks in her bag to take to Dodge's house.

"Dahlia?"

"Yes, the girl I've been seeing."

Jillian looked up from her bag and squinted. "Sesame Street girl?"

"Yes."

She smiled. "Well, my dear brother, my words of

wisdom are to *go and play, everything will be A-OK*."

"Real funny. But I'm not taking her virginity." Jackson stretched then interlaced his fingers behind his head.

"What's wrong? Mr. Snuffleupagus under the weather?"

"No. Her mom had a lesson today and asked me not to *go and play*."

Jillian's eyes bulged as she laughed. "Seriously? Her mom asked you to not sleep with her daughter?"

"Not directly. She just went on and on about how thrilled she is that Dahlia's dating someone mature, and because I have a cross tattooed on my arm she just knows I'm the type of guy who respects the sacredness of waiting until 'vows are exchanged' before taking a woman's 'flower.'"

"And of course you told her the reason you got that sacred tattoo ten years ago was to convince an unsuspecting virgin that you were a man of God who would cherish her forever if she gave herself to you."

Jackson shook his head. "You and your bullshit story. That's not what happened and you know it. I was going to get another tattoo anyway, and she wanted to watch. She told me if I let her pick out the tattoo, she'd have sex with me. I'd been eyeing the cross anyway. I wouldn't permanently mark myself just for some chick."

"You're pathetic."

He leaned against the counter, crossing his hands over his chest as Jillian stared at the cross. "I'll admit, that Jude guy had a way with the ladies." He pursed his lips like the cocky bastard he was.

"Male whore ... he was a male whore. So why the loyalty to Dahlia's mom? I'm sure her daughter won't tell her mom if you two have sex. It's not like she's underage."

Jackson shrugged and Jillian gave him a wrinkled face filled with distrust before leaving for Dodge's.

"It's the mom." She turned before closing the door, having an ah-ha moment.

"What?"

"You like the mom ... not the daughter. You won't sleep with both because you've never been the Benjamin Braddock type. And you like older women; rarely do you go for the young twenty-somethings. I'm right."

"You're not." Jackson firmed his jaw to contain his grin.

"I'm soooo right." Jillian winked and shut the door.

The knowing smile on her face faded as she passed AJ's house. In less than twenty four hours they'd fought twice and had sex three times. Whatever was between them was virulent, but too addictive to ignore. She needed him to remind her to not let her guard down and that was what earned him a bloodied nose. Any other guy would have filed a restraining order, but not AJ. Everything he did was a silent plea for more. *More,* that only Jillian could hear and only Jillian could give.

"Where's your Harley?" Dodge asked when he opened the door for her.

"Taking a nap, getting rested up for when I ride it hard later this evening." She grinned.

Dodge made several sounds but none of them formed into decipherable words.

"I'm relentless like that." Jillian elbowed his arm as she made her way inside. Lilith's smile came to life when she spotted Jillian. "Hi, Lilith. Did you eat?"

"Leftover steak from last night, but she's been bugging me to warm up the leftover apple pie Stan's wife made for *her*." Dodge grumbled out the last few words.

"You don't get any?"

"Stan's wife, Lynette, said I need to lose some weight or Lilith's going to outlive me. And it will be a cold day in hell before I drop dead first. She'd sell my golf cart to some schmuck that actually plays golf!"

Lilith smiled at Jillian.

"How do you communicate with her?"

Dodge shook his head. "Fist pumps, flying middle fingers, eye rolls, and scowls."

Jillian rolled her eyes. "I'll get her some pie. Maybe she'll share with me. It sounds better than the banana and granola bar I packed."

Dodge grabbed his raincoat. "That's a given. She likes you ... and she hasn't even seen you get the mail." Dodge wiggled his brows and snickered as he slipped out the back door.

"Dirty old man," Jillian murmured.

Lilith savored every last crumb of the warm apple pie, and Jillian found herself tempted to lick her plate too. Stan's wife may not have made a lot of sweet treats for him, but her apple pie was a true slice of heaven. Jillian handed Lilith her book and took their plates to the kitchen.

"I had sex with Sarge yesterday, then I nearly broke his nose today. Luke would be so disappointed in me." She kept her back to Lilith so she couldn't see the tears that filled Jillian's eyes.

"I don't even know who I am anymore. I'm not the sappy lovesick heroine that says a man 'completes' her, but I was the best possible version of myself with Luke. Everything I feared before him just ... vanished. I felt like a leaf falling from a tree and he was the wind whispering, *I've got you.* I'm here for my brother. I would have stayed ... I would have died. It's like the thrill seeker who goes full throttle all the time, never fearing death because eight seconds of that rush is worth more than eighty years of boring monotony. Luke was my eight seconds."

Day

KELLY WAS the closest friend Jessica had made since Four stole everything. However, Kelly knew nothing of that time in Jessica's life, nor her unconventional relationship with Dr. Luke Jones. In spite of the tragedy in Jessica's life, she never lost her sense of humor. Once she found out Kelly and Gabe were "cheating on her" by training part-time with Luke, Jessica decided to see just how uncomfortable she could make her dear friend.

Kelly: *Biking with Gabe tonight. Are we still running in the morning?*

Jessica bubbled with orneriness as she read Kelly's text.

Jessica: *Yes. Mind if I ride with you two tonight?*

It took Kelly much longer to text back than usual.

Kelly: *Gabe invited a friend to go with us.*
Jessica: *Great! The more the merrier! Meeting at your usual spot?*
Kelly: *Ugh! This is so awkward. We totally want you to come too, but the "friend" is actually Luke.*
Jessica: *What?!!!*
Kelly: *Sorry, hun. I know you two didn't hit it off, but he's still Gabe's friend.*

Jessica: *I see ... Well I still need to bike so Dr. Stuffy Pants is just going to have to deal with me coming along too!*
Kelly: *O-kay ... BTW please don't call him that when we're all together. I really like Gabe and if our two best friends can't get along then it's not going to be easy on us.*

Jessica giggled to herself.

Jessica: *I'll be on my best behavior. I won't even bite him this time ;)*
Kelly: *OMG! Wasn't that crazy! I can't believe he said that. Like you would ever bite someone.*

It *was* crazy, considering Jillian kept her blood drawing technique to fingernails only with anyone Kelly fixed her up with. Biting was crazy to most normal guys, and they wouldn't hesitate to call her out on it to everyone who would listen, but breaking the skin was not something that made the gossip loop. Most guys simply refused to endure the pain and the lasting marks, so those one-night stands ended with irreconcilable differences.

The devil pulled at the corners of Jessica's lips as she ended the conversation and got ready for an evening bike ride with "friends." She was the last to arrive which was unfortunate. Jessica wanted to see the look on Luke's face when he found out she'd be joining them. Instead, her obsessive primping at the last minute made her a little too late for the surprise.

"Hey, Jess. You remember Luke." Gabe scrunched his nose like she was a grenade and someone just pulled the pin.

Jessica's brain sighed as she let her eyes drink in the vision of Dr. Luke Jones in his biking attire that hugged every line of his fit, lean body. She was still in a miserable dry spell and needed sex more than food by that point.

"Jessica." Luke nodded with a polite smile as he fastened his helmet.

"Jones." She smiled with a wink of mischief.

"Call me Luke." His brow tensed a fraction, but only enough for Jessica to notice.

She shoved her two bottles of water in their holders. "Nah ... I'll stick with Jones."

"So ... shall we?" Kelly faked a smile that didn't hide her eagerness to get going and end the awkward reunion between Jessica and *Jones*.

Gabe followed Kelly and Luke gestured for Jessica to go.

"After you, *Jones*. I want to look at your fine ass. It's the best part of your personality. Besides, you'd never keep up with me, so I'll let you set the pace."

"You're contumacious." Luke pushed off on his bike.

"Whatever the hell that means," she mumbled just loud enough for Luke to hear.

"Stubbornly disobedient."

Jessica scowled at just how well Luke was playing the part.

"Catch me if you can." He looked back and smiled. It was playful, flirty, and the sexiest look Jessica had ever seen.

"Hey! Where are you two going?" Kelly called as Luke buzzed past her and Gabe with Jessica closing in on him.

"See ya at the finish!" Jessica yelled.

"It's not a race!" Kelly's voice faded in the distance.

Jessica drafted behind Luke for miles. Aside from Jude, no one had ever physically pushed her so hard. The pace was intense ... insane. They passed so many other cyclists

Jessica lost count, all she knew was it felt like the final stretch of a major race and she would not come in second.

"Ready to have your ass handed to you by a girl, Jones?" Jessica hollered as she moved left to pass him.

"Wait!" he yelled, but it morphed into nothing more than a fading echo.

Jessica didn't wait for anyone, but she should have. It happened in less than a breath. His voice, her name, stabs of pain, blurred scenery, then black.

She woke to his voice and flashes of red light.

"Don't try to move, Jessica."

"L-Luke?"

"Yes. I'm here."

The earth beneath her shook and then she realized it was the bounce of the gurney surrounded by strange faces.

"What's wrong with my neck?" She tried to reach for her neck but a pain shot up her arm. "Ahh!"

"You fell off your bike. We're taking you to the hospital. Your neck's probably fine. It's just a precaution," one of the paramedics reassured her.

"Kelly—"

"They'll meet us there." Luke climbed into the back of the ambulance with Jessica.

"What happened?" her voice slurred.

"The pothole was big and you were contumacious." Luke simpered and in spite of the pain, Jessica smiled.

"Contumacious?" the paramedic questioned.

"He's an ... o-overeducated idiot." Jessica let her eyes close.

THE EMERGENCY ROOM visit lasted two hours, then turned into an overnight stay for observation. Jessica dodged any major injuries, receiving only stitches in her arm and some sexy road rash along her legs and her other arm, but by some miracle nothing was broken—except her pride.

"I don't have phone numbers for anyone in your family." Kelly rubbed Jessica's hand.

"My parents are out of the country for their anniversary and Jude is at a conference. No need to call anyone and worry them."

"I'll stay with you."

Jessica shook her head with an appreciative smile. "No need. I'm a big girl. Besides, they're sending me home tomorrow."

"I do need a shower." Kelly pinched the front of her shirt, pulling it to her nose. "Are you sure you'll be okay?"

"Positive."

"Call me if you need a ride when they release you tomorrow. I can take off work."

"Thanks, Kelly."

"Get some rest, showoff."

Jessica rolled her eyes. "I wasn't showing off ... I just wasn't going to let a guy show me up."

"I still don't understand why you two didn't hit it off. You're perfect for each other."

"Good night, Kelly."

Kelly grinned. "Night, Jess."

Jessica leaned her head back against the pillow and closed her eyes. The medication they gave her began to numb the pain and slow her thoughts. The soft echo of Luke's voice lulled her to sleep. *Yes, I'm here.*

A dull ache clenched Jessica's body when she woke early the next morning, the physical impact of her accident magnified without the influence of pain medication. The gentle light of the distant horizon welcoming the morning sun illuminated the room. As everything came into focus she noticed the sleeping body in the chair next to her hospital bed. Luke.

He was still wearing his biking attire. Jessica's heart swelled in her chest. Luke stayed all night with her, without her asking, without her knowing.

"Shit!" she whispered, trying to sit up.

Luke's eyes fluttered open and he startled a bit as she grimaced trying to reposition. "Let me." He jumped to his feet and adjusted her pillow to support her back. "Good morning." He smiled, his face inches from hers for a brief moment.

"You stayed."

Luke sat back down. He nodded, scratching the back of his neck. Then he smoothed his hand over his ruffled hair. She had never seen Dr. Jones look in such disarray. She liked it ... a lot.

"I stayed."

"Don't you have patients today?"

"Eve rescheduled my day."

Unwanted emotions crowded in Jessica's chest then constricted in her throat. "You rescheduled your day?"

"Yes."

"For me?" she whispered, rubbing her dry lips together.

"For you."

"Why?"

He sighed. "I feel responsible."

She shook her head. "Oh God! I've mastered the ability to push your pity buttons. That's just great. Please, go to work. My body has taken bigger hits than yesterday's incident. You didn't put the pothole in the road. It's not your fault." She made a shooing gesture toward the door. "Go, I hereby absolve you of all responsibility."

"All?" Luke raised his brows.

"No, not all. I'll see you tomorrow. I gave you three months of my soul and then you tried to dump me. So for *that* you are not absolved."

"First, it is 'tomorrow,' second, I have yet to see your *soul*, and third, I didn't dump you."

The soul comment stung a bit. She couldn't blame him. It was possible she no longer had a soul to be seen. "I must look like a sewer rat."

"What?"

Jessica blew a stray hair from her face. "Me. I need a shower..." she whipped the sheet off her legs, exposing the mottling of road rash "...and then there's the ugly that won't disappear any time soon. But you've never looked better. You probably need a shower, but I swear to God I can still smell that soap or cologne of yours, and your hair has escaped the confines of its normal gel coating and it's giving me inappropriate thoughts. I go from visually tolerable to offensive and you go from *GQ* to *Sports Illustrated*."

"Jessica, you look fine."

She rolled her eyes. "Yeah, you mean white boy fine, not like when a brother says his woman looks *real fine*."

"I *am* white and you're not my *woman*."

Her gaze slipped. Luke was perceptive and always stated the obvious as if she was somehow always missing it. "Thanks for staying, but you can go now."

"I'll get your doctor to release you, then I'll take you home."

When he left the room, Jessica closed her eyes. "You're killing me, Jones." There was never a magic wand around when she needed one. With a few waves and some magical words she would be normal and irresistible in his eyes. Her whole   I-make-men-bleed-because-I-watched-someone-murder-my-best-friend thing was really getting in the way of the whole I-need-Jones-in-my-bed-NOW thing.

"Jessica, how are you feeling this morning?" Her doctor and his nurse filed in the room with Luke behind them.

"I feel and look like roadkill."

"Nothing that won't heal over time," her doctor reassured her with a kind smile.

"I don't know, my ego took quite a hit."

Luke glanced up from his phone, biting back a grin.

Cheeky bastard.

The doctor checked her over then released her. Luke waited outside while she dressed.

"Ready?" he asked as the nurse wheeled Jessica down the hall against her will.

She nodded. "Did you call a cab?"

"No. Gabe and Kelly brought my car last night. Then they took yours home. Nice friends we have." He relieved the nurse of her chauffeur duties and pushed her to the elevator.

"The best." Jessica nodded.

In the elevator she glanced up at him. "Why are you looking at me like that?"

"Like what?"

"Like you're studying me."

Luke chuckled as he leaned against the wall with his arms crossed over his chest. "Probably because I am."

"Have you figured me out yet?"

"Not completely."

"And when you do?"

"Then I'll have to start doing my own cleaning again."

Jessica held her breath to keep from gasping. His words

185

were a means to an end. She'd come to rely on her time with him, not his professional knowledge ... *him*.

"What will you do without me to entertain you?" She controlled each word, stripping them of the nervous emotion they wanted to convey.

"Whatever I want."

The elevator doors opened. He pushed her to the entrance as her shoulders sagged in a slump of defeat.

"Wait here. I'll pull my car around."

Jessica stood and waited by the curb; her mind reeled with panic. Luke was supposed to be her incentive to get better, find normalcy again. If getting better meant saying goodbye to Luke, then the incentive was gone.

She looked up as the vibrating roar of an engine approached. "What. The. Hell?"

A cherry red, mint condition 1967 Pontiac GTO pulled to a stop. It was the ultimate car porn and Jessica nearly convulsed right there on the spot. The driver's window cranked a turn. "Get in, Jessica. It's not a date."

She feathered her fingertips along the shiny chrome handle then opened the heavy door. Jessica felt Luke's eyes on her as she closed hers and slinked into the black leather seat, one slow inch at a time. "400 cubic inches ... 360 horsepower ... I'm in love," she whispered.

"Sorry, it's not a Jetta—"

"Shh! Don't—don't ruin this moment for me."

Luke laughed a little. "I thought you'd like her. Buckle up."

She opened her eyes and fastened her seat belt. "You're going to let me drive her, right?"

He shifted into first and eased up on the clutch. "Not a chance."

CHAPTER NINETEEN

KNIGHT

DAYS PASSED and again it appeared as though AJ had vanished. Jillian helped with the grounds upkeep during the day and sold battery-operated sex by night. She took punishing runs sometimes as late as midnight and sparred with Jackson until her bones melted into jelly under her fatigued muscles.

While her brother seemed to be flourishing in his role as Jackson Knight, Jillian warred with her emotions until her world spiraled on the edge of control. She hated Luke for making her love him. She hated Jackson for making her live. She hated AJ for making her care.

"Great night for a ride," Stan hollered over the rumble of her Harley's engine.

Jillian smiled and slipped on her helmet, grateful for a night to herself.

"I'll leave the notes from the association meeting here on your work bench."

She nodded again then pulled out of her garage. With less-than-perfect timing, AJ made an appearance. Getting out of his jeep, he signaled for her to stop. Jillian flipped him the bird and kept going with a fuck-all-men attitude that had been brewing for months. They weren't necessary anyway, and she had a catalog full of PPDs to prove it.

Shortly after finding some open road she tracked a black jeep in her mirror. A full tank of gas assured she wouldn't be stopping to listen to his meaningless words for many miles. AJ followed her, keeping a safe distance for close to two hours before she stopped at a lookout point up a gravel road atop a bluff.

"I'm not in the mood," Jillian said as she pulled off her helmet, looking out over miles of grassy terrain in the shadows of the sunset.

AJ stood behind her, keeping his distance. "I'm sorry."

His words brushed her nerves like sandpaper. "I'm not. I only regret not actually breaking your nose and a couple of ribs."

"Jill—"

"Don't!" She turned. "Go *fuck somebody else today*. I'm not in the mood for your crap."

"I'm not your knight in shining armor." AJ pumped his fists. He did it often.

Of course he wasn't. Her knight wore argyle socks. "I'm not Cinderella."

The tension between them built. It always did. It was undeniable, uncontrollable, and unpredictable.

"I hurt my wife," AJ gritted each word through clenched teeth. It was pain woven with anger.

"I hurt everyone I touch." She spoke with resolution, stating a fact without apology. Acquitting herself of responsibility came too easy. She surprised herself with just how well those old victim's shoes fit.

"I'll hurt you." He swallowed hard, each breath coming faster.

"I'd like to see you try." She took two long strides and fisted his T-shirt, pulling him to her lips.

The kiss was hard, sensual, and desperate. Their hands warred as each fought for the other one's clothes—pushing, pulling, tugging. AJ lifted her up to his waist and she wrapped her legs around him. Leaving her black jacket and both of their shirts in the dirt, he shuffled to the passenger's side of his jeep with his jeans at his ankles.

"You..." he breathed heavily setting her sideways in the passenger's seat "...I need to fuck *you* today."

Her own breath chased his as he tugged off her right boot, dropping it to the ground as she lifted her ass to let him peel down her jeans and panties, releasing them from the same leg. AJ stepped between her open thighs at the edge of the Jeep. Their eyes locked with the intensity of two wild animals tracking each other's every move. Jillian curled her fingers around the waistband of his briefs and slid them down. The moment she took his erection in her hand he rested his hands on the roof and dropped his chin to his chest, lips parted while he watched her stroke him.

Jillian's eyes flitted between her hand and the large muscles of his torso and arms flexed like steel as he rocked his pelvis towards her. The high that shot through her veins from seeing him like that was dangerously intoxicating. But it didn't satiate her need to make him bleed, and for that she felt a pang of nostalgia as Luke's voice seeped from her conscience.

AJ's eyes grew heavy as she tightened her grip, circling her thumb over the engorged head of his erection. "I'm going to make you bleed and then you can fuck me," she whispered, and for the first time her words held an edge of regret ... a breath of shame. Once again, he made her care.

He met her gaze, brushed the pad of his thumb across

her bottom lip, then nodded once as he slid his hand behind her head and claimed her mouth. Only a self-loathing man would offer himself to a monster. She clawed at his skin as though the earth was trying to bury her alive—desperate, lost. AJ released her mouth as she gasped for air a split second before digging her teeth into the muscled flesh of his shoulder.

Not a flinch, not a sound, just a statue of strength, AJ let her teeth melt into him. Like the air that filled her starving lungs, she felt the reprieve—the control she needed. The wet crimson smeared along his skin as she laid a gentle kiss on his neck.

"Now?" he whispered.

"Now."

AJ flipped open the glove compartment, retrieved a condom, and rolled it on. "I'm sorry ... I can't be gentle today."

Jillian scooted to the edge of the seat and spread her legs wide. "I know."

JILLIAN LEFT AJ WITHOUT A WORD. The guilt on his face said enough. Truth? He was somebody's knight in shining armor. Luke had once said people are exactly what they say they're not. Expectations demand accountability and accountability only matters in the presence of another. Denial is the road to solitude.

On the long ride home under a shimmering canopy of stars and in the watchful headlights of a black Jeep, Jillian contemplated her own accountability. By the time her bike was covered and her hand was reaching for the door handle to her house, the answer came to her. Jillian pushed the button to the garage door and raced out, jumping over the beam. She looked up and froze. AJ stood in his driveway, hands shoved into his pockets, a heartbreaking mix of sadness and relief stealing his handsome features.

"This is a mistake," he said as his gaze sank to the concrete.

Something so dark resided in AJ that at times she swore she felt it bleeding from his soul. "An epic mistake." Jillian ran into his arms.

It was a crushing embrace. She'd never felt anyone cling to her like their life depended on it. AJ needed her, maybe even more than she needed him. She physically needed him. He emotionally needed her.

"I'm due for an epic mistake."

AJ released her and cradled her face. "Me too." He smirked. "Stay..." he brushed his lips across hers "...stay with me tonight."

Blood surged through her heart like a freight train in her chest as she willed herself to take a few slow breaths to suppress the fear. *You're Jillian Knight. Fin de journée.*

"Okay," she whispered.

She felt like a child when he took her petite hand in his. AJ was strong and towered over her small stature. Any other woman would have felt protected in his presence, but not Jillian. She experienced a constant rush of adrenaline, a need to stay alert that could not be tamed. The feeling was equally exhilarating and exhausting.

"Can I get you something to drink?"

She smiled. Hospitable AJ was charming.

"Wine? Beer?"

"Beer, please."

"Not a wine drinker?" AJ grabbed two beers out of the refrigerator.

Jillian's smile faded a bit. "No, I'm not into wine." It was the truth. Jillian Knight did not drink wine.

They stood in the kitchen leaning against opposing counters while an awkward silence settled over them.

"Maybe we should drink our beers naked."

AJ choked in the middle of his long pull.

She grinned. "Only because we seem to be more comfortable with each other when we're naked."

AJ scanned her body with a stormy look brewing in his eyes as he set his beer down. "I do want you naked, beneath me, in my bed." He pushed off the counter and ran his hands through her hair as his lips descended to hers.

Jillian reacted to him with a feral hunger. She pushed his shirt up until he grabbed it, breaking their kiss for a split second as it brushed past his face. He squeezed her breasts through her shirt and she moaned into his mouth, her hands making haste to unfasten his jeans. Then ... the doorbell rang.

"Fuck!" His forehead pressed against hers. "Don't. Move."

She nodded as the moist heat from their labored breathing lingered between them. Her legs felt weak when he released her to answer the door.

"Surprise!" A female voice that Jillian couldn't quite place filled the air.

"Carin," he choked on her name.

Jillian found her legs and peeked around the corner. Carin stood at AJ's door in a long black trench coat that hung open revealing her red lingerie including a garter belt, black stockings, and stilettos. Carin eyed AJ's bare chest with a look that made Jillian want to do physical harm to her.

"Looks like you were thinking about me too." Carin wet her lips as she stared at AJ's unfastened jeans.

"Uh ..." AJ buttoned his jeans and yanked up the zipper "...did we have plans I forgot about?"

Carin stepped inside forcing AJ to retreat a step. "No, silly ... hence the surprise." She shrugged off her coat, letting it pool at her feet.

"You seemed distracted the last time I saw you. It was the first time we didn't..." she bit her lip "...you know. So I thought I'd spice it up a bit."

"I told you last time the arrangement is no longer working for me."

"But why?" She released her bottom lip into a pouty frown.

"Well, what a pleasant surprise." Jillian stepped around the corner.

Carin froze.

"Carin with a C, don't you look irresistible tonight." Jillian wedged herself between AJ and Carin.

"I told you to wait in the kitchen," AJ gritted.

"Victoria's Secret?" Jillian asked as she ran her finger along Carin's satin bra strap.

Carin shivered, eyes wide.

"How do you feel about being on the bottom?" Jillian sucked in her bottom lip.

Carin's gaze shot to AJ.

"Because Sarge thinks he's going to have me beneath him ... but I'm *never* on the bottom." Jillian turned to face a disgruntled AJ. "Will this be your first threesome, Senior ... Master ... Sergeant?" Jillian traced her fingertips along his firm abs.

"Are—are you *with* her, AJ?" Although weak, Carin found her voice.

When AJ and Jillian looked at each other, a half-naked Carin ceased to exist. Carin was the innocent party, and Jillian would have felt bad, but the truth was ... Carin was normal and deserved better.

"I'm his mistake," Jillian teased her fingers below his navel, keeping her eyes locked to his.

"An *epic* mistake," AJ whispered.

"Well ... I-I can't do this. I'm not that type of girl." Carin slipped on her coat and cinched the tie. Without another word she scurried down the drive to her car.

AJ kicked the door shut and had Jillian lifted with her back pressed against it before a coherent thought could form in her head or an audible word could escape her lips. Her hands slid up his neck and her fingers curled craving a fist full of hair, but his buzz cut denied her every attempt. He kissed her neck while an uncontrolled groan rumbled from his chest. Hugging her to him, he carried her to his bedroom. Before he set her down, she placed her palms on his cheeks until he looked at her.

"I *will not* be beneath you." She swallowed a lump of anxiety. How could one person be so messed-up? She knew he wasn't going to hurt her, but for some reason what she knew, what she felt, and what she feared were all at war.

His eyes searched hers. "I don't give a fuck about gravity when I'm inside you." He kissed her, drowning all her senses with his lingering words, his intoxicating taste, his powerful body flesh to hers. He sat on the bed and leaned back with Jillian straddling him.

AJ SLEPT. Jillian did not, although exhaustion fought to pull her under. The more the voice in her head tried to convince her to close her eyes, the crazier she began to feel. She slid off his chest.

"Where are you going?" he mumbled with his eyes shut. Jillian questioned if he was really awake.

"Bathroom," she whispered, grabbing her clothes off the floor. The reflection in the bathroom mirror still looked like a stranger. Dark roots pushed past the platinum blond, a reminder that she needed to schedule a hair appointment. Her tan line reflected the short denim shorts she wore while mowing instead of the bikini bottom lines Jessica Day used to have.

AJ's chest rose and fell with deep even breaths as she peeked around the corner. Jillian didn't want to leave. She wanted to feel his naked body next to hers in the morning. She wanted to share coffee and discover the labyrinth of detail that made him the man he'd become, but she was too tired and too weak to crawl back into his bed.

Tiptoeing up the stairs, she pushed open the door on her right. It was Cage's room. Behind the *locked* door, she slid between his sheets, then she set her phone's alarm to five a.m. and fell asleep.

Her body clock protested when the alert chimed at the break of dawn. She shut it off and made her way back down to AJ's room.

"Should I be worried that you'd rather sleep in my son's bed than mine?"

Jillian jumped as she reached the bottom of the stairs, wearing only her bra and panties. AJ sat at the table sipping coffee and reading the newspaper. He was showered and dressed in shorts and a T-shirt.

"Oh! Hi," she breathed out in surprise. Honesty wasn't a luxury Jillian had been granted. Deceit wasn't a lie; it was survival. She became an expert at revealing the truth cloaked in a lie. "You're up early."

AJ twisted the newspaper, glancing at his watch. "So are you."

Jillian took tentative steps toward him. AJ was far from an open book. His emotions were as subtle as the turn of the earth. She eased the newspaper from his grasp. He sipped his coffee as she straddled his lap, wrapping her hand around his to bring the cup to her lips. "Mmm ... hazelnut."

AJ nodded once as he set the mug on the table. He had yet to share even a faint smile, but his eyes gleamed with pleasure as they perused her body.

"I know you think I have control issues, but they're really more trust issues." Their eyes met as she released his tags. "Falling asleep, naked, next to someone takes a lot of trust. In fact, there's really nothing that feels more vulnerable than that."

AJ withheld all emotion, just a blank expression.

"Say something," she whispered.

He cupped the back of her neck and kissed her. His tongue slid against hers with lazy patience. It was as quick and simple as striking a match or flipping a switch. Jillian's body went from content to desperately insatiable. She rocked her pelvis against him, feeling a trickle of warmth at her core. He grabbed her hips to still her motion.

"Thank you."

She pulled back, eyes narrowed. "For what?"

"For not trusting me."

She frowned, resting her hand on his cheek. His pain was so palpable. "She left you?"

He nodded.

Questions swelled on her tongue, but she had no right to ask them.

The ghost of a man looked over her shoulder like he was seeing his past on a T.V. screen. "Brooke, my ex-wife, was my dental hygienist. My *former* dentist ... her boss, is now her husband. We fell fast in love and six months later we were married. Cage was born two years after that. We were never in the same place very long. When Cage started school we decided it was best for her to move back to Portland near our parents. We wanted Cage to have stability and make friends without feeling like nothing in his life was permanent, the way I felt growing up. By the time I came home for good, I wasn't the same person. It's like being on constant high alert. You just can't shut it off and it wears on you ... it affects everyone around you. She'd tap my shoulder and I'd have her pinned to the wall with my hand around her neck."

He sighed a shaky breath and ghosted his hands up and down Jillian's legs. "I broke her down a little every day. I broke *us* a little more every day." He shook his head. "I never hit her, but I lost my temper ... a lot. I frightened her. I didn't even realize how much until I found a locked box in her bedside drawer. Inside was a hand gun."

He shook his head. "What does that say about a man when his wife needs a gun by her bed to feel safe? We had sex, but we never made love again. She looked at me like she was looking at a stranger. I could almost hear her counting down the seconds until it was over. I never forced myself on her and she never denied me, but she'd curl up in a ball like I just raped her."

His voice broke and he swallowed hard. "I moved out when Cage was ten and we signed the divorce papers shortly after his eleventh birthday. I wondered if she'd been having an affair because of how quickly she remarried. But honestly it didn't matter. In some ways it was comforting to think that someone else was taking care of her and treating her with the respect and love she deserved."

AJ laughed. "How fucked up is that?"

His words were a clear warning, but they only made Jillian feel more drawn to him, not a moth to a flame—a flame to a stick of dynamite.

"It's not *you* I don't trust." She reached behind and unclasped her bra. AJ's hands slid up her stomach and cupped her breasts as her head fell back; a soft moan released. "It's me," she whispered.

CHAPTER TWENTY

THE KNIGHT's basement smelled like a gym, especially on the days Jackson wanted to sweat a lot. He turned off the air conditioner until the whole house began to feel like an inferno. Jillian stopped at the bottom of the stairs and watched her brother do one arm pushups. He defined the term physical specimen: muscles, tan skin, and a canvas of ink.

"Angry, bored, or sex deprived?"

Jackson grunted as he switched arms. "Yep."

Jillian sat down on the bottom step. "You're angry with me?"

"Yep."

"And bored?"

"Yep."

"Because I'm not here?"

"Nope."

"Because you're sex deprived?"

"Yep." Jackson growled through the last one that shook his whole body. Then he sat on the floor, arms resting on his bent knees, completely out of breath. "I don't like you with AJ."

"You didn't like me with Luke for quite some time."

He shrugged. "Why AJ?"

"I think he needs me."

Jackson laughed. "And who *are* you?"

"A single thirty-year-old woman with ghosts haunting her at every turn. AJ's haunted too."

"So two wrongs make a right? Or misery loves company? Or—"

"Or when I'm with him I feel close to Luke."

Jackson shook his head. "That's messed-up."

"I was messed-up. Luke saved me."

"So AJ needs saving?"

Jillian stared at the chipped polish on her toenails. "He needs somebody." Jessica Day needed *somebody*.

"Has he told you about his past?"

"A little."

"And has he asked you about yours? Your disturbing behavior that's reared its ugly head again?"

"Not really. Well ... that's just it ... he knows I need it, and he lets me ... but he doesn't demand to know why."

"Christ, Jillian! You don't *need* it! And he's one fucked-up son of a bitch if he voluntarily lets you do it. If a woman, no matter how good she was in bed, ever went all *Twilight* on me, it would be over!"

"What if *he* needs it? What if he's just as fucked-up as me? Huh? Maybe he needs to know that he can't hurt me. Maybe—"

Jackson hunched down in front of her, resting his hands on her shoulders. "You're not fucked-up. Okay? Jillian Knight lost her parents ... period. But she had a normal childhood and normal relationships, and is in fact *normal*. Got it?"

Tears swelled in Jillian's eyes. "But Jessica—"

"Is dead." Jackson kissed her forehead. "You have to let her go or she'll destroy you. You need to find normal. You need a guy that won't let you be anything *but* normal. You may think that AJ needs Jessica, but she can't save him and he can't have her because she no longer exists." Jackson wiped the tears from her cheeks. "Listen to me ..." he whispered "... you either have to let Jessica go or AJ."

"Dodge is waiting for me. I have to go." She pulled away.

"I'll go to my grave protecting you."

Jillian stopped midway up the stairs, but she couldn't turn around. A nod was all she could give without breaking down again. She felt the same. They had that unexplainable connection. When one was in trouble, no matter where the other was, they sensed it. They physically felt each other's pain.

Jackson was known for his cavalier attitude toward women. But someday he was going to be someone's jackpot. If the right woman came along and he decided to love her, she would be adored beyond words, protected to the ends of the earth, and given everything her heart could ever desire.

STAN STOPPED Jillian on the way to Dodge's place. He was drenched in sweat and sporting denim cutoffs, the right leg three inches longer than the left.

"Did you read over the notes from the meeting?"

"Uh ... yes." Jillian smiled. She'd lightly skimmed them a few nights earlier when she needed help getting to sleep.

"Oh, good. What are your thoughts on the speed bumps? Since we don't have sidewalks in our development a few people..." he rolled his eyes and waved his hands around "...namely my wife, wants speed bumps installed. I posted speed limit signs last year, but she doesn't think people notice them."

Jillian laughed a little. "You have like ... six of them posted. I don't think it's that they don't notice them. I just think they don't give a shit. It's a private drive, what are you going to do? Make a citizen's arrest?" Jillian shrugged. "I agree with your wife. Speed bumps are the way to go. Sometimes you have to physically control people's actions. I'm off to Dodge's, see you later."

"He's probably still watching wrastling."

Jillian turned. "You mean wrestling?"

"Yeah, that's what I said, wrastling."

She shook her head and kept walking. Dodge was indeed watching *wrastling* on the T.V. in his garage when she arrived.

"Who watches Lilith when you're out here, old man?"

"Hey, Jillian! Beer?" He lifted the lid to the cooler on the back of his golf cart.

"I'm good, thanks."

"No need to report me for wife neglect." He held up a baby monitor. "I've got ears on her. Never hear much, usually just her crop dusting ... thank God Almighty this thing doesn't transmit odor."

Jillian frowned, crossing her arms over her chest. "You do realize she's probably going to bludgeon you in your sleep and not a court in the country will convict her."

"Nah ... she's crazy 'bout me."

Jillian held out her hand. "Go get your stuff done. I charge double when you're inefficient."

Dodge grinned, handing her the baby monitor. "Yes, ma'am. I've been ignoring the rumors that you work at night in a black leather corset yielding a whip. But I'm starting to think there might be some truth to it."

Jillian opened the back door. "Whatever shakes your rocks."

Lilith smiled, looking up from her book at Jillian. Of course, after Dodge's comment, Jillian understood why Lilith always looked so happy to see her.

"Lunch?" Jillian pointed to the kitchen in her usual make-shift sign language.

Lilith shook her head, holding up an empty plate on the table next to her chair. Jillian took the plate to the kitchen.

"It's a beautiful day and the sun is no longer hitting your deck so I think we should go outside for some fresh air." Jillian looked inside the refrigerator. "Surprise, surprise, your crazy husband made some iced tea. And here I thought all he did was siphon beer from his cooler all day." Jillian chuckled to herself as she poured two glasses then cut up a lemon. "I'm basically talking to myself, so really, who am I to judge."

The sweltering heat that had plagued the previous weeks showed mercy that day. It was eighty degrees with low humidity. Jillian and Lilith nursed their iced teas and watched the ducks and geese play in the algae-infested pond. Before Lilith had a chance to finish her drink, she drifted off to sleep as Jillian drifted back in time.

Day

LUKE INSISTED Jessica take the day off to recover. No work, no therapy, no Luke. Jessica appeased him by playing the part of the good patient, only because she'd caught a glimpse of her hideous reflection in his GTO's window. Who was she kidding? Soap, deodorant, toothpaste, and a comb were the absolute minimum requirements before her charm and sex appeal would have a chance. And even then, she knew he was immune to her spells.

The loose-fitting cargo pants didn't turn any heads, but they also didn't rub against her road-rash covered legs. Her sleeveless blouse that revealed her cleavage, one of the few areas of her body that was unscathed, made up for the not-so-sexy pants. She left her hair down to veil the scrape high on her cheekbone. Armed with a pizza, Heineken, and a bottle of Riesling, she knocked on Luke's door.

"Jessica?" Luke answered wearing an authentic look of shock, but it didn't distract from his fitted button-down shirt, sleeves rolled up, and jeans that flashed like a neon 'fuck me' sign. At least, that was Jessica's humble opinion that was reaffirmed when she inhaled what she'd come to think of as Chanel No. 69 – Jones le fonder de culotte —*Jones the panty melter*.

"I'm not a take-the-day-off kind of girl, so ..." She shrugged.

"You should have called first." Luke's expression morphed from surprised to a reprimanding scowl.

She wrinkled her nose. "I wanted to surprise you. The call would have ruined it."

"True, but at least you would have known that I already have plans this evening."

"Plans? What plans? Your place is immaculate thanks

to yours truly and less than twenty-four hours ago your plans were with me?" Jillian leaned forward and sniffed, trying to decipher what she was smelling other than pizza and Chanel No. 69. "Are you cooking?"

"Yes," Luke answered, enunciating the word as if Jessica was deaf or just dumb.

"Luke?" A female's voice called from inside.

"Is that ... a woman?"

"Yes," he repeated his same enunciation.

"A date?" Jessica said with loud surprise.

"Shh ... yes, a date. Now, do you mind?"

"Where's your bottle open—Jessica?" A familiar body accompanied the mysterious voice.

Luke sighed as his date peeked around him.

"Ellie?" Jessica gritted her teeth.

"Wh-what are you doing here?" Ellie's gaze moved to the pizza box and sack of beer and wine.

"Jessica cleans my house." Luke smiled at Ellie.

"But, I thought Kelly and Gabe said they fixed you two up and it didn't work out."

Jessica smiled at Luke, waiting for his explanation.

"They did, and we didn't work out romantically, but I was looking for a cleaning lady and Jessica was looking for some part-time work so ..." Luke shrugged like that's all the explanation that was needed. "So, I take it you're both mutual friends of Kelly's?"

Jessica interrupted before Ellie could get one syllable out of her pouty lips. "We all went to college together."

"I dated her brother, Jude, for a while." Ellie flipped her blond hair over her shoulder as if dating Jude was worthy of a spot on her dating resumé.

"I think he said he screwed you in the alley behind a night club and couldn't remember your name so he referred

205

to you as 'the girl who would lick *anything.*' So if you call that dating, then sure ... you dated my brother."

Ellie laughed. "Oh, Jess ... you've always had such a great sense of humor." Ellie retreated from Luke's view and gave a pleading, wide-eyed look to Jessica.

"Well, listen up, Jones. I'm busy for the next two weeks so it's now or never for cleaning your place."

"Never." Luke squinted and started to close the door.

"Now? Great!" Jillian pushed it open and wedged her way between him and the door. "You don't mind do you, Ellie? I'll be done in no time. You won't even notice I'm here."

"Uh ... well..." Ellie stepped to the side "...what's with the pizza?"

"A girl's gotta eat." Jessica sauntered down the hall toward Luke's bedroom. She shut the door and leaned up against it, blowing her hair away from her eyes. "Ellie?" she grumbled. "Ellie fucking ... what is her last name? Lehman? Lawson? Lieberman? Lickey!" She laughed in spite of the frown on her face. "It's not Lickey, but screw it, I'm going with it. How could Kelly fix him up with *her*? Shit!" Jessica jumped as a loud knock vibrated the door just opposite her head. She turned and opened it.

"Jessica ..." Luke stormed inside his bedroom. It was more like a small gust. Nothing Luke did ever appeared out of control. "Once again you are crossing the line. I told you to stay home and rest. Now you're here crashing my date, which is completely inappropriate, and the web of lies keeps getting bigger and it's all going to blow up in your face—"

He turned, having been venting his frustration to the window. Jessica sat perched on his bed with her legs crossed, pizza box open, and in the middle of pouring a glass of wine.

"What are you doing?" His voice escalated. Incredulity etched in the lines of his forehead above his wide eyes.

"Eating..." she mumbled through a mouthful of pizza "... I'm starving."

"That's a fifteen-hundred dollar bedspread. Do you know what that means?"

Jessica held up a finger as she finished chewing, a sparkle of excitement in her eyes. "Oh, yes, I know this one. It means that you're an *idiot* for paying that much money for a semen towel."

He eased toward the open bottle of wine that she'd decided to balance on the bed next to the pizza box. A bit of relief washed over his face as he grabbed it without it spilling. "Out. Right now. Take your food and go. Ellie's waiting for me and I don't have the time nor the patience to deal with you and your antics right now."

"Oh God ... Ellie, right. Please tell me you're not seriously entertaining the idea of dating her."

"That's none of your concern."

"Come on, Jones! You can't be serious. She's a total slut. Are you really going to take her to dinner with your uppity shrink buddies, half of whom she's probably already screwed."

"She owns a daycare ... I hardly think that qualifies her as a slut."

Jessica took another bite of her pizza and shrugged. "She likes to recruit them when they're young."

Luke grabbed the box, leaving Jessica on the bed with just a lone piece of pizza in her hand. "Out. Now."

"Don't have sex with her."

"Once again..." he gritted his teeth "...none of your concern."

She scooted off the bed, wincing a bit as the friction irritated the raw skin on her legs that hadn't had a chance to form scabs yet. Luke's face mirrored her wince.

"You should be in bed, resting." He spoke with a softer surrender to his voice.

Jessica slipped on her sandals. "What do you think I was just doing?" She set her half-eaten piece of pizza on the box in Luke's hands. "Wash your sheets tomorrow. I don't want to sit on your bed after *she's* been in it." She opened the door.

"It's just a date." Luke sighed. "Here, don't forget your pizza."

Jessica frowned. "I've lost my appetite."

DR. LUKE JONES had a remarkable ability to focus even in the midst of chaos. He could dissect a problem, analyze it, mend it, and put it back together. Then he could walk away and forget about it. This is ... until Jessica Day landed in his office.

"Go away!" Jessica yelled at Luke's incessant knocking on her door.

In spite of the agitation in her voice, he kept knocking. That night was not supposed to play out the way it did. He had a date. A sexy date. An unattached date. A *willing* date. He wasn't supposed to be knocking on Jessica's door. He was supposed to be indulging in meaningless sex.

She tore open the door with a killer's wrath. "What?"

Luke flinched, but it wasn't from her words. Jessica

stood at the door in a sports bra and tight shorts, literal blood and sweat dripping from her body.

"What are you doing?" Luke stepped forward, struggling to hide a slip of uncharacteristic panic that tugged at his practiced and refined poker face.

"What does it look like, Einstein? I'm exercising." She turned and grabbed a towel off the couch by the punching bag that hung from the ceiling behind it.

Luke took the towel from her and pressed it to the exposed stitches on her arm, a few that had been ripped back open, then he moved it to dab the smeared blood that ran down her legs. She hissed as he blotted her wounds. Her stomach muscles clenched. This wasn't his fault and he knew it, but the finger of guilt still tsked at his conscience.

"You need help," he whispered, more to himself than to her.

"Then help me," she whispered back, confirming how far in over his head he'd become with her.

He stood and handed her the towel. "Why?"

"You said it yourself. I need help."

"No, why did you do this to yourself?"

"I was just exercising."

"Jessica ..."

She turned and walked to the kitchen. "I had to burn off some energy and Jude's out of town."

"You're bleeding."

"I couldn't feel it past the adrenaline."

"There's blood everywhere. Why did you do it?"

"I told you—"

"Tell me again. Where did you get all this energy since you left my house two hours ago?"

"Red Bull."

"Jessica."

She huffed. "You! Okay? You and fucking Ellie Lickey!"

"Ellie Liggett."

"Whatever! I was pissed that you kicked me out so she could do all her slutty shit to you. Is that what you want to hear?" Jessica leaned against her kitchen counter, arms crossed over her chest, refusing to meet his eyes.

"You were jealous?"

Throwing her arms in the air, she groaned. "No! Really, could you be more full of yourself? I'm starting to feel less and less guilty about not paying you for your 'expertise.' I said I was pissed, not jealous. I trusted you ... your judgement, but dipping your dick in San Francisco's communal pussy shows complete lack of judgment on your part—"

"Jessica?"

"And now I'm going to have to find someone else and start this whole process over again."

"Jessica?"

"And it's going to be a *woman!*"

"I didn't have sex with Ellie."

"But-but she sucked your dick, didn't she? God! She's such a man-eater."

Luke raised a lone brow.

She looked up at him. "Don't give me that look. I'm not a man-eater. I may take a nibble here and there, but I have discriminating taste. Ellie's just ... gross!"

Luke laughed a little. "Gross? Like ... icky or yucky?"

"So help me, Jones ... if you're making fun of me—"

"What? Are you going to bite me?" He knew his words were unprofessional and provoking. But with Jessica, Luke was caught in the crossfire between a man who desired her and a psychiatrist that needed to help her. The psychiatrist reminded the man every day that he could never have her.

Most days the man listened, but some days he told the psychiatrist to go fuck himself.

She swallowed. "Why didn't you have sex with her?" Jessica whispered.

Luke was drawn to her. His body detached from his mind as he moved toward her, pinning her against the counter with his hands on either side. "Because I have it on good authority that she ... gets around."

Jessica risked a glance at him. "I'll help you find a nice girl."

"You will?"

He could feel her heart pounding in her chest over and over as her breaths chased one another. Her proximity smothered his ability to think with any sort of clarity. He felt like a masochist in her presence.

"Yeah ... I have one in mind." She trapped her lower lip between her teeth, looking vulnerable without any resemblance to the Jessica Day he'd come to know.

"You do?" Luke's gaze shifted from her face to her chest, then the rest of her body. She looked like hell, the way she did at the hospital, and maybe it was her vulnerability, but in Luke's eyes all he could see was her beauty.

"I do. But she's very particular and I can't guarantee she'll like you."

Luke met her gaze again. "I can't guarantee I'll like her."

"Oh, you'll like her."

"How can you be so sure?"

"Because she's brilliant, and sexy, and athletic, and just ... a real catch." Jessica nodded with resolution.

"Well then I can't wait to meet her." He didn't recognize the raspy voice that floated past his lips, lips that yearned to touch hers.

"You're baiting me."

He squinted. "Baiting you?"

She ducked under his arm and scurried to the opposite side of the kitchen. "Yes, baiting me with your intoxicating smell, and evil sapphire eyes, and perfect skin, and thick dark hair that's been begging my hands to free it from its orderly confines." Jessica planted her hands on her hips. "And you show up here flaunting all of your ... your ... hotness! I'm completely sex deprived and the thought of you with Lickey should repulse me, but it doesn't! Because I'm SO. FUCKING. HORNY. The thought of you having sex, *naked*, with anyone, actually turns me on!"

Luke had an exorbitant vocabulary, yet not a single word in the English language came to mind. He felt like Kevin Bacon's character in *A Few Good Men* after Lt. Kaffee got Jack Nicholson's character to admit he ordered the Code Red. Eyes glazed. Mouth agape. Pulse barely detectable.

Jessica sighed on an eye roll. "I know what you're thinking ..."

Luke was impressed. *He* didn't even know what he was thinking.

"You think I just need to get laid, and you're right. But I'm trying so hard to not go all 'Hannibal Lecter' on anyone, so it's not as easy as just an innocent fix-up. If I can't have sex then I just need to ... hit something and get rid of all these emotions that feel so ... toxic."

He stared at her for a few silent moments, dealing with his own inner turmoil. "We're taking a field trip."

"Excuse me?"

He nodded. "This weekend we're going on a field trip. We'll leave Friday after we're both done with work and come back Sunday night. But you can't tell anyone."

"If this is a lock-in at the Y—"

He walked past her to the door, stopping for a quick second to press his finger to her lips. "Shh, no more questions."

She jokingly nipped at his finger. "Just one more."

Luke sighed before opening the door. "One."

"Is the chance of us having sex still less than zero percent?"

"Yes."

CHAPTER TWENTY-ONE

KNIGHT

Jillian loaded the back of Woody with her plastic containers of sex toys. In a short amount of time she had become the top seller of Lascivio products in her region. She was three grand away from receiving a new car and the bachelorette party she had on her schedule that night was sure to push her past her goal.

No one was more excited than Jackson. He was tired of loaning out Woody so she could haul her products. Jackson looked like sin on her Harley—muscles, tattoos, the whole package. However, he wasn't a bike guy. Women flocked to him in droves no matter what mode of transportation he used.

"What the *hell* are you wearing?" AJ's gruff voice sounded behind Jillian as she loaded the last container.

She smirked, looking back over her shoulder. "You like?"

AJ looked around.

"Relax, the neighbors have seen me in a lot less than this."

"You look like—"

"A whore?" Jillian shut the back hatch and turned. "You're such a romantic. Any other woman would be offended by your crass assessment. Lucky for you I know you like it rough and this is just your way of flirting."

"I didn't call you a whore and it's not my way of flirting. I want you to go change your clothes or *put on* some clothes."

She laughed. "Cute ... *Me Tarzan you Jane.* Yeah, nice try, big guy, but despite the rumors, I'm not really into role-playing.

Jillian looked down at her red corset, tulle miniskirt, thigh highs, and stilettos. "I'll slip on a trench coat for the ride, like Carin with a C."

"I'm serious." AJ stepped closer as if he thought he could intimidate her.

Jillian looked up at him, hands fisted on her hips. "Please tell me you see how laughable it is that you're trying to order me around like one of your soldiers."

"Jillian," he growled.

"Don't come home until you've secured that new car," Jackson said as he walked out of the house and straddled Jillian's Harley. "Woody's starting to smell like those girly candles you sell."

"You're just going to let your sister leave looking like this?" AJ gave Jackson a pleading look.

Jackson started the Harley. "I told her it was a bad idea to screw our neighbor, and as you know, she didn't listen to me. So ... good luck!" Jackson smiled as he rolled out of the garage.

"Go. Change."

Jillian rested her palms on his chest. "It's a themed bachelorette party. I'm pretty sure I'll fit right in with everyone else."

Her words didn't completely calm the beast, but AJ took a step back. "Didn't you go to college? Isn't there some other job you can get?"

"Kiss me, fool. I'm leaving." Jillian grabbed his shirt and pulled him toward her.

"You're killing me," he grumbled.

She kissed him with an eager passion, opening her mouth to invite his tongue to dance with hers. When he released her lips she whispered, "But what better way to die?"

JILLIAN DROVE Woody home for the last time. Her Lascivio party far exceeded even her expectations. The next time she'd be packing her boxes into the back of her new candy apple red Mercedes. Mary Kay reps in their pink Cadillacs had nothing on her.

It was nearly eleven o'clock by the time she got home. Jackson was still gone so she deemed it a good time for a booty call. By the tenth knock she gave up. As she walked back down the drive AJ opened his door.

"Not tonight, Cage is here." He squinted his eyes against the entry lights.

Jillian clicked back to his door in her stilettos. "You can't stand there in your shorts with your abs looking like you just did a thousand crunches and that tattooed serpent around your strong, sexy calf begging to be licked—which is weird I know—but I'm not sure I've ever seen such sexy calves on a guy before … but anyway, you can't say no."

"Cage is out with friends but he'll be home anytime now and I'm not ready to explain *us*."

"He's almost twenty-one. You're single and I'm the

neighborhood whore. I think he'd be shocked if you weren't having sex with me."

AJ frowned. "Don't call yourself that."

"Sorry, I didn't realize that's just your pet name for me."

"Jillian ... just ... I can't tonight. I need to talk to him first."

"I'll be quick."

"Jillian ..." AJ scrubbed his hands over his face.

"If you don't let me in I'm stripping right here on your stoop."

AJ gave her an annoyed looking smirk. "I know you're crazy, but I don't really think you're certifiably insane. Good night." AJ closed the door.

Clearly they each had their own definition of certifiably insane.

"If I get chewed up by bugs it's going to be your fault," she yelled.

AJ LUMBERED BACK to bed thinking about Jillian and how her evil temptress personality was twice as big as her little body. As he stared at the collage of shadows on his ceiling, he wondered what his chances were of getting back to sleep without jerking off first. That made two nearly naked women in one week that he'd turned away at his door.

Eventually he drifted back to sleep with his dignity intact, only to be awakened by Cage.

"Dad?"

"What?" AJ pulled the covers over his head to block the hall light.

"I just got home and ..."

"Good to know. Good night, Son."

"Uh … I think there's a package for you at the front door … and she's *naked*."

"What the fuuu-dge are you talking about?" AJ threw off his covers and jumped out of bed at fire alarm speed, nearly tackling Cage to get past him and to the front door.

"Oh and, Dad?"

AJ turned before opening the door.

"I'm an adult now, so what the *fuck* I'm talking about is Jillian. She's waiting for you naked and I'm not a genius but I think it's like a one hundred percent chance of you getting laid. And yes, it grosses me out a little and I swear to God if I hear you doing it with her I'll jab two sharp pencils into my ear drums, but I think you should invite her in for … whatever." Cage grinned. "You have my permission."

Stunned into a moment of silence, AJ watched Cage walk up the stairs. Reality was cruel. He couldn't remember when his boy became a man and sometimes the reminders were less than settling.

"You could get arrested for—" AJ opened the door to an empty stoop. No Jillian. No pile of sexy lingerie. "Oh for Chrissake!" he murmured.

He stepped outside wearing only his shorts and looked to the heavens for an answer. "I'm sorry. Whatever I did to deserve her, I'm sorry. Just … take her back. She's not the way I want to die." His words were mumbled to anyone who would listen and while common sense told him to be thankful that she was gone, whatever was malfunctioning in his brain propelled his legs to her front door step.

The lights were off and it was going on midnight, but AJ wasn't about to demonstrate social etiquette to someone who'd never heard of it.

"What'd she do now?" Jackson opened the door, covering his junk with a T-shirt.

AJ grimaced. "What is it with you two? This isn't a fucking nudist colony."

"Dude, I was in bed and you knocked on *my* door at midnight. You're lucky I even grabbed this T-shirt."

"Where is she?"

"In the bathroom. Help yourself ... not that you've ever asked my permission." Jackson turned giving AJ the full view of his naked, tattooed ass.

He had tattoos everywhere and there wasn't enough curiosity in the world to tempt AJ into staring at Jackson's naked ass as he walked to his bedroom. The door to Jillian's bathroom was closed but he saw flicking light under it and heard music playing.

"Aaron Joshua ..." Jillian said with a sultry voice as AJ opened the door. She was soaking in a bubble bath that AJ thought smelled like some sort of floral crap. A folded washcloth covered her eyes.

"Who the hell is Aaron Joshua?"

Jillian smiled. "Stab in the dark. I'll let you join me if you tell me what AJ stands for."

He shut the door and leaned back against it, arms crossed over his chest. "I'm clean, I already showered."

She laughed from deep inside her belly while removing the washcloth from her eyes. "Come on, Andrew Jasper, surely you know my intentions are for us to get dirty ... not clean."

"Wrong again, and I'm not really into bubbles and candles."

"Then why are you here, Anderson Jenkins? Because if you're in the tub with me, people would think of you as one lucky bastard. But if you stand there and watch me, I think that classifies you as one sick bastard."

AJ shook his head. "I'm not even sure why I'm here."

"Sex? You can just say it. That's why I knocked on your door earlier. But since I've been home I've given myself two moderately enjoyable orgasms, so at this point I can take it or leave it."

AJ pushed his focus past his arousal that was growing more painful by the minute. "How old are you?"

"Thirty. How old are you?"

"How old do you think I am?"

"Forty-two, seven months, and thirteen days ... give or take a few hours, minutes, and seconds." She rested her leg on the edge of the tub and ran a loofa along it.

AJ shot her a blank stare, surprised by her lucky guess. Then he thought about the seven months and thirteen days. "How the hell do you know my birthday? And how the hell did you calculate it to the day so fast?"

Jillian grinned. "I'm psychic and good with math, Abraham Jerusalem?"

AJ smirked while sliding off his shorts and briefs. "You're good with math and full of shit. How do you know my birthday?"

Jillian scooted up making room for him in the tub. "Condom, second drawer on the left."

AJ grabbed the condom and stepped into the tub between Jillian's legs.

"Put it on."

AJ shook his head. "I'm going to fuck your mouth first."

She raised a single brow, looking up at him. "Interesting choice of foreplay given my ... *need*. Besides, the only way your cock will be in my mouth is if your wrists are hand-cuffed behind your back." Jillian grabbed the condom from him and rolled it on.

AJ fought his clash of needs—the one to break her and the one to be broken. He wanted to punish her for refusing him ... threatening him. Then there was the part of him that wanted her to lose her own control. The look in her eyes when she broke his flesh was intoxicating. It had become almost as addictive to him as it was to her. Those thoughts weren't his, but they were in his head. He didn't know how they got there, or what they would end up doing to him, but they demanded his attention. The nagging, the taunting ... he wanted to shoot them, slide a knife along their throat, or blow them up, but they were too elusive.

"Nails..." her voice broke and she finished with a whisper "...or teeth?" She closed her eyes and swallowed.

AJ gritted his teeth, feeling that familiar tick in his jaw. He never pushed to know why Jillian was so messed-up. Not knowing took away accountability, and he didn't want to feel responsible for fixing her. If he couldn't fix himself, there was no way he could fix anyone else. But she had this need and the regret in her face proved that it wasn't a choice she was making. She was powerless to it.

His eyes drifted to the candles and soap bottles along the ledge of the tub. "Why not your razor?"

Jillian's eyes snapped open. "*Never* with a blade! Understood?"

He didn't ... he didn't understand any of it. But when he saw a tear trail down her cheek, it didn't matter. AJ tore off the condom and tossed it in the trash then sank into the water. He pulled her to him so her back leaned against his chest. Wrapping his arms around her, he kissed the top of her head.

"Don't hate me for not asking why," he whispered, feeling like a coward.

Jillian nodded.

CHAPTER TWENTY-TWO

JILLIAN CLOSED her eyes then opened them, over and over again. They were on springs loaded with anxiety and just wouldn't stay shut. The man showed complete detachment and restraint from prying into her behavioral issues, then crawled in bed with her. No sex. No banter. Just the simple offering of his warm body next to hers.

"You're not going to sleep are you?" He flattened his palm to her belly and drew her even closer. "You don't want me to stay."

Jillian wiggled in his arms until she was turned facing him. She kissed his neck. "I do want you to stay."

"But you're not going to sleep and it's already almost two in the morning."

"I'll go sleep on the couch, then come back in with you after I get a few hours of sleep."

AJ mumbled a few indecipherable words as he released Jillian and rolled to his back. "I'm not sleeping alone in *your* bed while you go sleep on the couch. That's too fucked-up … even for me." He circled his fingers over his temples. "You don't trust me."

Jillian sat up and straddled him, feeling him instantly grow hard between her legs. "I don't trust myself."

He grabbed her hips and slid her back and forth along his shaft. "You can't hurt me."

She closed her eyes and moved her left hand down her belly, pressing her fingers over his until he took the hint and started massaging her clitoris.

He rocked his hips up into her allowing his erection to slide against her wet sex. "You like this?" His voice was deep and growing thicker with each word.

"God ... yes." She felt so sleepy and equally as turned on. It may have been the spell cast by the early morning hour, or her body reaching its point of exhaustion, but she fell victim to his touch that felt like the whisper of a dream. "Please ..."

"Please what?" he stilled his hips and slipped two fingers inside her.

"Don't ... stop." She reached for his erection but he grabbed her hand.

"It's just for you." He moved her hand to meet his, both of them stimulating her sex. "You're so fucking sexy."

She rocked into his hand, wet with arousal. He slid a third finger in as she moaned, her muscles clenching him tight.

"That feels ... good ... so good ..."

"Show me, sexy. Show me how good." He slid his hand up her chest and circled her nipple with the pad of his thumb, syncing to the rhythm of his other thumb against her clit.

An orgasm seized her body, sending uncontrolled spasms so deep she felt them shake her bones. Her brain fogged like a night after Heineken, but her body spasmed with pleasure that came in waves until she collapsed on his chest. After a few minutes of AJ tracing circles on her back, she yawned and closed her eyes—for hours.

Jillian dreamed of her boys and her brother. She saw her parents alive for the last time and her friend's body mutilated and tossed aside like a piece of trash. Then she saw Four and his dark buzzed hair, hazel eyes, and perfect teeth. He was by all accounts sexy and alluring, especially in his combat fatigues. The Ted Bundy type that could manipulate girls into driving for hours to meet him. The kind that lived in a neighborhood of poverty but came from wealth and had a message to send to the world. He was the black sheep, the one that would never amount to anything. But he became more famous than anyone else in his affluent family ... he died a serial killer. He left his mark and he left it in blood.

As the sun first announced its presence, AJ shifted to scoot a sleeping Jillian off his chest. She felt large hands around her arms and became aware of her naked body. *Large hands gripping her arms. Naked arms. Naked body.* Her pounding heart sounded like an alarm. *"Sorry, doll ... but you were an unexpected surprise. Two for one."*

"Fuck! Goddammit! Oh ... fucking, fucking hell!" AJ roared.

"What the heck?" Jackson's voice drew near.

Jillian rapidly blinked as everything came into focus. Her naked body sat astride his. AJ's face was covered in blood—blood on his hands that were cupping his nose, blood on the sheets, blood everywhere.

"Sorry ... I'm so sorry ..."

"Get dressed." Jackson pulled her off AJ. "Let me see."

AJ shook his head, one hand stayed on his nose while the other grabbed for the sheet to cover his naked body.

"Jesus, AJ, just let me see!" Jackson pulled AJ's hand

away from his nose. "Looks broken and you're bleeding ... a lot. Jillian, get a towel and some ice."

Jillian stood naked behind Jackson like a statue. She couldn't move, not even a blink.

Jackson looked over his shoulder. "Jillian! Get some ice and a towel. Then get your ass dressed."

She swallowed and nodded slowly.

"I'm fine." AJ pulled himself up to sitting. More blood gushed from his nose.

"You're not, but you will be after we take you to the hospital."

Jillian returned with several towels and a bag of ice. "Oh God ..." she grimaced seeing AJ's crooked, bloody nose "...I'm so sorry."

He glared at her as Jackson brought the towel and ice to AJ's nose.

"Get his clothes," Jackson said.

"He just came over in shorts. No shoes or shirt."

"Just grab him something of mine."

Two hours later they left the emergency room. AJ's nose was reset and the bleeding finally stopped. Jillian had been incessant with her apologies, but AJ ignored her.

"It's been a long night, Jill. Just leave him alone. He'll come around," Jackson whispered as they walked to the car.

"He won't even look at me."

"Give. It. Time."

Jillian stared out her window the whole way home. Emotions blurred in her head like the city lights that passed by. Before Jackson had Woody in park, AJ hopped out and walked home.

"Don't," Jackson called as Jillian chased him.

"Go home," AJ mumbled.

"AJ—"

He turned. "You broke my fucking nose!"

Jillian blinked back her emotions and nodded once. "I'm sorry. I shouldn't have let you stay."

"No. You shouldn't have broken my nose."

"I was startled."

"By me?"

"By my past."

AJ closed his eyes and exhaled. "I'm not going to ask ... I just ... don't want to deal with it."

"I wouldn't tell you if you did."

He turned and opened his front door.

"I didn't bite you—" she murmured the words as if they mattered.

AJ turned.

"Or claw you," she whispered.

AJ laughed a little. "Tell my nose that."

THE WHINEY FIRST two stairs creaked announcing Jillian's arrival back home. He waited for her, knowing it wouldn't be long. No man with even half a testicle would let a woman break his nose then crawl into his bed.

Her posture sagged under a cloak of self-deprecation. "Break my nose," she mumbled, eyes cast downward.

"I'm not breaking your nose." Jackson unwrapped his hands.

She glanced up in confusion. "What are you doing?"

"We're not sparring. I thought you needed it, but now I see you just want me to punish you." He shook his head and walked past her. "I know you won't fight back. You'll stand there and let me beat the shit out of you. No thanks."

"Do you like your life here?"

Jackson paused halfway up the stairs. "Yes."

"Why?"

"Because it means I'm alive."

"Ask me." The sadness in her voice suffocated all other emotion.

"No."

"Why not?"

He closed his eyes. Why did she do this to him? Why did she do this to herself? "Because I know what you'll say."

"Then tell me."

"No." He continued up the stairs.

"Tell me!"

Leaning against the wall at the top of the stairs, he gently tapped the side of his head against it. "Do you like living here? No. Why? Because it means you're alive. Happy now?" He felt her at his back.

"What if I never find it again?"

Jackson turned, wrapping his arms around her body as she sank into him. "You won't find it again. What you had with Luke happens once in a lifetime. But I think you'll find something different ... something good."

She traced the cross tattoo on his arm. "When?"

"When you stop replaying your past."

"AJ hates me."

"He doesn't. But could you blame him if he did?"

"His face is going to scare people for quite some time. His eyes are going to be black and blue, *and* he's going to catch shit from everyone when they find out a girl broke his nose."

Jackson chuckled. "Yeah, that won't be happening. He'll say something like he singlehandedly saved Omaha from a terrorist attack, but I can promise you he won't be telling *anyone* you broke his nose."

"You men have such fragile egos."

He kissed the top of her head. "Yes, we do. But I'll deny that I ever admitted it."

"I'd better go clean up the crime scene."

"Jill?"

She stopped at her bedroom door. "Yes?"

"We can get you help. Knox said—"

"I've got this." She chuckled. "I know what you saw didn't look like progress, but had I not let him stay, he would have left unscathed."

"He's not without his own set of skills and *issues*. He could have hurt you."

"You wouldn't have let that happen."

"No, I wouldn't have, but I'm not always going to be in the next room when you're with him."

She sighed. "I've got this."

"I hope so."

THERE WASN'T a Hallmark card that expressed the appropriate sorry-I-broke-your-nose-yesterday apology. Instead, Jillian opted for brunch. She made a complete mess of the kitchen then packed everything in a bag to take next door.

"Lucky for you he probably can't smell anything today." Jackson tossed back a Red Bull.

"You act like I have zero cooking skills." She set the bag by the front door and shoved her feet into her red boots.

"I'm not acting. You do have zero cooking skills."

"I bet AJ and Cage like what I made."

"Are you wearing a bra today?"

"No."

"Then they'll gut it down with a smile. Well ... Cage

228

will. AJ has seen you naked; it's going to take more than a thin shirt and nipples to make him blow smoke up your ass today."

"Thanks for the tiara and fairy dust."

"Anytime, princess."

Jillian prayed Cage would answer the door. She needed an ally before facing AJ, in case the brunch and nipples weren't enough.

No such luck.

Jillian grimaced. "Hi. Uh, I made brunch for you and Cage."

"He's not here," AJ replied in a flat tone.

"Okay, then I made brunch for you."

"I'm not hungry."

She opened the screen door and set the bag by his feet. "I'm sorry. I know it doesn't change the way your face looks or feels today, but I am."

Jillian couldn't read his expression, probably due to the redness and swelling in his face. Regardless, he looked angry and unforgiving, and the moment bled awkwardness.

"So..." she shrugged "...I guess I'll go now."

AJ remained stoic.

Jillian stepped outside and took two steps before turning around and throwing open the screen door. "No. You know what? I'm not leaving. Be pissed at me, fine! Be a jerk about it, fine! But *do* something! Yell at me, cuss me out, hit me for God's sake, break my nose, but don't just stand here like you don't give a shit about me. I don't want to be *that* person—the one who broke your nose. But that's who I am right now."

AJ blinked several times like he was contemplating her words. She watched his hands clench and relax several times. He was going to hit her, she just knew it. AJ moved his arm and she flinched, closing her eyes to ready herself for the impact.

She sucked in a quick breath when his knuckles feathered across her cheekbone.

"What's in the bag?"

She opened her eyes and smiled as a wave of relief soothed her nerves. She covered his hand on her cheek and turned her head, pressing her lips to his palm. "Frittata, blueberry muffins, and orange juice."

He bent down and kissed her slowly. Jillian felt tears sting her eyes. A punch would have hurt less.

"You forgive me?" she whispered against his lips.

"Yes." AJ trapped her bottom lip between his teeth. Jillian's eyes widened. His lips curled into a grin as he released her, then he carried the bag to the kitchen.

"Where's young buck?"

AJ handed her a plate and sat down at the table. "He went for a jog."

"What did he say about your nose?" Jillian poured the juice into their glasses.

"He hasn't seen me yet. He left a note."

"What are you going to say?"

AJ held his juice glass up to the light. "I don't know what I'm going to tell him." He shook his head. "What is this?"

"Orange juice."

"It's barely orange."

Jillian took a sip of hers. It tasted like shit, but she swallowed and smiled. "I thought Cage would be here too and I only had a third of a jug left so I just filled it to the top with water."

AJ set it back down without taking a sip. Then he took a bite of the blueberry muffin after inspecting it for a few moments with apprehension in his eyes. His face wrinkled. When he took a swig of the orange juice to swallow it down, she knew he wasn't impressed.

"What did you put in these?"

She pinched off a piece of hers and dropped it in her mouth. It was shit too. "Multigrain raisin bread, almond milk, eggs, sugar, olive oil."

"Bread? Why did you use bread to make blueberry muffins and where are the blueberries?"

She shrugged. "I didn't have any flour so I used bread, which is made from flour, and I didn't have any blueberries so that's why I used the raisin bread."

"They taste like crap."

Jillian popped another piece in her mouth and gagged it down just to prove that they didn't taste like crap, which of course they did. "Whatever you do don't sugar coat it."

"I won't." AJ poked his fork at the frittata. "Are there eggs in here?"

Jillian rolled her eyes. "*Yes.*"

He took a small bite. "What the ..." He spit out the bite into his napkin. "It's gritty and crunchy and what the hell is the brown stuff?"

"Fake bacon. And the gritty stuff might be egg shells. A few of them got away from me."

He grabbed both of their plates and scraped everything into the garbage.

"Hey, I wasn't done."

He put the plates in the dishwasher and emptied the juice down the drain. "You know those people who say they can't cook but still manage to throw a decent meal together?"

"I suppose." Jillian watched him, not knowing where he was going with that question.

231

"Well, you're not one of those people."

"Ouch." She crossed her arms over her chest and fake pouted.

"And the only thing you're worse at than cooking is acting. I'd *love* to offend you. Maybe then you'd stop selling all those kinky toys, or start wearing clothes to the mailbox, or censor your words around strangers. So don't act offended that I think your cooking tastes like shit."

Jillian started unbuttoning her white sleeveless blouse.

AJ made a nervous glance at the door. "What are you doing?"

"I don't think we verbally communicate that well, so show me your thoughts and I'll show you mine. Besides, this *is* something I'm good at ... at least you've never complained."

"Don't do this. Cage could walk through that door—oh for the love of..." he massaged his temples "...where is your bra?"

Jillian smiled as she exposed her bare breasts. "Take your shirt off. Let's see who has a better 'half dozen.' Greta said—"

"Stop! Don't say her name with your shirt off."

Jillian giggled.

He grabbed her shirt and began buttoning it up. She snaked her hands under his shirt and let her fingers trail along his abs that were worthy competition.

"Tell me what AJ stands for," she whispered, brushing her lips across his T-shirt over his pecs.

"No."

She moved her hand down and stroked him over his jeans. AJ closed his eyes and sucked in a tight breath as his hands lingered on the middle button of her blouse.

"Tell me your name and I'll scream it when you're fucking me against the wall."

"It's Aric James, and please wait until I'm gone to scream it."

Jillian bit her lips together and closed her eyes as AJ jumped back like she burned him.

"Cage—"

It was the first time Jillian had ever seen AJ that flustered.

Cage grinned at Jillian as she peeked open one eye. "Told ya he likes you."

She nodded with a bit of a grimace as her fingers made nimble moves to finish buttoning her shirt.

"She didn't mean—" AJ stumbled over his words.

"I did," she deadpanned, shooting AJ a don't-you-dare-pretend-this-isn't-happening look.

Cage looked around the corner at his father. "Jeez, what the hell happened to your nose."

"My foot slipped out of my hanging giddy-up stirrups and broke his nose."

"Jesus, Jillian!" AJ rested one hand on his hip and scratched his head as he bowed it in embarrassment.

"Forget I asked." Cage pointed toward the stairs. "I'm going to go shower." He headed up the stairs. "By the way, if he won't let you scream his name, I'm good with you screaming mine." Cage shot her a cocky smirk over his shoulder.

"Cage!" AJ growled.

After they heard the bathroom door shut, Jillian sauntered over to AJ.

"Aric James..." she tugged on his shirt until he bent down a breath away from her lips "...and here I thought it must stand for something like Alice Jane because your parents were hoping you were a girl."

"Shut up."

Jillian grinned. "Make me," she whispered a second before his mouth covered hers.

CHAPTER TWENTY-THREE

JILLIAN SPENT the next three nights with AJ, or as Jackson learned the hard my-sister's-next-door-screaming way, "Aric James!" The sex was intense, sometimes brutal. It was never slow love making; it was a battle, a war of emotions in physical form. Eventually, they'd find solace in the entanglement of their exhausted, naked bodies until it was time to sleep—in separate beds.

Jillian wanted to believe that she was helping AJ, but mostly she felt like she was using him. And maybe he was using her. And maybe that made it OK.

"AJ asked me to go with him to Portland. His dad is giving Cage his truck so he asked me to keep him company since Cage can't go because of practice." Jillian looked up from the pile of laundry at Lilith asleep in her recliner. "I haven't told Jackson that I'm thinking of going because he will freak out. I might just leave him a note."

She hugged the warm towel from the dryer to her chest and sighed. "It's just been sex and banter ... lots and lots of banter, but now this trip invite changes things. I'm going to meet his parents and that's where I lose it. Meeting the family and seeing a guy through his parents' eyes changes everything. Sometimes for the better, sometimes for the worse. With Luke it was both. They made me love him ... then they made me leave him."

Day

JESSICA WAITED by the curb with her purse and a small suitcase. Her whole body trembled with excitement. She was going to Tahoe with Luke *and his GTO!* It was a close tie as to which one excited her the most. The powerful engine rumbled before she saw the black top come into view. She swore the ground beneath her shook like a mild earthquake as Luke pulled up next to the sidewalk.

"Can I drive?" She jumped up and down as he got out and opened the trunk. It was very uncharacteristic behavior for her, but Luke *and* the GTO had her ready to do cartwheels down the hill.

"No." He grabbed her suitcase and tossed it in the trunk.

She got in and felt the familiar car orgasm building as the seat vibrated to the purr of the engine. "But at some point you're going to let me drive, right?"

"Nope." Luke looked over and smiled all GQ at her: perfect hair, sexy shades, killer smile, plaid short-sleeve button down shirt, dark jeans, and Nike's that looked fresh out of the box. Her panties were doomed.

"You look edible." She winked at him then slid on her sunglasses as he put it in gear.

Luke flipped down his visor to block the setting sun then pulled away from the curb. "Thanks. It's a bit of a disturbing compliment from you, but you're still not driving."

"So what's in Tahoe? You've been so vague this week about our 'field trip.'"

"You'll see."

"Are you secretly whisking me away for a weekend of sexual healing with your magical penis?"

Luke didn't even crack a smile, which was unfair because her comment was not only flattering but funny.

He made a quick sidelong glance. "How did you find out about my magical penis?"

Jessica grinned. That's all she could do. Luke had a way of making her talk, but he also had a way of rendering her speechless. Those speechless moments ... they were the ones Jessica mentally logged into her *Reasons I'm Falling in Love with Dr. Luke Jones* journal that she kept in her head, and every time she added to it she moved it down a shelf closer to her heart.

"I think it was your Tumblr page ... Cockfessions of an Argyle Sock Addict. It was just by accident that I *came* across your page. I've never seen so many animated GIFs of girls having sex with argyle socks pulled up to their knees. That's some serious kink, Jones."

"So you're into online porn?"

She slipped off her shoes and hugged her knees to her chest. "Absolutely. It's a reminder that there are people in the world that are fucked-up more than me. Pun intended."

"Why do you think you're fucked-up?"

She looked out her window and shook her head. "I don't know. Ask my shrink."

"And what do you think he'd tell me?"

"*She*. My shrink is a female. There's no way in hell I'd

see a male shrink." Jessica smirked. "I've been down that road before. He made me iron his underwear."

"*Socks*," Luke corrected.

"Then we had sex in his closet."

"*Kissed*."

"Then he shoved me off my bike ten feet from the finish line because he didn't want me to win."

"You were never going to beat me."

"I totally would have. Then he came to my apartment and I think had I not been covered in my own blood we would have had sex that night."

Luke didn't respond. Instead the air became thick and heavy until he cranked down his window. Jessica had drank and bled too much that night to make sense of Luke's visit. He left his date—a sure thing—to come to her apartment. She remembered feeling something from him that wasn't empathy, or the need to fix her, or anything that she'd ever felt with him before. That night all she saw was a man who wanted a woman ... plain and simple. But until that very moment she hadn't let herself believe it ... she hadn't let herself *hope*.

The rest of the ride was filled with nothing but the high-pitched scream of the tires over worn pavement. They stopped for gas and drinks, but the conversation never ignited again.

"We're here."

Jessica opened her eyes while sitting up. She blinked away the sleep, then squinted at the lit sign, the only thing she could see in the surrounding darkness. "We're staying at a bed and breakfast?"

"Yes, but it's under renovation so it's not open to the public."

"So ... we're squatters?"

Luke chuckled. "No. I know the owners."

"Oh, friends?"

"Sort of." He shifted in the driver's seat so he was facing her. "What I'm about to tell you, you have to promise not to read into it, or get too excited, or anything like that. Okay?"

"Is it haunted? Just going to be honest. I used to love haunted houses, but Four kind of ruined them for me."

A sadness stole Luke's facial features for a brief moment. "No. It's not haunted. It belongs to my parents."

Jessica's eyes widened. "Oh ... you brought me to meet—"

Luke shook his head. "No. That's what I was afraid of. That's why I told you not to read into this. While technically you will meet my family, I didn't bring you here to meet them. I brought you here because I thought you needed to escape for a couple of days and this is where I come when I need to decompress."

"But they know you're coming this weekend?"

"Yes."

"And they know you're bringing me?"

"Yes."

"So you told them I'm your patient?"

"No. You're not my patient. I told them you're my friend and you've been dealing with some personal issues and that you needed to get away for a few days."

"Do you bring a lot of female 'friends' here?"

"No."

"So just be honest. They're going to think I'm your girlfriend."

"Possibly."

"And you're okay with this?"

"No. But it's only for two days and so if they don't want to believe me, in spite of the truth I've told them that there's nothing going on between us, then I'm not going to make an issue of it. They'll get the picture when they never see you again after this weekend."

Jessica unfastened her seatbelt. "Ouch! That's a little harsh. You make it sound like I'm dying."

They grabbed their suitcases out of the trunk.

"What are you going to do when *they* fall in love with me?"

"Hypnosis." Luke opened the front door.

"You can do that?"

"How do you think I got you to iron my socks."

"Shut up," Jessica mumbled when she stepped inside.

"Luke is that you? We're in here," a woman's voice echoed to the entry.

Luke deposited their bags by the stairs and led her down the hallway.

"Luke," Jessica whispered.

He turned.

"What if they ask us how we met?"

"Hmm ... we train together. Good?"

She nodded.

"There's our brilliant son," the same woman's voice cheered.

A mumbling of "gee thanks" rang in unison from the unexpected gathering. Jillian made a quick count of the group that sat around the table playing cards—eight.

"Oh, you know what I mean." The tall woman with short black and gray hair tried to quiet the group as she stood to hug Luke.

"Hi, Mom." Luke kissed her cheek. "Everyone, this is my friend, Jessica Day."

Jessica smiled at *everyone*, exactly six more than she thought she'd be meeting.

"Hi, Jessica." His mom offered her hand. "I'm Felicity." Her eyes lingered on Jessica's arm. "What happened?"

Jessica twisted her arm to look at the cut. "Oh, just a little spill on my bike. My legs are much worse."

Felicity looked down but Jessica's scars were covered by her capris. The man beside her cleared his throat.

"Sorry." Felicity winked at him. "This is Tom, Luke's dad."

Tom nodded with a bright smile. "Nice to meet you, Jessica." He shared Luke's deep blue eyes but his hair was thick and blond, very Robert Redford.

"Next to him," Felicity continued, "is our son Lane, and his wife, Anne, then our daughter Lara, and her fiancé, Drake, then our youngest son, Liam, and his girlfriend, Zoe."

Jessica struggled for words. "Um ... nice to meet all of you." She nudged Luke's arm and gritted her teeth through a huge smile. "You didn't tell me you have three siblings ... all with names that start with L."

Everyone laughed.

"We were high on something." Tom winked at Felicia.

"Actually, I have four siblings," Luke corrected. "Where's Lake?"

"She's staying at a friend's house tonight," Lara answered.

"You two want in on the next game?" Felicity asked.

"Sure, we'll go get settled upstairs and be right back." Luke motioned with his head.

"You're both in the adjoining lake view rooms." Felicity called as they reached the top of the stairs.

Luke plopped Jessica's suitcase on her bed. The room was a shades-of-yellow paint palate: the bedding, the curtains, the wallpaper.

"We'll share the bathroom that connects our rooms. So lock both doors when you use it."

Jessica looked out the window at the lake under the spotlight of the full moon. "I have nothing to hide, no need to lock the door." She looked over her shoulder and grinned.

"Jessica," Luke warned.

She turned and plunked down on the bed. "So ... Luke, Lane, Lara, Liam, and Lake. Oh. My. God."

Luke grinned like a shy child.

"And you're the oldest? And it's clear that you have your mom thinking you're the smartest. You're welcome by the way. I wanted to correct her on *that* one, but I didn't."

"Yes, I'm the oldest. And thank you for your self-control. Let's go."

BUTTERED POPCORN MIXED with laughter filled the air as the cards were dealt around the Jones's dining room table. The game was Hearts. The players were the most engaging and fun group of people Jessica had ever met.

"So, Jessica, what do you do?" Tom asked.

Jessica sorted through her cards. "Only the most extraordinary and exciting job in the world. I'm an actuary intern."

She looked up from her cards at the blank stares. "Basically, I'm a math geek that gathers and analyzes statistics to determine the consequences of risk in the future for insurance and pension programs."

The blank expressions continued. She needed to come up with something before the crickets took over.

"Can you believe *this* guy..." she jabbed her thumb in Luke's direction "...has like fifty pair of argyle socks?"

The room erupted into laughter. Luke looked at Jessica with a really-you-had-to-go-there look.

The evening progressed with Luke's family sharing some of his secrets, including his Star Wars obsession, his first time using a nail gun that ended in three of his fingers being nailed together, and his addiction to German chocolate cake. Jessica took mental notes for blackmailing him in the future. Everyone seemed content with their triathlon training explanation for their five month friendship.

"If you leave the windows cracked in the bedrooms it could get chilly, so there's extra blankets in the closet," Felicity called from the sofa where she sat cuddled in Tom's arms.

The rest of the family had left. Jessica was surprised that everyone except Luke lived in a ten mile radius of their parents' bed and breakfast. She loved their close family. It made her feel at home. Jessica only had one sibling, but their family of four was just as close. They were all survivors and always there for each other.

"Thanks, Mom," Luke called as he ushered Jessica toward the stairs.

"Good night." Jessica waved to Luke's parents.

"Jones ... Jones ... Jones ... Your family is amazing." Jessica flopped back on her bed as Luke stood in the doorway. "I don't even know where to begin. First, your dad's name is Tom Jones ... Tom ... Jones." Jessica rolled to her side, wearing a huge grin. "And all your siblings look like your dad with his blond hair, except you, the black sheep with your black hair, fifty pair of argyle socks, and fancy condo in San Francisco, which is way outside of the ten mile radius of the Jones' family circle."

Luke grabbed an extra blanket from the closet and tossed it on the bed. "Lake has black hair. I have *twenty* pair of argyle socks. My condo's not that fancy, and I'm far from the black sheep of my family. Now, good night."

"But your dad's name …"

Luke turned before exiting.

"*That's* pretty cool, right?"

Luke smirked before closing the door behind him.

He was a fucking unicorn. A unicorn with argyle socks, but no less a unicorn. It was a fantasy at best, but if she could catch him, Jessica knew her dreams would come true.

CHAPTER TWENTY-FOUR

Under four layers of blankets protecting her from the cool morning breeze, Jessica slept in past her usual waking time. A poking on her arm brought her out of her sleep like an animal under attack. There was a grunt, several snaps, and flailing limbs as she tumbled to the ground with a pool stick busted in three different areas.

"Good morning."

Breathless, she fought away the tangled hair that strangled her face, only to catch Luke sitting in a chair by the vanity mirror. "What are you doing?"

He smiled. "Waking you for our run."

"By poking me with a pool stick?" She grabbed one of the broken pieces and flicked it at him.

"Yes." He caught it and ran his finger over the splintered wood.

"Why?"

"Just a hunch."

"About?" She widened her eyes.

"About how you might react if someone or *something* brought you out of a possible dream state or startled you."

Jessica crawled back onto the bed. "And so?"

Luke waved the broken stick at her. "*And so* I was right to sacrifice the pool stick instead of one or all of my limbs."

She ran her hands through her hair. "Four kicked me in the ribs to wake me up. My hands and legs were zip tied, but I struggled to break free from the stabbing pain in my stomach and ribs so eventually the zip ties rubbed directly on my wrist bones." Jessica held up her wrists to show him her pearly faded scars. "The moral of the story is I don't like to be woken by touch. But you already knew that."

Luke shook his head. "I didn't. But anyone who scopes out a room for possible ways to kill everyone in it probably doesn't react well to surprises. I was just testing my theory."

"Are you afraid of me?" Jessica asked, just above a whisper as she dropped her chin to her chest. He was the one person she didn't want to scare.

"No."

She looked up. His eyes locked with hers. No flinch. Not even a blink of doubt.

"But then why—" She pointed to the broken stick.

"Who was the first victim to realize they shouldn't wake you?"

She sucked in a breath and willed all other emotions to stay in check. "Are we going for a run together by the lake?"

It was a rare occasion for Luke to let his professional mask slip and show any sort of emotion, but that was one of the few times Jessica saw sympathy in his eyes. She hated it.

"Yes." He stood and looked at her like a puzzle with a few missing pieces. "Get dressed. I'll meet you downstairs."

When the door clicked shut Jessica released the breath she'd been holding. Until Luke said it to his family the previous night, Jessica hadn't focused on the fact that they'd known each other for over five months. She wondered if any other psychiatrist would have known her whole story by that point. Was therapy like ripping off a Band-Aid or peeling an onion? The truth: She wasn't ready to tell Luke everything. Dr. Jones would have done his job and walked away. She didn't want Luke to walk away, but she feared giving him too much too fast would have him sprinting in the opposite direction.

Their relationship was a mystery. He let many unofficial days of therapy pass without her saying a word about her past. Maybe discussing random and completely irrelevant topics was a comforting white noise for him while he focused on his crossword puzzles. She wondered more than once why he allowed zero progresses for days and sometimes weeks, but as long as he kept opening his door to her she wasn't going to risk asking why.

"Good morning, Jessica. Can I get you some breakfast? It's my specialty." Felicity greeted her with a warm smile.

"Smells amazing, but can you save me some? Luke and I are going for a run."

"Absolutely. Oh..." she grimaced seeing Jessica's legs "... that does look painful."

"Nah ... Where is he, by the way?"

Felicity let her worried gaze linger a few more seconds on Jessica's legs, then pointed out the kitchen window. "He's out back with Tom."

Jessica nodded as she tied her shoes. "Thanks."

"How'd you sleep?"

"Too good. The room was cool and I was in a warm comfy spot under a heap of covers. I didn't want to wake up."

"You didn't miss the sounds of the big city?" Felicity handed her a bottled water.

"The city, yes, the sounds, no. I might send Luke back to reality tomorrow and stay here until you kick me out."

Felicity smiled with a playful wink. "Fine by me. Have a good run."

"Thanks, we will."

Jessica walked around the side of the house, coming to a stop when she saw Luke and Tom talking in front of an old shed, Tom sipping a cup of coffee, Luke fiddling with the cap to his bottled water. The sight of Luke in a T-shirt, running shorts, and a ball cap left her feeling warm and a bit dizzy. She closed her eyes for a brief moment. For every intelligent, strong-willed woman in the world there was one man that could render her speechless, make her sweat, and consume her thoughts. Luke was that guy for her.

"Hey, young lady." Tom noticed Jessica as he looked over Luke's shoulder.

She smiled and when Luke turned and gave her a huge grin that was so very un-Dr. Jones, she pleaded with her heart to calm down and play it cool so she wouldn't pass out.

"Good morning." She walked down the small hill toward them.

Tom grinned, his eyes making a quick inspection. "For the love of God, how'd you get all those muscles on such a little body?"

Jessica shrugged, surprised that it was her muscles that caught his attention and not her scabbed-over legs. "A few squats here and there, maybe a crunch or two."

Tom laughed. "Oh, that's all, huh?"

Luke adjusted his cap as if to hide his own wandering eyes. "We should get going before it gets too warm."

Jessica smiled. "Bye, Tom."

"Show him how it's done, young lady."

Jessica nudged Luke as they walked up the hill. "Oh, I will."

"You do realize I'm not Kelly and you're going to have to make two strides for every one of mine."

"God, I love it when you talk my language. You know numbers are my foreplay."

"Just get going." Luke shook his head and started jogging down the road.

Jessica followed a few steps behind. "Don't worry, Jones, I won't pass you until the last mile. The view is too good from back here."

"I feel violated."

Everything inside Jessica came to life. The playful side of Luke was like a shooting star—there and gone in a blink but leaving a lingering feeling of hope.

"I can take the lead and let you violate me if you'd like."

Luke glanced back at her.

"Don't give me that look, Jones. You know how long I've gone without sex. If I were you I'd lock my bedroom door tonight."

Luke picked up the pace as if he could prevent her from catching him. She toyed with him for nearly seven miles, sometimes allowing a sizable gap between them, other times riding on his heels. As the sandy oasis, an unofficial beach, just off the road came into view, Jessica closed the gap.

"First one to the beach gets to dive into the water naked."

"No."

Jessica pushed past him. "Yes."

"Jess—no!" Luke grunted the words through quick labored breaths.

Jessica finished with an all-out sprint. "Deep down ... I want you to beat me, Jones!" The second her shoes hit the sand, breaking the invisible finish line, she threw off her shirt and bra, continuing on toward the water.

"Jessica!"

A few feet before breaching the water, she turned and smiled as she removed her shoes and shorts. Luke dropped to his knees in the sand, bowing his head.

"I'm going in, Jones. Feel free to watch ... we'll call it your consolation prize."

A shrill squeal filled the air as she ran into the cool water several feet before making a shallow dive into the waves. For a few brief seconds she was free, liberated, and alive. She prayed to her God, *any* God that would listen. She prayed that the water would wash away all her problems and that she'd emerge a normal woman, a woman worthy of Luke Jones.

"Dammit, Jones," Jessica yelled with her first breath upon seeing him still kneeling in the sand, refusing to look at her. "You're such a killjoy." She pulled out her ponytail holder and rung out her hair as she walked toward him, collecting her clothes along the way. She stopped in front of him, clothes in one hand, shoes in the other.

"You're not supposed to get your stitches wet." At most he could've seen her feet, if his eyes had been open. But they weren't.

"You have a degree in medicine, yet you won't look at me?"

Luke remained still.

"Am I too short?" She slipped on her bra and top.

Headshake.

"Too many muscles ... too butch?" She stepped into her shorts.

Headshake.

"You prefer blondes?" She put on her socks and shoved her feet into her running shoes.

Headshake.

She squatted to tie her shoes. His eyes blinked open and met hers.

"Well then, I must just be too fucked-up in the head so I might as well tell you. The first person I attacked was my mother when she woke me up the day after I came home from the hospital. In turn, she spent two days recovering from a concussion and a broken rib."

That loving daughter turned monster bit her lips together, but it didn't keep the tears from bleeding down her cheeks as a sob escaped. Feeling required such vulnerability. It was all or nothing. She couldn't just take the good times, the happy memories. Life was an ebb and flow of pain and pleasure. One could not exist without the other.

With every blink, another teardrop faded into the sand between them. "I will never get married. I will never have children. I will never wake up in the arms of a lover. So here's what I have: a job that nobody understands, a random dating life where I never have sex with the same guy twice because really ... who sticks around after a roll in the hay with Count Dracula? My only option is some masochistic freak who gets off on that shit, but here's the thing: I don't. I don't want to be that person. I *hate* that person."

There was nothing but anger in her veins and a pounding pulse in her ears until Luke flipped her whole world on its head.

"You're so beautiful," he whispered.

"Fuck you. Don't you dare say that now." Jessica swiped away her tears as she stood.

Luke clasped her wrist and gave it a gentle tug like he was asking, not demanding. "Jessica?"

His paralyzing touch bled along her skin and seeped into her chest leaving a permanent mark. She lowered to her knees in front of him.

"I want to tell you that I prefer long dark hair, heavenly amber eyes, and a petite body: seductive, sexy, torturous. I want to tell you that a few minutes ago I would have rather gone blind than not looked at your naked figure. I want to tell you that I hate wine, yet I can't go to sleep until I've had one sip because that's what your lips tasted like that night we kissed. But I can't tell you any of that because what I want more than anything is to *help* you, and I can't do that from the bedroom." Luke rested his hands on her cheeks and his forehead on hers. "Because, Jessica, I *know* if I had you in my bed I would *never ... ever ...* want to leave," he whispered.

Jessica bit her trembling lip—hard. His words, the most beautiful pain ever, became the bane of her existence.

"I'll never be normal. Will I?"

Luke moved to his feet, dusting the sand off his legs then offering his hand to her. "Normal is subjective and boring."

She wanted to smile but it didn't quite make it to her lips. "Then I must be the most fascinating person in the world."

"You are. Let's go. I have a surprise for you." Luke lifted his hat, ran a hand through his matted hair, then repositioned it.

Jessica sighed. "I hope I like it more than you liked yours."

Luke grabbed his foot and stretched his quad. "I liked mine."

"Pfft ... you didn't even look at me."

Luke switched legs and smirked.

"What?" She tied her hair back again.

He turned, walking back toward the road. "I looked."

CHAPTER TWENTY-FIVE

KNIGHT

JILLIAN WAITED, fully dressed, under her sheets until she heard Jackson leave for his morning run. Then she retrieved her suitcase and purse from her closet. She knew there would be consequences, but the promise of them didn't stop her from saying yes to AJ. Yes to Portland. Yes to meeting his parents. Yes to everything.

"Good morning." AJ leaned against his Jeep. A rogue smile stole his lips.

She dropped her bags by their feet, wrapped her arms around his neck, and pulled him to her mouth. AJ hesitated for a second. He cared what the neighbors thought; she never did.

He kissed her, but pulled back when her tongue brushed his lips.

Jillian fisted his shirt. "Aric James, if you want me to get on the plane with you then you're going to have to kiss me like you fuck me."

His eyes searched hers. "How do I fuck you?"

She jumped up and wrapped her legs around his waist,

forcing him to hug her to his body. "Like your life depends on it."

Jillian kissed him again and AJ held nothing back. She loved the exhilaration she felt every time he claimed a part of her body with such unapologetic desire. A desire that felt like something much more than want. It was a need that brought her to life with a mind-numbing shot of anticipation and a heart-pounding jolt of fear.

"I want you," she breathed as his lips and tongue stroked her neck. He occupied her body. The perfect distraction from her mind.

He grazed his teeth along her carotid, teasing her, playing her game. "I know." He pulled her arms off his neck, releasing her to the ground.

"I know?" She gaped at him.

He grabbed her suitcase and tossed it in the back of his Jeep. "Yes, I know."

Jillian hopped in the passenger seat and he grinned at her as he turned the key.

"Cat got your tongue?"

Jillian pursed her lips to hide her smile. "Nope. We'll continue this conversation on the plane." She typed Jackson a quick message that he'd get when he got home.

Flying to Portland with AJ. Be back in 3 or 4 days. No need to worry.

"Who are you texting?"

Jillian slipped her phone in her purse. "Not that it's any of your business, Snoop Dogg, but I was just letting Jackson know about our plans."

"Snoop Dogg?"

"He's a rapper."

AJ pinned her with a quick sideways glance. "I know who he is." He grabbed her leg and squeezed it. "And just so you know ... I think over the past week I've definitely made you my business."

Jillian felt his touch like hot lava on her leg. With each passing day it became more difficult to tame her reaction to him. He'd come to know her in the only way anyone except Jackson could ever know Jillian Knight, and he accepted her —pierced lip-clawed back-broken nose type acceptance.

"We're having sex on the plane."

AJ removed his hand. "We're not."

"*Yes*, we are."

"I'm a highly decorated officer in the US Air Force. We will *not* be having sex on a commercial flight to Portland."

"What if I give you a merit badge for it?" Jillian smirked.

"No."

She squirmed a bit in her seat. All their talk had her vagina feeling very responsive. "Well you're at least going to get me off with your tongue."

AJ cleared his throat and adjusted himself. "You're not going to be able to talk this way around my parents."

"Well, then you'd better keep me satisfied so I'm not thinking about it all the time."

AJ didn't give her a verbal response, but his body was tense. There was frustration in his creased brow, and his jeans looked strained at the crotch. He was just how she liked him.

"Why didn't you tell Jackson about our plans before leaving?"

"He wouldn't have le—or wanted me to go."

"Were you going to say he wouldn't have *let* you go?"

"Yes, but that's not entirely true. There would have

been a verbal argument, a physical fight, and a monstrous guilt trip. I didn't want it ruining our trip, so I'm choosing to deal with him when I get back."

It was an uncharacteristically vulnerable move on her part. She didn't back down to Jackson, yet she found herself doing just that to protect her trip—her time—with AJ.

"Who taught you to fight?"

Jillian smiled. Could a lie be the truth if someone's life depended on it? "Our dad. He taught martial art classes and self-defense."

AJ nodded, seemingly content with her explanation. Every day he got a little more curious or bold with his questioning. He claimed to not want to know about her and why she was the way she was, but his actions and questions began to contradict his intentions to not care.

"So why is Jackson so overprotective of his sister who clearly has the ability to protect herself and a small village?"

Jillian chuckled. "Since our parents died, I'm all he has and he's all I have."

AJ's lips pulled into a firm line.

"Well, until you decided to make me your business."

"Business is good."

She laughed. "Cage would be proud. I do believe Mr. Serious is flirting ... actually *joking* with me."

In true Sarge style, AJ had to blow out the candle. "Well, don't get used to it. It never lasts."

Jillian stared at the entrance sign to the airport. Were she and AJ on that list of things that wouldn't last?

AJ MONAGHAN WAS TAKING a woman to his parents' house for the first time since his divorce. The invite wasn't to meet his parents, it was more for a travel companion. Meeting his parents was an unavoidable part of the trip. Dealing with Jillian's gifted talent of making him want to fuck her senseless with every word that fell from her snarky mouth also happened to be an unavoidable part of the trip.

"Do you mind if I sit by the window?" Jillian rested her hand on his chest as he lifted their bags into the overhead compartment. She did that a lot. It was an odd gesture and the hand of any other woman would have made him uncomfortable or even agitated, but he craved her touch. He craved everything about her.

"It's all yours."

"Thanks." She reached up on her toes and kissed his neck. He looked around to see if anyone was watching. Public displays of affection were part of who she was, never giving any consideration to onlookers. It made the promise or threat of her intentions for their flight that much more terrifying.

"Do you like to fly?"

She shut off her phone and shoved her purse under the seat in front of her. "I don't know. This will be my first time on a plane."

"You're kidding."

"Nope." She fastened her seat belt then gave him a smile.

"How is that possible?"

"Cars, trains, subways, boats ..." She leaned over and kissed him on the mouth, dragging his bottom lip between her teeth. "I'm so damn horny right now," she whispered over his lips.

He cleared his throat. "You're not nervous?"

"About sex on a plane?"

His brow tightened as he shook his head. "No, about flying. About not being in control of the plane."

"Nah, I'll be fine. I'll be in control of *something* or *someone*." She wet her lips.

The uncomfortable strain of his cock pushed against his jeans, growing worse by the second.

"Flying gets you there quicker."

Jillian stared ahead at the attendants making final preparations. "Maybe I like the journey better than the destination. Have you really never been in the Mile High Club?"

The older lady in front of AJ looked back. She wore a hearing aid that apparently worked just fine. He gave her a small apologetic smile. After she turned back around, leaving him with a nasty look, he leaned over and whispered in Jillian's ear.

"If you censor your words and the rest of your body for the duration of the flight, I'll find a place to fuck you nine ways to Sunday just as soon as we get off the plane."

She grinned, as only Jillian Knight would do. He made a warning and a promise, but from her smile he felt certain all she heard was the promise.

"I like the alliteration of seven ways to Sunday, grammatically speaking. However, in reference to your promise, nine is a much better number."

Ten minutes later they were in the air. Jillian showed no anxiety during takeoff and seemed content staring out the window. AJ leaned his chair back and closed his eyes, praying for an uneventful flight with the most unpredictable woman he had ever met.

Lulled to sleep by the mild turbulence, AJ woke when the flight attendant stopped in the aisle for their drink order.

She handed Jillian what looked like a mixed drink as Jillian handed her cash.

"Anything for you, sir?"

"Water." He glanced at Jillian. "Thought you were going to behave."

She took a sip then grinned. "Oh, I am—*Nine* ways to Sunday."

"Pretzels?"

AJ shook his head at the attendant.

"I'll take his." Jillian smiled.

"Are you enjoying your first time?" AJ asked.

She popped a pretzel in her mouth. "First time?"

"Flying."

"Oh ... uh, yeah, sure. Can you pilot a plane?"

"Not this one, but yes. I used to fly fighter planes."

"Missiles? Bombs?"

"Yes."

"And now?"

AJ tapped the empty plastic cup on his leg. "Now I advise with the Logistics and Readiness Squadron."

"Career military. Was it your dream?"

"I didn't sit around dreaming about my future. I just did it."

Jillian gulped the rest of her drink. "Yeah, my question was a bit more metaphorical, but whatever."

"Did you dream of selling ... what you sell?"

"Yes. My mom had at least a hundred erotica books in the study and my dad hid his subscription to Playboy in the bottom drawer of his tool chest. Our neighbor was a minister who was arrested for soliciting a prostitute, and my high school guidance counselor's ass landed in jail for selling photos online of the high school volleyball team taking showers in the locker room. No one ever figured out how he got them."

"There's a point to this?"

Jillian grinned. "Absolutely. My point is, I learned early on that sex sells. Like most people it took some time for me to follow my instincts, but here I am ... living the dream."

"You're not living the dream, but thanks for yet another entertaining story that I'm certain is one hundred percent fiction."

"What if it's not?" Jillian handed him her cocktail napkin that she'd been doodling on with a pen.

"What is this?" He knew what it looked like. Nothing about her should have been shocking any longer and yet, it was.

"Nine ways to Sunday."

He found the one person whose mind was more fucked-up than his, and she was hours away from meeting his parents. The only thing more messed-up than the drawing of two figures— one with its head between the legs of the other that was tied to a bed in four-point restraints—was how it stirred his cock to life.

AJ shoved it in his pocket. "God, you're twisted."

Jillian interlaced her fingers with his. "And yet, here we are ... together. Why is that?"

He released a heavy sigh. "I ask myself that question every damn day."

———

Hot stagnant air filled the room. It wasn't a five-star hotel, but for two hundred dollars AJ expected the air conditioner to work. Sweat beaded on his brow and trickled down his back that bowed from his arms being restrained behind the desk chair. The rope around each ankle chafed his skin every time he moved.

"You're a sadist."

Jillian rolled her eyes as she stood in her bra and panties, flipping through the TV channels. "Why does everyone say that?"

"I can only speculate why *everyone* says that, but I say it because you have me tied naked to the desk chair in a hotel room."

"Fair point." Her lips dipped into a frown at the screen. "There's nothing good on here." She left it on the hotel's information channel and turned up the volume.

"Does elevator music get you off?"

Jillian removed her bra and panties. "Asks the naked guy saluting me with a very impressive erection." She knelt down in front of him. "Hope you're not too uncomfortable. If you would have sprung for the suite with the four-poster bed, we'd both be more comfortable."

"I wasn't going to pay fifteen hundred dollars for a fucking blow job."

Jillian ran her hands up his legs then dragged them back down, letting her nails dig into his skin just shy of breaking it. AJ hissed.

"Then I'd say you haven't *really* had a blow job."

Jillian took him in her mouth and drew blood on his legs at the same time.

"Fuck!" he groaned, feeling the intense collision of pain and pleasure.

The chair creaked with protest as he bucked against the restraints. The rope sawed his wrists and ankles when he jerked his pelvis toward her, searching for a gag reflex she didn't seem to have. Her tongue licked and swirled as she kept her gaze locked on his. In that instant, she reached the pinnacle of sexy, unlike anything he had ever seen. His vision blurred a bit with each heavy blink as he felt himself getting closer.

She grinned with him still in her mouth then released him.

"For the love of God ..." he begged "... don't stop."

"Tell me you should have splurged for the suite."

"What?" He panted the word, feeling almost delusional. "Untie me."

Control—absolute physical control ran through his veins. It defined him, his career, his life. He'd never given such control to anyone before. Some perverse voice in his head convinced him to give it to Jillian. She was his kryptonite.

"Tell me you should have splurged for the suite."

"No." Every muscle fought the restraints. Every thought devised an escape.

Jillian glanced at the clock on the nightstand. "What time are your parents expecting us?"

AJ called his parents from the airport and told them not to pick them up because they had a few stops to make. The clock ticked with no mercy. He knew how it felt.

She slipped on his T-shirt and snatched the room key. "Have it your way. I'll be right back."

"Jillian!" he yelled over the nauseating elevator music.

She returned a few minutes later with a bucket of ice. "Now, let's try this again."

AJ was supposed to fuck her nine ways to Sunday. Jillian had other plans. Two hours later his dick felt in need of a cast and crutches, maybe even a wheelchair. Someone must have hypnotized and used word association with her. Nine ways to Sunday had to be a trigger for her horns to emerge, because she put him through hell. A woman sucking his dick with ice in her mouth gave new meaning to the word aroused. She brought him to the brink so many times until he conceded that he should have paid for the suite. Less than ten seconds later he came in her mouth, and even if the timing and purpose was inappropriate, he thanked God over and over again.

When she untied him, he charged at her like a bull out of its cage. What ensued after that was sexual grappling, both of them vying for the upper hand. It was—in its own right—combat, and that's why two-hours-and-nine-ways-to-Sunday later when they left the hotel room in shambles, AJ wondered if his dick had made its final performance ever.

Jillian signaled to the cab driver outside of the hotel. She looked perky ... fucking perky ... and full of energy. AJ looked and felt like a wounded soldier being dragged back to the barracks.

They slipped into the backseat of the cab. AJ managed to mumble his parents' address to the driver while Jillian nuzzled her nose in his neck.

"That was incredible. If I promise to be on my best behavior for the rest of the trip can we have an encore performance when we get home?"

There would be no encore performance—ever. At forty-two, AJ had the build and stamina of a thirty-year-old in top condition. Sadly, it was no match for Wonder Woman on steroids. He rubbed the rope burn marks on his wrists, which were nothing more than minor blemishes compared to the bite marks and claw scratches on other parts of his body. He looked like hell and the task of explaining any of it to his parents was daunting at best.

"Have you actually ever killed anyone?" he asked her.

The cabbie glanced at them in his rearview mirror.

She sat up straight. "Why would you ask me that?"

No, was the answer he was looking for.

"Look at me."

She stared out her window for a second too long. Then turned with a soft smile on her face. "Hmm?"

"You didn't answer my question."

"You didn't answer mine either." Her eyes shone bright with amusement as though the conversation was absurd.

Was it?

CHAPTER TWENTY-SIX

Jᴵᴸᴸᴵᴬᴺ Kɴᴵɢʜᴛ ʜᴀᴅ ɴᴇᴠᴇʀ ᴋᴵᴸᴸᴇᴅ anyone. Period. That
was the accurate answer to his question and to deliver that
answer, every thought, every move, every breath had to
embrace Jillian Knight. There was no room to flinch, pause,
or even swallow. Jillian Knight had never killed anyone.

AJ shook his head. "I shouldn't have asked that. I'm just
stressed about seeing my parents." He reached between the
seats and held her hand.

She stared at the red marks on his wrist. What kind of
barbaric person does what she did to him? How fucked-up
does a man have to be to allow a woman to do what she did?
Why did taking control feel like losing control?

"Are you stressed out because of me?"

"No. Yes … it's complicated."

She knew complicated. Jillian defined complicated.

"I'm sorry," she whispered.

"For what?"

"That you're taking *me* home to meet your parents
instead of someone more … normal."

AJ leaned over and kissed her cheek, and then her ear. "Normal's boring," he whispered back.

The pain in Jillian's chest from his words was almost indescribable. It triggered such vivid memories of Luke. She turned toward the window and the only thing she could see through the blurry passing of the city was Luke. Would he ever stop controlling her mind?

———

Day

IT WAS A SHED, not a surprise.

"Thank you?" Jessica's lips formed a tight smile as they stood in front of the old shed behind the house.

Lara loaned her a pair of work boots to go with Jessica's old jeans and faded red T-shirt.

"You ready to show the old man up?"

Jessica turned at the sound of Tom's voice. He handed her leather work gloves.

"Uh ..." she looked at Luke.

He grinned. "You're going to tear off the siding then reside the shed with my dad. Then I think he has an ax for you to chop down a few old dead trees."

"Felicity has a few easy projects inside too," Tom added.

"I-I'm good with this." She nodded. "But ... just to be clear. This is a gift and not a punishment for taking my clothes off in front of you, right?"

Tom cleared his throat. Luke's eyes darted to his, wide with surprise.

Jessica turned to Tom. "I took a dip in the lake. Luke did not."

Tom smirked. "I'll grab an extra crow bar." He gestured to the shed.

"You know he's old enough to be your father, yet because he's a guy and he can't help it, he's going to be picturing you frolicking in the lake *naked*. Thanks for that."

Jessica trapped her upper lip between her teeth. "Do you think any of the other Jones men will be picturing me naked today?"

His gaze rested on her, but he was somewhere else. It was a familiar look that elicited a slap of regret. Jessica wanted his affection, not his regret.

"It's a gift. I thought ripping something apart and whacking down a few dead trees would be a healthy release of all that energy you keep trapped inside."

She nodded; a soft, pensive expression masked her enthusiasm. Luke was trying to help her, but she hated herself for needing it in the first place.

He slid his palm against her cheek and threaded his fingers in her hair. She closed her eyes as his mouth brushed her ear. "It's not a punishment."

Her body shivered right to the bone. He smiled, It was weak, almost tortured.

"Where are you going?" She found her voice after he'd already turned and started back toward the house.

"I have a lunch date."

Panic stomped on her lungs forcing her mouth open in a silent gasp. How dare he say that? How dare he *do* that? She was too old to stick out her tongue and pound her feet so she flipped him the bird as he walked away. In her peripheral vision she caught Felicity looking out the back window. Jessica rotated her wrist and flattened her hand, palm up, then waved with a smile. Felicity's shoulders bounced a bit.

Jessica sighed, relieved that Luke's mom found the humor in her immature gesture.

"Ready to tear something apart?" Tom called from the door of the shed.

"Absolutely."

They ripped the siding off the shed. Then Tom gave Jessica instructions on residing it. She took down three dead trees with an ax, envisioning Luke's head as the trunk. By the time they finished the small projects inside the house, Jessica felt like a certified handywoman.

"You're a natural, young lady." Tom handed Jessica a cool lemonade as she pulled off her gloves. They stood side by side on the deck, watching the sun sink into the lake.

"I had fun."

He laughed.

"I'm serious. I used to work on cars and motorcycles with my dad. We still do occasionally. I love tearing things apart and putting them back together."

Tom sighed, keeping his gaze to the lake. "You're good for him."

"Luke?"

He nodded. "Taught him everything I know. I thought he'd stay around here, buy some land, and open up his own B&B. He originally went to college to pursue a business degree. Then ..."

Jessica's brow furrowed. "Then what? Did something happen?"

Tom nodded with a painful squint.

"Dinner will be ready in about an hour, if you two want to get showered up," Felicity called from the kitchen.

"Okay." Tom smiled at Jessica as if he wasn't just about to tell her something important. "That's her way of saying we're smelly and dirty."

"Yeah, we probably are." She stepped inside as Tom held open the screen door.

After grabbing her toiletries, she went into the bathroom and peeked her head into Luke's room. He was on his bed reading a book, looking casual in his shorts and T-shirt —both ironed and devoid of wrinkles of course.

"Hey."

He looked up, slipping his bookmark in his book. "Hi. My mom said you were a huge help to my dad today."

She shrugged. "Yeah, I suppose. He taught me a lot."

Luke nodded. "He knows his stuff, that's for sure."

They looked at each other for a silent moment. It felt like a stare-off. He was daring her, taunting her to ask about his lunch date.

"Did you have a good day?"

He smiled, a little too much. "Yes, I did. You'd better get in the shower. Dinner will be ready soon." Luke opened his book up and began reading again. "You're staring." He kept his eyes on the page.

"I'm thinking." Jessica replied.

"About all the things in this room that you could use to kill me?" Luke continued to focus on his book, not showing a bit of true concern.

"I did that yesterday and found six possibilities. But I just spied four more. That's ten, Jones. So maybe you should lock your door tonight." She freed her tangled mess of dark hair from its ponytail holder as she slid the door shut. At the last second, Luke glanced up. Jessica held her scowl until the lock clicked ending the showdown.

Livid.

Her level of frustration continued to escalate with each word he didn't say about his lunch date. Really, who brings a girl to meet—or not meet—his parents, and then goes out on a lunch date with someone else?

The shower was supposed to calm her nerves, cool her off ... but it didn't, even when she turned it to completely cold. By the time she stepped out and wrapped a towel around herself, she felt contemptuous heat simmering beneath her skin. Jessica was about to blow.

"Did you have wine?" She slid the door open until it jerked to a stop in the wall pocket.

"Excuse me?" Luke looked up, keeping his eyes on hers, in spite of her wet, naked body wrapped in a towel.

"Did. You. Have. Wine. At. Lunch?"

He smirked. "Get dressed. It doesn't matter."

Jessica took several steps closer. Luke tensed but continued giving his full attention to what must have been the most spellbinding book ever.

"It matters to me."

"Why?"

"Because if you had wine then you were trying to impress your 'lunch date.'"

"So what if I was?"

Luke had perfected the I-don't-answer-to-anyone attitude.

"I'm serious, Jones." She snatched his book and stomped back to the bathroom, depositing it in the toilet along the way. "Lock your fucking door tonight!"

JESSICA'S STOMACH screamed at her to hurry up as she applied some light make up and added a few curls to her hair. The aroma of fresh bread and savory herbs wafted up the stairs, enticing her to make her way to the dining room.

"Don't you look lovely." Felicity's welcoming smile eased Jessica's nerves.

Everyone else was already seated. She chastised herself for wasting so much time plotting Luke's death when she should have been showering and helping with dinner. Helping with what? Jessica wasn't sure. She could side a shed or fix a leaky toilet with minimal instruction, but baking fresh bread seemed as intimidating as flying around the world in a hot air balloon.

"Thank you, Felicity. Sorry I'm late."

"You're not. My kids are all vultures so they were all early."

A few chuckles and eye-rolling ricocheted around the table. Jessica made eye contact with Luke as she took a seat next to him. The appreciative smile that stole his lips settled like warm yet sour milk. The stiff, forced smile on hers confirmed it.

"Jessica, this is Lake, our youngest." Tom leaned over and wrapped his arm around the younger female version of Luke. She was quite possibly the most beautiful teenage girl Jessica had ever seen: high cheek bones, black hair that fell to her shoulders in a chic wedge cut, dark blue eyes, and a model's body.

"Hi, Lake. Very nice to meet you."

"You too. So you're the one who has caught my brother's attention."

Jessica placed her napkin on her lap. "I wouldn't say that. Then again, these days I don't think it takes much to capture his attention."

Luke sighed, but only enough for Jessica to feel his exasperation, his displeasure.

Liam cleared his throat. "Well he's thirty-two and you're only the second girl he's brought home ... ever."

Lake shoved a bite of food in her mouth and mumbled over it, proving her manners weren't as refined as her beauty. Jessica already loved her. "Yeah, but he was engaged to the first girl."

Like dimming the lights in a theater, silence invaded the room. Everyone's eyes were on Luke with caution, then Jessica with sympathy, and ending with a scowl for Lake.

"What?" She shrugged. "Sorry, I didn't know it was top secret."

"It's not," Luke intervened. "Jessica's not my girlfriend or fiancée, so ... it's fine."

Everyone relaxed and carried on with dinner, except Felicity and Tom. Jessica could feel their empathetic eyes on her, gauging her reaction to Luke's clarification. So he had a fiancée, and a lunch date, and possibly a glass or two of wine ... so what? He also had something happen to him in college, but what? Why would he tell Jessica, the "not girlfriend or fiancée," about his personal life?

"Mmm, this is amazing." Jessica focused on the food and found her smile after taking a bite of her herb-roasted asparagus.

"Thank you. Actually, Luke seasoned the vegetables."

Jessica dabbed her lips. "Well, looks like he'll have a talent to fall back on if the mind-manipulation thing doesn't pan out."

Laughter bubbled from his family as Luke's hand rested on her leg. Jessica turned to stone. Her pulse raced like he'd slammed down the accelerator to her heart.

"Ah, my dear friend, Jessica, has such a refreshing sense of humor." His grip on her leg tightened.

Was it a test? Jessica rested her fork on the table and curled her fingers into a fist, pumping it several times. She wanted to dig her nails into his hand instead of her own.

The growing need to throw him on the floor, tear off his clothes, and taste the saltiness of his flesh consumed her.

"Did your *lunch date* have a refreshing sense of humor?" she asked with a smile, but firmly clenched teeth.

"Aw, Luke ... you called me your lunch date. How sweet." Lake stuck out her pouty lower lip.

Luke smiled and released Jessica's leg. "Yes, I did. I don't get many lunch dates ... with all the 'mind-manipulating' that I do, so it was nice to have one with my favorite Lake."

Felicity melted in her chair, no doubt touched by Luke's sentimentality. Jessica, however, was ready to knock out a few teeth.

They coasted through dinner with Luke giving an occasional sidelong glance to Jessica, which she returned with absolutely nothing: not one look, one smile, one word.

"Thank you for dinner, Felicity. I need to go make a phone call." Jessica stood as everyone finished their dessert.

"You're very welcome. We're going out on the houseboat in a little bit so grab a jacket or you can borrow one of mine."

"Oh ... okay." Jessica retreated to her bedroom and collapsed on the bed.

Luke was heroin in her veins. Just his proximity made her world a better place, yet at the same time he felt like her imminent demise. She was going to need another psychiatrist just to recover from him.

"Jessica?" He knocked on the door.

"Go away ... *or* come on in." She sighed as he opened the door.

"Do you really have a phone call to make?"

"Yes. But God's busy right now. His mother/secretary, Mary, took a message. I'm sure he'll call back later."

"Do you want to talk?" He sat in the chair he'd been in that morning with the pool stick.

"Not really. Do you?"

"I think we should."

"Fanflippentabulous! You go first."

"You're angry."

Jessica sat up, pulling her knees to her chest. "You're judging me."

"I apologize. You're right, that wasn't fair."

"Why did you want me to believe you had a lunch date when in fact it was your sister?"

"To see how you would react."

She closed her eyes. "It was a test?"

"Jessica—"

"Did I pass?" Her words were slow and sharp.

Luke leaned forward resting his elbows on his knees. In casual clothes and his hair sporting a slightly-ruffled look, he had the appearance of a normal man capable of speaking uncensored words that hadn't gone through some politically correct filter.

He looked at her and she waited and waited.

"Sorry, Jones, I can't understand you, probably because I don't speak mute. So I'll just go while you make sure all your words are lined up in perfect order. I don't really give a damn if I let a few escape that haven't been given much actual thought. Sometimes emotions matter more than the right words, and if you overthink every goddamn word it's like suffocating it until all the emotion is gone."

She swallowed and took a deep breath, still riding that wave of courage. "I thought it was sex, you know? I haven't had it in ... forever: ten months, two weeks, one day, and a few hours. Yes, I'm counting."

Luke's attention jumped from the floor to Jessica. She returned a one-shoulder shrug.

"But even after you assured me we would never have sex, as in *less than* zero percent chance, I still wanted to be with you. And maybe it's because I can tell you anything, even if I haven't told you everything, but it feels like something more than that."

Jessica ran her fingers through her hair. "Does the thought of you on a date with someone make me jealous? Yes. Do I know that some completely put-together girl is going to steal your heart someday? Yes. Does it crush mine? Absolutely."

She bit her lips together until her eyes blinked back the impending tears. "Am I aware that no matter how brilliant and talented you are I will never be completely right ... normal?" She nodded as the words broke from her throat.

Luke would never give her normalcy. At best, he'd give her acceptance.

"You two coming?" Tom yelled from downstairs.

Jessica stood, blotting the corners of her eyes. "Good talk, Jones. Good talk." She grabbed a hoodie out of her suitcase and slipped it on.

"Jessica?" Luke grabbed her wrist as she walked by him.

"Don't." She gave him a sad smile. "You don't have to say anything. Think of everything I just said as off the record and ... forget about it." She pulled away and headed downstairs.

MILES OF GLASSY water under a blanket of stars greeted the Jones family as they all boarded the two-story house boat.

"Are they setting off fireworks tonight?" Lara asked.

"Yes. In about thirty minutes," Liam answered. "You're going to love this." He rested his hand on Jessica's shoulder.

She smiled, pulling the sleeves of her hoodie over her hands. "I can't wait. This house boat isn't too shabby."

"Our dad bought it at an auction, then completely refurbished it."

"I'm looking for a sailboat next. You should come help me work on it, Miss Fix-it." Tom wrapped his arm around Jessica's shoulders and gave her a squeeze.

"Sure." She forced as much enthusiasm into her response as possible, knowing it was probably her first and last visit to Luke's parents' place.

"There's drinks and snacks inside and chairs on both the upper and lower decks. Feel free to look around." Felicity tossed an armful of blankets onto one of the chairs as everyone else crowded inside to grab drinks.

"I'm going to take a look up top." Jessica pointed toward the stairs.

The view was picturesque from the top deck. Lighted boats dotted the water like glitter and some of the most magnificent homes Jessica had ever seen framed the nearby shores.

"Wine?"

Jessica turned. Luke stood behind her holding two glasses of wine.

"Thank you." She took one and watched him with a suspicious eye as he sipped from the other. "What are you doing?"

He swallowed, rubbing his lips together. "What do you mean?"

"I mean the wine. You don't drink wine."

"*Sometimes* I do," he replied, each word slow and laden with so much meaning ... so much intention.

The patient that wanted to be nothing more than a woman—his woman—stared at him. It had to be a joke, another test.

He took her glass and set both of them down on a small table.

"Jessica," he whispered as he moved toward her until her back hit the rail.

She blinked over and over. Her hands itched to touch him. Her skin ached to feel him.

"I don't want you to feel sorry for me."

He tugged at the hood strings to her sweatshirt. "I don't."

She no longer needed the hoodie. Her body heated like a furnace to a fever pitch, but she didn't dare move.

"Are you going to kiss me?" she whispered as he moved closer until the space between them evaporated.

"Yes," he breathed.

His promise caressed her body as much as his touch that moved from her sweatshirt to her face.

She drew in a quick breath and held it while her mind spewed silent chants to any and every God anywhere in the universe that could possibly hear her. She asked for strength and resistance.

"And, Jessica?" He stopped less than an inch from her lips.

"Huh?" she whimpered.

"You're going to stop before you make me bleed. Got it?"

Nodding in rapid succession, she would have sacrificed her right arm had that been the deal he wanted to make with her.

She jumped, even surprising herself, the instant his lips brushed hers. Her conscience had impeccably stupid timing. He paused, his eyes searched hers.

"What's the catch?"

"No catch," he whispered, brushing his lips against hers again: teasing, tasting, tempting.

She covered his hands and pulled back. "There has to be a catch."

Luke sighed, releasing her. "There's. No. Catch."

"You said 'less than zero percent chance.' Numbers are my thing, Jones. I know what that means."

"It's a kiss, Jessica. Not sex."

Her head jerked back. "Whoa ... clearly you don't understand. A kiss is a save the date, an RSVP to my vagina that says: You. Will. Be. There."

Luke rested his hands on his hips and looked to the heavens. Maybe God was taking his call that night.

"So you've slept with every guy you've kissed?"

"No! But I've never kissed a guy that in my head I've thought, 'less than zero percent chance.'"

"You two bay birds envious of our little lake?" Lane asked as he and Anne climbed the last few steps.

"I would be if you had my bridge." Jessica picked up her wine and took a sip, controlling the urge to gulp down the whole glass.

"Are you a San Francisco native?" Anne asked.

"Yes. I will never leave."

Lane locked his gaze to Luke's. "Sounds familiar."

"I'm attached to my job, not the city." Luke rested against the railing next to Jessica.

"Is Luke the rebel for not staying in Tahoe and opening a bed and breakfast?" The ten mile Jones' radius was interesting but the fact that Luke, Lara, and Liam all owned B&Bs too was crazy to Jessica.

Three somber frowns surrounded Jessica. What was she missing? And dare she ask?

"Nah, Luke did what he needed to do. It was for the best."

A pained expression disguised as a smile stole Luke's handsome features after Lane's comment.

"Look!" Anne pointed to the sudden burst of color in the sky.

Lane stood behind Anne, pulling a blanket around them. "There's another one." Lane nodded to the extra blanket Anne had set on the lounge chair.

Luke gave Jessica a questioning look.

"I'm fine." The heat from their moment still clung to her body.

The awkward, junior high dance feeling continued the rest of the evening until everyone arrived back at the house and said their goodnights. Luke followed Jessica up the stairs and stopped as she turned into her room.

"I'll lock my door."

She pulled off her hoodie and tucked her dark hair behind her ears. "Maybe I should go to the dungeon."

"What?" The perplexity in his expression matched that of his voice.

"A BDSM club. What if the only way I can be with someone is if they're submissive? Maybe I'm a dominatrix and I just don't know it. I'm sure you think that I have this need to cause pain, but that's not it. It's just about the blood." She plopped down onto the edge of the bed and stared at the floor.

"Does the blood arouse you?"

She shook her head.

"Then I don't think you're a dominatrix, and while I'm sure you could hold your own in a *dungeon*, it's not where you belong."

Jessica looked up. "Where do I belong?"

"I'm not sure, but it's not there."

They could have been making out like teenagers had she only kissed him on the boat. Instead Jessica was headed for a place far from his lips. She'd fallen in love with Luke and the fact that she didn't kiss him proved it. Love takes nothing but gives everything. Jessica hadn't given him everything yet.

"Do you believe in spirits?"

"Spirits?" he questioned.

"Yes, like when someone dies, do you believe they have a spirit that leaves their body?"

"I-I don't know. I've never given it much thought. Why do you ask?"

Her hands began to tremble. She clenched them together to make it stop as he moved to the bed and knelt in front of her. She felt the instant pull of her heart from his nearness.

"Tell me about the spirit." He tugged at her hands until she released her firm grip, then he held them in his.

"When Four died ... I think his spirit transferred to my body."

"Why?" Luke whispered.

"Because I killed him."

CHAPTER TWENTY-SEVEN
KNIGHT

THE MONAGHAN's lived in a small ranch style house with mature trees in the front yard and a stunning view of Mt. Hood from their back deck. AJ's father, Jim, was a mirror image of AJ aged another thirty years, except Jim smiled more. His mom, Charlene "Char," bubbled with personality as rich as her strawberry and gray hair that fell past her shoulders. She embraced Jillian with all the warmth of a daughter the second they walked through the door.

"I take it your parents don't buy that I'm your 'friend.'"

"Why do you say that?" AJ questioned as he set their bags at the foot of the bed.

"They have us sleeping in the same room, genius. Which you realize can't actually happen."

"They're not stupid. The last woman they saw me with was Brooke."

"Your ex-wife?"

He nodded, tossing the folded blanket from the end of the bed and one of the pillows onto the floor. "Don't worry, I'll be sleeping on the floor tonight."

Jillian pushed him back until he sat on the bed, then she

crawled up on his lap. "You told your parents the bruises on your face were from a training incident. Thank you."

"Yeah, well my mom used to counsel victims of domestic abuse. I'm not sure how she'd feel about her son being one."

She shoved his shoulders until he fell back. "Domestic abuse? Really? You think I'm abusing you?"

AJ stared at her as he slid his shirt up revealing the bite marks and scratches. Jillian feathered her fingertips over them.

"I'm—"

"Don't." He pulled her onto his chest, silencing her with his lips.

Desire stirred a need for him. She shifted her hips to feel his arousal between her legs. His acceptance and forgiveness turned her on as much as his body.

"Not now." He gripped her waist, ceasing her movement.

She buried her face in his chest and nodded. "You're right."

"Up you go." AJ sat up, lifting her with him and setting her on her feet as if she weighed nothing.

"I'm going to stop ... doing *that*. Okay?" She could do it. She could do it without Luke. There was no other choice. Jackson was right. She had to make a choice between AJ and Jessica.

He nodded, but his eyes lacked conviction. Hers did too.

"I hope your control is stronger than mine." He pulled her between his legs and rested his forehead against her sternum.

Jillian kissed the top of his head. Her feelings for him were intense and real. Comparing him to Luke wasn't fair.

Jillian had never been with Luke, Jessica had. As messed-up as making that distinction in her head felt, it was necessary. Luke was the love of Jessica's life. Jillian deserved one too.

"We're taking a walk before dinner. You two want to join us?" Char called down the hallway.

"Be right there," AJ answered.

Jillian placed her palms on his cheeks and smiled. "I like your parents."

"They're good people." He pressed his lips to her for a quick kiss. "There's something I need to tell you."

"You're adopted?" She smirked. "I'm not surprised. They..." she tipped her head toward the door "...are genuinely nice, *happy* people. And I've only exchanged a handful of words with them since we arrived."

"Exactly, give them twenty-four hours, and they'll be ready to kick your crazy ass to the curb."

She kept her smile firm in place. He had no idea just how "crazy" she really was.

"As I was saying ... I didn't mention their neighbors."

"You said Dodge and Lilith used to live next door."

"Yes, but on the opposite side is Brooke, her husband, and their twin girls."

"Oh ... that's ..."

"Strange. I know, but it's not as crazy as it seems." AJ pursed his lips. "Well, it may be, but long story short, we bought the house next to my parents so my mom could help with Cage. I gave her the house in the divorce since she had Cage more often, but honestly I figured she'd sell it and move."

"But she didn't?"

"No. She stayed, married her boss, and five years ago they had twin girls that my mom babysits since Brooke's mom passed away three years ago."

Jillian took a step back. "Wow. Cage never mentioned he had twin sisters."

"It is surprising because he thinks the world of them, but lately he's been distracted by football and the naked neighbor lady getting the mail."

"You realize you're funny when you want to be."

AJ shrugged. "I don't try to be."

"Yeah, I know that's why it works. So why the warning? Are we all having dinner tonight?"

"No, but you'll eventually see them."

"We're leaving tomorrow."

"I know, but I also know Brooke. Trust me, my mom told her about our visit and Brooke never misses an opportunity to throw her perfect little life in my face."

"And you're good with that?"

AJ stared at Jillian's feet with a pensive expression. "I loved her. The things I did to her were unforgivable and she hated me ... still does. But I don't begrudge her anything—not the house, not the relationship she's kept with my parents, and definitely not her new family. So if it helps her to flaunt everything she has as a reminder of everything I did and everything I don't have, then I'll gladly accept it. It's the least I can do."

Jillian held out her hand. AJ looked at it with confusion.

"Come on, they're waiting."

He stood and took her hand.

"For the record ... you, Aric James Monaghan, are a good guy. In spite of all your grumpiness and efforts to act otherwise. I see it and it's amazing."

He squeezed her hand and she felt the silent desperation in his grip. AJ needed her and that too was amazing.

"The twins will be staying with us when Rob and Brooke go to Mexico next month," Char announced as they walked up the street, passing the house where AJ used to live.

AJ had always found it odd that Brooke's new husband, Rob, would agree to move into a house where she used to live with her first husband—next door to his parents. In a small way he was proud of Brooke for taking charge, something he never allowed her to do. It was clear that Rob had tiny balls, but he adored Brooke so AJ found it easy to overlook his lack of a true man card.

"Beautiful house," Jillian commented.

"Jim and AJ built it."

He could feel Jillian's eyes on him, wide with surprise. It was easier and safer to let her see the monster inside. AJ prayed his parents wouldn't humanize him too much before they got the hell out of there.

"The boy has always been good with his hands," Jim added.

Jillian released AJ's hand and hugged his arm, begging for him to look at her, but it wasn't going to happen. He knew how her mind worked and it was headed in the definite direction of everything he'd done to her with his hands and fingers. His dick was growing hard just thinking about it. He didn't need to look at her fuck-me eyes to confirm it.

"I'll second that."

Too late.

"We're all flying out for Cage's pre-season game," Char said.

"*All*?" AJ asked.

"Your father and I, Brooke, Rob, and the girls. We'll stay with you of course, but they'll find a hotel closer to campus."

"They're more than welcome to stay with me and my

brother. We have two extra bedrooms and a bathroom in the garden level."

AJ gasped the word "What?" at the same time his mom squealed "Really?" in complete delight. How could she make such an offer?

"Absolutely. I adore Cage, so of course his family is welcome to stay with us."

"No way, that's … you can't make that offer." AJ's attempt to talk sense into a woman who, by all normal standards, was completely senseless.

"Why not?"

"You haven't even asked Jackson."

"Pfft, he won't mind. He'll probably make himself scarce anyhow." She waved a dismissive hand.

"I like her, AJ. I like her a lot." Char winked at Jillian, who looked like she just got accepted into the popular group at school. "I think she and Brooke will hit it off when they come over for dessert tonight."

Jillian rolled her eyes to his with an I-told-you-so smirk stuck to her face. He refused to admit he lied because he didn't … it wasn't dinner. It was dessert.

They continued their walk and revealing conversation that included Jillian's nighttime job. At first AJ was surprised that his parents took it so well, until his dad admitted that Dodge had already told them. Gossip wasn't always bad.

"Dodge speaks so highly of you," Jim said to Jillian as they sat on the deck waiting for dinner.

AJ grunted which earned him an elbow jab in the ribs.

"I love Dodge and Lilith. He's completely obnoxious, though. I'm sure being deaf doesn't seem like a blessing to Lilith, but with all his little digs I think she should feel grateful for the silence."

"Oh, I'm sure she hears him since she's only deaf in one ear, but I know what you mean. I'd imagine she pretends to not hear him most of the time." Char rolled her eyes and took a sip of wine.

All the color drained from Jillian's tan face.

"You okay?" AJ leaned over and whispered.

"F-fine," she answered with a stiff nod and quivering voice. "I-I just remembered I forgot to call Jackson when we landed. He's ... uh ... going to be worried." She stood as though her legs were having trouble holding her.

"Okay ... want me to come with you?"

She shook her head. "No ... I've ... I've got it. Be right ... back."

Not since the death of her parents had Jillian felt her heart struggle so hard for its next beat, her lungs deflate to the point of near asphyxia, or her stomach knot into a hard, brutal fist ... until Char revealed that Lilith could in fact hear.

The simple task of unlocking the screen on her phone proved to be a challenge with her shaky hands. What had she done?

"Way to not answer your fucking phone! What the hell were you thinking?" Jackson was livid about her leaving and flying, of all places, to the West Coast.

Tears mounted in her eyes as she thought about the consequences of what she had yet to tell him.

"Jackson?" Her voice shook as much as her hands.

"What's wrong? Are you crying? What happened? Did he hurt you? I swear I'll end his fucking life if he—"

"St-stop! It was m-me." She walked into the bathroom and turned on the exhaust fan to drown out her voice.

"Just calm down ... tell me what happened. Did you see someone? Did someone recognize you? Dammit! Knox is going to kill you for being so reckless."

"No ... that's not it." She took a deep breath. "It's Lilith."

"Dodge's wife?"

"Yes."

"Did something happen to her?"

"She's not deaf, Jackson. She can hear."

"I'm not following."

"She knows ... she knows about me ... about us."

"What do you mean she knows? How the hell could she know?"

Jillian sat on the toilet seat and batted away her tears. "I told her."

"You told her? How? Why? I-I don't understand."

"I needed to tell someone ... someone who wouldn't tell anyone else and who would just let me talk without judgement. She never said anything, never acted like she could hear me." Her words weren't entirely true. Looking back there were many clues that Lilith could hear, but Jillian was too blinded by her selfish needs to see it or even question it.

"I'll take care of it."

"What? No! Don't you dare do anything until I get home."

"Jillian, we don't have the luxury of time right now. It could already be too late. God knows who she's told. I need to end this and let Knox know there's been a breach."

Uncontrollable panic set in. Jillian jumped up. "No! No! No!" *Taking care of things*, meant eliminating the source. "You lay one fucking hand on her and I swear I'll—"

"What? Kill me? Really, Jill? You're going with that one?"

Jillian clenched and pulled at her hair. "She's not a threat. Don't do this. Wait for me or I swear I'll never forgive you."

Silence filled the line, suffocating Jillian in that tight little space waiting for Jackson to respond.

"Are you willing to bet your life on the chance that she's not told anyone?"

Jillian leaned against the door and closed her eyes. She played back all the sympathetic looks, kind smiles, and soft hand squeezes that Lilith had given her. She thought of how excited Lilith always was to see her.

"Yes."

"Fine. But if you're wrong—"

"I'm not, Jackson. I just ... I just know."

"You have to get your shit together. If you're fine, then be fucking fine, but if you're not then we have to get you help because I don't want to live this way."

"I know. I'm sorry."

"We can put bullets in our heads tomorrow if that's what you want, but don't self-destruct on me. Not after everything we've been through."

"I'll see you in a few days."

"Jill?"

"Yeah?"

"I love you."

"I know. I love you too. Bye."

CHAPTER TWENTY-EIGHT

STUNNING. It was the only word to describe Brooke. Jillian by no means was vain, but she considered herself to have some attractive traits ... until Brooke. She was Jillian's opposite in every way which left Jillian wondering what the opposite of stunning was.

Brooke was a Victoria's Secret runway model, at least in Jillian's eyes. She had to be older than Jillian for Cage to be her son, but the angel didn't look a day over twenty-five. Three kids ... she'd given birth to *three* children. It didn't seem possible.

"So how did you two meet?" Brooke asked Jillian as the women sliced up pie and scooped ice cream into bowls while the men and the twins waited on the deck.

"I'm his neighbor."

"I'll start taking these out," Char said as she grabbed several bowls and headed outside.

Brooke poked at the ice cream with the scoop, wearing a look of contemplation on her face. "I know it's no longer my business, but you seem like a nice person so I have to ask if you're aware that he's ..." She looked up at Jillian.

"He's?"

"Not right."

Jillian nodded once. "I assume you're referring to the PTSD?"

"Yes. Has he talked about it with you?"

"A little."

"Well, I'm not trying to cause any friction. All I want is for him to be ... *fine*, but I just couldn't bear to see you get hurt and wish I would have said something."

Leaning against the counter, Jillian took a bite of the warm pie. Brooke wanted him to be *fine*, not happy. Her pain and anger were clearly still raw. "I'm stronger than I look."

Brooke smiled, but it had a condescending feel to it. "Just be careful. He can turn on a dime."

Char entered the kitchen. "Did Jillian tell you that you, Rob, and the girls can stay at her house when we all fly out in a few weeks?"

"Really?" Brooke's perfect eyebrows peaked in surprise.

"Yes, we'd love to have you."

"We?" Brooke questioned.

"I live with my brother, Jackson."

"Oh ... well, sure. That's so nice of you. But only if you're sure."

Jillian wasn't sure of anything since dealing with Jackson and the Lilith revelation.

"Positive."

"Amazing pie, Mom." AJ brought in the empty bowls.

"Jillian's graciously invited us to stay with her, AJ. Are you okay with it?" Brooke crossed her arms over her chest.

Jillian noticed her doing that whenever AJ was in the same room. Maybe it was habit—protection of sorts. Regardless, there was no denying the tension between them.

"It's her house. She doesn't need my permission to invite you to stay. I would have asked you to stay with me, but I don't have enough beds."

Jillian looked at AJ with a slight twitch of her brow. Would he really have offered to let them stay with him? Would Brooke have agreed to sleep under the same roof when her tolerance for sharing space in the same room as AJ seemed minimal?

"We'll talk as it gets closer, but I really do appreciate the offer, Jillian." Brooke gave her a genuine smile. "We'd better get going. The girls have to be to camp early in the morning."

Brooke gathered her family and they said their good-byes. She whispered "Don't let your guard down," in Jillian's ear before leaving. It should have sent chills racing down Jillian's spine, but instead she felt sorry for Brooke and how she still grieved the man she'd loved and feared the man she hated.

"I'll have breakfast ready by seven," Char gave both AJ and Jillian hugs before they went to bed.

"Sounds great. We'll have to hit the road right after that."

"Good night," they all chimed.

AJ locked the bedroom door behind them. Jillian's body shivered with promise.

"Brooke is gorgeous."

AJ toed off his shoes and peeled off his socks as he looked at Jillian with his head cocked to the side. "You're not the jealous type."

Jillian shrugged as she undressed. "No. Not usually." He was right. Jealously was an unnecessary emotion, toxic and destructive—but entirely human.

"Well don't start now. When I fuck you it's fifty percent

your body and fifty percent your attitude. It's a close tie as to which one arouses me the most."

Jillian wet her lips and rubbed them together as he sauntered toward her in just his briefs and a dark look in his eyes. She slipped off her bra.

AJ shook his head. "Not tonight." He picked up the blanket from the floor and spread it out by the pillow.

"You're joking right?"

"No. My parents are just down the hall and you're too loud." He settled onto the floor, giving his pillow a quick fluff. "And my body is still recovering from the post-flight beating."

"I won't make you bleed."

His brow peaked.

Jillian swallowed, searching for conviction in her words. "I won't ... and I-I won't make a sound." She slipped off her thong and tossed it on his chest.

He brought it to his nose as his eyes perused her naked body. Men were such dogs. She loved smelling Luke's clothes, but never in her life had she considered taking a sniff of his underwear.

"No." He slingshotted the thong back to her. "Besides. I'm fighting a headache." Closing his eyes, he rubbed his temples.

"Isn't that supposed to be my line?"

"Believe me, I'd gladly give you this headache."

"You're such a gentleman. Come here." She slipped on his T-shirt and knelt on the bed.

"I'm good down here."

"I'm not going to break your nose. Get your ass up here ... on your stomach and I'll give you a massage."

He peeked open his eyes, then crawled up onto the bed.

"Have you taken anything for it?"

"Yeah, right after dinner. But it's not doing the job."

Jillian straddled his butt and kneaded his muscles.

"You were nervous earlier before you left to call Jackson. Was there a problem?"

"What makes you think I was nervous?"

"I'm good at reading people. You looked terrified."

She dug her fingers into a knot under his shoulder blade and he moaned. "I said I would call him as soon as we landed and it occurred to me that it had completely slipped my mind. I guess I was just thinking of how worried and pissed he probably was."

"And was he?"

"Of course. But everything's fine now."

"Why were you crying?"

"I wasn't."

"Your eyes were red when you came out."

Jillian had met her match in so many ways. "He yelled at me about leaving without telling him first. It hurt my feelings."

"Bullshit," AJ mumbled.

"Excuse me?" She paused for a moment.

"It would take a helluva lot more than that to hurt your feelings. Try again."

"You make me sound like a cold bitch." She shoved her thumb into the back of his neck, her nail making claim to his skin.

"Watch it," he warned. "I'm sure you have a warm and fuzzy part to your heart ... I think I've caught the occasional glimpse, but I don't see you sharing it with Jackson. You two beat the crap out of each other for no reason at all. He must have said something you're not telling me."

"And since when do you care? I thought we were going by the don't-ask-don't-tell motto for our relationship."

"I *don't* care. I'm just trying to keep you awake so I can escape to the floor without a physical confrontation."

She leaned forward and pressed her lips between his shoulder blades. "I'm sorry. I ..." She closed her eyes.

AJ rolled over with her still straddling his waist. "You?"

A sad smile was the best she could manage. "I don't like that person. This sounds ridiculous, I know, but when I look at the scars that bear my name..." she feathered her fingertips over one of the bite marks on his shoulder "...I don't recognize them. I don't recognize the person who made them. I'm not her ... yet she's me."

Jillian scooted down, resting her cheek against his chest. "But I wish she weren't."

DID JILLIAN SOUND RIDICULOUS? Someone with their sanity fully intact would have said, yes. AJ was not that someone. Her words struck a chord that vibrated to his soul and that said a lot for a man who contemplated its existence.

"Do you think I'm an asshole for not asking?"

He felt her body relax into his. "About my past?"

"Yes."

"No."

"Why? Don't women want men to care?"

"I don't know ... if you see one you should ask her."

AJ chuckled. He found himself doing that often with Jillian. "Don't fall asleep. The sheets are white and my nose bleeds red."

"I won't," Jillian mumbled in an already-half-asleep voice.

And then she did just that. He dared not move or even breathe. She may have fallen asleep as Jillian Knight but she would wake as someone else ... a frightened, dangerous animal. AJ closed his eyes and focused on the unforgiving pulse in his head until the pain nearly broke him and he deemed having his nose broken a welcome distraction from the assault on his brain.

He had to be quicker than her, not an easy task but a necessary one for self-preservation. All at once he wrapped his legs around hers, one arm around her body including both arms and his other arm over her head. Then he rolled like they were on fire, pinning her entire body to the mattress under his.

In an instant she fought with her whole body. "Dammit, Jones!"

"Shh ... it's me. You're fine." He covered her mouth.

Her eyes opened into saucers as she fought with life-threatening intensity to escape.

"If I release you will you calm down?" he whispered.

She nodded. AJ could almost hear her lungs screaming for air as her heart sprinted out of control. He rolled off her.

"What the fuck?" she whispered with the intensity of a yell as she sat up to catch her breath.

AJ gripped his pounding head, as if he could physically keep it from exploding. "I'm sorry ... I didn't want to startle you."

"Well then, I'd call that an epic fail on your part."

He rolled his head from side to side, searching for any position that would relieve the ache, even just a fraction. "Fine, then I didn't want to see the guilt on your face as blood squirted from mine."

She sighed. He didn't have to open his eyes to see the regret on her face. It happened too slowly to remember an exact moment, but none the less it had happened—at some point he started caring about her feelings.

"Let's get in the shower," she whispered, clasping his hand.

Nausea. Blurred vision. An angry pulsing. None of it compared to the painful feeling that he didn't deserve to have anyone treat him with such compassion. Jillian guided him, undressed him, and helped him in the shower until the sweet relief from the heavy stream of hot water pelting his head dulled the sharp edge of agony.

He stopped the massaging motion of her hands on his scalp by covering them with his. "Why?" he whispered.

She planted soft kisses all over his face, stopping at his ear. "Because everybody needs somebody."

A KNOCK on the bedroom door brought AJ from his sleep. Total disorientation. He wasn't able to remember much after getting out of the shower.

"Breakfast," his mom said with a soft voice.

He sat up in bed with caution, praying his heart would only beat in his chest and not in his head.

"Feeling better?"

AJ blinked the sleep from his eyes, searching for a body to go with the voice. "You slept on the floor?" He looked at Jillian curled in a ball on her side. There had been a time when seeing her sleeping on a hard floor would have brought a feeling of revenge or satisfaction to him. That time had passed leaving him with guilt. The whole caring-about-her-feelings thing had softened, tainted his hardened attitude.

"So it would appear." She grinned, eyes wide.

"Sorry—"

"Don't." She climbed on the bed, straddling his lap.

"You look like you're feeling better." Her hips wiggled with all kinds of suggestive seduction.

He ran his hands up her legs and under his T-shirt she'd worn. Her bare ass greeted him. A deep groan of appreciation vibrated from his throat. "Yes, I'm feeling better."

"How much better?" She slid her hand into his briefs.

With a thick swallow he closed his eyes. "My mom's—"

"Aric James, so help me … if you ever say the word 'mom' again while I have your cock in my hand, I'll break it off. Condoms?"

"B-bag." His lungs seemed to be controlled by her grip on his dick.

She started to move off him. He grabbed her waist.

"I can't …" The words were there and he didn't regret them, but he wasn't sure how she would react.

Jillian looked between them at the head of his erection peeking out above his waist band. "I think you can."

He shook his head. "I can't get you pregnant."

"O-kay …" Her brows knitted in confusion.

"I've had a vasectomy."

She nodded. Her face a blank page. AJ wasn't going to apologize, even if she had happily-ever-after dreams of marriage and a gaggle of babies. He was forty-two, irreversibly fucked-up, and done with that part of his life.

Jillian pushed down the front of his briefs and stroked him a few times. "I can't make you bleed anymore." Her eyes shifted from her hand to his eyes.

It was an odd statement or maybe it was the way she said it with such agony and regret.

She rose on her knees and positioned him at her entrance. "But you have to look at me the whole time. And … I know this is going to be hard for you, but I need to feel some sort of adoration, safety, contentment. Okay?"

His hands slid up to her breasts. "Okay." He stripped the shirt off her body, the impulse to taste her was too unbearable. Sucking a nipple into his mouth he looked up at her, surprising himself—the look, the feeling—it was automatic. He did adore her.

She sank onto him one slow inch at a time. The warm pressure made it hard to keep his eyes open and on her.

"Aric James ..." she whispered, "look at me."

He opened his leaden eyelids and bit her nipple. Their bodies rocked together in a slow rhythm. She swallowed over and over again. Her body reacted in pleasure while her eyes bled the pain as she fought to keep her *need* at bay. How long could he continue to ignore her pain? The questions grew louder in his mind every day.

"Aric Jam—"

Thwarting her effort to announce their morning activity to his parents, he crashed his mouth to her. Their tongues explored and probed, heavy, labored breaths desperate to escape. Jillian's nails dug into his shoulders so he grabbed her fingers and interlaced them with his, keeping his gaze locked to hers the entire time.

Control began to slip as their movements became more erratic. "Find it," he gritted through his teeth as he thickened and spilled into her.

She circled her hips—grinding, rocking, searching.

"Aric—" She spasmed around him and moaned into his mouth as he massaged her clitoris with the pad of his thumb, drawing every last bit of pleasure from her.

He dropped his head to her shoulder. "Good?" he mumbled into her neck as he licked and nipped at her salty skin.

She nodded. He looked at her again, flinching at the glassy tears in her eyes.

"What's—"

"Don't ... just don't ask." Jillian shook her head. "You'll ruin it..." she kissed his shoulder then rested her cheek on it "...and it was too good. Words will spoil it."

He hugged her to him, not wanting to break their connection. Of course he couldn't love her—not yet, maybe never—but he loved that she pushed him for less and not more. He loved that she used her compassion as her greatest strength, and he loved the way her acceptance made him feel normal. Was it possible to love so much about her and not actually love *her*?

"Your mom's probably wondering where we are."

He teased his teeth over her shoulder and up her neck. "If you ever mention my mom again while my dick is lodged inside you, I'm certain it will fall off."

She laughed. "Touché."

CHAPTER TWENTY-NINE

DAY

LUKE NEVER FORGOT the feeling of rescuing someone from a fire. He also never forgot the feeling of being a few seconds too late. Some days he could feel Jessica in his arms, just seconds from that breath of air. Then there were the moments he felt like he had her by the hand but she was slipping ... falling ... fading into the darkness—the point of no return.

"Luke?"

He searched her eyes for something, maybe a clue to why she was doing this to herself.

"Luke?" she whispered. "Say something."

"You didn't kill him."

She narrowed her eyes. "What ... I-I did."

He rubbed his lips together. "No. Edwin Harvey committed suicide."

Jessica shook her head. "What are you talking about? Who's Edwin Harvey?"

"The man who killed your friend."

"He's Four ... that was his name because he cut my best friend *forty-four* times!" She yanked her hands from his and scooted back on the bed. "Don't you dare call him that! Four. His name was Four. He wasn't human. He was a goddamn piece of shit without a heart or soul. He didn't deserve one single breath of oxygen, let alone a name to make him sound like a person with feelings and parents and a fucking life!"

Luke surrendered with his hands up. "You're right. He didn't deserve any of it, and he deserved to die..." his face winced into a pleading expression of pain as his chest tightened "...but you didn't kill him, Jessica. It wasn't your fault."

She looked at him with a vacant stare, lips slightly parted, knees hugged to her chest. "Who told you that?" Her voice was flat and eerily calm.

"A friend of mine did some research. It was on the news, in the papers, viral online. His parents are very wealthy. I'm sure that's why he was out on bail. The police report ruled it a suicide. He left a note before he drove off the bridge. They never found his body. Why would you think you killed him?"

"Because I did and I need you to believe me."

"Jess—"

"I'm not crazy."

"I didn't say—"

"Do you believe me?"

Luke moved toward her and she jumped off the bed like a frightened animal, easing toward the door.

"Stop."

She shook her head. "I trusted you ..." She turned and ran down the stairs then out the front door.

Luke followed her, calling her name. She hopped along grabbing one sandal and then the other, tossing them into the ditch before surging forward in an all-out sprint. His casual loafers were no match for her insane determination.

Eventually, she disappeared, *fading* into the darkness. He slowed in breathless defeat, bending over with his hands propped on his knees. He tried to save her, but instead she slipped from his grasp.

Defeat heavy on his shoulders, Luke returned to the house. He closed the door and looked up with a heavy sigh.

"She's in love with you," his mom said, sitting on the bottom step in her grey terrycloth robe and slippers.

Luke blinked, staring at the floor. "She's troubled. I'm not sure she knows how to love like that."

Felicity stood, walking to her son. She rested her palms on his cheeks until he looked at her. "I love seeing you through her eyes. Not Dr. Jones, but my beautiful, *troubled* boy." She smiled "Good night, love." Felicity walked up a few steps and turned. "Loving you, Luke ... it might be the only thing she knows how to do."

His mother knew virtually nothing about Jessica, but somehow she felt everything. He went upstairs and waited in Jessica's room, letting his mind battle with the fear that she was unstable, distraught, and alone in a strange place late at night. No shoes, no jacket, no phone, no Luke.

He sat in the chair by her bed for over two hours. Just as each blink struggled to recover, heavy with exhaustion, Jessica walked in the room. Without the slightest glance in his direction, she stumbled to the bathroom, pools of sweat covered her heat flushed skin. Luke stood. Leaving the door open, back to him, she turned on the shower and peeled off her clothes.

He moved toward her—regretful, conflicted, *aroused*.

Jessica froze as he stood a breath away from her naked body. She balled her fists, pumping them over and over.

Long dark hair veiled tan skin pulled taut over defined muscles, the kind that served a purpose far beyond what a young woman in her twenties should ever have to fathom. She was fear wrapped in strength greater than anything Luke had ever seen. He broke into a million pieces. Every piece was hers. He was ready to walk through the flames, sacrifice everything for her ... one woman ... *the* woman.

A lone drip of blood splattered on the tile at her feet. Luke's eyes retraced its path. Several more drips pooled at her hand where her fingernails broke the skin.

"Do you believe me?" she whispered, like every last ounce of hope evaporated with her words.

He gathered her hair, pulling it off her neck. Pressing his lips to her skin he answered, "Yes."

She turned, a stream of tears melting down her cheeks. "Luke." Her voice cracked as her lower lip quivered.

Maybe his mom was right. Maybe the thing that he'd been holding back was the one thing Jessica needed more than anything else. It felt like the most inexplicable thing ever. Their relationship had surpassed inappropriate several lifetimes over. Yet, he swept away her tears and kissed her. It was a kiss that told all reason to fuck off.

Luke crossed his arms, grabbing the hem of his shirt.

"No," she murmured against his lips.

He pulled back, eyes narrowed.

"I'll have to make you bleed first." She held up her hand, tipping her chin down in shame.

It was spelled out in front of him—in blood. All or nothing.

"Are you on birth control?"

Jessica lifted her gaze, searching for his intention. She nodded once.

Luke shrugged his shirt off and unfastened his pants, shoving them down his legs. His lips craved her ... all of her. "Then make me bleed." He wrapped an arm around her waist, pulling her against his body as he lifted her into the shower.

"Luke—" she began to protest.

"We're done talking." He kissed her again, his tongue tasting her—claiming her.

Jessica's hands tangled in his wet hair. His hands slid up to her breasts.

She broke their kiss, head falling back. "Oh … God," she moaned, arching her back into his touch.

"Do you have any idea … how beautiful you are?" he whispered in her ear, each word accented with truth, need, and complete reckless abandon.

Her fingers curled into his back. He closed his eyes and waited, questioning whose addiction he was feeding—hers or his.

"I can't." Her legs buckled.

He held her to him as she sobbed into his chest.

"I'm not beautiful. I'm ugly because of him … he did this to me. He's inside me and I hate him. I hate myself."

"Shh … don't say that." He kissed her hair.

Once her sobs subsided, he wrapped them in towels and carried her to bed. Leaving the towel around her body, he covered her with blankets and kissed her forehead.

She opened her swollen eyes and he could see past everything—straight to her soul. "I love you," she whispered then closed them again.

THE GUSTY WIND rattled the windows as an early morning storm rolled through. Jessica peeled open her eyes to look at the time. It was a few minutes after ten in the morning.

"Well done, Jessica," she mumbled to herself.

Her vagina had been dreaming of Dr. Luke Jones for months. The less than zero percent chance felt like a life sentence behind a chastity belt.

Naked. They were naked in the shower, a one hundred percent chance of sex. *Sex* with the man who had become the pinnacle of her life's purpose.

"Stupid!" She sat up, letting the towel and blankets fall from her body. "Jesus, Jessica! You're so stupid!"

An internal grimace tugged at her conscience and gave an upper cut to her ego knocking it back into last week. She had cried, actually cried. Why couldn't she have simply spread her legs and said thank you very much?

Jessica grabbed her clothes and headed to the bathroom. The opposing door was open. Luke's bag was packed and set by the door. The quilt and pillows were neatly folded by the headboard and the dirty sheets were piled at the foot of the bed. They looked more folded than wadded. Of course Jones would fold dirty sheets. Wadding probably made him visibly cringe.

She showered and packed. Almost an hour later she swallowed her pride, which was virtually non-existent by that point, and headed downstairs. The soft voices faded into silence as she rounded the corner.

Luke and his parents were sitting at the table with coffee mugs and kind smiles.

"Good morning," Felicity shot Jessica a quick wink.

"Hi. Sorry I overslept. Kinda rude on my part."

"Not at all. It's the weekend and you worked your butt off yesterday." Tom nodded to the empty chair by Luke. "Have a seat, we'll get you some breakfast. Coffee?"

Jessica nodded. "Thank you." For the first time that morning, she allowed herself to look at Luke.

"Good morning," he said without a single inflection in

his voice or the slightest clue on his face that the previous night ever happened. "I think we should head out after you eat. I have a few things to attend to when I get back."

"Yeah, sure." She smiled, letting her eyes linger on him as she sat down.

She ate while Luke and his parents talked about the renovation, his siblings, and other random topics. The hey-so-you-two-almost-had-sex-last-night topic never came up. She couldn't keep her eyes off him. Had she dreamed it? How could he not give her the tiniest hint of acknowledgment?

"I'll grab our bags." Luke deposited his coffee cup in the sink as Jessica finished the last bite of her omelet.

"I packed some goodies for you two to take on the road." Felicity held up a bag.

"Thanks, Mom." Luke took it from her and kissed her on the cheek.

When he took the bags out to the car, Felicity drew Jessica in for a hug. "He adores you."

Adore. It was an interesting word choice. Could Dr. Mind Fuck *adore* her? Unlikely.

"Thank you for everything."

"You're welcome. I hope you come back."

Another unlikely.

"The sailboat offer still stands." Tom lifted his coffee cup toward Jessica and grinned.

"Absolutely." She smiled past the lie.

They pulled out of the drive with his parents waving at the front door. Jessica waited for Luke to speak as the GTO tore down the paved road. When the silence became too torturous, she broke it.

"About last night ..."

"Yeah, there's nothing to say. It was an error on my part. I apologize."

It felt like a knife being lodged into her stomach. How could he say that? If almost having sex was an error, she hated to think of what having sex would have been in his mind. Then there was the whole professing her love to him.

"I wanted to make you bleed as much as I didn't want to make you bleed."

"I know." He kept his focus on the road.

"I can't remember the last time I *didn't* want to make a man bleed. It felt like progress in a very painful way."

He nodded. One. Cold. Single. Nod.

Jessica wasn't in the mood to beg. Groveling was a pathetic behavior she saved for extreme circumstances. She tipped her head back and enjoyed the best part of the trip— the cherry red GTO.

Luke wasn't kidding when he said there was nothing to say. Neither one spoke a solitary word the rest of the way back to San Francisco. She unfastened her seat belt before the car came to a complete stop in front of her place.

"See ya around." She jumped out and waited with her arms crossed over her chest as Luke retrieved her bag.

"Jess—"

She snatched the bag from him. "No ... don't start now. If there was nothing to say three hours ago, there's even less to say now." Taking the stairs two at a time she fled to the safety of her home.

Jessica slammed the front door shut and waited. Waited, of course, for Luke to knock on it because she was certain he would ... but he never did.

A SLEEPLESS NIGHT expedited the delivery of Monday. Jessica worked until noon, grabbed lunch, and made a quick dash across town to take another test. Some days her quest to become an actuary seemed insane, and the Monday after the Jones' weekend qualified as one of those days.

Exiting the building, brain exhausted, she checked her phone, coming to an abrupt halt which earned her a few expletives from the person who bumped into her back.

Jones: *My place, 7:00.*
Jessica: *No thank you.*

There was a less than zero percent chance of her showing up at his place that night. She got her laps in at the pool and met with Jude to spar for an hour before grabbing dinner on her way home. Climbing the stairs to her apartment, she glanced at her watch: 8:15. A deviant smile tugged at her lips. OCD Jones was getting a taste of his own bitter medicine.

"Good evening."

Jessica looked up as she reached the top of the stairs.

"Mind telling me what you're doing?" She fished out her keys.

Luke stood by her door, ankles crossed, smug bastard mask in its usual place, and a bag slung over his shoulder. "I wanted to apologize again about the other night."

She turned the key and shoved the door open like she wanted to shove him down the stairs. "Oh for the love of sex-deprived women everywhere, please don't."

The door shut behind him. "I was out of line."

Jessica whipped around. "Yes, you were out of line for pretending that nothing happened. You were out of line for sitting in the driver's seat the whole way home acting like a freaking iceberg. And you were especially out of line..." she narrowed her eyes as her chin jutted out "...for not letting me drive your car."

"I—"

"No..." she shook her head "...I'm not done."

Luke closed his mouth.

"But if you try to tell me you were out of line for what happened or almost happened in the shower, then I'll count to five and you'd better get your ass going otherwise you won't be leaving in one piece."

His brows peaked while humor twisted his lips. "Are you done?"

She huffed, nodding to the black duffel bag. "What's in the bag?"

"You'll see, but only if you trust me."

Jessica grabbed the sandwich from her bag and unwrapped it, attacking it like a shark. "I shouldn't ... but I do," she mumbled over the massive bite. Wiping the corners of her mouth, she swallowed. "I just don't trust myself."

"That was the reason for my apology. I want you to trust yourself with me—not for me, for you."

"That's funny, coming from the guy who threatened me with a muzzle and straitjacket."

Luke shrugged as he dropped the bag on the floor with a thump and a rattle. "I also said there was a less than zero percent chance of us having sex."

Jessica stared at the bag. "We didn't have sex."

Luke moved closer with the calculated moves of a predator. "But we kissed," his gaze locked on hers holding it hostage.

"So," she whispered.

He ducked to her neck and teased his lips along her

skin, landing on her ear. "So, a kiss is an RSVP to your vagina that says: I. Will. Be. There."

The sandwich in her hands fell to the ground as her heart stopped and all the air evaporated from her lungs.

"Close your eyes."

Jessica blinked. It was the only part of her body that could move.

"I said ... Close. Your. Eyes."

She did and he kissed her cheek. "Good girl. Now don't open them until I say."

She nodded. "I don't like surprises."

"It's not a surprise."

"Then why do I have to keep my eyes closed?" She shivered feeling his nearness again.

"It's therapy."

"Are you going to hypnotize me?"

"No."

"Have you done this before?"

"No."

"Have any of your fellow shrinks?"

He chuckled. "I highly doubt it."

"Then how do you know it will work?"

"Shh ... we're done talking." He kissed her the same way he had before—patient yet commanding, never letting her take more until he was ready to give it.

She gasped for air when he released her mouth. He brushed his thumb over her breast, pebbling her nipple beneath the thin material of her dress and lace bra. Then his hand slid lower. She reached for him.

He tsked her several times. "You can touch anything ... but me."

"Luke," she pleaded, squeezing her eyes shut even tighter while balling her fists at her sides. "I can't do this."

His hand slid between her legs and her breath caught in her chest as her nails made claim to her palms.

"Do you want me *here*?" He massaged her clit over the cotton skirt of her dress.

She jerked her hips toward him. "Y-yes."

"What will you sacrifice to have me here?" He continued with firm small circles.

"Any-anything," she breathed as her hips circled with his touch.

He kissed her again, easing her hands behind her back. She tensed a bit until his tongue dove deeper making her moan. He broke the kiss, leaving her feeling weak and dizzy. His tongue trailed down her neck.

"I want to taste you here." His thumb brushed over her nipple.

"Yes ..." she breathed.

"Then I want to taste you here." He pressed harder against her clit until she whimpered.

"Luke ... please ..." Her hands clawed at his shirt.

He grabbed them, pushing them behind her back. They stared at each other—her breathless and fighting fear, him focused and taunting.

"Call me when you're ready." He pressed a soft kiss to her cheek before he released her wrists and walked out the door.

Once again, her mind was thoroughly fucked. That wasn't the part of her body she'd hoped would feel thoroughly fucked when he left. If *anything, yes,* and *please* didn't say she was ready, then what would?

Homing in on the black bag he left behind, she squatted down and unzipped it. "What the hell, Jones!"

CHAPTER THIRTY

KNIGHT

I<small>T RAINED</small> for four hours straight when Jillian and AJ left his parents' house in the truck. She was surprised that AJ let her drive, but after he slept for the first three hours it was obvious what a physical toll his migraine had been on his body.

"Hungry?" he asked as they stopped for gas and to switch drivers.

"Yes. You fill up and I'll grab some grub."

AJ nodded as he got out. Jillian used the bathroom and bought a variety of junk food. Climbing in the passenger seat, she handed him the bag.

"For Chrissake, you call this shit food?" He tossed the bag in her lap and started the truck.

"Uh ... it's a gas station not a farmer's market." She looked in the bag. "Peanuts?"

"Too much fucking salt."

She mouthed a silent *okay*. "Twizzlers or M&Ms?"

"If I want to be a diabetic by the time we reach the next state."

Jillian sighed. "Water?" She held up a bottle.

"You paid for bottled tap water?"

She gritted her teeth. "No ... I paid for the bottle since we're not camels."

AJ shook his head, murmuring something indecipherable.

"Well, then you're out of luck, buddy. Because all I have left to offer is a sack of suck your own nuts and a spray can of fuck off."

Keeping out a bottle of water, she tossed the bag into the backseat, then she Googled PTSD on her phone. Her instinct was to beat the crap out of him, but he was driving so that seemed like a suicide mission. Instead, the confines of the truck held her captive to his abuse for the next several hours until they reached their hotel.

If there was a record for most car trips taken, least words spoken, then the Day/Knight duality that encompassed Jillian held the record. What was it with the ride home after meeting a guy's parents for the first time?

They parked the truck for the night and checked in at the front desk of the hotel.

"Reservation for Monaghan."

The lady behind the counter glanced at the computer screen. "Yes. Two double beds?"

"Actually. We're going to need another room," Jillian smiled at the lady.

"No, we don't," AJ growled.

"*Yes*, we do." Jillian handed her a credit card.

The lady's eyes volleyed between them as she took the card with hesitation. After a few moments of Jillian refusing to acknowledge his crabby scowl, he huffed off toward the elevators. The tension coiled between them as the elevator made its accent to their rooms on the fifth floor. AJ could have pissed all over Jillian, the lobby floor, and the mirrored walls of the elevator and she still wouldn't have given him the satisfaction of a single quick glance.

She shot out ahead of him the second the elevator doors opened, dragging her suitcase like a hostage behind her.

"Stop!" He grabbed her arm and swung her around.

Her eyes shot to his hand. "Let. Go. Of. Me. *Now.*"

He released her, but the anger that rippled his muscles and burned in his eyes remained. "I warned you."

Jillian felt her own jaw tick as she envisioned him bleeding. "Good night," she said with a stiff voice. Drawing in a quick breath, she turned. AJ out of control was enough. One of them had to keep it together. His game was to draw a reaction from her, maybe to lessen the burden of guilt. She refused to play it as her brain chanted: *walk away, walk away.*

She slipped the keycard in the door and hurried inside. The door slammed, but not shut—it slammed open against the wall before she made it halfway inside.

She closed her eyes for a brief moment then turned. The man before her looked like AJ, but the vacant look in his eyes and hardened features of his face were those of a complete stranger.

"I don't recognize you right now, therefore my natural instinct for self-preservation will kick in and you'll be taken out of this hotel on a gurney."

The wrathful smirk he tossed her would have made anyone else cower.

"Go to bed."

His eyes narrowed. "Don't tell me what to do. I'm not afraid of you. I've looked fucking psychopaths in the eye and not blinked. You and me..." he tipped his chin "...let's see who's left standing."

"You hate yourself right now, don't you?"

"Stop..." He shook his head.

"Are the voices in your head fighting? Do you want to tell them to just shut up?"

"Don't act like you know how I'm feeling," he seethed, taking a step closer.

Jillian stayed rooted to her spot. "You want to hit me right now, don't you? But not for the same reason I've made you bleed; you want it because the messed-up person inside your head is pissed that you *ever* let me make you bleed. For God's sake, you let a *woman* break your nose. Senior Master Sergeant let a little woman break his nose."

He balled his fists and clenched his jaw, taking yet another step.

"So here's how I see it. You can tell that voice to fuck off and kiss me because even after that ridiculous episode in the truck ... I'm still here. Or, you can hit me and I'll even let you draw first blood." Jillian held up her index finger. "But that's all you'll get. One. Shot."

It was a risk that could have gone either way. Jessica once had Luke to teach her mind-body control and it was a conscious battle she fought everyday of her life. But AJ had nobody so Jillian would be that somebody even if it left a mark ... which it did.

The blinding pain was bearable—just—and the blood was minimal as she tasted the familiar metallic tinge that pooled on her lip. She hid her smirk. Jackson treated her as an equal when they sparred. Backhanding was something men with small dicks and overinflated egos did to women they wanted to control. She expected more from someone with AJ's experience and dick size.

"Fuck!" he yelled, holding his fisted hands to his head.

She didn't touch him. She didn't have to. The sacrifice was for the impact and with one slap, it was done. Her heart broke for him as realization pooled in his eyes. Nothing bled quite like regret.

"Oh, God ... I-I'm sorry." He squeezed his eyes shut and shook his head.

"Good night, AJ." Jillian kept each word steady like walking across a tightrope.

His Adam's apple bobbed as if he was choking on something. Pride? Turning, his shoulders curved in as he drudged through his self-made pit of misery to the door.

"Aric James."

He glanced back over his shoulder.

She dabbed the blood at her lip. "I forgive you."

AJ winced as if forgiveness was a burden—sometimes it was.

AJ WRUNG his hands together as he sat on the edge of the bed, feeling nauseous, dizzy, and plagued with shame and regret. Never in his life had he hit a woman. He despised the PTSD label. It was an excuse and he didn't want an excuse. There was no excuse for the razor edge to his words or the lash of his hand against Jillian's face. Who the fuck was that person?

Why would she offer to let him hit her? Why would she forgive him? Why would she stay? The questions were infinite and the answers were enigmatic. He'd caused pain to the one person who took his away. Glancing at his watch he thought of two skipped meals and Jillian's petite body that couldn't keep fat on it for anything.

Twenty minutes later he knocked on her door, holding the biggest bouquet of flowers he could find in a ten mile radius. It was pathetic and an ocean short of the grand apology she deserved, but it's all he had at the time.

She opened the door, her face stone ... her lip swollen. The dagger of regret twisted. Without a second thought he fell to his knees. Jillian had said she'd bring him to his knees and for the second time that's where he landed.

"The flowers are overkill for a slap on the cheek." Jillian rolled her eyes. "And get up off your knees unless you're proposing, in which case the answer is no." She grabbed the flowers.

"It was more than a slap and your face shows it. And you're the only woman in the history of the world that would say that to me." AJ stood and followed her inside the room.

"Yeah? Well, women can be sensitive and a bit persnickety. You had a moment ... everyone has their moments."

AJ tried to smile through the anguish. "What happened earlier, that wasn't me. It's not a *moment* I'm proud of." He rubbed the back of his neck and sighed while closing his eyes. "Or maybe it was me. God! I hope not, but ... I just don't know anymore. It's so damn frustrating—the unpredictability. One minute I'm in control, in the next ... agitation at the whole fucking world rips through my body like a tornado."

AJ rested his palm on her cheek. She closed her eyes and leaned into his touch. "I'm so damn sorry. It will never—"

"Shh." She rested her hand over his. "Never's a long time. But next time—"

"There won't be a next time." He sat on the bed and pulled her between his legs, resting his forehead on her chest while cupping her ass.

"As I was saying ... next time put some balls behind it."

"My God, woman. You have a knack for verbally castrating men. If I spend much more time with you, I'm not certain I'll still have a pair." He bit at her nipple through her top.

Jillian moaned bringing his dick to attention.

"Let's go." He smacked her ass.

"Go where?" She climbed up on his lap, perching her crotch on the bulge in his jeans.

"I'm taking you to dinner for some real food." His fingers dug into her hips to still her efforts of dry humping him.

Jillian kissed his neck as if food wasn't even close to being on her radar. "I think if I tied you up again and sucked on your cock that would tide me over until morning."

"No way in hell." He lifted her from his lap and stood, adjusting his erection.

She laughed. "I don't think that's a normal reaction to a blow job offer."

AJ cleared his throat and held open the door for her. "I don't think you know how to give a 'normal' blow job."

She waltzed past him with a smirk. "You mean boring?"

"Boring's not always bad," he grumbled to himself, letting the door slam behind him.

"Yes it is," she called from twenty feet down the hall.

The woman had the hearing of a dog.

"My tongue will keep you young, Sarge. You don't want your ball hair going gray yet, do ya?"

Jillian had impeccable timing. AJ turned at the giggling sound behind him. Three doe-eyed teenagers froze, holding their breath while covering their mouths. His piercing glare sent them scurrying in the opposite direction.

THEIR DINNER at the hotel's tavern was two cloth napkins short of a real date.

"We had drinks, appetizers, a main course, and dessert. It was a real date," AJ argued in the elevator on the way back to their rooms.

"Sorry, no cloth napkins."

"But I brought you flowers."

"That was an apology." Jillian stepped off the elevator.

As she unlocked her door, he smoothed her hair off her neck and brushed his lips along her skin. "It was a shitty apology," he whispered.

Goose bumps bloomed along her flesh as she shivered from his touch. "Good night, AJ."

"Wait." He hooked his arm around her waist as she pushed open the door.

"Just like that? No kiss goodnight or—"

She turned and planted a kiss on his cheek. "Sweet dreams."

He tightened his grip as she began to pull away. "I think my ball hair is going gray."

She laughed. "About that ... I think you should just wax that whole area. I'd be happy to do that for you when we get home."

AJ released her, buckling over like she just kicked his junk. "Guys don't do that shit."

"They do." She tossed her purse on the bed. "I suppose you could shave it instead. I think Jackson has a straight edge we could borrow."

"I'm messed-up, but not completely insane. I think I'd gnaw off my own hand before I'd let you near my dick with a straight blade."

"I told you, I'm not into cutting." She smiled past the knot in her stomach after realizing the words in her head actually came out of her mouth.

The jovial mood evaporated leaving a heavy, suffocating feeling in its place. She could see the question brewing in AJ's mind as his expression became more focused, eyes searching, lips firming with a deep swallow.

"Who's Jones?"

All the blood pulled from the surface of Jillian's skin leaving a cold sweat in its place.

"What?"

"Jones. When I pinned you down and woke you after you fell asleep last night, you yelled 'Dammit, Jones.'"

Complete honesty wasn't a luxury Jillian would ever have again. Lying was survival. "My dog. I used to have a dog named Jones." No lie.

"He died?"

She turned and opened her suitcase, needing something to hide the way her hands were shaking. "Yes, he died," she lied.

"I'm sorry."

Jillian fought the tight grip of emotion in her throat that felt like it was trying to asphyxiate her. "Me too." She could hide her thoughts, her words, and on a good day her tears. But her heart demanded acknowledgment, there was never enough Heineken to numb the dull ache in her chest.

AJ huffed a heavy sigh. "I'm not good at this."

She sat on the edge of the bed with her hands tucked under her legs. "Good at what?"

"This..." he motioned between them "...this relationship stuff. I should care enough to ask you more about your past, the blood thing, the ridiculous profession you've chosen, the reason why you're living with your brother ... but I'm too fucking selfish. I can barely deal with my own pathetic life, I just—"

She shook her head. "It's fine. I have nothing to tell."

His head jerked back a fraction as his eyelids fluttered with rapid blinks. "What is that supposed to mean?"

Jillian lifted a single shoulder. "You act like I'm on a cliff's edge just waiting, *begging* you to ask me about my past and my 'issues,' but I'm not. The fact that you don't ask me about it is why this..." she mimicked his motion between them "...relationship works."

He nodded with an absent stare.

She'd gone too far. It was a slippery balance between too much and not enough. It's human nature to desire what's perceived as the unattainable. Was she making her past seem too unattainable?

"Don't."

AJ's gaze snapped to hers. "Don't what?"

"I was simply stating a fact. Don't interpret it as a game. I'm not playing hard to get with my emotions. It's not a trap."

He rested his hands on his hips and stared at his feet.

"It's a gift, AJ. You will never have to be my gallant knight on his trusty steed, drawing your sword to defend my honor. I will never gawk at sparkly diamonds in the jewelry store window or ask you where you see our relationship going."

"You sound callous, but I know you're not. I've experienced your compassion."

"That's a gift too. I've never been compassionate toward you with an ulterior motive. I'm not callous. I'm strong. It takes a lot of strength to give unconditionally because the ego is a savage, demanding beast."

He narrowed his eyes a bit. "So nothing ... you don't want anything from me in return."

Jillian smirked, prowling toward him. "I'm compassionate, not a saint." She slid her hands under his shirt, tracing the definition of each firm plane of muscle.

He quirked a brow. "So you want me for my body?"

A provocative smirk stole her lips as she pushed up his shirt and teased her teeth over his skin. "I think we both know it's not for your stellar personality."

"You're such a bitch," he growled, grabbing her ass and lifting her up.

She wrapped her legs around his waist and laughed. "But an honest bitch."

CHAPTER THIRTY-ONE

DAY

Jᴇssɪᴄᴀ ᴄᴏᴜʟᴅ ɴᴏᴛ ʙʟɪɴᴋ. A thousand jolts of panic coursed through her veins.

It was fire.

It was ice.

It was insanity.

Panic seized her heart sending it into a pounding arrhythmia. Inside the black bag was an assortment of restraints: handcuffs, ropes, satin gags and blindfolds, and *zip ties*. She stepped away as if it were filled with poisonous snakes. He wanted to torture her. Maybe he did believe Four's spirit was in her and he was planning an exorcism.

He'd been right all along, and maybe it was all part of his mind games. The chance of them having sex was once again less than zero percent. Period.

The bag was his final point. He'd been studying her, therefore he had to know there was no way she could ever be restrained. They'd hit an impasse and there would never be a bridge long enough to gap the distance. No matter how much she loved him ... the bag and what it represented was too much.

She shoved it in the front closet, tossed her sandwich in the trash, and went to sleep alone—the way she would for the rest of her life.

AUTOPILOT.

Jessica fell back into her pre-Dr. Luke Jones routine: exercise, work, study, test, repeat. After two weeks she gave up trying to pretend that he didn't exist. After all, it would be difficult to do since they were both in the Long Beach Triathlon with Kelly and Gabe.

"You have a lot of explaining to do." Kelly barged through the door.

"Nice to see you too." Jessica set her bags by the door.

They were all riding down to Long Beach in Gabe's SUV. Aside from a few texts from Luke asking if she was coming to clean, which she answered with a simple "no," they hadn't had any other communication since the black bag incident.

"Ellie said you're Luke's maid now. I told her she was full of shit, but she insisted she wasn't and it's a weird thing for her to make up on her own, so what gives?"

"Oh, Ellie ... yeah, um ... it's true. I was doing some light house cleaning for Jones—I mean Luke. But I'm not anymore."

Kelly looked at her like a third eye had sprouted above her nose. "That ... that doesn't make any sense."

It really didn't.

"You're a disaster." Kelly looked around Jessica's cluttered apartment. "And everything at his condo is immaculate. What could you possibly be doing to help him?"

"I'm not doing anything. I was, but now I'm not. Are you ready to go?"

Kelly narrowed her eyes. "Why not?"

Jessica grabbed her bags and lifted her bike on her shoulder. "We—I—he ... fired me."

"What?" Kelly opened the door.

"Well, what I mean is he let me go. Actually it was more me than him." She handed Kelly her keys to lock up then headed down the stairs. "He was too ... *demanding*. I didn't want to feel so *tied down*."

"Jessica Mauve Day, I don't believe a word you're saying. This whole situation reeks of lies and ... something else."

"Hey, Jess," Gabe greeted her at the curb and took her bags and bike.

Kelly tracked Jessica with an evil eye as they both got in the backseat.

"What's with the sour grape look?" Gabe asked Kelly as he shut the door and adjusted his mirror.

"Our *friends* are up to something."

Jessica shook her head and ignored Kelly's distrustful scowl all the way to Luke's condo.

"Hey, man!" Gabe jumped out and grabbed Luke's bike.

Jessica looked out the opposite window, digging her nails into her palms just short of breaking the skin.

"Oh ... you're sitting in back?" Luke asked Kelly as he opened her back door.

"Why? Do you want to sit back here with your ex-maid?"

Jessica whipped her head around to look at Luke. He squinted a bit, flitting his eyes between her and Kelly.

"*Ex*-maid?"

"Yes. You fired her, didn't you?"

"Uh ..."

"I quit."

"Oh, that's right." Kelly nodded. "You were being too ... what did you say, Jessica? Oh, now I remember. You were being too demanding and she didn't want to feel so tied down."

Luke's wide eyes sought confirmation from Jessica. "Is that so?"

She grimaced.

"Get up front. I'm sitting back here with my *ex-maid*."

Kelly seemed to dismiss the edge of anger to his words, but Jessica did not.

"Everyone ready?" Gabe asked as soon as Kelly closed her door.

With a unison of yes, they were off to Long Beach.

Kelly dominated the conversation with her pre and post triathlon meal plans for everyone, the map of the course, check-in times, and basically everything else from the website as if she were the only one in the group who could read.

Luke pulled his phone out of his pocket and focused on the screen. Jessica drummed her fingers on the arm rest, stealing an occasional sideways glance. Those hands that held his phone and fingers that slid over the screen were the same ones that cupped her breast, brushed over her nipple, and slipped between her legs. She adjusted in her seat, feeling warm and tingly.

Her phone vibrated. Slipping it out of her bag she smiled.

Jones: *Hi.*

Jessica: *Hi.*

She rolled her eyes to the side, but his face remained stoic as if he were messaging someone a million miles away.

Jones: *I've missed you.*

Her heart galloped.

Jessica: *Missed you too.*
Jones: *Did you lose my number?*

She stared at the screen.

Jessica: *Just my nerve.*
Jones: *Because of the bag?*
Jessica: *Yes.*
Jones: *I miss your lips.*

She shifted again in her seat. How he sat there like a statue was beyond comprehension.

Jessica: *They miss you.*
Jones: *Why no bra today?*

She dipped her chin. Her hard nipples were molded in twin peaks against her grey tank top. Tossing any sort of discreetness out the window, she turned and stared at him, silently demanding him to look at her. But he didn't. He showed absolutely no outward signs that they were having any sort of interaction.

Jessica: *I'm against suppression.*
Jones: *It's distracting.*

Jessica: *So are your socks. How did you end up wearing two right ones today?*

Jones: *They're crew socks. There is no right and left. They're ambidextrous.*

Jessica: *If I wouldn't have cried in the shower, how many times would we have had sex by now?*

She stared at her bold words, letting her finger hover over the send button. She had to know, so she let her thumb tap the screen. Then she waited, but within seconds there was a return message.

Jones: *More than you can count.*

Gulp.

Jessica: *Fuck me …*

Somehow her fingers typed what her brain was thinking, not what she really meant to say.

Jones: *When and where?*

She turned to him again. Nothing. Not one look. Not one flinch.

For a brief moment she wondered if she had the right "Jones." What if he lost his phone and got another one with a new number? What if she was having this conversation with a sick and twisted stranger? Even worse … what if she wasn't?

Jessica: *Ever had sex in the restroom of a restaurant?*

Jones: *What do you think?*

That's just it, she didn't know what to think. Before that day she would have said no. But when her orderly, completely irresistibly sexy, mindfuck of a friend answered "when and where?" to her fuck-me comment—all bets were off.

Jessica: *I think if the restaurant where Kelly has planned for us to stop for lunch has a restroom door with a lock on it we …*

"Are we stopping for lunch soon? I'm *starving*," Luke called up to Gabe and Kelly.

No need for foreplay. That was it. The heavy ache between her legs grew with such intensity from his voice—his words—she feared just getting out of the vehicle would detonate her impending orgasm. The more she thought about it the more certain she was that she'd never make it. The feeling was ten times worse than a full bladder on a bumpy road. Her pulse was nonexistent in her chest; every beat was at her sex. How would she explain going weak in the knees in the middle of a parking lot from an orgasm?

"There's road construction so we're going to detour. I'll have to look for a different stop, so it might not be for another hour or two. The bag on the floor between you two has some snacks in it," Kelly said.

Jessica salivated like a dog. Her entire body was in zero hour meltdown. If it were a bladder issue she could request they pullover and let her squat in the ditch. But how could she ask them to pull over and step out of the car while she had emergency sex with Luke?

Luke: *wet your finger*

She squinted her eyes at his text. What did he mean?

Brushing her finger over her lip, her tongue darted out to wet it.

Luke: *lower*

His all-consuming eyes finally met hers, sucking her into his sensual vortex. All of her senses sprang to life: the brush of her cotton shirt along her nipples, the salty taste from her own finger that was destined to slide between her own legs, and the sudden rush of Channel No. 69 that infiltrated her nose like a drug.

Under his manipulative trance, controlled only by his eyes, she pulled up her cotton skirt and slid her finger under the crotch of her panties, being careful to not touch her painfully sensitive clitoris. One wrong move and she would have exploded. A single swipe and her finger was drenched.

Luke bent down. With one hand he ruffled the snack bag and with his other hand he clasped Jessica's wrist. Keeping his head ducked behind the front seats he brought her wet finger to his lips and slid it into his mouth. It was a modest gesture with a monstrous effect.

Jessica panted through it ... fighting for control and dying to release soft moans of pleasure. He pulled her finger from his mouth and circled the tip of his tongue along the pad of it and It. Was. Over.

She squeezed her legs together, dropped her chin to her chest letting her hair fall like a curtain over her face. Then she bit her lips and closed her eyes as an orgasm pulsed in rippling waves along her sex, clear to her toes curling them in her flip-flops.

How did he do that? Some guys could fondle a woman's body for hours and—nothing. Luke texted *where and when, wet your finger*, then sucked said finger for less than ten seconds. Bang!

With his hand in the bag he went ahead and retrieved an apple before releasing Jessica's wrist and sitting up straight again.

"Those are so good." Kelly looked back at the apple in Luke's hand.

"Mmm ... yeah, my mouth is already watering." He took a big bite with a smirk on his face, eyes on Jessica.

She narrowed her eyes. Cocky wasn't becoming of him. Well, maybe it was.

THE RESTAURANT BATHROOM did not have a locking door. Just as well. Luke wasn't entirely certain how he and Jessica's first time would play out. The close call in the shower at his parents' was the weakest moment he'd experienced in years, a real diving-into-the-shark-tank move. He had been ready to bleed again if it meant being with her, until she cried and his selfishness hit him in the chest like a wrecking ball. How could he have lost sight of the regret she would feel?

Gabe let Kelly and Jessica off at the hotel entrance while he and Luke looked for a parking spot.

"So who's the girl?" Gabe asked.

Luke glanced at him in the rearview mirror. "What girl?"

"Our parents had dinner the other night. I heard you took a girl home for the weekend."

Luke nodded. "I did."

"Why didn't you tell me?"

"It wasn't a big deal."

Gabe laughed. "That's not how your parents described it."

"What did they say?"

"They said she's *the one.*"

Of course they thought that, whether it was true or not. She was the girl you hate to love and love to hate; either way she was nothing short of an addiction. He was out of control with her and desperate without her.

"So who is she?"

Such a simple question.

"A friend of a friend."

"Really? I know most of your friends. Maybe I know her." Gabe pulled into a parking spot.

That seemed one hundred percent probable.

Luke got out and slipped on his sunglasses. Gabe shut the door and rested his hand on Luke's shoulder. A shit-eating smirk not-so-elegantly graced his lips.

"I'm giving ya shit, man. God, it's exhilarating for once to watch the great Dr. Jones squirm a bit. I know you took Jessica home and you have some serious explaining to do."

"Does Kelly know?"

"Nope. She'd be pissed that Jessica hasn't said anything."

"How long have you known?"

"About a week."

"Why didn't you say something before now?"

"I assumed you'd tell me. You *were* going to tell me, right?"

"It's complicated."

"I don't get it. We fixed you two up. Why the secrecy?"

Luke turned and started unloading their gear. "As I said, it's complicated."

"Listen, dumb ass, I have a PhD in physics. I can handle

'complicated.' You won't even have to talk slow or use elementary vocabulary."

Luke sighed. "It's ... it's not that you won't get it or understand. It's that I can't tell you everything."

They weighted themselves down with bags and bikes. The car beeping when Gabe locked it was like a lightbulb going on in his head.

"Oh fuck! She's your patient, isn't she?"

The guy really was too smart for his own good.

CHAPTER THIRTY-TWO

KNIGHT

DAY two on their journey back to Omaha went much better than the previous one. AJ ate the salty peanuts and diabetic Twizzlers then washed them down with bottled tap water.

"There's a rest stop coming up. Want me to pull off?" AJ asked.

"Sure."

There was only one other vehicle as they pulled to a stop. They stretched and hobbled a bit toward the bathrooms, legs stiff from so many hours on the road. AJ was already in the truck by the time Jillian came out.

She froze.

Two of the lights along the walk were burnt out, leaving her nearly blind to anything on either side. Someone was lurking in the distance. She closed her eyes so she could focus on the faint rustling of footsteps in the brush.

"I know you."

The initial fear that clenched her heart was replaced with a killer's rage the second she processed the voice.

"Your hair is different, but I'd recognize that body anywhere."

The truck was twenty yards away. She could see the outline of AJ from the light of his phone screen. His chin was tilted toward his chest. Jillian needed to keep walking, but Jessica could not.

"You killed my friend. I know it was you. He wouldn't have committed suicide."

It was Jessica Day's opportunity for closure. She could walk away and let him decide his fate, but the license plates on the truck would lead him to AJ's family. Her identity could lead him to Omaha. Nobody wakes up and decides to be a killer, certainly not Jillian Knight, but Jessica Day was trained to defend herself and that training had made her a killer.

He laughed. It was the same sadistic laugh that filled Jessica's ears as Four cut her friend, Claire.

"I think this is fate. Of all the rest stops in this goddamn big ass country, what are the chances of us reuniting here, tonight? What are the chances of your boyfriend over there saving you before I put a bullet in your head?"

He moved closer and she closed her eyes again, hoping AJ couldn't see her in the shadows.

"I'd fuck your tight little ass first, but I don't trust you. I saw the news. You died and I don't trust ghosts." He inched closer.

Knox had blindfolded her over and over, sharpening all her other senses and removing the humanly guilt that came from taking the last blink of life from a victim's eyes.

It was too easy. All those years later, she remembered everything with exact precision. Two moves in less than five seconds later, he was disarmed and limp on the ground with a broken neck.

Her heart pounded as one lone tear trailed down her

cheek. It wasn't for him. It was for her—for Jillian. Jessica died a killer, but Jillian would have to live as one.

Taking a deep breath she balled her fists that were a bit shaky, opened her eyes without looking at the body even once, and walked to the truck.

AJ glanced up from his phone as she got in the driver's side. "You okay?"

She started the truck and nodded.

"They need to replace some lights around here. It's black as sin."

Jillian didn't acknowledge him. Some things were better left in the *sinful* dark.

They managed the last twenty-four hours of their trip without any more casualties. It was an awful thought, but Jillian was oddly grateful for the migraine that seized AJ on the last night. As hard as she tried to be herself, whoever Jillian Knight was supposed to be, it felt too forced. AJ would have noticed had his head not been dealing with such a pounding distraction.

As soon as they arrived home, AJ nearly overdosed on pain meds and collapsed onto his bed. Jillian went home.

"I'm so unbelievably pissed at you," Jackson scolded her the second she walked through the front door.

She dropped her bags and looked up at him, tears racing down her cheeks. The strength it took to make it home without falling apart in front of AJ almost killed her.

The anger in his eyes vanished the second he saw her pain. "Jesus! What happened?" He pulled her into his arms.

She fisted his shirt while sobs wracked her whole body. "I k-killed him."

Jackson gripped her arms and held her back. "Who?" he yelled, eyes wild.

"T-T-Trigger." She sagged in his hold.

"What? How? Look at me!"

"H-he was at a-a rest stop."

Jackson lowered them both to the floor and brushed his thumb over the mark on her lip from AJ.

"He hurt you. Where the fuck was AJ when this happened?"

She shook her head. "He didn't hurt me."

"Your lip—"

"That was AJ."

Jackson's body went rigid. "AJ hit you?"

"I told him to—"

"You what—"

"Stop!" She grabbed Jackson's face "Listen to me..." she sniffled "...this isn't about AJ. We stopped at a rest stop in Wyoming last night and AJ returned to the truck before me. It was dark and I heard someone in the distance. It was him, Jackson ... it was Trigger."

"You saw him?"

"No." Pain washed over her face. "I heard his voice. He recognized me."

"But you didn't look at him?"

She slowly turned her head side to side, keeping her eyes locked to his. She didn't have to say it. They both knew.

"He had a gun."

Jackson nodded once.

"AJ didn't see anything."

"He was following you?"

"No. His car was there before us. He was just as surprised to see me."

"Come on, you're smarter than that. There's no fucking way it was a coincidence."

"His car was there before we pulled off. There's no way he was following us."

"Did you see him get in or out of the car?"

"What?" Jillian tried to shake the confusion from her mind.

"What was the license plate number?"

"I-I don't know."

"There was only one other car in the lot and you didn't get the license plate number?"

"No! I didn't. It was late at night and we were in the middle of nowhere. Why the hell would I need to sweep the area?"

"Because that's what you were trained to do. It's been ingrained in you."

"It was him!"

Jackson held her head, forcing her to look him in the eye. "But was it his car? Is it possible he did in fact follow you? Could he have parked somewhere else?"

"Oh God!" Her jaw trembled. She couldn't say for sure if it was his car. It was just an assumption—a hasty, bad assumption. "We should call Knox."

"I'm sure he already knows. It's been almost twenty-four hours. They have eyes and ears everywhere. Knox knows what move you're going to make before you do. I'll search it up."

Jackson stood and pulled her up then grabbed his computer. Jillian turned her back to him. She didn't want to see any photos.

"Man found dead at Wyoming rest stop along I-80 East Wednesday night. The thirty-five-year-old male has been identified as Matthew Green from San Diego, California. Investigators don't suspect foul play but are waiting autopsy confirmation. Green has been on the FBI's most wanted list

*for over a decade. He is believed to have been the accomplice
of the infamous serial killer, Edwin Harvey."*

"Enough," Jillian whispered as one last tear rolled down
her cheek.

"The autopsy report will say heart attack."

Jillian swallowed. "I know."

"But you broke his neck." It wasn't a question.

She shook her head. "I didn't. Jessica Day did." It was
what she had to believe to keep her last shred of sanity.

TAKING the life of another never came without permanent
sacrifice. Everything had a balance. In exchange for Trigger
and Four's last breaths, Jessica had to let a piece of her soul
die, a soul that she shared with Jillian.

She left Jackson to deal with Knox and the high proba-
bility that she had been followed. None of it made sense.
Extraordinary coincidence was more comforting than the
idea that their identity and whereabouts had been compromised. But how and by whom?

"Welcome back!" Dodge greeted Jillian as she stepped
inside their house escaping the blistering temperature and
suffocating heat index.

"Thanks, it's good to be back."

"So you and AJ huh?" Dodge grinned.

Jillian felt an uncharacteristic blush heat along her neck
and cheeks. "Yes, we've become ... close."

"Well, Lilith and Char talked the other day and they're
both real smitten with you. Said they haven't seen AJ
looking this happy since he returned from his last tour
before the divorce."

Of course Lilith and Char talked because Lilith could

hear just fine out of one ear.

"You must have a lot of things to catch up on since I've been gone."

"Mainly drinking in peace, but yeah, a few other errands too." He winked and waved before leaving through the back door.

Lilith sat in her chair reading a book.

"Why did you let me believe you're deaf?"

Lilith raised her head an inch and placed her bookmark inside. "I hadn't planned on it."

Jillian sat down on the sofa beside Lilith's chair.

"But then you started telling me a story ... your story."

Jillian couldn't hide the pained look on her face. "No one was supposed to know ... I shouldn't have—"

"I'll take it to my grave, sweetie." Lilith held out her hand and Jillian took it.

Her heart squeezed with anguish, thinking how close Jackson had come to ending Lilith's life to save theirs. "If you ever tell anyone it would put your life in danger."

"It's not my story to tell. I promise."

Jillian nodded.

"Why are you in Omaha? I have to know why you left the love of your life," Lilith pleaded with her own pained expression.

Jillian felt the burden of Lilith's sympathy and knew the right choice, the only choice, was to never say another word to Lilith about Jessica Day.

However, Jillian thrived on bad choices.

"I didn't leave the love of my life. Jessica did because she died."

The soft wrinkles around Lilith's eyes deepened with confusion.

"It's complicated." Jessica made lemonade and then

made Lilith swear on the lives of her grandchildren that Jessica Day didn't exist.

CHAPTER THIRTY-THREE

DAY

"I swear to God ... if you say a fucking word—" Luke glared through narrowed eyes at Gabe.

"You'll lose your license. I get it. Once again ... not stupid. Wish I could say the same about you," Gabe mumbled as they trekked to the hotel like oxen hauling full loads.

"For the record, she's not my patient anymore, and we've never had sex."

"Thanks for that, but just so you know, I'm not keeping record. I'm your best friend. I know more about you than you know about yourself. But I think Kelly might be my *one,* and I don't want to screw it up because our best friends can't get their shit together."

"I'm working on it."

"Well, work faster. And tell Jessica she needs to say something to Kelly about your trip to Tahoe before she hears about it from my parents when we go to visit them next week. Got it?"

"Yeah, I got it."

Kelly and Jessica were waiting in the lobby.

"So, Jess and I were going to share a room, but she said we could stay together." Kelly leaned up and kissed Gabe. "The other room has two queen beds, are you okay with it too, Luke?"

"Yeah, are you two okay with staying in the same room?" Gabe gave Luke a tightlipped grin.

Luke looked at Jessica who was staring at her feet. "We'll survive."

Jessica looked up, wetting her lips then rubbing them together.

"Let's go then, ladies. We're not going to stand here holding all this shit forever," Gabe said.

"Oh ... here, babe." Kelly took a few bags from Gabe as Jessica jumped to ease Luke's load as well.

They took the elevator to their rooms and made plans to meet up for carbo-loading after Kelly and Gabe took a "nap."

"So..." Jessica shoved open the curtains to their ocean-view window "...I think I'm ready to talk about the bag you left at my place."

After weeks of the silent treatment since he'd left that bag, Luke was rethinking his unconventional plan to find intimacy with Jessica that didn't involve him losing blood.

"Is this the point in our 'relationship' that you confess you're into kink?" she asked, turning back toward him.

He grinned with his lips twisted to the side. "Yeah, about that ..."

She plunked down in the swivel chair, throwing her feet up on the desk, reminiscent of their time at his office— minus the leather chair.

"No. I'm not into bondage. You were going to be my exception."

"You're afraid of me?"

345

"No." He leaned against the wall, hands shoved in his pockets. "It was intended for you not for me."

"So ... you thought after my experience with Four that I might like to be restrained during sex?"

"I thought you might want to be with me and not feel guilty for making me bleed. I thought we could use the idea behind bondage to establish trust."

"I see. So you don't trust me?"

"I trust you implicitly."

She drew in a slow breath. "How can you say that?" she whispered.

"Because I believe you."

"What do you believe?"

Luke pushed off the wall and bent over, resting his hands on the arms of her chair—his face inches from hers. "I believe you love me."

He looked at her lips and she looked at his.

"Kiss me, Jones."

How COULD he trust her when she didn't trust herself? His lips met hers and it didn't matter. Jessica needed him beyond passion, beyond reason, beyond breathing.

Her hands went straight for his hair as she dropped her feet to the floor. She fell so deep into his kiss her lungs screamed for air, yet her tongue reached for more. The harder she tugged, the louder he moaned. His taste brought her to life. His smell drowned all thought. His touch felt like a whispered promise.

"Luke ..." His name floated from her lips—a fervent plea —a prayer. The heat of his mouth drifted down her neck.

She arched her back begging to feel him anywhere and everywhere all at once.

Luke wrapped her tight in his arms until their bodies cursed the clothes between them. He laid her on the bed, her hands tugging and pulling at his pants, his drawing the straps to her top down her arms.

She closed her eyes. "What if I—"

"Do it." He freed her breasts and sucked one nipple while kneading the other with a firm grip. "I'll die if we stop."

Want.

Need.

Trust.

"I'll hate myself if we don't."

He stilled. Releasing her breast, he closed his eyes and sighed.

"You hate me?" She grimaced, not really wanting him to answer.

Eyes still shut, he shook his head.

"But I'm killing you."

He nodded then looked at her. She rolled to her side and sat up, pulling her top back in place.

"Dammit!" she yelled and pounded her fists into the bed. "What is wrong with me? I've been thinking about this for months. I'm a freaking statistical phenomena. Who goes from less than zero percent to one hundred in two weeks' time?"

He reached for her but she stood and pulled away. "Jessica ..."

"No." She began to pace the room. "Don't try to down play this. I'm a cock tease, plain and simple. How did this happen? I'm the RSVP girl and you did. You RSVP'd and both times you've been denied access. Cock. Tease!"

"Jessica ..."

"I'm not a procrastinator. I get the job done. It may get a little bloody, but I do it. Be damned the consequences!" She ran her fingers through her hair. "You gave me permission to make you bleed. Nobody does that. Why did you do that? I don't need your permission ... that negates the whole point of it. You've completely messed with my mojo."

Luke fought back a smirk. "Your sex mojo?"

"Yes! Exactly." She steepled her fingers against her lips. "Now the question is why? Why are you messing with my sex mojo?"

He rolled onto his back and flopped his arm over his face. "This is the weirdest conversation I've ever had ... and I've had some *really* weird conversations."

"Come on, Jones. Show me your stuff. In your expert opinion why is this happening to me?"

"I'm not doing this."

"Why not?" She planted her fists on her hips.

"Because I'll come across as some conceited jerk."

"Say it."

"No," he grumbled.

"Say. It!"

"Fine!" He sprang up, ramrod straight. "You can't have sex with me because you're scared. I'm probably the only person who completely trusts you and that scares you because you love me. You care what I think and the idea of hurting me and breaking that trust scares you to death because you don't. Trust. Yourself."

She blinked at him, over and over again. "It's not the pain. I know you could handle my nails and teeth breaking your skin. It's the embarrassment ... because nobody in their right mind does that. And I know how ludicrous it must sound saying this to my *ex-psychiatrist*, but I don't want you to think that I'm crazy."

She bit her upper lip and sighed. "Sometimes it works. In the throes of passion, drawing blood can heighten the desire, intensify the lust. But afterword, the scars and bite marks are no longer sexy … they're insane. The so-called 'control' I need during sex, it's emasculating to normal men. I've never slept with the same guy twice."

"You think I'll leave you if we have sex?"

"Yes," she whispered.

"I won't."

"You don't know that."

"Then let me prove it."

She slipped on her shoes. "I'm hungry. Let's go snack while we wait to have dinner."

Luke stood and fastened his jeans. "Do you realize I think about you all the time? When we first met I couldn't wait to get away from you and the moment you were gone I couldn't wait to see you again. You already control my thoughts … does it really matter if I let you control my body at this point?"

Jessica opened the door and glanced back over her shoulder. "So you're obsessed with me?"

Luke smirked. "Yes."

She shrugged. "I can live with that."

"Okay, gentlemen, place your bets." Kelly grinned, spinning her pasta around her fork as they enjoyed an early dinner.

"Bets?" Luke's face twisted in confusion.

"Yes. Will Jess finish in first place tomorrow?"

Jessica rolled her eyes.

"Have you ever finished in first place?" Gabe asked.

She shook her head.

"I always beat her, and I've never taken first place. But Jess always says she could finish first if she wanted to, she just doesn't care what place she takes."

"It's true." Jessica shrugged.

"Bullshit. It's a competition. The whole point is to try and finish first." Kelly's voice peaked a few pitches higher in disbelief.

"A thousand dollars says Jessica finishes first tomorrow." Luke looked up from his plate at three sets of eyes gawking at him.

"A *thousand* dollars?" Gabe asked.

Luke stared at Jessica. She narrowed her eyes at him.

"Yes. You in?" Luke challenged.

Gabe shook his head and grinned. "Sorry, Jess, no offense but I can't say no. This is money in my pocket."

"I'm in too. But only if she loses. If by some freak-of-nature chance she wins, I don't really have the thousand dollars." Kelly giggled.

Everyone laughed, except Jessica. "What's in it for me?"

"A medal and bragging rights." Kelly winked.

Jessica returned her glare to Luke. He was using her to hustle his best friend. "The bet has to be two grand and Luke gives me half if he wins."

"What?" Kelly exclaimed.

Gabe chewed on the inside of his cheek, eyes flitting between Jessica and Luke. "What do you say, babe? Do I have anything to worry about?"

Kelly shook her head and grinned. "Jess is full of shit. Take his money."

Luke leaned back in his chair. "If I lose, Ms. Day, you'll be paying half."

She shoved another bite of pasta into her mouth, already having eaten everyone else under the table. "Deal," she mumbled.

Gabe checked his watch. "We're getting to bed early. But you two feel free to order dessert, drink too much, and stay up late. By this time tomorrow you'll both be passed out and two grand lighter."

Kelly kissed Jessica on the cheek. "Sweet dreams, hun. No pressure."

As soon as they walked away, Jessica grabbed the rest of Kelly's pasta and started in on it. Luke eyed her.

"Don't judge me, Jones."

"Why would I judge you? Just because you're eating your body weight in pasta tonight, and I have a sizable bet placed on you finishing first tomorrow?"

She shrugged. "It was your idea, not mine. But for what it's worth, I count cards too if you want to take me to Vegas and use me for some more quick cash."

He chuckled. "You don't count cards."

She paused, spaghetti hanging down her chin.

He looked to the ceiling with a slight head shake. "Of course you do."

After slurping the last piece of spaghetti, she wiped her mouth and folded her hands over her stuffed stomach. Their table was off in a corner away from other patrons. Jessica took a quick glance around then rested her gaze on Luke.

"The incessant thoughts in your brain are deafening, Jones. Just ask me."

"Ask you what?"

"I don't know, it's your brain. But you always look at me

with this strange curiosity. I suppose you'll say you're studying me, but I sense it's more than that. So what is it?"

"Tell me about your training."

"For tomorrow?"

"No, the training that led to a broken pool stick at my parents' house the morning I woke you up."

"You mean the information that I can tell you but then I'll have to kill you?"

Luke smiled. "Yes."

Jessica nodded. "Well, we all have to die somehow." She took a sip of water. "Okay, here we go ... Once upon a time there was a DEA agent who went undercover to bring down a powerful drug lord. Two days before he was going to have the evidence to bring the whole operation down, his cover was blown. Three hours later his pregnant wife was abducted from their home. A week later her body washed up on the shore. The shitty part? The DEA agent knew his cover was going to be blown and he requested his wife be taken into protective custody. His request was denied based on lack of evidence that there was an eminent danger."

She stared at Luke, waiting for him to process everything.

"Is there more to the story?"

"There's a moral to the story. The government can't be trusted to keep its employees and their families safe. So now what I'm about to say is just hypothetical because I kinda like ya, Jones."

They shared flirty smiles.

"I'd hate to have to kill you. I can't imagine there are too many other shrinks in this city that would barter with me."

Luke frowned. "You're probably right."

"So imagine this for a moment. What if a group of highly trained, high ranking officials from various branches of government, including the FBI, CIA, DEA, the military —SEALS teams etc., formed a secret group? And this group included immediate family members and the sole purpose of this hypothetical group might be to train its members in a very elite type of self-defense."

"Is that what happened?"

"Please, Jones ... I said this was hypothetical," she scoffed.

"Okay, *hypothetically* what type of self-defense training?"

"Depends. Some might be trained to avert or possibly escape capture. It would depend on their physical and psychological capabilities. Others might be trained to protect and defend."

"Like an unofficial army?"

"Hypothetically, yes. If there were an emergency, say a kidnapping or hostage situation involving a member, there would be no political hoops to jump through, because after all—the group doesn't exist—therefore, the 'elite' members who are not officially employed by the government could be called upon to *extract* the captured member from the dangerous situation."

"So are we talking martial arts training?"

"For the elite members?"

"Yes."

"Everything. They would be trained by the best and taught everything they know. Think of it as a special forces boot camp on steroids."

"These members are trained to kill?"

"Yes."

Luke nodded, his Adam's apple bobbed with a hard swallow. "So *hypothetically*, if you were part of a group like this would you be considered an elite member?"

"Most of those members would be trained from an early age ... say fourteen. They would be single and in top physical and mental condition. You have a two thousand dollar bet with Gabe that I'm going to finish first tomorrow. So I think you already know the answer to your question."

Luke nodded again.

"So now I have a question for you, *Dr. Jones.* As you can imagine, someone who watched their friend die would no longer be considered in top "mental condition," and would therefore no longer be called upon to save someone's life. My question is ... how long would it take this person to walk in a room and not think of weapons or the means to kill the people in it?"

He rested his chin on his fist. "I honestly don't know. Maybe never."

She appreciated his honesty. Luke had become her truth. But it was just another confirmation that she would never be the same again. That confirmation from the doctor himself left her with two options: bow out gracefully in a woe-is-me-you-deserve-someone-better way, or get the guy with a fuck-it-I-deserve-happiness-as-much-as-anyone-else attitude.

On the precipice of a lethal carb-coma, it was best to delay that decision until after the triathlon.

CHAPTER THIRTY-FOUR

KNIGHT

THE "STREAK" of Peaceful Woods in red rain boots and not much else zipped through the yards wielding a weed eater. Normally she tried to set pace with Bill on his mower to make her negotiated wage seem justified. But on that particular day she set a new record, staying a notch above the subpar quality the residents had come to expect from Bill's complete lack of attention to detail.

"It's here!" she squealed, while hanging the weed eater in Bill's garage.

The sexy lawn lady channeled her inner child on Christmas, chasing her new red baby down the private drive, boots smacking, hands waving.

"She's so damn sexy!" Jillian grinned as Sara, her training consultant, climbed out of Jillian's new red Mercedes.

"You're something else. I don't think in the history of the company anyone has ever earned a car this fast." Sara handed her the key and waved to her husband who pulled up behind them in a minivan. "I'm proud to say I trained you."

Jillian took the key. "Yes, I couldn't have done it without you." A lie, but Jillian reserved her arrogant gloating personality for Jackson and only Jackson. "You didn't need to deliver it. I could have gone to the dealership."

"Nope, I trained you so it's tradition that I deliver the car to you." She opened the passenger door to the minivan. "Enjoy it while you can. Someday your chariot will have dual sliding doors and a DVD player on the ceiling."

"Bye, Sara." Jillian laughed.

She ran her hand along the shiny paint.

"It's an overpriced Jetta," Jackson chimed.

"Shut it." She grinned while feathering her fingers over the glossy red coating. It *was* an overpriced Jetta. "But it's a gift so who cares."

"Speaking of gifts. I talked with Knox."

Jillian stiffened.

"As we already assumed he took care of the *incident*."

"Why does he think Trigger was there?"

"Coincidence."

Jillian turned. "But you don't believe that."

Jackson shook his head. "And I don't think you do anymore either."

She didn't know what to believe. If it were a coincidence then the universe dropped her a gift ... the gift of closure. What had she done to deserve such a gift? Nothing.

"It wasn't coincidence. I'm not that lucky. But if Knox doesn't believe it then what can we do?"

"Wait."

She sighed. "Yeah, wait like sitting ducks. Fabulous."

Jackson raised his chin. Jillian turned and waved at AJ pulling in his garage, wearing a timid smile.

"I'm going inside. Don't be pissed."

"About?" She cocked her head to the side.

"Nothing." He pivoted and walked in the garage, turning just before closing the door. His face wrinkled into a slight grimace.

She skipped across the yard and into AJ's garage. He eased out of his Jeep checking out her yard work attire, or lack there of.

"See something you like, Sergeant?"

He grabbed his messenger bag from the backseat. "Yes. I just wish everyone else weren't seeing it."

"Are you grumpy today?"

Head shake. "I have some work to do. Maybe I'll call you later."

Jillian watched him with confusion as he went in the house. She followed him.

"I said I have work to do." His words carried an edge as he set his bag on the counter.

She moved toward him.

"Stop." He held up a flat hand.

Jillian stopped. "Um..." she sniffed one of her arm pits "...I put deodorant on. I wasn't going to stay. I just wanted to give you a reason to call me later." She gave him a sexy grin and continued toward him.

"Jillian," he warned, retreating a step.

"Do you want me to beg?"

"No. I want you to go home."

"Kiss me." She inched close as the worried look of discomfort deepened along his forehead.

He grabbed her arms, holding them to her sides, and gave her a quick kiss. Then he turned her around and gave her a gentle nudge toward the door. "Now off you go."

"Aric James!" She whipped around and shoved him against the wall.

"Fuck!" he hissed.

She jumped back, eyes trailing up and down his body until landing on his hand pressed gently to his ribs. She slid his shirt up. "Your ribs are bruised."

"Brilliant, Dr. Knight."

"What hap—" Her eyes grew wide. "Jackson. He did this, didn't he?" She turned and AJ grabbed her arm.

"Stop. He was looking out for his sister."

"I gave you permission to hit me. Did you give him permission to do this?"

"No, but he earned my respect. If you were my sister, I'd beat any guy a breath away from his last for laying a hand on you. I think he let me off pretty easy."

"Did you hit him back?"

He shook his head. "It wasn't a fight. It was an understanding."

"An understanding?"

"Yes. I understand that I answer to him when it comes to your wellbeing."

She fisted the collar of his jacket. He winced as he bent down to her.

"You two Neanderthals answer to me, not each other. Got it?" She kissed him hard, feeling the pain in his ribs through the reluctance of his lips. "Now, take something for the pain or sex later is going to make the infamous blow job seem like a trip to Disneyland." Pivoting on her signature air of confidence, she waltzed out the door like a queen.

"We're not having sex la—" The door shut before AJ could finish his not-so-confident declaration.

Of course they weren't having sex later, but ruffling his grumpy feathers had become her new favorite pastime.

JILLIAN ALWAYS TOLD JACKSON EVERYTHING— EVENTUALLY. And what she attempted to bury in her emotional tomb that she'd take to her grave, he knew that stuff too. Though out of respect, he kept that knowledge to himself. She needed that illusion of control and he gave it to her. It kept her on the right side of sanity—most of the time. AJ was the wild card. Jackson wasn't sure where he fit into Jillian's level of sanity. Her asking to be punished, no matter her reasoning behind it, was a hard limit. Jackson never crossed it, and he sure as shit wasn't going to let anyone else get away with crossing it.

"Where are you, dick face?" she yelled as the door slammed shut.

And so it began. Her love for him was so touching.

He pumped through pull-ups in the doorway to his bedroom. There was no need to answer. She'd smell his sweat and pain like a bloodhound.

"Mother fucker!" He fell from the bar, landing on his side in fetal position, gasping for his next breath through the intense pain radiating in his stomach and groin. "Below the belt..." he gritted through his teeth "... not ... cool."

"Yeah, well lucky for you, once you stop gagging on your testicles you'll be fine. AJ's ribs are going to be sore for weeks. What is wrong with you?"

Every nerve in a guy's body connects to his balls. It was both a blessing and a curse. Once the nausea and lightheadedness faded, all that was left was the dull ache.

Jackson fought his way into a sitting position against the wall. "For reasons that have somehow slipped my mind at the moment..." he continued to grimace "...I feel responsible for the evil demon that is my sister."

She crossed her arms over her chest and leaned forward, looking down on him with said evil demon's glare. "AJ has

PTSD and suffers unimaginable migraines. I've hit him in the nose twice, broken it once, and left an embarrassing and most regrettable collage of claw and bite marks tattooed over his body. I think it's best we refrain from any more bodily harm before he slaps a restraining order against both of us. Agreed?"

Jackson nodded. Jillian turned to leave.

"Jill?"

"What?"

"I think you've had enough too. Don't let him hit you again. Agreed?"

"Agreed," she whispered.

Jackson's phone rang. It was on his bed, ten feet away. A *long* ten feet. He crawled through the pain to answer it.

"Yes?" he groaned.

"Hey, pookie. My mom's out of town. Want to have a playdate?"

It was a good possibility that any girl inviting him over for a playdate might be too young for him. That and Mr. Snuffelupagus was not feeling so pookie that night.

"Sorry, Dahlia, I'm a little under the weather right now."

"Oh dear ... need me to come over and take care of you?"

"No, no, no ... I'm good. I'll call you." He ended the call and rested his head against the bed. "Dammit, I've *got* to keep my dick out of that girl's mouth and cut her loose."

HALLMARK REALLY NEEDED to make a *Sorry I Beat the Shit Out of You* card. The Knights would have purchased them in bulk. In lieu of the nonexistent poetic gesture,

Jillian opted for breakfast in bed delivered to AJ, at the ass crack of dawn since that's when he awoke.

She retrieved the well-hidden key under his planter and let herself inside.

"Your lack of conscience or morals when it comes to breaking and entering is disturbing," AJ mumbled from behind the morning paper. At five a.m. he was already showered and dressed.

"I brought you breakfast in bed as a peace offering for Jackson's irrational behavior. So if you wouldn't mind getting naked and under the sheets, I'll set this on a plate and surprise you with it in about two minutes."

AJ folded the paper and tossed it aside. Taking a sip of his coffee he made a quick assessment of her attire—black lace panties, a grey and white polka dot tank top, and her favorite red rain boots.

"I'm fairly certain whatever you managed to throw together for my breakfast is the opposite of a peace offering."

"Thanks for the vote of confidence."

"You're welcome." He couldn't keep his eyes from wandering over her body.

"If you don't stop looking at me like that, the only thing you'll be eating for breakfast is me."

He raised a brow like a sexy accent to his sly smile. "I already know you taste better than anything in that bag." He shoved the newspaper on the floor. "Hop up and spread 'em."

She sighed. "Nice job calling my bluff. Actually, it's cinnamon coffeecake—"

"Oh Lord ... I bet you actually put coffee grounds in it, didn't you?"

She set the bag on the table and straddled his lap. He

tensed, bending as far back into the chair as he could to keep a safe distance between her and his ribs.

Pinching his lips together like a duck's, she narrowed her eyes. "As I was saying ... it's cinnamon coffeecake that Greta made for Jackson while I was gone. Apparently she was under the impression I do the cooking and therefore he was going to starve if she didn't offer him sustenance until I returned.

AJ jerked his head to the side, freeing his mouth from her grip. "I've had Greta's coffeecake, it's the best. Now..." he grabbed her hips and lifted her off his lap with a small, painful grimace "...move your rump so I can have some."

"Rump?"

AJ pulled the foil off the coffeecake. "It means ass or buttocks."

Jillian leaned her hip against the table, arms crossed over her chest. "I know what it means. You sounded like an old man using that term. It wasn't sexy."

He shrugged then hummed—*that* sounded sexual, but it wasn't about her rump ... it was Greta's food porn. "Need I remind you that I am older than you, but I'd rather you not call me an 'old man.' And I'd imagine you don't come across the word rump much in the fake meat aisle at the store, but it's a meat term, like rump roast."

Jillian picked off a chunk of the crumble topping and popped it in her mouth. It was orgasmic. "So you like rump roast?"

"Yes, I do."

"Well then, I'm going to take rump as a compliment coming from you. I do believe in your *older*-man way you just told me I'm a fine piece of ass."

AJ grinned around his fork as he slid it from his mouth. Sexy. As. Fuck. Jillian's panties fainted to her ankles.

"Did you hear about Matthew Green?" AJ nodded toward the newspaper.

Jillian froze. "Who?" She cleared her throat to mask the shakiness of her voice.

"Edwin Harvey? He died over a decade ago, but surely you've heard the name. He was a serial killer from San Diego. I think he killed over fifteen young women—stalked them on the internet. Anyway, he had an accomplice, Matthew Green, who disappeared. He's been on the FBI's most wanted list for years. He was found dead at a rest stop in Wyoming. It was the rest stop we stopped at late Wednesday night. His body was found early Thursday morning."

"W-what are you saying?" She swallowed hard.

AJ chuckled. "Just that it's crazy. What are the chances that we were so close to crossing paths?"

Jillian shook her head. "Yeah ... crazy."

CHAPTER THIRTY-FIVE

DAY

LUKE AND JESSICA looked at the two queen beds and then each other.

"What's my safest bet?" Sleeping in the same room with the woman he desired to the point of physical pain was not going to be an easy feat for Luke.

She pursed her lips to the side. "Hmm ... I'd say the one closest to the door. If you get up in the middle of the night to use the bathroom you won't accidentally bump my bed and startle me. That might not end well."

"My prostate's not sixty years old, but good plan anyway. What about in the morning? I didn't pack a pool stick."

She laughed. "I wake fine to alarms, voices, serenading ... just don't touch me."

"Serenading?"

"Yes."

"Any requests?"

"Tony Bennett, *I Left My Heart in San Francisco* will do just fine." She grabbed her toiletry bag and squeezed past him to the bathroom.

His dick twitched just from the brief brush of her arm against his. He. Was. In. Trouble.

"So if you could live anywhere in the world you'd choose San Francisco?"

"Yes."

"Why?"

She mumbled over her toothbrush. "I've lived there my whole life and it feels like a physical part of me. If I ever leave it will not be willingly and my heart will seriously be ripped from my chest."

Luke loved the city by the bay too, but he'd never felt a physical connection to it beyond his address ... until he met Jessica.

"What about you, Jones?" She stepped out of the bathroom wearing lacy panties and a pink camisole top that hid absolutely nothing.

Not good.

"If you could live anywhere in the world where would you choose?"

Her bed.

"Uh ... it's hard..." he was hard "...to say. I haven't traveled the world. I probably haven't been to paradise yet."

Her bed.

"Well, let me know if you find it."

He wouldn't have to tell her, she would know.

She slipped under the covers. "You're staring, Jones."

"You're half naked, of course I'm staring." He gripped the back of his neck and groaned while grabbing his bag and escaping to the bathroom.

He prayed for her to fall asleep so he wouldn't have to deal with an awkward goodnight situation, but ... no such luck.

"Pajama pants? Really?" she teased.

"They're lounge pants and I don't usually sleep in them, except when I'm traveling."

"What do you sleep in at home?"

He climbed in bed and shut off the wall light between them. "I don't wear anything in bed at home."

A soft whimper came from her side of the room. His heart hammered in his chest but not nearly as hard as it was in another area of his body.

"I can't get to sleep. I'm too ..."

He swallowed. "Too?"

"Turned on, horny, in need of a release."

"I don't want to know that." He gritted his teeth, willing his hand to not slip into his pants.

"Well I didn't want to know that you normally sleep in the nude."

"Then you shouldn't have asked."

"I need my sleep, Jones, or we're both out a grand tomorrow."

He massaged his temples. "Well what do you want me to do about it?"

"Ugh ... I don't know. Let's just do it. Let's have sex."

It was a brilliant idea. She read his mind.

"Good night, Jessica." His conscience was an evil, blue-balling bastard. "What the hell?"

"I *need* it, Jones," she whispered in his ear while climbing on top of him.

His dick was so hard she nearly snapped it clean from his body while grinding her pelvis into his. The situation was volatile and extremely time-sensitive. Four layers: her barely-there lace panties, the cotton sheet, his pants, and his briefs that were wearing thin against his erection and the rowing motion of her hips.

"N-not a good idea," he lied.

She thrust her tongue into his mouth and clawed at his chest. "Mmm ... do you have a better idea?" she murmured against his neck, working her mouth down to his shoulder.

He didn't.

Starting at her hips, he slid his hands up her body, stopping at her breasts, squeezing them as she moaned in response.

"Oh God, Jones ... I need this so bad."

It was impossible to abandon a woman in need. Luke shoved her top above her breasts and sat up with a desperate jerk as his mouth devoured her. She cried his name, arching her back, as his tongue slid across her nipple. The desire to crawl inside her body and never return sucked every last coherent thought from his brain.

The sensible doctor was nowhere to be found. A man with his own needs clenched her small waist and guided her body over his, cursing all four of those damn layers. Her head dropped to his shoulder as her hands clutched the muscles along his back.

It happened so fast—without warning.

Luke flipped her over and kissed her, pinning her to the bed with the weight of his body.

A deep grunt that sounded like an animal catching the fatal end of an arrow vibrated from Luke's chest as he rolled to the side.

"Oh my God!" Jessica flipped on the light. "I-I'm so ..." she stuttered with her hand cupped over her mouth, kneeling on the bed beside him. Tears sprang from her eyes as her words lodged in her throat. The regret on her face cut so much deeper than the bite on his shoulder and the torn skin on his back.

She broke down before his eyes because *he* couldn't control himself. Him ... not her.

"Jess." He pulled her into his arms.

"Not you..." she sobbed "...I w-wasn't supposed t-to do that ... n-not to you."

"It's okay. *I'm* okay."

She pushed away from his grip—blood on her lips, blood on her fingernails. "It's not okay! You rolled over on me, pinning me down, and ... and I-I lost it because I'm a fucking psychotic monster."

"Jessica," he said in a reprimanding tone.

She shot out of bed and ran to the bathroom.

"Jess." He knocked on the locked door, unable to hear anything but water running. "Open up."

"I just ... just ... give me a minute." Her words, a mournful plea, gutted him.

He sat on the end of the bed and waited. Every accolade he'd ever earned weighed heavily on his conscience. He was a fraud and the broken woman behind the door was proof. They couldn't go back to a doctor-patient relationship, yet every step forward felt like a detour.

She opened the door. In that moment he knew it would be his life's purpose to give her everything—his body, his mind, his soul, his very. Last. Breath.

"I'm so sorry." She sucked in a shaky breath, holding it together, once again proving her immortal strength. Crawling on the bed behind him, she pressed a warm wash cloth to the cuts.

He held his breath, stopping time to commit to memory the way his heart ached for hers. It was the most incredible feeling in the world. He'd never felt more alive. She eased off the bed and stood between his legs, cleaning the bite mark on his shoulder.

"I don't expect you to forgive me." She kept her eyes on his shoulder.

His hand covered hers. When she looked at him, nothing else in the world mattered. "Jessica Day ..."

She bit her lips together, a new round of tears swelled in her eyes, her breath captive in her chest.

He took the washcloth from her and brought her hand to his lips, kissing the inside of her wrist. "I'm so ... very ... one-hundred percent ... madly in love with you."

Relief flooded from her eyes in uncontrolled tears. He pulled her into his arms and held her like his life depended on it.

"What if—"

"Shh." He kissed her just below her ear then whispered, "No what-ifs. I've got this. I've got *you*—I'll always have you."

THE GOOD NEWS? Luke loved her. The bad news? Luke loved her. It had been the most emotionally draining and romantic night of Jessica's life—until they crawled into separate beds and went to sleep. Maybe they could live like a ninety-year-old couple—forego the sex, sleep in separate beds, but eat together and hold hands on long walks.

At two a.m. the alarm sounded. She crawled out of bed and grabbed their two fruit smoothies from the small refrigerator. Luke didn't even open his eyes when she nudged him to wake up, but he followed her orders: drink this and go back to sleep. Her regimen for race day started with breakfast at two, sleep, wake, hydrate, and kick ass.

Several hours later, Tony Bennett serenaded her in her dreams about hearts being left in San Francisco. It was so real, as if her mind had a volume button allowing each word to get louder and louder until she opened her eyes.

"Good morning." Luke grinned, sitting on the edge of his bed at a safe distance. His phone was on the nightstand beside her and Tony Bennett was indeed serenading her, but not in her dreams. "I called Tony and told him it was a big day for you so he agreed to be your alarm clock."

Jessica smiled. "But he had a prior engagement and couldn't fit me into his schedule so you downloaded his song from iTunes."

"Are you going to call me out on such inconsequential details for the rest of our lives?"

Her heart stumbled over its next few beats. *The rest of our lives?* She sat up in bed as he moved over to her, cupping his hand behind her head and pulling her to his lips.

"Oh, uh ... wait." She ducked out of his hold and crawled out of bed.

"What are you doing?"

"Brushing my teeth," she mumbled over a mouth full of suds while internally frowning at the puffy eyelids in the mirror.

He peeked around the corner. "Really? You won't kiss me until you've brushed your teeth?"

"Really. That shit's only sexy in movies and books." She wiped her mouth with the towel then wrapped her arms around his neck.

"So you wouldn't kiss me if I had morning breath?"

"As long as I didn't then yes."

"That makes no sense."

"It does. I'm human. My shit stinks and my mouth tastes like rotten mothballs in the morning. You, however, always smell like sin and sex mixed with some expensive soap. I think you could bottle your sweat and sell it for a hundred dollars an ounce."

"Shut up and kiss me." He plunged his tongue into her minty-fresh mouth confirming his sinfully sexy appeal that left her feeling tipsy and breathless.

He released her and she grabbed the vanity to steady herself.

"I'm going to go a week without showering or brushing my teeth to see if you change your mind."

"You do that. I bet you'll have a harem trailing you as your pheromones multiply and age like a fine wine."

He shook his head. "Get dressed. We've got some money to win."

KELLY TEXTED Jessica that they'd meet them in the lobby after she and Gabe grabbed breakfast. They didn't follow Jessica's well-researched nutrition plan for race day. Their loss.

"You need to tell Kelly that we went to Tahoe together," Luke said in the elevator on their way to the lobby.

Jessica pulled the bottle of Smart Water she'd been nursing away from her mouth. "Why?"

"Because my parents had dinner with their neighbors, who happen to be Gabe's parents. Basically everyone *except* Kelly knows I took you to Tahoe."

"Gabe didn't tell her?"

"Nope. Said she'd be less than pleased if she heard it from anyone but you."

"Got it."

The elevator doors opened.

"Good morning!" Kelly squealed, jumping up and down. All that energy was wasted on a greeting and she wasn't going to be able to retrieve it on the last leg of the race.

Jessica grinned. "Luke took me to Tahoe a couple weeks ago. Sorry, I forgot to mention it. Are we ready to go?"

Kelly's eyes bugged out. "Wait ... what?"

"I was stressed about *things* and he thought I could use a getaway so we went to Tahoe. I did some manual labor with his dad. Luke sat on his ass reading and then took his sister to lunch. We watched fireworks from the houseboat, and I unsuccessfully tried to seduce him by skinny dipping in the lake. Felicity packed us a to-go bag for the road and we arrived home Sunday night. Now ... is everyone ready to go?"

Crickets.

"I'll take that as a yes." She slung her bag over her shoulder, grabbed her bike, and gestured with her head toward the hotel entrance. "Lets go, peeps. I've got some ass to kick and names to take."

They found parking at the event, checked in, and got all their equipment and energy packs in place. The women were going first.

"I just sat on my ass reading all day, huh?" Luke pulled Jessica into his arms, earning a gasp from Kelly behind them.

"I call it like I see it, Jones."

He grinned, the adoration shining bright. "See you at the finish."

"Be careful and don't die on me." She leaned up and kissed him.

"Die?"

"Yes, it happens. Usually during the swimming."

"The adrenaline surge."

She nodded. "A shitload of adrenaline. Everyone racing

into the unpredictable waves, idiots swimming over the top of you or kicking you in the face, so just ... be careful."

"I'm flattered you care so much."

She shrugged. "Don't be. I'm really looking out for myself. If you die I may never find another guy who 'gets' me."

He smacked her ass. "Show Kelly how it's done."

"I heard that," Kelly yelled as Jessica jogged to catch up to her on the way to the start.

Gabe rested his hand on Luke's shoulder, giving it a firm squeeze. "Ready to pay up?"

"Wanna up it to three grand?"

"You're insane," Gabe chuckled. "But hey ... I'll take your money."

Several hours later Kelly and Jessica waited at the end of the course, watching the men's group trickle through the finish line.

"I'm ready to crash." Kelly drizzled the last few drops of her sports drink into her mouth and leaned against Jessica. "Those waves were brutal today and I swear the wind about knocked me off my bike. By the time I started running, my tank was completely drained."

"Yeah, it was a hard one today."

"Shut up," Kelly grumbled. "I feel like you've been scamming me for years."

"Here they come." Jessica lifted on her toes to get a better view.

"See ... Gabe was nice enough to wait for Luke so they could finish together."

Jessica laughed. "What makes you so sure Luke didn't wait for Gabe?"

The guys crossed the finish line far from first place, but the weak grins on their faces said they were in fact pleased to have made it to the end still standing. Luke spotted Jessica first with his unspoken question. She played the somber defeated part long enough for Gabe to take a look and get his hopes up. He patted Luke on the shoulder with a can't-win-'em-all look of arrogance on his face as they ambled closer to Kelly and Jessica.

Kelly shook her head at Gabe as Jessica held the finish line tape above her head. Her grin was wicked.

Luke's grin was knowing. "That's my girl!" Luke yelled, picking up his pace to a weak jog. He bear-hugged her, swinging her in a circle. "You're so damn incredible." He kissed her until his lungs demanded air again.

Jessica didn't need the medal, the tape, or the money. *"That's my girl!"* was all she needed and the adrenaline rush she got from those three words exceeded anything she felt during the race.

"No way ... not possible." Gabe looked to Kelly for confirmation.

"Sorry, babe ... she played both of us."

Gabe slumped, resting his hands on his knees. "Three. Thousand. Dollars."

"What?" Kelly questioned. "Two."

Gabe shook his head. "We upped it ... just before the start of the race.

Jessica looked up at Luke, who was smirking behind the mouth of his water bottle. "Fifty-fifty split, Jones," she warned.

Luke laughed. "Take it all. You earned it. That..." he gestured to the ugly defeat morphing Gabe's face "...that's all I needed." He took her hand and pulled her toward the tents in search of some energy. "I had complete faith in you, but I'm not going to lie ... when you held up that tape I nearly fell to my knees in awe of you. That's ... impressive."

"Truth?" Jessica looked up at him.

"Yeah, what?"

"The course, the wind, my recent distraction from training..." she narrowed her eyes at him "...it all kicked my ass today. I stopped counting how many times I thought I was going to die. And those women who were on my heels the entire time ... they wanted it. They wanted it more than me."

"Yet you still finished first."

She turned into his embrace as they stood in line. "I finished first for you, not me."

CHAPTER THIRTY-SIX

KNIGHT

LILITH STARED at Jillian with her head slightly tilted, eyes glazed in a dream state. After a few moments of silence, she blinked from the realization that story time was over for the day.

"I get chills every time you tell me about Luke." She sighed with a wistful smile. "I'm living vicariously through you and life is good."

They both laughed.

"You took first place in a triathlon. That's amazing."

Jillian nodded. "The only first place medal I ever took. I wasn't lying to him. It was excruciating, but I wanted him to be proud of me because there was just so much that I'd done that was not worthy of his respect. It's a cliché, but he made me want to be a better person. Unfortunately, it wasn't so black and white. The mind is too complicated and emotions, impressions, and feelings are stronger than anything. I couldn't just flip the switch and declare myself cured. Jessica Day's past will haunt me for the rest of my life."

Lilith gave her a sad smile. "Tell me about Sarge."

Jillian grinned, trapping her lower lip between her teeth like a ridiculously giddy teenager. "What can I say? He's sexy, intense, overwhelming, grumpy as hell most days, and stuck in either an emotional or physical war with his past on a daily basis."

"So you're crazy about him?"

Jillian squinted one eye. "You already know I'm 'crazy.'"

"Oh stop it, dear. You are not."

"It's hard to say. I like him ... a lot. The sex is ..."

Lilith's eyes grew big as Jillian winked at her.

"Anyway, the problem is ... Jillian's having trouble letting Jessica go, or maybe Jessica's angry with Jillian for trying to move on. I don't know yet. AJ reminds me, almost on a daily basis, that he's not my Prince Charming, which is fine because I don't own any glass slippers."

Lilith smiled.

"So it's hard to assess what we are to each other. I think whatever it is we have works *because* we're both messed-up, not in spite of it."

"Sounds tragic or perfect."

Jillian huffed a small laugh. "It is ... it's perfectly tragic."

THE DOUBLE STANDARD in regard to the Knights was entirely too 1970's-ish. If Jillian showed off her body she was a home-wrecking whore, but when Jackson beached out in the sun smack-dab in the middle of the driveway wearing only a pair of low-hanging shorts, flaunting his muscle-bound, tattooed body to all the women, it was completely acceptable.

"Have you dealt with the Lilith issue?" Jackson asked, not bothering to open his eyes as the sun kissed his body.

"It's a non-issue."

"So did you go with accidental drug overdose or will she be labeled 'missing' indefinitely under the unsolved mysteries file?"

"You really lost your scruples along the way, didn't you?"

"We're trained in survival, sister-dearest, not in baring our souls over tea and cookies."

"She's not going to say anything."

"You willing to bet your life on it?"

"Yes." She headed toward the front door.

"You willing to bet *my* life on it?"

She stopped. The stab hurt, it always did. Jackson carried around this I-love-you-more-than-you-love-me attitude and trying to prove him wrong was exhausting. Declaring it a lost cause, she continued inside. As she kicked off her shoes, her phone buzzed with a text. She pulled it from her back pocket.

Mark 13:32-33

"What the hell?" she whispered to herself.

The sender was unknown. No name. No number. No further explanation.

The door opened behind her. "Ike Turner just pulled in his drive," Jackson jabbed.

"How are your testicles today?"

He squeezed by her, covering his junk.

"That's what I thought, so just *shut it* about AJ."

He tugged on his shirt. "You look confused."

She nodded. "Mark 13:32-33?"

"*But of that day and hour no one knows, not even the*

angels in Heaven, nor the Son, but only the Father. Take heed, watch and pray; for you do not know when the time is."

Jackson never missed a Sunday. As long as God turned a blind eye to his sexual indiscretions, it was possible her brother was worthy of the cross he wore on his arm.

"Did you see an unusual clearing in the clouds?" He laughed.

She shook her head and held up her phone.

"What's that?"

"A text?"

"From whom?"

She stared at him and shrugged. He grabbed her phone, clicking from one screen to the next.

"Everything's traceable."

"What do you think it means?"

His brow furrowed deeper with frustration at her phone. "Biblically speaking?"

"I don't think it's a reminder text from our childhood pastor. So no, not biblically speaking."

"Then I don't know. Dammit! Fucking phone." He tossed her phone back to her. "I'll call Knox. They're monitoring our phones."

"Great. Just what I need, another big brother butting in on my business."

"Don't forget, *Sis*, how hard your big brothers work to keep you alive."

"You know what I mean." She walked toward the bedroom. "I'm going for a ride."

"Super ... great. I'll just be here doing what I do best. Keeping you alive."

Jillian changed into her jeans and black boots then grabbed her leather jacket. "Did you reach Knox?"

"I did." His fingers tapped over the keyboard to his computer.

"And?"

"And he said he'd look into it."

She zipped up her coat. "I wouldn't worry about it."

He looked up at her. "Of course you wouldn't."

"What's that supposed to mean?"

He shook his head. "Nothing."

"No, not nothing. Tell me."

He blew out a long breath. "You're just messed-up."

"Agreed. Is that it?" She shoved her hands in her jacket pockets.

"It's not that I don't get it. We were trained to deal with a lot and nobody could have predicted that you'd watch your friend die the way she did. Every fucked-up part of your brain is completely justified in my opinion. But lately I question your decisions: AJ, your reckless trip to Portland, sharing information with Lilith that you weren't supposed to tell anyone ever again, and now this text that honestly scares the shit out of me. Yet you don't want to worry about it."

"What do you want me to do?"

He rested his elbows on the table and rubbed his eyes. "I don't know ... just be careful. Okay?"

"I will," she answered in a small voice. Moving behind him she wrapped her arms around his neck and kissed his cheek. "I love you."

He squeezed her arm.

Jillian needed the wind and miles of open road to let her thoughts fall away into oblivion. She pulled on her helmet and threw a leg over her Harley.

"Want some company?"

She turned. "Aric James." Her eyes smiled more than her lips.

"Rough day?"

"What makes you ask that?"

He moved to the front of her Harley, resting his hands on the handle bars. "You call me Aric James when you're feeling vulnerable."

"Vulnerable?" She was vulnerable—vulnerable to his earlier questioning about Trigger, Matthew Green.

"Yes. It's usually when I'm inside you." His gaze moved over her body and for a brief moment she could *feel* him inside her. "But sometimes you say it like a prayer, and I think it's when your emotions begin to consume all your strength."

Like in that exact moment. It was in her mind, all coincidence. AJ read the paper every day, of course he would mention Trigger's death at the same rest stop. It didn't mean anything more. How could it?

"Get on."

"Scoot back."

"My bike. I'm driving."

"I'm not riding bitch behind you."

"You are." She shoved his hands away and gripped the handle bars.

"If I'm on the back now, you're on bottom later."

"You're being presumptuous that there's going to be a later."

"You put my face in a headlock between your legs this

morning and *begged* me not to stop, and two seconds ago you called me Aric James. I'm pretty sure there'll be a later."

AJ had this gritty, almost angry confidence that was most likely mistaken as arrogance by anyone who couldn't see past it to the raw vulnerability he hid beneath the surface.

"Move back," he repeated.

"So I'm supposed to ride bitch?"

"Yes."

"Why?"

"Because you are my bitch."

Jillian laughed, a lot. "I love when you sweet talk me. It makes me very wet for you." It wasn't a lie. Pathetic? Maybe. She relinquished her spot by scooting back.

He hopped on.

"Have you ever driven a motorcycle before?"

He brought it to a roaring start and had them zipping out of Peaceful Woods in a matter of seconds. She had her answer. It felt oddly reminiscent of his tongue dragging along a certain area of her body earlier that morning— controlled, arousing, and irresistibly sexy.

AJ gave her a tour of the city beyond what she'd received on her "date" with Cage. She felt like a tourist. Omaha wasn't home. She could live there for the next fifty years and it would never be home. Her home ... her heart would always be in San Francisco.

They chased the sunset back to Peaceful Woods two hours later. AJ parked in her garage. Even after he killed the engine, she held on to him.

"Are you asleep?" he asked without making any sudden movement.

Smart guy.

"Mmm ... no, but you feel perfect hugged to my chest."

He peeled her arms off his waist. She groaned then slid off the back.

"You going to win me a new car too?" He gestured to her Mercedes.

"Will it earn a more favorable opinion of my job from you?" She pulled off her helmet.

"Not likely."

"Then I think my next bonus will go to Jackson. He supports my profession."

"I doubt it."

"Don't. He chose it."

The pained please-tell-me-you're-bullshitting-me look was worth revealing that minor detail that wasn't intended to ever be shared.

"You both need to be committed."

She snaked her hands up his back, resting her forehead on his chest. "Shh ... don't tell anyone. I don't want to scare off Brooke and her family when they come next week."

He pulled away. "What are you talking about?"

"Cage's game ... next week."

He narrowed his eyes for a moment then nodded, pulling her back into his hold. "His game ... next week."

CHAPTER THIRTY-SEVEN

DAY

Jessica returned to San Francisco with fifteen-hundred dollars, a medal, and the biggest motivation ever to overcome her issues. In true Mr. Stuffy Pants fashion, Luke insisted they keep up their arrangement: cleaning and counseling.

"Miss Day." Luke smiled while holding open the door to his condo.

They hadn't talked since returning from the race. Not even their newfound relationship could distract from the post-triathalon coma they fell into, sleeping for almost eighteen hours straight.

"Jones," she reached for his neck, craving his touch.

"No, no, no..." he dodged her advance "...work then play."

Her jaw dropped. "Are you serious?"

"Deadly." He turned, walking toward the bedroom.

"Did you not say you were madly in love with me?"

"I did and I am." He turned into his bedroom and continued to the closet.

The reaffirmation gave her a giddy shiver. "Just one kiss."

His unexpected one-eighty degree turn had her bumping into his chest. Chanel No. 69 poisoned her thoughts as he looked down at her. "It could never be just *one* kiss." Those dark blue eyes held so much promise, so much expectation.

"Fine. But I don't want to do any chores."

"Why not?"

"Because it will distract me from what I'm going to tell you.

Luke leaned back against his closet door, hands in his back pockets. "What are you going to tell me?"

Her eyes locked to his. "Everything."

JESSICA AND CLAIRE had been friends since the first day of kindergarten. They were ketchup sisters since Claire was too scared to poke her finger to be certifiable blood sisters. Claire nearly passed out when she got her first period, and she wore clip-on earrings because the thought of having her ears pierced made her queasy and ashen in the face.

It was all kinds of fucked-up karma that she died in the bloodiest way possible—one slow cut at a time. By the final cut, the one that sliced through her femoral artery, Edwin Harvey sealed his fate. Something shifted in the universe, an imbalance that had to be set right. An eye for an eye. His death would be cataclysmic and at the hands of Jessica Day.

"You're next." Edwin tossed the bloodied knife on the card table and wiped the remainder of Claire's life from his hands with an old rag.

Trigger cursed when he discovered their cocaine stash

had been depleted. "Eddy, I'm going out." He grabbed his phone. "She's mine when I get back. You've had yours." He smirked at Jessica.

Claire's blood pooled along the floor, seeping through Jessica's soiled shorts. It was still warm—a last kiss goodbye. There should have been tears. Any normal person would have been screaming and crying in a fit of hysteria. But when Claire released her last breath, something broke inside of Jessica. A piece of her humanity, the innate part of her that was programmed from birth to do no harm. It was severed and her grief remained buried under the desire—the need—to end Edwin's life.

"H-how many days h-has it b-been?" Jessica rasped through her dry, raw throat, feeling a new wave of dehydration seizing her body. The dog bowl had been dry for quite some time.

"Three, bitch. Why? You have a date or something?" Edwin continued to scrub at the blood under the single light that hung from the basement ceiling. The wretched smell of death and other bodily fluids hung stagnant in the dungeon air.

"Yes..." her eyelids fought to stay open "...with Jude. H-he's going to try and k-kill you, b-but I w-won't let him." It wasn't hope, it was certainty. Jude tracked her phone at all times and it was on when she and Claire arrived at the hellhole. He'd know her last location, even if the battery died.

Edwin laughed. "I don't know who the fuck Jude is, and I don't really care, but I'm touched that you're going to save me, sweetheart. Why the sudden love for me? Your slutty friend steal your boyfriend and therefore deep down you're grateful that I ended her pathetic little life?"

Jessica rolled her head side to side. "No, because *I'm* going to k-kill you."

His laugh grew to a roar. "Well this will be interesting. You can't talk without stammering all over the place and you're sitting in a puddle of blood and piss with your arms and legs restrained, yet you're going to kill me?"

She forced her tired eyes to meet his sadistic gaze and then she nodded once before passing out. Voices mixed with jolting sounds echoed like a tunnel, and random flashes of light blurred into hazy outlines—then black.

———

"WAKE up so I can fucking kill you," a voice whispered in her ear.

Jude came into focus as she peeled her eyes open.

"Stop it!" her mom pushed him aside. "Hey, honey." She rested her palm on Jessica's cheek. "You're going to be fine. Two broken ribs but thankfully they didn't puncture your lung." Tears swelled in her mom's eyes despite the smile of relief on her face. "Dad's in the waiting room handling some things. I'll go tell him you're awake." She kissed her forehead.

Jude moved to her side again, greeting her with a scowl. "I'm serious, as soon as you get out of the hospital I'm going to kill you."

She managed a faint grin through the residual effect of whatever drugs they'd given her. "At least I'll die at the hands of a worthy adversary."

Jude's expression softened. "Claire is ..."

"I know." Jessica averted her gaze, guilt-ridden that she had yet to shed a single tear. "Did you kill them?"

"Them? You mean him?"

Her eyes shot to his. "Them. There were two."

Jude shook his head. "One. When we arrived there was only one, Edwin Harvey."

"No there was another. He left, I think for drugs. Trigger, he called him Trigger. He carried the gun and waved it around with an itchy finger."

"Claire ... who killed—"

"Eddy or 'Edwin' ... he cut her—only him. But I think ..."

Jude sat on the edge of her bed. "You think what?"

"I think I somehow belonged to Trigger. I was his toy and it was going to be his turn." She sucked in a shaky breath. "You didn't answer me. Did you kill him?"

"No. I wasn't alone. Dad was there too and you kept coming in and out of it, but the only thing you said was 'don't kill him.'"

"He's alive?"

"Yes. He'll never see the outside of a prison cell, but he's alive."

"Good." She nodded.

"Good?"

"Hey, baby girl." Their dad walked in the room.

"Hi, Dad."

He kissed the top of her head. "We need to talk."

She nodded.

LUKE POURED her another glass of wine as they admired the view of the city's lights welcoming the sunset from the balcony. He listened to every single word, but it wasn't enough. She held the pain too tight and too close to her heart and he couldn't take it from her. It was a part of her and it always would be.

Mostly she stared into the night as if she were looking at everything and nothing at the same time, but she'd give him an occasional glance filled with worry, searching for judgment in his eyes.

"Jessica ..." he held out his hand, having reached his limit, no longer able to resist. He needed her touch.

She looked at it for a moment before taking it. He pulled her over onto his lap.

"I'm all in. Do you get that?"

She worried the edge of her lip between her teeth, giving him a barely detectable nod that lacked true conviction.

"You don't *really* get it, do you?"

She frowned. "It's ... well, I just told you that I didn't cry for my dead friend and that I wanted to kill a man. And I'm not done. The story's not over. I made good on my promise." Her brow drew tight. "That's a lot to be 'all in' for: the truth, the person I became that day—and to some extent always will be—my twisted mind, and morbid obsession. Can't you see how hard it is to 'get' that any person with even half my sanity would willingly be all in?"

"Well, I am."

"Well you shouldn't be!" She shot off his lap.

He felt his heart rip from his chest, confirming that she had it, at least part of it.

"What is wrong with you? I'm getting ready to tell you I killed a man, but I'm not going to stop there. I'm going to give you every sadistic, gory, fucked-up detail about it. And then I'm going to tell you that I walked away and in the past decade I haven't regretted it for one. Single. Second."

"It doesn't change anything." He felt her agony, the torture, the unforgivable guilt that left a permanent mark on her heart, her conscience, and her self-image.

Jessica huffed a sarcastic laugh. *"Really?"* She paced the length of the deck several times before settling with her back to the railing, resting on her hands. "I wanted to die after I attacked my mom when she woke me the first morning home from the hospital. I was so messed up. My father worked round the clock to assure Four would never taste freedom again. But he was privileged, born into a family with an obscene amount of money, so he was released on bond. My family was outraged ... everyone but me."

Luke refused to cower under her glare, the one that said she couldn't imagine how he could love her ... all of her.

"His family sent him to stay at their private beach house to protect him from the media. It was almost too easy, too perfect. I'd been a mess for weeks, and Jude knew I needed something more than a guilty verdict. He was my decoy for getting into the beach house and my backup if anything went wrong. But it didn't. In less than five minutes I had him restrained with *zip ties*. I was there for two hours and even that was too merciful. Forty-four ... I cut him forty-four times, the final cut was to his femoral artery. He begged for mercy. I showed none—not one second of hesitation, not one moment of regret, not one tear."

He waited for her to continue, but she just looked at him. Whatever awful reaction she expected him to have, he didn't. She killed the man that stole her emotional innocence and murdered her best friend. He deserved everything he got. It wasn't the professional opinion of Dr. Jones or even well-thought-out logic. It was simply Luke's raw human emotion in that moment, his truth.

"He had it coming, Jessica."

"Bullshit! How can you have a fucking degree in psychiatry and say that? Yes, he deserved to die, but it doesn't make what I did right." Her voice cracked as she fisted and pulled at her hair, squeezing her eyes shut. "My hands *didn't* shake. Do you *get* that? I was a damn surgeon with every cut, immune to his pain, immune to his cries, immune to my own humanity."

He sighed. "What do you want from me?"

She shook her head, tears growing heavy in her eyes. "I want to deserve your love and I want it to make sense."

"Jessica—"

She wiped her tears and walked back inside. His muscles ached to run after her. But then what?

CHAPTER THIRTY-EIGHT

Jᴇssɪᴄᴀ ɪᴍᴀɢɪɴᴇᴅ ᴛᴇʟʟɪɴɢ Luke everything would free her. It didn't. Saying the words aloud, hearing them herself, and reliving the events only confirmed her insanity—how unworthy she was of anyone's love. She could be the strongest most confident woman in the world, but it wouldn't change her past, it wouldn't change the truth. Edwin Harvey sealed his fate the day he took Claire's life and Jessica sealed hers the day she took his. She was destined to live without love and the kind of happiness normal people dreamed about. That was her life—her prison.

On the way home she stopped for alcohol, but not her favorite bottle of wine. Beer. She needed beer. The six pack of Heineken called to her. It seemed like the right choice, a tribute to the man she loved but could never truly have. The first bottle tasted like piss and so did the second. By the third, her taste buds were as buzzed as the rest of her, and it went down like a smooth analgesic.

She stared at the ceiling fan from corpse position on her living room floor. The couch must have moved on her when she tried to lie on it. Just as well, the cool floor felt like heaven beneath her warm tingly skin.

"Why did you leave?"

"Jones?" She laughed. It was more fun than crying. "I didn't hear you come in."

The door slammed shut.

"Yep. I heard that." The ceiling fan had her in a trance. "Why did I leave? Hmm ... I'm pretty sure I left because I love you." Another laugh. "Isn't that just fan-fucking-tabu-lous? You're the boy I dreamed about when I used the back of my hand to practice kissing as a young girl." She smiled at the fan. The fan smiled back. "Bet you didn't know that girls did that? Well we did—the back of our hand, a pillow, the wall, each other."

Luke stepped over her, straddling her waist with his feet, arms crossed over his chest while he looked down on her like a god. "You kissed other girls?"

She pressed her lips together and grinned. "I love that you're still a guy, Jones. Did you hear me say I kissed the wall?"

"How many girls did you kiss?"

"I'm not sure. How many did you kiss?"

"I've only kissed one that matters."

She was several bottles of Heineken short of that comment not affecting her heart. "They say if you truly love someone to set them free. I'm setting you free, Jones. This is a huge step for me. If I didn't love you, I'd keep you around, use you, abuse you, then cast you aside."

"Well, I'm here and I can't leave."

"Why?"

"Because you're drinking beer which in your words is an SOS. You need me. Where's my bag?"

Jessica squinted. "What?"

"The bag I left here. Where is it?"

"Entry closet."

He bent down and grabbed her, hoisting her over his shoulder.

"What are you doing?" She laughed.

He opened the entry closet and grabbed the bag.

"Jones, answer me!"

"Quiet!" He smacked her ass, continuing to her bedroom.

"Dammit, Jones! You did not just spank me."

"I did and if you don't shut up I'm going to do it again." He tossed her on her bed. "No more questions. Take off your clothes."

She shook her head. "I told you, I can't do this. And this is not the answer to an SOS."

He unzipped the bag and riffled through its contents. "Then I'll cut them off you."

"What? I'm not talking about—"

"Lie back." He tossed handcuffs and rope onto the bed. "Choose one."

She stared at them and then lifted her gaze to him. "Why do you think I'll submit to you?"

He grabbed her ankles and jerked her body so it was centered on the bed. "Because you trust me."

She gripped the sheet beneath her. "But I don't trust myself."

"That's the point. You don't have to."

"Rope?" He grabbed one ankle.

She tensed. They had a brief stare down.

"This is happening ... *We* are happening," he said it like a warning and a promise.

She relaxed her leg, submitting to the *this* part. The *we* part was still very much in question. He tied her legs to the bedpost, leaving enough slack to allow her to bend her knees a little. After she was secured in four points to the bed, Jessica tugged at her restraints. She wasn't going anywhere.

"The kiss. Were you talking about me. Is my kiss the only one that matters?"

He worked the buttons to his shirt while bending over and pressing a soft kiss to her lips. "Yes," he whispered.

"What does that say about your ex-fiancée we've never talked about?"

Luke continued unbuttoning his shirt, his brows pulled close in thought. "If it mattered enough she wouldn't be my *ex-fiancée*, she'd be my wife."

"But you loved her?"

"Of course." He draped his shirt over the chair next to her night table.

"But you love me more?"

His gaze brought a flood of chills to the surface of her skin, like a stadium crowd doing the wave. "Unequivocally."

Her next breath caught in her chest. "You can't mean that."

There was such a sadness in his eyes. "I loved her which is why the word suddenly feels monumentally inadequate for you. I gave her my love, but you ... you took it. You took everything. I never had a choice. You tore into my life ... into my heart, wrecking all sense of the man I was before you. Being with you is the best part of my day ... every day. You think you're broken, but you're not. And if you were ... it wouldn't matter. I love every. Single. Piece of you."

"Luke—" she pleaded.

"Shh ... let me love you. Let me show you that in this crazy world *we* make sense." He grabbed the scissors from his bag.

Jessica pulled on the restraints. "No! I'll take off my clothes."

He shook his head. "I think it's better this way."

"I-I don't think putting a blade anywhere near my skin is a good idea. And this is an expensive dress."

"I'll replace everything." He kissed the skin just above her knee next to the hem of her dress. "There's nothing I wouldn't give you." He kissed a little higher. "There's nothing I wouldn't do for you."

"Luke ..." she moaned as his tongue brushed along her skin.

"Now, do you trust me?"

She met his piercing gaze then looked at the scissors he had ready to slash her dress. He was it. Luke was absolutely, *unequivocally,* her everything. Swallowing hard, she nodded.

He sliced up the middle and she closed her eyes. It was terrifying, exhilarating, and so fucking seductive all at the same time. With the last cut, her dress was nothing more than scraps of material beneath her. Three snips later her bra disappeared, and two after that her panties followed suit. He'd cut everything *but* her.

"Open your beautiful eyes."

She blinked them open. The scissors were gone.

"You're—"

Her chest vibrated with a nervous laugh. "Don't be cliché, Jones. Whatever you're going to say, make it count because I'm so far out of my comfort zone I could rip off my own limbs just to escape." She was nervous, scared, aroused, and in love ... in so much love.

"You're—"

"And don't make it sweet or sentimental, not with me tied to my own bed."

He smirked. "You're—"

"I swear to God, Jones ... if you make me cry and rob me of my last bit of dignity with some you're-so-beautiful-you're-the-mother-of-my-children bullshit I will break your cock. Do you understand?"

He ran his finger along the instep of one of her feet. She jerked. Then he did it to the other, eliciting the same response. Leaning over the foot of the bed, he rested on his elbows, his face inches away from her sex. She tipped her chin down to see him, all four restraints pulled taut in anticipation.

Luke grinned. It was filled with mischief. He kissed the inside of her thigh. "You're ..." he kissed the other side "... going to get thoroughly fucked." Slyest. Smile. Ever.

"J-Jones!" she cried, her body arching from the bed as his mouth covered her.

Luke hummed against her sensitive flesh. The need to make him bleed was building with fury. He was in complete control. The vulnerability threatened what little sanity she still had.

"Too much ... I-I can't." Her heart pummeled against her chest, driven by fear. She fought the pleasure that peaked in waves, growing in intensity.

"Kiss me, please ..."

His hand replaced his mouth—two fingers slid into her as his palm pressed against her clitoris.

"Kiss me!" she demanded between labored breaths.

"I am," he murmured over her skin as his mouth drifted along her body, paying a beautifully, torturous homage to every inch of it.

"This ... this is a bad idea." Her voice broke under the duress of pleasure poisoned with a crippling anxiety.

He flicked his tongue over her nipple.

"Oh God ... stop ... my mouth ... I need your mouth on mine."

He squeezed her breast—sucking, biting, and moaning.

"Now!"

He laughed. The bastard laughed. "My God, I love you. I know this is killing you, but I'd rather you feel tortured with need than with guilt."

She writhed beneath him as his fingers brought her closer to losing all control.

"Kiss me."

"Not on the mouth," he whispered in her ear.

"I won't bite you."

"You will." He dragged his tongue down her neck.

"Fuck ... no ... stop. I can't come."

He'd stripped her of nearly all physical control. She'd completely shatter if he took the rest.

"Please ..." A lone tear slid down the side of her face.

"You can and you will. You'll give me *everything*" He slid his fingers out and sucked her clitoris.

"No!" The posts to her bed creaked in protest as she jerked against his warm, wet mouth—losing *everything*. The pleasure was so. Damn. Painful. Hot tears spilled over and bled down her cheeks.

He sat up, kneeling between her knees. She blinked out more tears as he slid down his pants and briefs. Grabbing his erection he pumped it a few times giving her a look so dark and chilling she shivered.

"I'm going to take you the way you took me—by surprise, relentlessly ... *completely*."

Beyond the steely eyes, the hard lines of muscled flesh, and the promise of more pain and pleasure that he pumped just inches from her sex, she saw so much love and adoration it sent a flood of more tears rushing down her face. Closing her eyes, she nodded.

"Ung!" She groaned as he lifted her hips and pushed into her with one quick thrust.

"Fuck," Luke moaned, pausing a few seconds.

Her breaths came quick and shallow as she waited and waited ... and waited.

"Jessica?"

She opened her eyes, first looking at the sexy-as-fuck sight of him completely impaled in her. Then she met his gaze.

"I need you to acknowledge that *this* is happening ... that *we* are happening. I need you to feel me, see me ... *trust* me."

She drew in a shaky breath. "Okay," she whispered.

He pulled back and pushed right back in over and over until the slow rhythm built into something more. Faster. Harder. Desperate.

With each passing second, one muscle at a time, she relaxed—surrendered—until she no longer recognized where her body ended and his began. He slowed his movements and untied her ankles. Then he leaned forward and released her hands. She hesitated.

"Now ... trust yourself," he whispered, pulling her body up to his.

She wrapped her arms around his neck and he kissed her. *He* trusted her. Their two bodies moved as one, both finding control in absolute surrender.

She felt a tinge of panic again as another orgasm approached the brink. "I-I'm close. What if—"

"I've got you—I'll always have you." He kissed her with complete abandon as their walls of resistance came crashing down with sweet relief—sweet surrender.

CHAPTER THIRTY-NINE

KNIGHT

Lɪʟɪᴛʜ ʜᴀᴅɴ'ᴛ ʜᴀᴅ much sun, but her cheeks were flushed a nice rosy red. Jillian poured her another glass of tea and handed it to her.

"Oh ... thank you." She smiled and blinked for what seemed like the first time in over an hour.

"You're blushing."

Lilith fanned herself with her hand. "Why, yes I am. It might have something to do with your very steamy story."

Jillian smiled. "What Luke and I had was ... not of this world." The memories were painful, but they owned so much of her heart, without them she'd feel like an empty shell.

"So he cured you of your *ways*?"

"Hmm, so it seemed at the time. He taught me how to trust myself, but later I found out that trust was contingent on him. Without him, I've sort of ... lost it." Jillian frowned.

"Maybe Sarge needs to tie you up." Lilith winked.

Jillian twisted her lips to the side. "No. I don't trust myself around AJ for good reasons. However, I have been trying to channel Luke when I'm with AJ."

Lilith's eyes widened.

Jillian smirked. "That sounds bad. I know. Luke's voice in my head calms me. I can't completely let my guard down with AJ, but I've been trying to control myself ... my reaction. Basically having an appropriate reaction to him, which is hard because AJ and his PTSD are unpredictable."

"Oh, has it been getting worse?"

"No. Well, I can't say for sure. It feels like his migraines have been more frequent and sometimes his mood is all over the place, but that's the only AJ I've ever known so I'm not really the best judge."

Lilith nodded in thought. "He's lucky to have you."

Jillian smiled. "It goes both ways."

JILLIAN ARRIVED home to her dear brother working at an obsessive pace trying to figure out who sent her that text. It pissed him off that Knox dismissed its possible threat. A lot of things about Knox pissed him off.

"Everything is a fucking dead end."

"Maybe it was sent to me by mistake. You know, wrong number," she murmured as she sent AJ a text.

Jillian: *Still on for dinner tonight?*

She'd texted him earlier about grabbing dinner before her Lascivio party.

"The average person doesn't have an untraceable number. Even private numbers are easy to break if you know what you're doing."

AJ: *Dinner?*

Jillian: *Yes ... we agreed on Thai.*
AJ: *Right, sorry. Long day.*
Jillian: *Coming home soon?*
AJ: *Yes, see you in an hour.*
Jillian: *OK*

"Well, I'm going to dinner with AJ tonight. I think you should come with us. You need to get out and shut your brain down for a few hours."

"No thanks. I'm too on edge. He'll look at you the wrong way and piss me off. It's better if I don't witness your fucked-up relationship any more than I have to."

"Real nice, Jack. Speaking of fucked-up relationships ... how is Sesame Street girl?"

"That's over." Jackson kept pounding the keys to his laptop.

"Sorry to hear that. What happened? Did she want to enhance Mr. Snuffelupagus with Play-Doh? Or did you screw her mom on Black Beauty?"

Jackson looked up. "First, you haven't seen Mr. Snuffelupagus since we were like ... five. If you had then you'd know there's no way in hell I need enhancement in that department. Second, I have a little more respect than having sex on my piano."

"Respect for your piano, not the woman, right?"

"Yep."

"Typical. I'm going to shower before AJ gets home. Guess you're on your own for dinner tonight."

"Greta gave me a standing invite to dinner, or any meal for that matter, at her house. And *she* can seriously cook."

Jillian shut the bathroom door. "Yeah, yeah ... so I've heard," she grumbled to herself.

She stepped into the hot shower letting it rain over her head while closing her eyes. It had been months since she'd let herself remember that day with Luke—the bed, the ropes, the most emotional sex she'd ever had. The first time in her life she *made love*.

Letting her hand slide between her legs, she replayed the way he touched her body. They spent hours in her bed, indulging in every part of each other. It was raw carnal need. It was sex. It was the most beautiful destiny. It was a worshipping love ... a once-in-a-lifetime love. She leaned back against the wall and let a soft moan escape as she had one last orgasm for Luke.

She emerged from the shower as Jillian Knight: woman on a mission to find her own life, her own love. What better way to forge ahead with that journey than dinner with AJ at a Thai restaurant with *cloth* napkins.

"What do you think?" Jillian twirled around in her short black racer-back dress and heels.

Jackson dropped from his pull-up bar. "For dinner or work tonight?"

"Both."

He nodded. "Yeah, you won't make it to work if you wear that to dinner. AJ's an old guy, but I've gathered from your incessant 'Aric James' cries that his dick still works."

"So you're saying I look hot?"

Jackson's face morphed into a sour look. "No. God no!"

"But if I weren't your sister you'd totally do me, right?"

"Jesus, Jill!"

The admittedly sick and twisted sister turned on her high heels and giggled all the way to the front door, peeking out to see if she could see AJ's Jeep. The seventy degree evening invited her out to sit on the stoop while she waited for him. He was a half hour late and she tapped her heel on the concrete feeling a little upset and a lot disappointed that they were probably going to miss dinner. She had to be back by seven for her party.

"I'm feeling stood up, Sarge. I have to work at seven, and I'm dressed for sin. Your loss buddy." She pressed *End* and headed back in the house.

"That was quick. He forget to take his Viagra?"

"Funny, Jack-*ass*. He's being such a guy today, like you. It's as if he forgot we even had plans until I reminded him. Now he's late, not answering his phone, and he hasn't called me back."

"Are you pissed or worried?"

"Both." She frowned. "But more worried than pissed."

Jackson chuckled. "Welcome to my world."

She slipped off her heels and plunked down on the chair next to him. "This worrying crap sucks. That's why I don't do it very often."

Her phone chimed.

Jackson's brows perked. "And there he is."

Jillian looked at her phone. "It's not him." She swiped her finger across the screen. "Hello?"

"Jillian, it's Cage."

"Hey, what's up?"

"My dad ... I just got a call from the hospital. He's been in an accident."

"Oh my God," she whispered.

"I'm on my way there now. The nurse said he's stable, but other than that she couldn't elaborate on the extent of his injuries. They're running some tests now."

Jillian jotted down the hospital information as Cage gave it to her. Then she grabbed her purse and slipped back on her shoes. "I'll see you there."

Jackson stood. "What happened?"

"AJ ... he's been in an accident." She looked around. "Dammit! Where's my purse."

Jackson tugged the strap already on her shoulder. "I think it's best if I take you."

She sighed, closing her eyes, and nodded.

———

As EXPECTED, they arrived before Cage and were refused any information about AJ's condition because they weren't family.

"I should have said I'm his wife." Jillian paced the waiting room.

"Don't even go there," Jackson deadpanned.

"You know what I mean," she huffed.

"Jillian." She turned. Cage stepped off the elevator.

She frowned. "They won't tell me anything." He gave her a hug.

"Wait here." Cage checked in at the nurses station then came back. "He's done with the tests and in a room now. You can come in with me."

Jillian looked back at Jackson.

"I'm good out here."

She nodded.

The doctor was just leaving as they entered the room. He gave them a somber nod.

"Dad. Jesus, are you okay?"

A faint smile pulled at AJ's lips. He had gauze wrapped around his head, but no other visible injuries. Jillian stayed back a few feet, giving them space.

"Yes, nothing major. A few stitches..." he pointed to the side of his head "...and a mild concussion."

Cage's shoulders relaxed. "What happened?"

"Some idiot t-boned me. Totaled my poor Jeep." AJ gave Jillian a fleeting glance as if he couldn't hold her gaze.

Something felt off.

"When can I take you home?"

"Not until tomorrow. They're keeping me for observation and to run a few more tests."

"Okay. I'll call Grandma and Grandpa."

AJ nodded, giving Jillian another quick glance. "Can you call them in the waiting room? I need to talk to Jillian."

"Sure." Cage gave AJ's shoulder a gentle squeeze. "I'm so relieved you're okay."

When the door closed, Jillian eased toward AJ. "Hey, I was worried and rightfully so."

AJ reached for her hand. "I'm sorry. I didn't mean to worry you." He forced a smile. "You look incredible. Too damn sexy as usual."

She sat on the edge of his bed. He rested his hand on her bare knee.

"If you were willing to endure a concussion and a few stitches just to keep me from going to my Lascivio party tonight, I could have accommodated you."

He smiled. Once again it was forced—a nervous smile. The look someone has when a million thoughts run through their brain, crashing into each other.

"What's wrong?" She rested her palm on his cheek, brushing her thumb over his stubbly chin.

"I need to tell you something."

If she wouldn't have known better—wouldn't have known his iron-fisted personality, she would have thought the glassiness in his eyes was tears.

"O-kay. You're scaring me ... just say it."

He nodded. The pain in his face conveyed the weight of his unspoken words. When he said them, his voice cracked and so did he. "Jillian ... I love you."

To be continued...

PREVIEW OF MIDDLE OF KNIGHT

CHAPTER ONE

Knight

The signs were everywhere. That twenty-twenty hindsight was an evil, gloating bitch. What incentive was there to ponder a question that had already been answered? The PTSD *was* a catch-all. AJ knew it. Jillian dismissed it. Fate seized it.

I love you. Why would he say those words? Jillian Knight pondered that question while her brother, Jackson, drove her home from the hospital.

"So you just ran out?" Jackson asked, making a quick sideways glance.

"Walked. I walked out. I told AJ I needed to do something."

"And what was that?"

"I needed to get the hell out of there."

"Why?"

"He said ... 'I love you.'"

"I see ... Actually, I don't. You're going to have to help me out on this one."

"Why would he say that? Was his accident some near-death experience that brought about this rush of irrational feelings? And it wasn't just that he said it. It was the way he said it. It's like someone had a gun to his head."

"Do you love him?"

"No ... I-I don't know. That's just it. What was I supposed to say? *Thank you,* or *I'd rather you wouldn't?*"

"So what now?"

She sighed. "I don't know. Food, beer, and then I'll face him tomorrow."

By eleven o'clock that night, with the help of four bottles of Heineken, Jillian had an epiphany. It was a new record for her. Most epiphanies didn't happen until the end of the sixth bottle of Heineken.

"Jackie?" she whispered, opening Jackson's bedroom door.

"What the hell did you call me?" he grumbled with his head buried in his pillow, the bed sheet draped low on his waist.

Jillian giggled, then hiccuped. "Jackie ... I figured it out."

He flipped over, raising up on his elbows, eyes squinted against the hall light. "Call me that again and I'll knock you out before the beer gets to it."

"Scooch over." She stumbled to his bed.

"I'm naked."

"So ... scooch." Jillian wedged her way into his bed.

Jackson retreated to the other side, securing the sheet around his waist.

"I've decided to love AJ."

"Decided?"

Jillian rolled onto her side facing Jackson with her cheek rested on her folded hands. "Yes. Why not? Right? He's mature, and good in bed, and he gets me, and he's good in

409

bed, he's strong and grumpy, which I find oddly sexy. Oh ... did I mention he's good in bed?"

Jackson stared at the ceiling. "Yes, you mentioned that." He chuckled. "Sex doesn't mean love."

"I never said that. God ... all you guys think about is sex," she slurred each word. "I'm serious. He's my chance. You're going to find that happily ever after and she's not going to want me living with you forever. AJ will take me."

"God, you're so drunk right now. That's it, huh? You can just decide to love him like love's a choice? And you're basing this deep emotion on the possibility that he 'gets' you, or even more pathetic ... that he'll 'take' you. You're making yourself sound like a stray dog. You need to get off the booze. It's beginning to rob your self-esteem."

"It doesn't matter. I'd rather he love me than hate me. He's had a vasectomy so he's not looking for a baby mama, and he's definitely not clingy so in some ways he's the perfect guy. And I have these feelings for him and maybe they're love. I'm not going to lose him because my head is messed-up. When Cage called me earlier, I swear my heart stopped. It has to be love."

Jackson rubbed his eyes. "You're thirty years old and just like that you're making the decision that you don't want a family?"

Jillian tried to roll her eyes but it was hard to do behind heavy eyelids. "That makes no sense coming from my twin brother that doesn't want children."

"I never said that."

"You said you don't like kids."

"Misquoting once again. I don't like other people's kids. *My* kids will be awesome."

"*Will be?*"

"Yes. The whole slew of them. My wife is going to be so

hot I won't be able to keep my dick out of her. She'll be knocked-up all the time."

Jillian laughed. "I can't wait to see that. My nieces and nephews ... not your dick in my sister-in-law."

"If you don't want to see my dick then get the hell out of here."

"Fine. Good night." Jillian bumped into the bed stand and then the wall, trying to maneuver her drunk self out of Jackson's room.

Morning didn't care that Jillian had too much to drink the previous night. Neither did the incessant knocking at the door.

"Jackson!" she called.

Nothing.

Unaware of the time—fifteen minutes after noon—Jillian grumbled about the poor etiquette of someone knocking on the door so early. She winced at the throbbing side effect of too much Heineken as she shuffled her bare feet to the front door.

"Cage, hey."

Cage cleared his throat, forcing his eyes to stay on hers instead of her barely covered body.

"Uh ... hey. I just brought my dad home from the hospital. He wants to see you. I have to get back to campus but I'll be back this weekend."

"Yeah ... I ... um, yeah." She nodded through her rambling of nothing that made any sense. "I'll shower and be over."

She started to close the door.

"Jillian?"

"Hmm?"

"Thank you."

She narrowed her eyes. "For what?"

"For being here and putting up with him. Even if he doesn't say it. I know he appreciates it. But mainly for me. It eases my mind to know that someone is ... looking out for him."

"Oh ... sure." She shrugged as if it were no big deal. "How's he doing today?"

"Fine. I think. He's quiet. Seems a little distracted. I think the accident really shook him up, which is a little weird because he's been in crashes, around gun fire, and even ejected from a plane that was shot down."

Jillian frowned. Cage had confirmed her earlier suspicions that AJ wasn't quite right. "I'll talk to him. Drive safely back to campus."

"Thanks. I will."

After a long, procrastinating shower that included a review of the previous night's declaration made under the heavy influence of alcohol, Jillian slipped on a sun dress, her red rain boots, and her best smile to mask the courage she was having difficulty mustering. She considered taking him something to eat, but decided one near-death incident that week was enough.

"AJ?" Jillian called, letting herself in his house.

"On the couch."

She peeked around the corner to the great room. "Hey." Her voice was unusually small. Damn nerves. "Are you drinking? Before five?"

AJ tipped back a bottle of beer. Just the sight of it caused Jillian's stomach to roil.

"Yeah, why not?" He flipped off the TV.

She slipped off her boots and sat on the opposite end of

the couch, lifting his feet up to sit and resting them back on her lap.

He nursed his beer, staring at her, but not saying anything.

"About yesterday—"

He shook his head. "Don't worry about it."

"I'm not ... or I was, but I'm not now."

"Doesn't matter. Just forget about it."

Jillian traced her finger along the serpent tattoo on his leg. "What if I don't want to forget about it?"

"I don't give a fuck what you do."

She glanced up at him, lips parted, eyes wide. "Do you need a minute to rethink that?"

He took another pull. "Nope."

"Would you like me to come back later?"

"You don't need to come back at all. That's all I wanted to tell you."

The twenty-four hour whiplash left quite a sting. Especially since she'd prepared to reciprocate his expression of feelings. Those feelings had taken a backseat to his anger.

"Are you having a moment or is this about me leaving yesterday?"

"Don't be so fucking condescending with me. I'm not having a *moment* and I told you to forget about yesterday."

Scooting out from under his legs, she stood. "Call me if you need anything." She didn't even look at him as she pulled on her boots and walked to the door.

"I won't—" His voice slurred.

She turned. "AJ!"

He was shaking and his body tumbled from the sofa with a thunk.

"Oh my God!"

A seizure racked his body, stealing him from consciousness.

Jillian grabbed his cell phone off the sofa table and dialed 9-1-1. They talked her through it and sent an ambulance. She followed it to the hospital, leaving a message on Jackson's phone, but waited to call Cage, assuming it was most likely a side effect of his accident and the concussion.

They treated him in the ER but no one would give her any information because she wasn't family. An hour later they let her see him.

"Why are you still here?" he said as she entered the room. His tone had lost a little edge compared to what it had been at his house. It sounded more defeated.

"Because I love you, you idiot." It's not how she'd planned on telling him, but it came out and she couldn't stop it. The word didn't feel right, but it didn't feel wrong either. It just felt like a word.

He closed his eyes and turned his head side to side. "Don't."

She sat on the edge of his bed. "I shouldn't have left yesterday and I'm sorry. What you said scared me. I don't feel worthy of that kind of love and—"

"Stop ... just stop." He opened his eyes. "I meant it when I said it doesn't matter."

"What doesn't matter?" Jillian's voice escalated. "Me? Us? Your love for me? Mine for you?"

"All of it," he said in a deathly monotone voice.

"It mattered yesterday. You said—"

"You didn't let me finish!"

Jillian jumped.

AJ sighed. "You didn't let me finish yesterday. You left too soon."

She shook her head. "I don't understand."

"I needed you to know that I love you, but then I was going to tell you that I can't be with you anymore."

"Yeah, that makes perfectly no sense whatsoever. You need help. I know you don't want to talk about the PTSD, but it's eating you up inside. You may not think anyone can help you, but maybe you just need another opinion." She refused to back down, refused to be kicked to the curb like an old sofa up for grabs. He could be harsh and hurtful but she could deal with it.

"Goodbye, Jillian." He looked away.

"I'm not leaving, you stubborn SOB." She grabbed his face and forced him to look at her. He was it—her last chance at love and she was determined to take it. Her past had taken too much already. It wasn't deserving of him too. He was her future—a future she would fight for.

"Is this a bad time?"

Jillian turned.

A doctor in a white lab coat stood at the door.

"No ... sorry, come in." She smiled past her anger and released AJ's face as if she hadn't just manhandled a patient.

He nodded, walking toward them. "I'm Dr. Rinehart, the oncologist."

Every last bit of air evaporated from the room. Jillian couldn't find a single breath.

"Hi, Doctor. This is my friend, Jillian."

Jillian looked at AJ, not Dr. Rinehart. "W-why do you need an oncologist."

"Tell her, Doc. Why do I need you?"

Dr. Rinehart gave Jillian a regretful smile. "AJ has a brain tumor. It was discovered on his MRI after his accident yesterday."

The air. Where was all the fucking air? The migraines,

the personality that flipped without warning, the PTSD pigeonholing for everything ... how could everyone have missed it?

"Cancer?" she whispered.

"We're not sure," Dr. Rinehart replied.

"When will you know?"

Dr. Rinehart looked at AJ.

"When I'm dead and an autopsy is done to confirm it."

Jillian turned, glaring at AJ. It wasn't the time to be mad at him but she was. How could he say that? Why would he say that?

"You're not dying!" She looked to Dr. Rinehart for confirmation.

"I've consulted with the neurologist that saw AJ yesterday. The tumor may be inoperable."

"But ... you can do radiation or chemotherapy or something else, right?"

"Yes, there are other options."

"But the neurologist confessed that the success rate is lower with tumors like mine. And I'm sure as hell not going to be a guinea pig, so—"

"So what?" Jillian snapped at AJ. "You're just going to do nothing? Wait until your headaches get even worse? Wait until you're having seizures every day? Wait until you —" The pain in her chest was too familiar. She didn't notice the tears streaming down her cheeks until she tasted their salty presence.

"Die?" AJ grabbed her hand and squeezed it so hard the pain in her chest exploded into something irreversibly destructive. "Yes, Jillian. I'm going to die."

ALSO BY JEWEL E ANN

Standalone Novels

Idle Bloom

Undeniably You

Naked Love

Only Trick

Perfectly Adequate

Look The Part

When Life Happened

A Place Without You

Jersey Six

Scarlet Stone

Not What I Expected

Jack & Jill Series

End of Day

Middle of Knight

Dawn of Forever

One (*standalone*)

Out of Love (*standalone*)

Holding You Series

Holding You

Releasing Me

Transcend Series

Transcend

Epoch

Fortuity (*standalone*)

The Life Series

The Life That Mattered

The Life You Stole

Receive a FREE book and stay informed of new releases, sales, and exclusive stories:

Mailing List

https://www.jeweleann.com/free-booksubscribe

ABOUT THE AUTHOR

Jewel is a free-spirited romance junkie with a quirky sense of humor.

With 10 years of flossing lectures under her belt, she took early retirement from her dental hygiene career to stay home with her three awesome boys and manage the family business.

After her best friend of nearly 30 years suggested a few books from the Contemporary Romance genre, Jewel was hooked. Devouring two and three books a week but still craving more, she decided to practice sustainable reading, AKA writing.

When she's not donning her cape and saving the planet one tree at a time, she enjoys yoga with friends, good food with family, rock climbing with her kids, watching How I Met Your Mother reruns, and of course...heart-wrenching, tear-jerking, panty-scorching novels.

www.jeweleann.com

Printed in Great Britain
by Amazon

34555744R00236